DIARY OF A HAUNTING SERIES

DIARIES OF A HAUNTING

M. VERANO

DIARY OF A HAUNTING AND POSSESSION

SIMON & SCHUSTER BFYR

NEW YORK LONDON TORONTO SYDNEY NEW DELHI

SIMON & SCHUSTER BFYR

An imprint of Simon & Schuster Children's Publishing Division
1230 Avenue of the Americas, New York, New York 10020
Diary of a Haunting copyright © 2015 by Simon & Schuster, Inc.
Possession copyright © 2016 by Simon & Schuster, Inc.
Cover photographs copyright © 2020 by Erin Cadigan/Arcangel and Tracy Collyer/Arcangel
Diary of a Haunting interior images on page 15 copyright © Getty/Stuart Fox; page 26 copyright © Trevillion/Stephen Wilson; page 31 copyright © iStock/Auris; page 41 copyright © Trevillion/Andrew Sanderson; pages 81 and 284 copyright © Shutterstock; page 84 copyright © Arcangel/Hayden Very; pages 123, 142, 183, 217, 231, 235, 237, 296, and 315 copyright © Thinkstock; page 128 copyright © Masterfile (flies) and copyright © Arcangel/Mark Owen (hands with jar); page 135 copyright © Getty/Escobar Studios; page 139 copyright © Getty/Stephen Webster; page 156 copyright © Arcangel/Douglas Black; page 261 copyright © Trevillion/Frank Losay; page 267 copyright © Getty/Adam Papadatos; page 275 copyright © Trevillion/Susan Fox; page 279 copyright © Trevillion/Christophe Dessaigne
Possession interior images on pages 335, 359, 367, 372, 390, 402, 404, 415, 430, 489, 494, 519, 524, 527, 538, 557, 574, 579, 627, 629, 640, and 665 copyright © 2016 by Thinkstock; interior images on pages 381, 425, 437, 441, 465, 479, 490, 500, 509, 513, 536, 543, 562, 605, and 639 copyright © 2016 by Amy Danziger Ross
All rights reserved, including the right of reproduction in whole or in part in any form.
SIMON & SCHUSTER BFYR is a trademark of Simon & Schuster, Inc.
For information about special discounts for bulk purchases, please contact Simon & Schuster Special Sales at 1-866-506-1949 or business@simonandschuster.com.
The Simon & Schuster Speakers Bureau can bring authors to your live event.
For more information or to book an event contact the Simon & Schuster Speakers Bureau at 1-866-248-3049 or visit our website at www.simonspeakers.com.
Cover designed by Sarah Creech
The text of this book was set in Berling Std.
Manufactured in the United States of America
First SIMON & SCHUSTER BFYR bind-up edition September 2020
2 4 6 8 10 9 7 5 3 1
Library of Congress Control Number 2020934669
ISBN 9781534473836 (pbk)
ISBN 9781481430708 (*Diary of a Haunting* eBook)
ISBN 9781481464437 (*Possession* eBook)
These titles were previously published individually.

CONTENTS

DIARY OF A HAUNTING

EDITOR'S NOTE

For as long as I can remember, I have been fascinated by the supernatural, and for years sought any evidence of its existence. Indeed, it is for this reason that I entered academia, and began my inquiry into the peculiar faith and practice known as Pronoica. From the first I learned of it, I had a sense that there was more to this strange relic of an earlier era than was obvious at first sight—that here at last, in the story of this movement, I would find the tokens that would confirm to me, if to no one else, that there was more to this life than the mere material.

Although I caught glimpses suggestive of a shadow world beyond our own, there was nothing to render it visible to human eyes. Nothing to convince me firmly, let alone anyone else. All was evanescent—enough to breed in me a hope, a curiosity, and drive toward knowledge, but nothing I could share.

In all that time, I wished for anything that would validate my theories and make them worthy of publication. I never dreamt that what I found would come at such a terrible price.

The shocking events of this story have shaken me more than I can possibly express. I have lost . . . No. What I have lost cannot be quantified. To even try would be a terrible insult to the memory of the departed.

Nevertheless, now that this documentary evidence has fallen into my life, the tragedy that brought it to my attention cannot be reason to hide it from public knowledge. It is vital, for the sake of human understanding, that this information be released to the world. I wish that the evidence were stronger. I know that many—most, perhaps—will read this account and view it as fraud, or worse yet, as entertainment. I can only hope that a few will see this document for what it truly is: a tragic testimonial concerning the dread workings of the spirit world upon our own.

Some names have been changed to protect the privacy of the bereft.

Montague Verano, Phd.
Professor, Department of History
University of Idaho

THURSDAY, JANUARY 1, 11:14 A.M.

New year, new journal! Or well, new attempt at old journal.

I haven't posted here in forever. I can't believe I even remember the password. All my old posts are so ridiculous. I'm not even friends with those people anymore. I used to get so worked up about this or that boy, or who was passing notes in math class. All that stuff seems far away now, ever since Real Life came along and punched me in the face.

From now on I am only posting locked entries—I don't think anyone I know is still on this site anyway, but just in case. It'll be kind of a relief to have one place where I can be completely honest . . . even if it doesn't always make me look that great.

But really, it's everyone else who look like assholes right now. I just . . . I cannot believe my dad. My *dad*! The person I loved and admired most in this world, who I looked up to . . .

It's been six months, but I still can't wrap my head around the fact that he was having an affair. That now he has a new wife, that he has no interest in even seeing me and Logan anymore. I mean, he says he does, but that seemed like it was more for the judge than for us. I can hardly blame the new girl for not wanting to deal with stepkids, what with her being all of TWENTY-TWO.

Disgusting.

And the worst thing is what a cliché it is. It's not like I completely lived in a bubble. I was semi-aware that Hollywood producers don't have the greatest record of staying married to one woman their whole lives . . . especially when that woman was a beautiful young movie star when they got married. And that's exactly what all the industry rags are saying, *obviously*. It feels like everyone outside these four walls is actually *yawning* at how lame and predictable this divorce is, my dad trading Mom in for the younger version.

I don't know, I shouldn't be shocked, but I am. Call me naive, but I really believed our family was different. We used to joke about it around the dinner table, how all that Hollywood gossip would never affect us because Mom and Dad were real people, not like the stereotypical plastic LA-types. They even named me Paige and not, like, Starfruit or Crash or some absurd celebaby name. But *haha*, turns out the joke is on me. And I'm the only one who didn't see the punch line coming a mile away.

Well, me and Mom. If anyone is handling this worse than I am . . .

And that's the thing. Part of me is really glad to see her starting to get back on her feet at last. It's definitely a step up from alternately sobbing and staring off into space, or screaming into her phone at her lawyer—though that was good in a way, because it got her a fat settlement (another good thing about my parents being "real people" is they didn't have a prenup, like the rest of Hollywood). So there's that at least.

Does that sound awful?

Mercenary. That's what the New Girl called Mom, according to TMZ (which I have stopped reading, obviously, but the kids in school insist on feeding me every gross detail).

But whatever, the whole point of this journal is for me to be able to say these ugly things and not feel bad about it. So there it is: I am glad that if Dad has to be a scumbag and ruin everybody's life, at least we get some money out of it.

And I'm glad Mom is doing better. I really am. But I wish she could find a way of getting better that's less disruptive to *my* life. Haven't I been through enough upheaval this year? Now, in addition to losing my family, I'm also about to lose all my friends, my school, my room, everything that is familiar to me, all so Mom can follow her dream out in . . . God, it makes me cringe to even say it. Idaho.

IDAHO. Is that not just . . . completely psychotic or what? Is that even a real place? I guess Cassie and Mackenzie went there last year to ski, but I don't think we're moving to the ski-resort part.

SATURDAY, JANUARY 3, 9:30 A.M.

It looks like Mom really means it about this Idaho thing. We leave in less than a week!

I totally get the desire to get away from Hollywood for a while, but couldn't she have applied to graduate school in normal places? Like NYU, or London . . . or even *Seattle* or something. But I guess when you're obsessed with the environment and ecology, "middle of nowhere" is pretty much your only option. Don't get me wrong, I do think it's cool that after all those years being a stay-at-home mom, and saving owls for charity on the side, Mom is now really going for it, studying natural resource conservation so she can make the world a better place. Sure, Dad and I like (liked!) to tease her about being such a hippie-dippie do-gooder, with all her "trust the universe" and "stewards of the earth" and "law of attraction" silliness, but I really do admire her.

Maybe more now than I did when they were together.

Mom's always been such a positive, open "spirit" as she would say, and that grated on me, because I take after my dad more, with the cynical sardonic personality . . . but it was weird and kind of terrible to see her so wretched for the past few months, because it was so not her. Like living with a stranger. And now she is finally coming out of it, which is a relief, but can I just say it one more time? IDAHO. Who does that? Who does that to her innocent children? I just can't even.

Come on, where's that positivity, Paige? *deep breath*

Okay, maybe it won't be so bad. Nature, right? It's supposed to be beautiful there. Maybe I'll get to see a moose or something. And it will make Mom happy. That's the important thing.

THURSDAY, JANUARY 8, 10:04 P.M.

Having serious second thoughts about this Idaho business. I cannot believe that this morning I woke up to 70-degree cloudless weather, and willingly got on a plane to take me to *this*. Though saying "willing" might be a slight overstatement.

I am trying to put a good face on everything for Mom and Logan, but holy crap, it is miserable here. For the past few days Mom has been feeding us fantasies of our first real snowfall, and how we were going to make snowmen and snow angels and have snowball fights. I admit I was getting a teensy bit excited about going to this winter wonderland. Then we get off the plane and we're greeted with *slush*. Dirty wet slush that gets in your shoes and soaks the bottoms of your jeans. And wind! I have never felt so much wind. It's like being on a mountaintop even when you're in the middle of downtown. Not that there *is* a downtown, really. Just one street with a few college bars I can't set foot in. Plus an indie movie theater, an indie bookstore—Jesus, hasn't anyone heard of chain stores here? Apparently Barnes and Noble hasn't made it to the frontier.

Our new house is a big hulking gray monstrosity, which is what you get when you rent a place sight unseen from six states away. Though you could almost imagine it being kind of pretty, once upon a time, with the big wraparound porch and the little turret on one side. If it were in better shape, it might look like something out of a storybook. Inside, everything is centered around a big staircase, and there's a massive room on the first floor that I guess was once a ballroom? Crazy. Mom and I agreed to leave that room empty because we would be, like, shouting at each other across it. There is a smaller room with a nice fireplace that I think we'll make the living room. In the back is a kitchen, which is pretty small compared to our place back in California, though it does have a big pantry behind it. Then another couple of random rooms, one of which will be Mom's study, and the others will inevitably fill up with junk, I bet.

It must have been a mansion when it was built, probably a million years ago, but now it's just old and rickety. And drafty. They don't seem to have heard of insulation here. The wind whistles through the walls so much that you can feel it indoors. Even with the heat all the way on and my heaviest sweater, it still feels like I'm standing outside. Except when I *am* outside, and it feels like I'm in Siberia. And so far the moving truck hasn't arrived with our stuff yet, so in the meantime we are making do with just sleeping bags and air mattresses. Logan thinks camping indoors is awesome. Wish I could share his enthusiasm . . .

The house is on the outskirts of town, though to be honest

that's only about a mile from the, uh, inskirts of town. On one side it's a normal street with other houses and cars and stuff, but you go around back and the town just ends. Normally don't cities and towns sort of peter out, the houses getting farther apart from one another until eventually you are looking at open fields? Not here. Step out into the backyard and you can see for miles. Not that there's anything to see.

Before I came, I spent some time looking up pictures of Idaho online, and there were all these super pretty landscapes of snowcapped mountains and crystal clear lakes. Well, that must be some other Idaho, because all we've got here are these weird little stubbly brown hills, extending out all the way to the horizon. And nothing on them—no houses, no trees, no roads, just the occasional broken-down barn, or the towering shape of a grain elevator outlined against the sky. Oh, and the sky here isn't blue. It isn't even gray. It's pure white like cotton, and it seems to go on forever. Makes the whole world feel sort of muffled.

That's what I see from my window. At first I wanted the room at the front of the house, under the turret, but Logan claimed it on his run through. Mom shot a look over at me—on the plane she had promised me first dibs on the rooms, since I'm older (and maybe since I'd been whining about the move)—but it didn't feel right pulling rank. Not when Logan seemed so excited. Plus, there was something weird about that room. I don't know what it was, but the minute I walked in, I felt this sort of buzzing, like a vibration coming up through the floor, or maybe through the air even. It set my teeth on edge, and after just a few minutes helping Logan dust the place, I had a bit of a headache. I wonder if there's some kind of transformer or something just outside? But Logan and Mom didn't seem to notice it.

Anyway, after that I was just as happy to pick a room at the back of the house, even if it's a little smaller and looks out over those endless brown hills.

FRIDAY, JANUARY 9, 9:37 A.M.

The house is infested with vermin.

I don't know why I didn't notice it the first day. Maybe they were in hiding? But today they definitely sent out the welcoming committee.

I went out early this morning for a run (bad idea, btw— all that slush from the other day had frozen overnight into a solid sheet of gray ice), and when I came back in through the front door, I felt something tugging on my ponytail. At first I thought it must be Logan messing with me, so I yelled "quit it" and turn around to swat him away, and that's when I see some *thing* caught in my hair. Ugh.

Just inside the front door, there are these three sticky, yellow-orangey strips hanging from the ceiling—right where anyone walking in would get snagged on them. Mom says

it's flypaper, which I've heard of but never seen before, and she says she hasn't seen it since she was a kid. How do we deal with flies in the civilized world? I don't know, but we must somehow, because you hardly ever saw them in California.

Anyway, I let out a yelp, which brings Mom to my rescue. She manages to disentangle me, and we both look closer and realize the strip is *covered* in flies. Dead fly bodies, all up in my hair. That's cool, I guess.

So obviously I scuttle away in revulsion while Mom says not to worry because she is going to take the strips down. And Logan, who must have been drawn like a moth to the bright light of my discomfort, shows up and is like, but then won't there be more flies? But Mom says no, it's the middle of winter, there's no need for flypaper now. That it must be left over from summer.

"So why are these ones moving?" says Logan. And I am so sure he is messing with me that I lean over to look and it's true. It's. *True*. Flies with their wings stuck to the paper, and their wretched little legs waving around in the air.

"That's weird," says Mom, ever so helpfully.

She thinks she's an expert in all things to do with nature, but apparently she skipped the chapter on the life cycle of winged insects. But of course I know what's coming next. Mom is all upset, not because there are half-dead zombie flies in our house, but because she is *concerned* for the welfare of the flies. Yes. So she goes off on a huge speech about how cruel flypaper is, and how flies are living creatures who feel pain and fear death, and okay fine, now I am feeling kind of bad, because I see her point, but still. Ew.

So she declares, no more flypaper, nor any other poison or anything that could harm the flies. Come summer, she'll have someone take a look at making the screen door fit a little tighter, and that, according to her, should solve the problem. We'll see.

SUNDAY, JANUARY 11, 11:14 A.M.

First day of school tomorrow. Mom is the happiest I have seen her in ages, getting all her stuff ready to start classes. What a lunatic! Did she not get the memo about how all normal people dread school? But maybe it's different when you get to go by choice, instead of people forcing you.

I'm still working on being cheerful and supportive about everything, but it is hard not to be homesick for my queen-size bed and big closets and sunshine and our pool. No one has a pool here, because it is the North Pole, basically.

Oh well, better make the best of it. I can only hope school tomorrow won't be too awful.

Oh, who am I kidding? Getting plopped down in the middle of junior year in a school where everyone has probably known each other since birth? It's going to be excruciating.

MONDAY, JANUARY 12, 6:40 P.M.

Okay, so it wasn't that bad. Wow! Imagine that. This journal was supposed to be a place for all my bad thoughts, but I have to be honest and admit I had an okay time at school today. Yes, it's true that everyone here has known each other since forever, but weirdly that kind of worked in my favor. "The new girl from LA" was the big news all over the whole school, and everyone wanted to meet me. And they were all super nice! So strange . . . is this how people act outside of LA? Because at my old school we pretty much shunned any new person for at least a month or two.

Anyway, I could get used to this. I got invited to sit at the cool girl table—not LA cool, but within the context of Idaho I could tell it was the best of the available options. And they wanted to know all about Hollywood and what celeb parties I had gone to. Oh, and there was this ridiculously cute guy in my math class, so I flirted with him a little, and after school he came up and asked me if I needed a ride home! Which I couldn't accept, unfortunately, because Mom was going to pick me up and take me out for coffee and a chat about my first day, but still.

I don't know. It's not home, but it's nice to be thought of as special and exciting.

WEDNESDAY, JANUARY 14, 4:10 P.M.

Well! Scratch that last post. Everyone at school hates me now.

I guess that cute guy in my math class is dating one of the girls from the cool table. I don't know how I was expected to know that, but now she hates me, and told everyone that I am stuck-up and slutty. And everyone in school believes her, because that's what it means to be the cool girl. Everyone just unthinkingly goes along with whatever you say.

So now in addition to living in the middle of nowhere, I am also a social pariah. Fun!

In other wonderful news, it was a big mistake for Mom to take down those fly strips because the front entryway has now become Grand Central Station for flies. Big black, ugly suckers too. They've taken to hanging out in a lazy swarm right inside the front door, so it's impossible to go in or out of the house without wading through a *cloud* of flying, buzzing beasts. But Mom still won't do anything about them. She says they have as much right to the space as we do.

I pointed out that they aren't paying rent, and then Mom pointed out that neither am I.

Point: Mom.

But I have this creeping feeling like there might be something else in the house too. Something even worse. I kind of don't want to say it aloud (or even put it in writing) because it freaks me out, but I think there might be . . . . . . (((((spiders))))) in here. Oh God, pretend I didn't say that. I don't even want to think about it.

Getting really sick of living without furniture. But let's end this on a positive note: the movers will be here soon with all our stuff!

THURSDAY, JANUARY 15, 4:38 P.M.

So, episode 3 of Paige's Humiliating Life. I thought nothing could be worse than everyone in school shunning me for no reason, but it turns out something is. The Weird Girl (you know what I mean, every school has one) wants to be my friend.

Seriously awkward. This girl—Chloe, I think?—dresses all in black and camo, and wears super heavy eye makeup. And her hair! Well, her hair is just ludicrous. Like, dyed black with a pink streak, but not a normal streak—it's *leopard* print. Is that not a cry for help? And obviously everyone else agrees, because no one ever talks to her, and she never talks to anyone either. Except me!

I now have that honor, since she came up to me at lunch and started asking me all kinds of creepy questions. Everyone else here (back when they were speaking to me) wanted to know about California and the movie business and all that. This girl just asks me about my new house. I'm like—this is *your* town, and the house has been sitting here for at least one hundred years. You probably know more about it than I do! Okay, I didn't say that, because I'm not a complete jerk. But I thought it.

How did I sink so low? What pathetic stench am I unwittingly giving off that makes this girl think I am an appropriate friend match for her? Although I guess she's right. Given the current situation, it's not like I'm going to do any better.

A part of me wants to blow her off in hopes that I can claw my way back into a respectable friend group at some point. But another part is like, eh, who cares? I've done the whole popular girl thing before, and it's not like it brought me a ton of happiness. Maybe I should experiment with being a weirdo outcast. I don't have much to lose, at this point.

(Drawing the line at leopard print hair, though.)

FRIDAY, JANUARY 16, 11:20 P.M.

I'm going to kill that little jerk.

The movers finally came with all our stuff (thank God!) and I was so happy and excited to see my bed and all my stuff again, you wouldn't believe. And I was trying to help out, carrying this big box full of lamps and picture frames and stuff, when Logan comes up and is like, "Hey Paige, look what I found." So I glance over at him and he rubs something sticky and gray on my sweater, and then he holds up his hands and they are covered with spider webbing.

So of course I drop the box and probably break forty things.

Uggggggh, trying so hard not to freak out. I mean, it's an old house, and old houses have cobwebs, right? It comes with the territory. But the spiders probably all died off a hundred years

ago. It totally doesn't mean there are legions of eight-legged monstrosities skittering in between the floorboards at night.

(oh, nice image, Paige. way to give yourself nightmares.)

deep breaths

It's okay. At least we have our stuff now, and the house is beginning to look like an actual place people live, and not like some hobo encampment. It is soooo nice to be able to curl up on a couch again, and cook real meals, and watch TV. Although the TV is acting weird—must be a problem with the cable hookup. I'll talk to Mom about it.

SUNDAY, JANUARY 18, 11:03 P.M.

Saw Weird Girl (Chloe) walk past my house twice this weekend, and stare up into the windows. Why is she so weird! I think I officially have a stalker.

MONDAY, JANUARY 19, 4:32 P.M.

Okay, I did it. I talked to Chloe after school today and it was okay. Don't get me wrong, this isn't some Lifetime movie where it turns out that the weird girl is nice and normal and just in need of a little kindness. She's *real weird*. But at least she's interesting.

For example, here's an actual conversational exchange we had today, on my walk home:

[Chloe lights a cigarette.]

Me: You smoke? Don't you know how bad it is for you?

Chloe: People say that. But it's only true if you think death is something to be avoided, rather than embraced.

Me: [. . .]

Then she goes back to asking me about the house. She's all, "So, what's it like?" What does that even mean? But she clarifies: "Is it really haunted?" And I think, ohhhh yeah, I should have seen that coming. Of course death-obsessed gothy girl wants to know if my creepy old house is haunted. Obvi.

So I roll my eyes, but she doesn't let it go. She's like, "Really? Nothing? No strange sounds, or lights flickering on and off, or random cold spots?" At that, I had to laugh. I explained to her that it's hard to find cold spots when the whole house is a freaking refrigerator. As for the noises . . . at first I was going to brush it off, but then I remembered the buzzing sound in Logan's room. So I mention that to her—how sometimes I can feel it in my teeth, and I'm not even sure if it's a sound or a feeling or what, but no one else seems bothered by it.

Her comment: "Wow, intense."

So I'm like, no, it's weird, but it's not supernatural, okay? Why would you even think that?

Chloe shrugs. "Maybe because of all the dead bodies."

So now there's that.

And she's like, the landlady didn't tell you? Back when this town was first founded, this house used to be the hospital. The basement was the morgue.

I admit, I might have gotten a few goose bumps. But I was pretty sure she was screwing with me, because I have been all up and down that house, and I never saw a basement. I tell her this, but Chloe gives me a weird look.

"Of course there's a basement," she says. "You can tell even from looking at the outside." We're half a block away from my house at that point, so she could show me. "See? There are little windows all along the bottom. There's got to be something down there."

And what do you know, she's right. I'd never even noticed.

That's when I remembered something slightly weird. There's

this random door in a kind of an out-of-the-way place right next to the kitchen. Or rather, there *was* a door. You have to look carefully, because it doesn't have a handle or anything. In fact, it's really just a doorway that has been walled up. I would never have noticed it at all if Mom hadn't been trying to hang a picture there and discovered that there was brick behind the plaster instead of wood like the other walls.

As I tell Chloe this, she raises her eyebrows as if this somehow constitutes proof that my house is haunted. Which it does not.

Except . . . when Chloe asked about funny noises in the house, there was one I didn't mention. In fact, I didn't even mention it here, I guess because I didn't want to admit it even to myself. But there's something about Chloe—weird as she is, she makes it feel sort of okay to admit that there is weird stuff in the world.

So I told her: One night last week I had fallen asleep on the couch downstairs and didn't wake up until after midnight. As I was tiptoeing up to bed, the wind died down just as I was passing in front of that walled-up door, and . . . I heard something. Chloe didn't say anything, she just raised her eyebrows in that way she does, as if inviting me to go on. It's hard to resist those eyebrows.

"Okay, this is going to sound crazy, but . . . it sounded like voices."

Chloe's expression didn't even change. It was as if she had been expecting this all along. "What were they saying?"

"I don't know, I couldn't make it out. And I'm not even totally sure it *was* voices. I'm not even sure it was anything at all, or if it's just my imagination playing tricks on me. I didn't exactly stick around to find out."

Chloe gazed at the house thoughtfully, her skirt whipping

around her legs as the wind blew in over those hills.

"Well, what do you think?" I said at last, trying to strike the right tone between serious and sarcastic. "Definitely haunted?"

"I don't know," she said. "I've heard things about this place all my life, but I've never been inside."

"Oh. Do you want to come in? But it usually seems pretty okay during the day. I mean . . . except for the gross cloud of flies hanging out in the entryway."

"Flies? In the middle of winter?"

I shrugged. Good thing the only person speaking to me is deeply weird, because I'm pretty sure any normal person would have freaked out when I announced that my house has an insect infestation. Chloe just raised her eyebrows slightly.

"Do you think I could stay overnight?" she said. "This weekend, I mean."

So, yup. That's the story of how I invited the Weird Girl over to my house for an awesome haunted house slumber party. Hope all my new zombie friends can make it!

WEDNESDAY, JANUARY 21, 11:05 P.M.

I am 300 percent done with Mom's stupid "the universe is a breathing organism" crap, and "we have to be stewards of the earth" and "every living thing is sacred," and yeah yeah that's all really beautiful but come on. We have to have some exceptions. We have to have an exception for spiders.

Because yes, we have spiders. I don't know how I didn't see before—some kind of mental block maybe? I think I just *so* didn't want to see them, didn't want to know, that I shut them out of my mind and out of my perception. But ever since Logan's little stunt with the cobweb, I have been seeing webs in every corner of the house. And they aren't always empty.

I thought I could handle it, I really tried to be stoic, but today I was sitting at my desk typing and one crawled over my *hand*. All those impossible little legs scurrying across my skin as if it was heading somewhere vitally important and I happened to be in its way.

So I may have screamed. I didn't even realize I was doing it until Mom came running into my room, obviously convinced I had broken a leg or been bitten by a raccoon or something. And she went into serious Mom mode and was all, "Paige, what happened, show me where it hurts, do I need to call an ambulance." Of course then I started crying and I pointed to the spider and . . . that's when she gave me the look.

The look that says, "You're kidding, right?" Where she sets her chin, and her lips make a thin line, and she just looks like she can't even believe I'm her daughter.

And I feel like the most worthless person in the world. But just . . . she doesn't get it. She thinks I'm being unreasonable, or unkind even. I can see the disappointment in her eyes when we talk about it, like she can't believe she produced someone so different from her, someone who doesn't see the world in the beautiful hippie earth mother way that she does. And I try to, I do. As much as I can. But spiders are . . . spiders are different.

This isn't just me being some tacky California girl and freaking out over every creepy crawly thing just to make myself seem feminine or cute or whatever. I'm pretty sure that what I have is a legit phobia. It's the legs—the way they coordinate in constant motion, all those pointy legs creeping and feeling, touching your flesh . . .

Then there's the way they crawl around where you can't see them. How they always crop up where you don't expect, dangling from a thread on the doorframe or in a cabinet. It's like they make safe, comfortable places suddenly threatening. Rationally, I know the spiders around here won't hurt me, but they still trigger my urge to cleanse the house with fire.

And Mom *knows* this about me. I have been like this ever since I was a little kid. Since before Logan was born. I remember back in our old house I went up to the attic once to dig through the old boxes and see if I could find some toys or clothes to play dress-up or whatever, and there was a spider-web on one of the boxes—not even a spider, just a web!—and I basically lost my mind. Had nightmares for weeks. So it's not like this is news to her.

Anyway, she did calm me down some, and made me sit at the kitchen table for one of her "talks." Basically, she lectured me. All the Goddess's creatures, that whole bit. Tenderhearted Mom, cares more about the eight-legged freaks of the ~~animal insect~~ arachnid world than her own daughter! But she did at least promise that she and Logan would scour the whole house and sweep out all the cobwebs, and that should solve the problem.

And she did point out that spiders eat flies . . . and wasn't I just complaining about the flies?

Somehow that is cold comfort right now.

SATURDAY, JANUARY 24, 12:13 P.M.

Well, that was unexpected. And not entirely awful.

So, as arranged, Chloe came over to my house after school on Friday. It was definitely a little awkward at first, since we're not exactly friends. We don't really have anything in common except this house—Chloe because she's curious about it, and me because, well, I live here. So it's not like we had a lot to talk about. I kinda wished I could be like Logan and his new friends. All he has to do is show them to the video game consoles and they are set for the afternoon.

Luckily, Mom was there to smooth things over a bit, though that was also kind of embarrassing because she started doing her routine about how we come from this long line of mystics. Uggggggh. The whole thing is ridiculous, and not something I believe in at ALL, and just makes Mom look either crazy or gullible. It's one thing to believe in respecting the earth and stuff, it's another to actually believe (contrary to ALL evidence) that you can control the universe with your mind.

I don't mind indulging her little hobby when it's just us, and it's been years since she did this in front of my friends because I told her how much I hated it, but I guess she decided that old rule didn't apply here, since Chloe was so clearly weird herself. I hadn't noticed before, but of course my mom remarked immediately that Chloe was wearing a pentagram around her neck. And it seems Chloe *was* interested, because while I sat there feeling awkward and trying not to roll my eyes, Chloe asked all kinds of questions about the family history, and Mom told all her stories that are either completely or largely made up, about my great-grandma being some kind of druid back in Ireland, and how there is this ancient energy that flows through our family line. Blah blah blah.

I finally got them to stop by inviting Chloe on a tour of the house. I knew she would go for that, since she has been curious about it for so long. Too bad there isn't all that much to see . . . It's not like we've got ghosts jumping out from behind corners. She didn't seem bored, though. She stood watching the flies swoop around for about five minutes. How's that for weird? And she asked a lot of questions about the history and structure of the house, most of which I couldn't answer.

I brought her into Logan's room because I wanted to see if she could hear the noise, but she had something else on her mind. "Where are the boarded-up windows?" she said before I could ask her about the buzzing. I had no idea what she was talking about, but she was like, "I can see from outside, some of the windows in the house look like they are boarded up."

I told her it must be a trick of the light or something, because no way would we leave any windows covered. Northern Idaho in the middle of winter is dark enough, and we're always trying to drag every ray of sunshine we can into the house. Then Logan came and kicked us out before I got a chance to draw her attention to the sound.

Anyway, that got us through the evening until Mom finally put the house to sleep and we wordlessly crept down to the secret door. It's funny but I was actually a little worried that we *wouldn't* hear anything. I think I was more nervous about looking like an idiot who imagined this whole thing than I was of actual ghosts. But sure enough, as we put our ears against the wall, there it was: a sound like muffled voices in conversation.

At first I felt a flutter of excitement. It was a relief to share this experience with someone, and not feel like I was completely crazy. But when I looked over at Chloe's shadowed face and saw her wide-eyed expression, I felt fear crawl back into my body and grip my guts.

"What do you think it means?" I whispered to her.

"I don't know. It seems crazy, but . . ." She pulled away from the door and stared at it, her expression set as if she was solving a puzzle. "The windows to the basement," she said. "Have you ever looked in them?"

Amazingly, that had not occurred to me, but now it seemed pretty obvious, and I led the way out of the house. A part of me knew I should be afraid, but excitement had taken over again, and I felt a lot more confident with Chloe by my side. We slipped down the front stairs and crept around the house toward where the windows were. I looked at Chloe, screwing up my courage, but she hesitated only a second before cupping her hands around her eyes and peering into the window. I followed suit.

After a few seconds I pulled away. "I can't make out anything," I said. "It's too dark." Chloe was still looking in the window, and she told me to look again. "Over there, toward the left," she said. "Do you see that?" I looked, and suddenly my fingers went numb with fear. Just faintly visible, off to one side, was a strange blue glow.

Without even thinking, I reached out and grabbed Chloe's hand. I realized right away that was a weird thing to do, what with us having just met and not particularly liking each other. But she didn't pull away, she just squeezed it back. My only thought at that point was to run back inside and hide under my covers, or wake up Mom and make her deal with it—whatever *it* was. But Chloe clearly had other things in mind. Dropping my hand, she took a few steps backward, as if to take in a view of the whole house in the moonlight. Again, she had that look on her face like she was in algebra class. "Paige," she said at last, "there's a door."

It took me a moment to even process what she meant. For a second I thought she was talking about the walled-up door inside. But then I followed her eyes and saw it: Tucked away around the back of the house and down a small flight of stairs was another door. A basement door.

I followed Chloe down the stairs and she tried the knob. The door gave way, groaning slightly as it opened. She gave me the briefest of looks over her shoulder, then stepped into the darkness. I took as deep a breath as my fear-constricted lungs would allow and joined her. At first, compared to the moonlit night outside, the basement seemed fathomlessly dark, but after a moment I noticed the same blue glow we had seen through the

windows. Chloe obviously saw it too and moved toward it, though I remained frozen in place. I was aware of her dark form blocking the glow as she progressed, until it became clear that she had made it to a doorway. I heard her give a strangled yelp, and that was all it took to free me from my paralysis. I screamed.

"What the hell?" I heard a voice through my scream, and it wasn't Chloe's. It was a guy's voice. "What are you doing in here? Calm down, Jesus, calm down."

A bright light came on, and I stopped screaming. Chloe's black-clad form came into view just in front of me as my eyes adjusted. And in front of her, slightly blocked by her, was a pale, lithe guy with a tangle of dark, curly hair flopped over his forehead. His eyes were dark and serious, and were framed by straight, sharp eyebrows. He was standing in his underwear. And he was staring at us.

"It's okay," said Chloe. "He's just a . . . I don't think he's a ghost."

"Pretty sure I'm not a ghost," the guy said. "Who are you?"

I didn't know what to say, and not because I was distracted by his incredible body. Definitely not that. "I live here," I tried.

"No," he said. "*I* live here. Look, can you hold on a sec? I want to have this conversation with pants on." He disappeared from my view a minute, during which time I realized that the blue glow we had seen must have come from a TV or a laptop in his bedroom. The boy came back wearing jeans and pulling a white T-shirt on over his head. He gave us both a once-over.

"You live upstairs, don't you?" he said to me. "I saw you when you moved in. And you . . . you're the weird girl who walks past this place three times a day and always stares at it."

"She's not weird," I said, feeling suddenly defensive on

Chloe's behalf. But Chloe apparently didn't need my support.

"Sure I am," she said. "It's kind of my thing."

At least she owns it. As the less weird member of our investigative team, I went ahead and introduced us both. He said his name was Raph (short for Raphael, I guess), and when he shook my hand, I may have trembled a little.

"Why did you scream?" said Raph. "You broke into *my* apartment, I should be screaming."

"Your door was unlocked," Chloe pointed out.

"Small-town Idaho. Who locks their doors? That's not an invitation to come wandering in at all hours of the night." A dark smile flickered across his face, his lip curling wickedly. "Small-town Idaho. You're lucky you didn't get shot for trespassing."

I couldn't help grinning back at him. "I'm sorry," I said. "I just, I didn't know anyone was living here. I didn't even realize this house had a basement until a few days ago. Why *are* you living here? Does anyone know?"

"I'm not a squatter, if that's what you're asking. I pay rent." Raph suddenly looked a little sheepish. "Most of the time, anyway. Sometimes. My mom owns this place. She's your landlady. I go to school," he said, nodding vaguely in the direction of the university. "The previous owners refinished this basement to be a mother-in-law apartment, and then my mom took over the house, and last year when I . . ." He combed a hand roughly through his hair. "Well, I decided to move off campus, and my mom said I could move in here. I help out around the place, fix stuff up when it needs it."

"There's a lot left to be fixed," I said, then blushed at my rudeness.

"You should have seen it before." He explained how the

43

place had stood empty for years, and was falling apart when she bought it. Raph had patched the roof and fixed up some of the plumbing, repaired some holes in the stairs. Guess he hadn't gotten around to insulation yet.

Chloe, ever on the prowl for macabre mysteries, asked why the house had been abandoned. "Did something bad happen here?"

"What, like a murder?" said Raph.

Chloe didn't say anything, but she gave me a meaningful look. Raph snorted in amusement. "Yeah, something bad happened here," he said. "Something bad happened everywhere. It's called the housing crisis. Ever pick up a newspaper? There was a family that lived here a while back, but the guy's store went out of business and they couldn't pay the mortgage and the bank foreclosed on them. The whole family moved in with his wife's parents."

"So the bank kicked them out, even though no one else wanted it?"

"It's what banks do," said Raph with a shrug. "Once it started to look run-down, the price went down, and my mom had the idea that she could turn it into a bed-and-breakfast. I didn't think she'd find anyone to rent such a big, weird old place in the meantime, but then you and your mom came along."

"It wasn't a morgue, then?" said Chloe.

"You've heard about that, huh? Yeah. There was a morgue down here in the basement once, back when it was the town's hospital. Is that why you guys thought it was haunted?" He looked between us, obviously amused. "Cute," he said. "But who would haunt a morgue? Think about it. A morgue is really just a way station. A place bodies rest a little while, between when they died and when they get buried. If you were a wandering spirit, why would you hang around a morgue? You'd probably go to the place you died, or where something bad happened, or go find the person who wronged you. A morgue would be boring."

"You don't believe in ghosts," said Chloe, clearly disappointed.

Raph pressed his lips together. "There are no ghosts down here."

After that, Chloe and I left Raph alone and snuck back into the house and up to bed. It was very late by then, but we lay awake for some time, discussing what Raph had told us about the house. As for me, I found it kind of a relief to hear his stories. I was just as happy to hear that this house is not haunted, and it was just our overactive imaginations playing tricks on us. Chloe, though—I think she was actually disappointed. Maybe that's what it means to live in a small town. Life is so boring here, you start wishing for supernatural evil just to liven up the weekends a bit. Easy for her to say—she doesn't have to live here.

Eventually the spaces between our comments grew bigger, and I got the idea that Chloe was just about asleep. I closed my eyes, but before I drifted off, I put forward one last topic of conversation.

"Chloe?"

"Yeah?"

"Raph is kind of cute, I think."

"Um," said Chloe. "If by cute you mean devastatingly gorgeous, then yes. Kind of."

"But he's too old, right? I mean, how old do you think he is?"

Chloe considered. "Well, he's in college, obviously. And I

don't think he's a freshman . . . so he's probably like 20, at least."

"That's totally gross, right?"

"Gross and illegal," she confirmed. "Still . . . as ghosts go, Raph is definitely sexy."

Ha! Raph the sexy ghost. I like that.

MONDAY, JANUARY 26, 5:15 P.M.

The flies aren't gone, and neither are the spiders. If Mom's theory about spiders eating flies were correct, you'd think we'd see a diminution in one or the other. But this morning I saw five of the spiders standing together in the corner near my book bag, almost like they were plotting. And the flies just kept swooping around without a care in the world.

I'm really trying not to be such a baby about this stuff, but when I saw the spiders, I couldn't help it: I yelped. Logan came over to see what was wrong, and without even flinching, he just leaned down and scooped them up and tossed them outside. God, I have never been so grateful for my annoying little brother.

I felt a bit stupid as we walked to school together, and I was like, "You must think I'm pretty pathetic, huh?" But he was cool about it. He said he got used to dealing with gross stuff because of all the science experiments he does. It's not that he doesn't get creeped out, it's just that he's learned to control it. When you turn it into science, it stops being scary or gross, and just becomes data.

I asked him how I could turn the bugs into data, and he said to keep a notebook.

Ha. Is it really that simple?

TUESDAY, JANUARY 27, 4:10 P.M.

Spiders: 2 in the shower, 1 on the windowsill in my bedroom.
Flies: Too many to count, but maybe there are fewer? In any
case, the cloud seemed a little thinner this morning. So maybe
the spiders are pulling their weight around here after all?

Which really just begs the question: Which is better, spiders
or flies? Or let me rephrase that: Which do I loathe least? On
the face of it, this seems like an easy choice, because I have a
phobia of spiders, and no phobia of flies. I don't love flies, God
knows, but I'm not morbidly terrified of them either.

But the flies in this house . . . it's just that there are so *many*
of them. And they're so unavoidable. It's weird how they cluster
by the door. I can't see what is drawing them there. Wouldn't you
expect them to be near the food, or the trash? A drain, maybe?
But they insist on hanging out at the front door, which makes

every trip into or out of the house into a kind of horror show.

Spiders, on the other hand . . . well, at least they keep to themselves, mostly. You catch sight of them out of the corner of your eye, but you don't have to go swimming through vast hordes of them (ugh, that thought, why did I even think that?). But maybe it's not the spiders I see that worry me. For every spider you see, you know that there are at least a dozen more, hiding and waiting for you to go to sleep so they can walk on you and nip at you with those awful fangs . . .

shudder

I wonder if I could get the flies to eat the spiders? Or maybe they can both eat each other in a revolting free-for-all.

I'm not sure this is what Logan meant about thinking like a scientist.

Right. Moving on to cheerier subjects . . . we got our first real snowfall since I've been here! I woke up yesterday morning and my room was so much brighter than usual. I couldn't figure out why at first, but then I realized—the rolling brown hills outside my window weren't brown anymore. They were sparkling white! A big improvement, though it did make walking to school a bit of a pain.

Maybe after school tomorrow Logan and I can have that snowball fight we were promised.

Classes are fine, though I am still the school outcast. I guess one nice thing is that I pay a lot more attention in class now than I used to, when I was popular. Makes my homework easier.

TUESDAY, JANUARY 27, 11:30 P.M.

Mom continues to be annoying. She got into this weird thing with me this evening when I was unpacking groceries. I was just trying to be helpful! But instead of thanking me, she started nagging about where I put stuff away. She was going on about how she bought two jars of pasta sauce and a whole crate of granola bars a few days ago, and now she can't find them anywhere in the kitchen. Like, how is that my fault? So she is micromanaging me about where to put all the stuff away, and I open a cabinet and there are SIX jars of pasta sauce. Ha! I have no idea why she bought so much pasta sauce, though. And apparently neither does she, since she swore she only bought two.

Then Logan was like, "It was probably ghosts." I laughed. What kind of ghosts mess with marinara? But Mom seemed to like the idea that we might be sharing the house with some "restless spirits." She is such a freak sometimes.

It's weirder from Logan. He's never shared in any of Mom's otherworldly interests. He's the scientist of the family, and pretty much always has been. I pointed this contradiction out to him, but he just shrugged. "Science means trusting the evidence of my senses." Whatever that means . . .

But Logan *has* been acting a little strange lately. He's been having trouble sleeping. I think it's because of the move and the divorce, not to mention the flies and the spiders and the wind screaming in the walls every night. But Mom seems a bit worried about him. I think mostly she feels guilty—under the circumstances, I guess it's easy for her to blame herself. No wonder she's a little absentminded . . . I guess I should cut her some slack.

Oh, but I did manage to ask her about Raph. I tried to be all, "So, uh, there's a dude living in our house, *jsyk*," but it turns out she did know, so then I felt dumb. Then she got on my case, and was like, "Paige, I *told* you the landlady's son lived downstairs, but you never listen to anything I say," blah blah. Why is it that the minute someone says, "You never listen to a word I say," I immediately start to tune them out?

Weirdly enough, Mom seems to be a total fan of Raph. Apparently she has been going down to his place now and then while I'm at school to bring him proper meals, because he's "much too thin." Hmm, that's one way of putting it. I would have gone with "lean" or "svelte" or maybe "outrageously gor-geous." Wait, ~~does this mean Mom has been checking out Raph's~~

~~body?~~ Ew, I don't know why I even thought that. Don't think about that.

Anyway, she actually told me that he "seems like a nice boy" and that I should get to know him. Mom wants me to cozy up to a scorching hot college boy? Uh, okay, don't mind if I do.

SATURDAY, JANUARY 31, 3:15 P.M.

Sooo that was awkward.

The good news is, I figured out an excuse to go see Raph again. (Mom's permission or no, it felt weird to just knock on his door and be like, hi! wanna make out? ahem.) So yeah, I was trying to log on to the Internet to update this journal, but the stupid Wi-Fi has been crapping out lately. I don't know what is up with it. I reloaded a million times and kept getting different error messages. Rebooted the router, blah blah troubleshooting, but each time it would work for like a minute and then fritz out again. I need to bug Mom about it, along with the cable, which is still cutting in and out. (And doing odder stuff too—like the other day I was watching the end of a show, and instead of the next show coming on, the same episode started playing. I'm lazy, so I watched the whole thing again. But then it started playing again! And I know there was another show that was supposed to be on. The weird thing is, we don't even have a DVR.)

Anyway, I was checking the Wi-Fi network for the fiftieth time when it suddenly occurred to me that this situation might have a silver lining. There was this other network, very strong, called "The Morgue." It had to be Raph. Password protected, of course, but what better excuse to wander down and strike up a conversation? I know, pretty crafty!

So I head down there (after putting on some makeup and my best pair of jeans) and he answers the door in this pale blue T-shirt and was just looking . . . delicious, and I'm trying to be all supercool, like um, hey, my Wi-Fi is out, can I borrow your password? And he's like, yeah, if you want, but mine's been all over the place today too. Is it windy today? Sometimes the wind messes with the wires or something. So I'm like, mmm, yeah, wires. And he gives me the password and then we're, like, staring at each other.

So obviously I start babbling like an idiot, because I have nothing to say but I don't want to leave. So I say, "I hope I'm not bothering you. My mom told me to come down and ask. She really likes you or something, I guess." WTF am I even saying. So he's like, "Whaaa?" and I'm trying to think of a single flirty thing to say that doesn't make me look like an idiot, and I settle on, "Yeah, normally she is kind of uptight about me hanging out with older boys. Especially ones who . . ." and then right there I lose my nerve to say what was on my mind, so I just sort of peter out. I'm so cool.

Raph had been smiling pleasantly, adorably, through this whole performance, but right then, when I didn't end the sentence, he . . . I don't know, he looked serious all of a sudden. Or more than that, he looked . . . nervous? I kind of want to say haunted, but that's probably just because I have hauntings on the brain, thanks to Chloe. Anyway, I expected him to just smile and move on, maybe give me an "Okay, weird girl" look, but instead he gets this very intense look about him. I can see the muscles in his shoulders and arms tense up (not that I was checking out his body! okay, I was), and he's like, "Ones who what?"

Now I *really* don't want to say what I was thinking, except whatever *he's* thinking is apparently even worse, so I kind of have to. So even though I am feeling entirely flustered and awkward and embarrassed, I try to sound nonchalant as I say, "Ones who look like you." And then obviously blush like a dork.

But it wasn't allll bad because it brought the smile back to his face, and his shoulders relaxed, and then he looked down and ran a hand through those amazing curls and omg but HE WAS BLUSHING TOO. And it was pretty much the cutest thing I have ever seen. "Oh," he said. "Um . . . thanks."

And right then I was probably the happiest person in the world.

Yeah, that didn't last.

"I think I know why your mom is cool with us hanging out," he said, still looking all sweet and bashful and incredible. And I'm like, mmmm? And he says, "Probably because I told her I'm gay."

I know. I know. What is my life even.

But the best part is my brilliant response is to be like, "Oh. OH. Oh. So . . . wait. Are you? Gay?"

"No," says Raph, "I just told her that for shits and giggles."

"Oh," I say, and AGAIN my brain starts reeling before finally he figures out that I am a moron and need sarcasm explained to me.

"Paige," he says. "Yes. I'm gay. So your mom doesn't need to worry. And neither do you."

Hahaha FML. Ferreal.

SUNDAY, FEBRUARY 1, 10:28 A.M.

Flies: About the same, I think. No more or less. Except they seem . . . bigger, somehow. Maybe they have taken my suggestion after all and started to eat the spiders?

Spiders: 4 in the shower, 6 in my bedroom, 1 in my bed.

The less said about that the better.

Moving on. This is weird. Mom was freaking out last night (but not over spiders, which any reasonable person would freak out over) because she couldn't find her striped sweater. Not just any sweater, her *favorite* striped sweater. Which she suddenly needed to attend some department function. As if those eco-geeks care what anyone wears, as long as it's made from hemp.

Anyway, she came into my room and accused me of stealing her sweater. Unfair! Okay, yes, I have borrowed it on a few occasions. True. But in my defense, it looks better on me than on her. And anyway, I didn't take it! It's not like I've got anyone to impress here in Idaho—not even eco-geeks. Well, I guess there's Raph, but . . . yeah, it would have to be a pretty magical sweater to turn him straight, so. Point is, I did not take her sweater. Swear to God.

And I told Mom this, but she didn't believe me, so she opened up my closet to look for it, and in very dramatic fashion she turns around, holding up the missing sweater like she's Sherlock Holmes or something.

And that's weird, because I swear I have not even seen that sweater in months. But what's even weirder is that I notice over her shoulder . . . there are three other sweaters. Three other striped sweaters. That are totally identical to the one in her hands.

I pointed this out to Mom, and she agreed that it was weird, but idk, she deals with this stuff better than I do. Because while my whole body went cold and clammy, she just laughed. "Guess our astral roommates were a little bored tonight," she says in a too-loud voice, as if she figures they are listening. And I just cannot deal with that. I'm like, MOM. This isn't funny, this is seriously freaky. Isn't it?

But all she says is, someone just gave you free clothes, honey. Are you really going to complain?

Point: Mom.

WEDNESDAY, FEBRUARY 4, 5:20 P.M.

Flies: Big
Spiders: 16 since my last entry. I think.

I might have missed a few. I've been keeping track of them on a sticky note next to my computer, but that mostly only works for the ones I see in my room, or else I have to remember them until I get back to my room. You would think a person like me would have no trouble remembering seeing a spider, but sometimes other events do push them out of my head.

For example, it snowed again. A lot this time, so it's really deep. It's pretty when it falls, but I am getting a little sick of dealing with it on the ground. Guess I shouldn't complain too much, though, because when I got home, Raph was shoveling our porch and front walk. Glad I don't have to do that.

He looked really cold—he was all bundled up, with only his

eyes and the tip of his nose visible, and his nose was pink—so I asked if he wanted to come inside for some hot chocolate. He pulled the scarf down to uncover his mouth.

"Inside," he repeated. "Your place?" Like, duh. He looked up at the house, then back at me without answering. I sighed a little.

"It's just a warm drink," I said. "I get it, you're gay. Look, I don't bite."

At that, his cheeks blushed to match his nose. "It's not that," he said, "it's . . ." He broke off, huffing white vapor as he got his breath back from shoveling. "I used to spend a lot of time alone in that house," he said at last. "It . . . kind of got to me. The basement feels okay, but . . ."

"Really?" I said. "Not you, too. Am I the only person not convinced this place is haunted?"

"You mean Chloe?" he says. And I explain no, not just Chloe—Mom and Logan are always saying it too. And this, I guess unsurprisingly, does not seem to make him feel less uneasy. At last I roll my eyes and tell him I'll just bring it out to him. Which I do.

So then I'm handing him the chocolate and feeling like I have to make conversation now, so I mention that I don't think I've ever seen him out of his apartment before. He just nods at this, so I follow up with, "When do you go to class?"

Instead of answering, he takes a big gulp of hot chocolate and winds up choking on it. Adorably, but still pretty dorky. Anyway, he tells me he's taking a "light schedule this semester." So I ask what his major is, and he says history. "I mean, English. It was English, and then it was history. I guess." Which is kind of a weird answer.

"Oh," I say. "And now?"

"Now it's . . . I don't know. I guess not history anymore."

This conversation seems to be derailing fast, so I struggle to get it back on track. "So . . . English, then, or . . . ?"

"Maybe? We'll see. Technically I don't have a major." He takes a deep breath and looks out at the snow. "Technically I'm not a student."

This is odd and unexpected. I only just met the guy, and practically the very first thing he said to me was that he was a student at the university. And now he says he's not . . . Kind of awkward to catch someone in a lie within, like, the first hundred words they say to you. So now I don't know what to think. Or say. Luckily, he goes on.

"Medical leave of absence. Technically."

"Oh," I say, suddenly feeling like a huge jerk for mentally calling him a liar. "So you're like . . . sick? What's wrong with you?" Which is the most appallingly rude thing I could possibly have said, but he doesn't seem fazed. He just taps his forehead with one finger. "Oh God," I say, "brain tumor?"

He laughs. "No . . . I'm not dying, just crazy. Or so they tell me. Something happened last semester. I was working on this project with a professor, and . . . things got weird. Or I got weird. Or—I don't know. Anyway, it was decided that I needed some time off. To regroup."

I nodded sagely as if this all made complete sense, even though not any of it did. "What was the project?"

Raph just looked up at the house, as if something in the peeling gray paint was suddenly very fascinating. "I should get to that one of these days," he said. "It could cause problems down the road. If it's not repainted."

So I'm like . . . uh, okay. Why are we talking about paint now?

"You were about to tell me about the project?" I prompt him.

"I wasn't, actually." Raph gives me one of his long, intense looks, which still make me feel a little trembly. "You're pretty dense, aren't you?" he says. "When someone changes the subject like that, it's a way of saying 'I don't want to talk about it.' Got it?"

"Right," I say. "Sorry."

Guess someone's got a secret.

THURSDAY, FEBRUARY 5, 5:40 P.M.

Flies: About the same
Spiders: 8 since yesterday, I'm pretty sure.

I wonder if anyone has created an app to help people keep track of their spider infestations. If I could enter the sightings on my phone, I could keep my data more precisely, which I am told is important for science.

I suppose it wouldn't have to be specific to spiders. You could use the same app to keep track of all sorts of things that happen to scare the bejeezus out of you. Snakes. Rats. Clowns. Maybe there is someone out there right now writing an app to keep track of how many clowns he runs across every day, in hopes of calming his irrational fear of them. If so, I hope he makes it publicly available.

Not that it would do me much good these days. My phone is being a complete bastard.

God, why can't things just work? The Wi-Fi is sort of working now, since Mom called the ISP. I mean, the signal looks good, but there are weird dead spots all over the house, most particularly in my room! Which is really annoying. So basically if I want to be online at all, I have to hang out in the kitchen or one part of the living room. It's the strongest in Logan's room, which is weird because his room is, like, on the opposite side of the house from the router. I don't even know. And I hate going in there because of that buzzing noise.

But when I try to use my cell phone to go online, that's no better—my signal craps out at the randomest moments. Is this what it means to live in the middle of nowhere? It's fine when I'm at school, though. Raph says it has something to do with where the house is, but that makes no sense to me because we're at the top of a hill. Shouldn't that make the connections clearer? But then he says something about the wind.

Mom and Logan are even worse. If I bring it up with them, they just giggle that it's our "invisible roommates" messing with us. I can't tell if they really believe that, or if they just know it annoys the heck out of me. I'm leaning toward the second.

And the really annoying thing about the dead spots is that the minute I walk into a live spot, my phone gets flooded with all these messages that I obviously haven't been getting. I had three from Dad the other day, which I felt terrible about, because as mad as I am at him, I don't want him to think I'm giving him the silent treatment or whatever. Just because of some technological glitch. Missed a bunch of texts from Chloe, too. Oh, and I think I also got some actual friend requests but my stupid phone won't open them, so I can't even tell who they are from. So much for making any friends outside Chloe, since this is only going to confirm everyone's suspicion that I am stuck-up.

Then the other obnoxious thing is that when they do come through, I get a lot of double (or even triple or more) texts . . . so I'll feel like, woo, my phone is blowing up, but when I go to look at them, it's, like, five of the same text from Logan, asking if I know when Mom's going to be home. And sometimes the double text will come much later than the original text, like I'll get one every hour. Oh, and the latest nuisance is that I'll get texts from people but they show up blank. Or garbled, like maybe it's an autocorrect problem. But sometimes it looks like such gobbledygook that it's like they didn't even have auto-correct on. So I think it must be a virus or something. That reminds me, Chloe mentioned that some of my texts to her had come in garbled too. Gah, just what I need.

I don't know, should I try to download a virus scan thing? Or wipe the phone completely? Or make Mom call the service provider again?

Sorry, this is probably going to win some award for the most boring entry ever. Since I am the only person reading this, I will bestow the award myself. Hear ye hear ye, I hereby declare this journal entry an utter waste of electricity and pixels.

FRIDAY, FEBRUARY 6, 3:10 A.M.

Flies: About the same
Spiders: 8 since yesterday, I'm pretty sure.

I wonder if anyone has created an app to help people keep track of their spider infestations. If I could enter the sightings on my phone, I could keep my data more precisely, which I am told is important for science.

I suppose it wouldn't have to be specific to spiders. You could use the same app to keep track of all sorts of things that happen to scare the bejeezus out of you. Snakes. Rats. Clowns. Maybe there is someone out there right devil now writing an app to keep track of how many clowns he runs across every day, in hopes of calming his irrational fear of them. If so, I hope he makes it publicly available.

Not that it would do me much good these days. My phone is being a complete bastard.

God, why can't things just work? The Wi-Fi is sort of working now, since Mom called the ISP. I mean, the signal looks good, but there are weird dead spots all over the house, most particularly in my room! Which is really annoying. So everyone basically if I want to be online at all, I have to hang out in the kitchen or one part of the living room. It's the strongest in Logan's room, which is weird because his room is, like, on the opposite side of the house from the router. I don't even know. And I hate going in there because of that buzzing noise.

But when I try to use my cell phone to go online, that's no better—my signal craps out at the randomest moments. Is this what it means to live in the middle of nowhere? It's fine when I'm at school, though. Raph says it has something to do with where the house is, but that makes no sense to me because we're at the top of a hill. Shouldn't that make the connections clearer? But then he says something about the wind.

Mom and Logan are even worse. If I bring forgets it up with them, they just giggle that it's our "invisible roommates" messing with us. I can't tell if they really believe that, or if they just know it annoys the heck out of me. I'm leaning toward the second.

And the really annoying thing about the dead spots is that the minute I walk into a live spot, my phone gets flooded with all these messages that I obviously haven't been getting. I had three from Dad the other day, which I felt terrible about, because as mad as I am at him, I don't want him to think I'm giving him the silent treatment or whatever. Just because of some technological glitch. Missed a bunch of texts from Chloe, too. Oh, and I think I also got some actual friend requests but my stupid phone won't open them, so I can't even tell who they are from. So much for making any friends outside Chloe, since this is only going to confirm everyone's suspicion that I am stuck-up.

Then the other obnoxious thing is that when they do come through, I get a lot of double (or even triple or more) texts . . . so I'll feel like, woo, my phone is blowing up, but when I go to look at them, it's, like, five of the same stone text from Logan, asking if I know when Mom's going to be home. And sometimes the double text will come much later than the original text, like I'll get one every hour. Oh, and the latest nuisance is that I'll get texts from people but they show up blank. Or garbled, like maybe it's an embodied autocorrect problem. But sometimes it looks like such gobbledygook that it's like they didn't even have autocorrect on. So I think it must be a virus or something. That reminds me, Chloe mentioned that some of my texts to her had come in garbled too. Gah, just what I need.

I don't know, should I try to download a virus scan thing? Or wipe the phone completely? Or make Mom call the service provider again?

Sorry, this is probably going to win some award for the most boring entry ever. Since I am the only person reading this, I will bestow the award myself. Hear ye hear ye, I hereby declare this journal entry lies an utter waste of electricity and pixels.

SATURDAY, FEBRUARY 7, 9:17 A.M.

Huh, that's weird. I just realized my last entry posted twice. I must have hit the post button funny or . . . but it's weird because the time stamp is hours and hours later than the original post. How would that even happen?

Anyway, just logged on to record my bug tracking.

Flies: The cloud seems denser today.

Spiders: 10 this morning

WEDNESDAY, FEBRUARY 11, 3:22 A.M.

Woke up to the sound of screaming.

At first I thought it was me, waking myself up from a nightmare with my own shrieks. But even after I lay in bed a moment, letting my heart rate calm, I could still hear it. Feel it like it was coming from inside me, but my mouth was closed.

It's just the wind, I think. There's another massive storm raging outside, shards of lightning splitting the empty landscape outside my window, whirling gusts of snow billowing against a purple sky. And when the wind picks up, it pierces every crack in this old house and howls and moans like a dying animal.

And under it all I can still hear that buzzing from Logan's room. It's getting worse, like it's drilling in my head, making my teeth vibrate. It doesn't even feel like it's separate from the wind. Maybe it's because my head is still fogged with sleep, but somehow the sounds feel linked, or like one is a version of the other.

I guess while I'm up, I might as well tell the funny story of the missing packages. So a couple of days ago, Mom busted a taillight on the car while backing out of our driveway. I'm going to remember that next time she gives me a hard time during my driving lessons. Anyway, rather than trust an actual professional with the repair, Mom got it into her head that she could just order the new taillight off the Internet and install it herself. So she paid extra for the one-day shipping, but the package didn't come. And didn't come. And didn't come, so finally she sent a complaint, and they said they would send another one out right away. And that one didn't come either, so she sent another complaint, and they apologized again, etc. etc.

Well, the upshot is, yesterday we got SEVEN taillights delivered to our house. And guess what—every one of them is

Okay, that was weird. Logan just came into my room, and we had a seriously oddball conversation. I couldn't even tell if he was awake or asleep, to be honest . . . although he has never been a sleepwalker. Insomnia is his gig lately, which I knew from my mom, but I guess this was the first time I was up in the middle of the night to experience it firsthand.

Anyway, he came in and sat on my bed and stared at me. I was sitting up with my laptop in my lap. And I was like, Logan? What are you doing? Go back to bed. He didn't say anything, but he sort of shrugged, so I think he heard me. Normally if he comes into my room, I tell him to scat in no uncertain terms, but he seemed so weird that I tried to be gentle . . . I told him he'd feel better if he went back into his room and got into bed. And then he goes, "I can't go back in there." And I'm like, why? And he's like, "The wall." And I'm like . . . wha?

"There are words in the walls. Or some kind of . . ." He looks around. "Your room doesn't have them."

So at this point I'm like, okay, the kid had a bad dream, thought he saw something scary in his room. Typical little kid stuff, though Logan isn't so little anymore—I don't think kids are supposed to be seeing monsters in the closet at his age. But hell, everyone in this household is on edge these days. So I'm like, "It's okay, Logan, I'll go back to your room with you and show you there is nothing wrong with your walls. It's probably just a shadow or a water stain or something."

He seems cool with this, so I take his hand and we go over to his room and I look around quickly and I'm like, "See? No one in here. Perfectly safe." And he doesn't say anything, he just . . . points. Toward the wall, which is different from mine, he has wood paneling in his room, where I just have plaster. So I walk over to where he's pointing and I'm like, whatever, these are just normal swirls in the wood, but then I get closer and . . . it's weird, because suddenly I can see it. It really does look like there is some kind of writing in the paneling.

But if it's writing, I should be able to read it, right? But I can't, exactly. It's like, if I glance at it askew, I get a sense that there are words there, but when I look at it directly, they lose all definition and it doesn't even look like proper letters. Although maybe in another language? Like Arabic or something? Or symbols of some kind?

But what it's really like is dream writing—you know, when you're dreaming and you pick up a book or look at a sign and you know there are words there, but they swirl and run together

73

and writhe on the page and you can't make them resolve into actual language? I used to always use this trick to tell if I was dreaming—if I thought I was, I'd pick up a newspaper or something, and if I couldn't read it, I knew I was in a dream.

But this isn't a dream. Right?

I couldn't send Logan to bed after that. Hell, I wouldn't sleep in his room after that (not to mention the annoying buzzing noise in there that always makes my head ring). Instead I asked him if he wanted to watch TV, and I took him downstairs to the living room and put on a movie for him. And I got my laptop and now I am keeping him company, or maybe he is keeping me company, because I sure as hell am not going to sleep anymore tonight.

Oh, I guess I never finished my story from before. So yeah, the punchline is that all seven of the stupid taillights that came are for the wrong side of the car. That seemed funnier an hour ago.

FRIDAY, FEBRUARY 13, 5:04 P.M.

Flies: Bigger? I'm not sure. Qualitative measures are a bit hard to judge, especially when I don't have the specimens side by side. I wonder if I should start capturing and storing flies, for purposes of comparison.

Wow, I really am losing it. Who knew there was such a thin line between "scientist" and "batshit insane"?

Spiders: 10 since last time

I told Chloe about the words in the wall and she was like, whoa, that's so cool! You have to show me. So I guess that's a thing.

I was annoyed at first, because I'm really worried about Logan and this seemed like a pretty traumatic experience for him. I mean, it's not a joke. And then, hell, I'll admit it, I was pretty freaked out too—I don't even have to sleep in that room, but I see those words behind my eyelids as I'm drifting off to sleep most nights now, and let me tell you, it's unsettling.

So I was kind of pissy with Chloe about it at first, and not interested in hearing her stupid goth enthusiasm for everything spooky, as if this was some Halloween theme park run by the local church or something, rather than our actual lives. But even though I was kind of moody about it, she kept pressing for more details and descriptions, and wouldn't let it drop, and . . . well, I guess her enthusiasm is kind of infectious, because after a while I got into telling the story, and I got excited about bringing her home to show her. She was telling me about these websites where people post pictures of this kind of thing—messages from the beyond or whatever—and she said most of them are either really dumb looking, like you can't see anything at all, or else they are so obviously edited by some troll just looking for attention. And I wound up kind of excited about sharing this weird experience with the world.

On the one hand . . . I don't really want anything in my life to support the idea that I live in a haunted house. I just don't need that. But on the other . . . well, it seems less scary and more fun when a whole bunch of other people are invested in the question too.

I just hope I can sell Logan on the idea.

Thursday, February 19, 11:16 P.M.

Flies: About the same
Spiders: 9

Is Logan's advice working? It's definitely not making the flies and spiders go away. Is it helping me deal with them? I don't know. A little, I guess. Counting them at least gives me something to occupy my mind when I start to freak out.

I've been sweeping out the spiderwebs whenever I see them, but it doesn't seem to do any good. And I'm not sure everyone else in the house is totally supportive of my efforts.

I get that Logan's not freaked out by spiders like I am, which is good for him, I wouldn't wish this annoying phobia on anyone, but . . . sometimes I think his interest is more than purely scientific.

Like lately, I don't know if I'm just imagining it, or if my mind is playing tricks on me, but it seems like sometimes I catch him . . . *playing* with the spiders. I don't know, I've never seen anything, not really, and it feels crazy just to say it. It's just that sometimes I'll go in his room and he'll be really quick to usher me out of it. Which is totally normal little brother behavior, and there could be a billion normal things he is hiding in there from me.

But then there were a few times when I saw him, late at night or early in the morning, sitting on the stairs, or on the landing where the stairs turn, and sort of . . . poking around something in a corner. Why would he do that? And when I asked him, he wouldn't talk about it. But I know there are some holes in that area where the floorboards don't quite meet, and that's one of the places where I know I've seen spiderwebs that come back even after you've swept them away.

And a couple times, out of the corner of my eye, I saw Logan doing something weird with his hands, and I don't know if I'm just hypersensitive or something, but it looked like he was letting them crawl on him, like, deliberately. And just sort of watching them with this interested look on his face.

But that can't be. God, where do I come up with this stuff? It's like I'm actively trying to freak myself out. If I can get the damn Internet to work, I'm going to watch a bunch of kitten videos and try to get this horrible thought out of my head.

SATURDAY, FEBRUARY 21, 11:52 A.M.

Ugh, I am trying to get in touch with Chloe to figure out when she can come over to look at Logan's walls, but my texts keep disappearing into the ether. Or else they show up garbled beyond deciphering—just nonsense words and key mash. Though she told me the other day that last week she got six messages from me over the course of an hour and they all said "blood on the tail of the pig." Haha, what? Where the hell did that come from? Mom would say the universe is trying to tell me something, but damned if I know what.

MONDAY, FEBRUARY 23, 3:32 A.M.

It is impossible to get a decent night's sleep in this house!

I guess I shouldn't complain, since Logan clearly has it worse than I do. Though between being an insomniac and being woken up from a lovely dream in the middle of the night by your insomniac little brother, I'm not sure which is preferable.

In any case, it was right around 3 a.m. that I woke up to Logan messing around in my room, going through my closet and drawers. I asked him what the hell he was doing, and he just mumbled something. I asked him again and he turned around with a fierce expression, just visible in the moonlight streaming in through the window.

"I'm looking for my game."

For a minute I couldn't even answer this, it was so absurd. His video game? That had to be what he meant, but . . . in the

middle of the night? And what would it be doing in my room? It didn't make any sense. But he didn't seem concerned with logic.

"I've looked everywhere else and I can't find it. It has to be somewhere. Help me look."

I got out of bed and crossed the room to him, planning to grab him by the arm and haul him back to his bed, but before I reached him, he gasped in amazement and I stopped short.

"What is it?" I said.

He pulled his hand out of the trunk he'd been rifling in, a trunk I hadn't even opened since a day or two after the movers brought it, and in his hand was a video game disk.

Surprise was written across his face, and his hand trembled a little, but he was smiling triumphantly none the less. "Yes," he exclaimed. "I found it! I knew it had to be somewhere." Then, as he took a closer look, his expression shifted to confusion, and he dove back into the trunk, muttering to himself about how that "couldn't be right."

As I watched, he pulled another disk out of the trunk, then another, and another. Finally he sat back on his heels and looked at me. "Monster Party," he said. "All Monster Party. All I want is my Polybius disk, and instead I find four copies of a game I haven't played in five years."

I stared at him mutely. I couldn't figure out why any of his games would be in my trunk, let alone four copies of one.

Suddenly his face screwed up with rage, and he hurled the games across the room, where they smashed into the wall and fell to the floor.

"What the hell," was all I could say.

Logan got up and left the room.

SUNDAY, MARCH 1, 5:04 P.M.

I can't believe we just got another six inches of snow, on top of the three inches we got last week. It's March! Isn't it supposed to be spring? Oh right: Idaho. It's probably never spring here.

It is really pretty, especially the view out my windows over the rolling white hills, but enough is enough already. I'm tired of feeling like a captive in this house. I want to go running again. I want the walk to school not to leave me sore and exhausted. I want it to stop being so damn cold all the time. I want to wear pretty floral dresses and sandals, not sweaters and boots.

Hold on, Logan is freaking out about something. I better see.

Heeeeeeeey, school got called off tomorrow! Logan just told me they announced it on TV. I've heard about snow days, but I don't think it had occurred to me as a thing that might happen

in my life. Okay, I guess I don't mind if winter sticks around a *little* longer.

Nice to see Logan in a good mood, too. And not acting . . . however you'd describe what he's been like recently. He's been all right lately. Maybe it's out of his system.

WEDNESDAY, MARCH 4, 7:30 P.M.

Chloe's over right now. She and Logan are blathering on about occult messages, so I thought I'd update my journal.

She came over tonight for dinner, which was awkward to begin with because Mom didn't remember even though I reminded her this morning. Not that she minded, but it seemed to throw her off her game a bit—inasmuch as Mom has a "game" at the best of times, which is not much. So she was futzing around in the kitchen, going through her cookbooks and opening and shutting the cabinets absentmindedly as she asked us our plans for the evening. And Chloe immediately starts telling her about the words in the walls, I guess assuming Logan and I had told her about it. Which we had not.

So Chloe's babbling on about this website and how we're going to send in some photos, and Mom turns around with this concerned expression, and she's like, are you sure this is a good idea?

And I try to signal to Chloe to let it drop, but she is so excited she starts describing the website to Mom, and meanwhile Mom's concern-face is deepening steadily. And finally she sighs and she's like, "I really don't think this is a good idea."

So I'm like, "Aren't you always saying that the spirit world is nothing to be afraid of?"

And she has to concede this, but she still looks unthrilled. And as she goes back to opening and closing all the cupboards, she lectures us a little vaguely about being respectful toward the dead, and not exploiting the energy in the house for our own personal glory, etc. To which I snark, "If you think having a pic posted on a website equals glory, you might want to recalibrate your measures of fame a little."

I was just kidding around, but right then she slams the cupboard and turns around and shouts, "I don't believe it!"

Which, like . . . it's not like I've never seen my mom mad before, but it's definitely a rare occurrence, given how committed she is to peace and patience and whatnot. So I definitely jumped. And I was about to defend my little joke when she starts going off about these vegetables. I guess she had gone to the co-op (basically, the fancy, pricey grocery store) yesterday and gotten all these fresh veggies and health foods and was planning to make some elaborate meal tonight, but now she can't find any of the stuff she bought in the fridge or the pantry.

So then Logan breaks the tension by saying, "Maybe it's the ghosts. They really want us to have spaghetti tonight. We've still got plenty of that, right?" And Mom kind of sighs and can't help grinning a bit, and she does make spaghetti, because what else is she going to do?

But after dinner she makes me help her with the dishes while Chloe chats with Logan, and she's wearing her concerned-mom face again. And she's like, Paige, is there something you'd like to talk about?

And I just . . . I got kind of teary, because there is so much I want to talk about. So much we never talk about. About Dad, and what's happening with Logan, and this house, and all the weird stuff that's been going on . . . But I don't even know where to begin, so I don't say anything, and then Mom starts in on my *food intake* of all things. It was completely out of left field, except she was bulimic for a while in her 20s, when she was in the movies and there was all this pressure on her to be thin and gorgeous. And she's always worried that I would pick that up at some point, but like . . . I'm not in the movies. And it's not like anyone is looking at my body here in Idaho, where everyone has to wear 17 layers all winter or they'll freeze to death. It's just . . . yeah, I used to diet sometimes back in LA, but lately, with everything else on my mind, it's not something I've been thinking about.

But I guess she read some mom-pamphlet somewhere that said if food goes missing from your house, your teenage daughter probably has an eating disorder. I think they probably had cupcakes and cheese curls in mind rather than bulgur and quinoa. Why would I hoard that? But in any case, I'm not hoarding anything. And I'm trying to convince her of this, but everything I say comes out sounding defensive, which just makes her look even more concerned, until I feel like I'm at my wits' end.

So finally, just to move the conversation forward, I'm like, have you ever considered it might be Logan? And she rolls her eyes, like Logan has an eating disorder? Yeah, right. So I'm like, well, maybe not an ED exactly, but . . . I've seen all these stories about people who eat when they sleepwalk. Sleep-eat. And Mom points out that Logan doesn't sleepwalk, and I'm like, yeah, but . . . you have to admit, he's been acting weird. And he's up for so many hours when no one else is. What does he do with all that time?

And Mom says, "You think he's making quinoa tabouleh salad?" She has a point. This kid only just learned how to use a can opener so he can microwave himself some ravioli. He's not a genius in the kitchen, and he's definitely no health food guru. And it would be really out of character for him to clean all the plates and pots and counters and everything when he was done . . . but maybe his insomniac self is a neat freak, I don't know.

Anyway, she clearly doesn't believe my story, and is still acting all suspicious toward me and keeps prodding me about where the food went, like she's convinced I'm lying to her and she's not going to leave me alone until she gets to the bottom of this. And that's when I'm like, well, you're the one who had seven wrong taillights sent to the house. Are you going to blame me and Logan for that, too?

And Mom looks deeply annoyed at that jibe, and she's about to respond when we're both distracted by a noise behind us. And we step out of the pantry to look, and there's a big bag of vegetables in the middle of the kitchen floor.

Mom goes over to the bag and starts pulling stuff out of it—peppers, zucchini, onions. And she's got this look on her face of, like, complete bewilderment. I think something really shifted for her in that moment. All the other stuff that has been happening . . . she called it spirits, but she didn't *really* believe it. But sitting there with those onions in her hands, it's like she couldn't deny it any longer.

She raised her eyes toward the ceiling. "Thank you?" she said. But she sounded a little unsure of herself.

Chloe and Logan are totally absorbed in the wall writing now, but I'm still a little weirded out by what happened with the veggies.

I asked Logan if he could explain it according to scientific principles, and he says, "Well . . . all matter is made up of atoms, right? And atoms are made up of subatomic particles. And subatomic particles are constantly moving. Normally, their movement is so tiny and so random that all the different movements of all the subatomic particles cancel each other out. But if, by random chance, all the particles suddenly moved in the same direction, that could make the vegetables move on their own. Scientifically."

Um, what? Am I supposed to believe that?

Logan says no, not really. Which is why he is going with an

alternate explanation. But somehow I like that alternative even less.

At least that annoying noise in Logan's room isn't bothering me as much as usual. Maybe having Chloe here, and the two of them laughing and talking, is drowning it out. I can still feel it through my body like when you're leaning against a car with the engine running, but it's not noisy, and it's not uncomfortable.

Anyway, Chloe and Logan have been talking and taking photos for ages now, but Chloe isn't happy with how any of them are turning out. I guess she wants to try it with the lights off and her flash, so I'll end this now.

WEDNESDAY, MARCH 4, 11:36 P.M.

I never want to talk to Chloe again. He's just a kid! And now—

I need to calm down. He's going to be okay. The doctors are saying he's fine. But God, I don't ever want to see something like that again. One minute Chloe was snapping some cell phone photos in the darkness of his room. Then all of a sudden I started feeling that buzzing build up again . . . It started in my stomach muscles, then spread into my chest and my head, and this time it didn't sound like someone screaming, it sounded like a dozen people screaming . . . or wailing . . . but not human at the same time. Mechanical, somehow.

I shut my eyes tight because the vibrations were making me queasy, and then I heard a loud thump, and Chloe was yelling Logan's name. I opened my eyes in the darkness and felt for him while Chloe ran for the light switch. When the light came on,

Logan was on the floor, and he . . . he didn't look right at all. His limbs were stiff and extended, his muscles tensed, and he was shaking and drooling, with his eyes rolled so far back I could only see the whites.

I screamed for Mom, who came running, and the rest is kind of a blur of 911 calls and ambulances and stuff.

So now I am at the hospital updating on my phone, and Mom is meeting with the doctors and Logan is in some room strapped to all these wires and machines, and no one is really telling me anything, except not to worry, and that everything is going to be fine.

I want to believe them, but this doesn't feel fine.

I've fallen behind on my Science Duties.

Flies: Annoying

Spiders: A dozen or so

God, what a week this has been. Chloe feels terrible, of course. The doctors agree that Logan's seizure was probably brought on by the flash from her camera phone, and for a while I was furious with her for that, but . . . how could she have known? It's not like Logan had any history of this sort of thing. It could have just as easily been me with the camera in my hand.

The weird thing is, the doctors aren't even sure it was really a seizure. I don't know, I don't totally understand, but they ran their tests, the EEG or whatever, and they say there's no evidence of abnormal brain activity. But how can that be?

The neurologist said it was a "pseudo-seizure," and that from the outside they look indistinguishable from regular seizures, and the victim can't tell the difference either. They're not intentional or anything, but she said they could be caused by stress or anxiety. She acted like this was good news, and of course it's good that there's nothing biologically wrong with Logan's brain, but I don't think Mom was too happy to hear that it's stress-related, either.

Anyway, the neurologist referred Logan to a new doctor now. A shrink, Dr. Louisa Clyde, who says that it's probably a side effect of the ADHD drugs he's on. Which she says also probably explains the insomnia . . . which I guess makes sense. Those pills are basically speed, aren't they? No wonder he can't sleep.

In any case, they taught us what to do if it happens again: roll him on his side, loosen his clothes, slip a pillow under his head. It's good not to feel so helpless, but I hope I never have to use this information. I don't want to see him like that again.

Dr. Clyde's big idea is that we should just take him off the pills for a while and see if he stabilizes a bit. Lack of sleep is also a pretty common trigger for seizures . . . The doctors were pretty shocked when me and Mom couldn't tell them when the last time Logan slept was. I mean, I think I always assumed that he slept *sometimes*. When I wasn't looking. When I was sleeping. But God, yeah . . . it's been a really long time since I *saw* him sleep. They said normally people with insomnia make it up somewhere. Naps during the day or whatever. The body's not designed to go completely without sleep for a long time. They actually seemed more concerned about that than the seizure.

Anyway, hopefully getting him off the medication will help him sleep, and stop the seizure thing from happening, and make him . . . okay again.

It's all really scary and upsetting, except . . . this is terrible to say, but a part of me was really glad to hear the thing about the medication. It was just such a relief to get an actual, like, scientific reason for some of the stuff that's been going on. I know the veggies in the kitchen story is silly and seems like a joke, but at the same time, how the hell does this stuff keep happening? All we can think to do is blame each other for each weird event, but none of it adds up, and it just makes us snipe at each other all the time. I'm sick of Mom not trusting me, and I'm sick of not trusting her or Logan. Not that I think they are deliberately messing with me, but it's upsetting to think that I can't trust them to be normal. To be sane. To not be moving stuff in the middle of the night or forgetting things or getting confused all the time.

For that matter, it's upsetting to not really be able to trust myself. I mean, what if I'm just as bad? What if I'm the one hiding video games and stealing sweaters and sending garbled text messages, and I just don't remember?

I don't like thinking about that.

I'm hoping, with this change, that everything will settle down for a bit.

TUESDAY, MARCH 10, 4:07 P.M.

I can't believe the weather today. Finally the snow melts, but instead of blue skies and warm spring breezes we get . . . WTF is this, anyway? A sandstorm, I guess. All I know is that it's impossible to walk down the street without getting buffeted by the wind, and no matter how tightly I tie back my hair, by the time I get to school, my cheeks hurt from where it has come loose and whipped me in the face.

And even worse is the sand—or maybe dust, or grit—that blows into town from those big empty fields and stings my eyes and crunches between my teeth no matter how snugly I wrap my scarf around my face. This can't be normal. There is a deep-seated evil in this place, I swear.

On a more positive note, I can see just a hint of green on the hills outside my window, though mostly the landscape still looks muddy and brown. Delightful.

SUNDAY, MARCH 15, 3:25 A.M.

I'm up in the middle of the night again. And I'm not alone.

Ugh, wasn't everything supposed to be better now?

I guess Dr. Clyde's new routine for Logan hasn't exactly kicked in yet. I woke up around 3 a.m. with strange sounds in my ears. Mixed in with my dream state it sounded almost like children playing, or maybe like fairy laughter . . . but eerie somehow. Anyway, I tried to ignore it and go back to sleep, but it kept annoying me, so finally I got up and followed the noise out to the hall. The whole house was dark, except for a blue glow coming from downstairs, and I was unavoidably reminded of the blue glow Chloe and I saw that first time we met Raph.

The sight of it gave me a chill at first, just remembering how frightened I had been that night. But then I reminded myself of how that turned out—not scary at all, right? And this must be the same thing, just the TV on in the middle of the night. Not scary.

So I went down the stairs and into the living room, and . . . well, I was right. In a sense. Logan was sitting in front of the TV, playing one of his video games. That was the music that had been haunting my dreams, of course. But I was wrong to think it wasn't scary. I don't know, I can't explain it. Logan was just so transfixed. But so what? Everyone looks transfixed when they're playing video games, right?

But this was different, somehow. More like that time he came into my room, and I couldn't quite tell if he was in a trance or what. It was like he wasn't even really playing the game—his thumbs were moving, but his brain didn't seem to be engaged.

So I was like, "Logan? Are you okay? Why don't you come to bed, honey?" But he just ignored me. It was creeping me out, for real. So finally I went over to him and sat behind him on the couch. My knee was touching his back, but he didn't react to it at all, so I laid a hand on his shoulder and tried to shake him gently. But he didn't . . . he didn't move the way a sleepwalking person would. He resisted me, like he was playing statue or something. Held himself perfectly still and straight, and didn't make any response to me at all.

So then I tried to be like, "How about we just finish this level, and then back to bed, okay?" And I figured I would watch along and give him tips, both to relate to him, and hopefully to get him to finish faster. But as I watched, I realized something. Logan . . . wasn't really playing. I mean, he was—his fingers were moving on the buttons, and they were affecting the stuff on the screen—but he kept dying like every minute or two. He hadn't gotten beyond level 1! And this is Logan—I've seen him play this game a million times. He's basically an expert. He could make it to level 9 in his sleep . . . at least that's what I would have said until tonight.

Because now, as I watched, he just kept dying, over and over and over. Misjudging a jump or meeting up with a bad guy or just running headlong off a cliff. He wasn't playing like himself at all. And each time, he would just go back and start again, as if nothing was wrong.

Eventually I left him and came back up to bed, but I sure as hell can't sleep now. How long is he going to be like this?

Flies: LOUD. Were they always this loud? bzz bzz bzz.

Spiders: 16ish

Is there really any point in me keeping track of the spiders? For every spider I see, I know there are loads that are invisible to me, so what exactly am I recording? (For Science!) How brave they are? How bold? How deeply they want to piss me off? I suppose the point was to give me something to do other than shriek and run from the house in terror every time I see one, and I guess it has worked, in that respect. But that makes me feel more like Logan is studying me for some kind of psych experiment, instead of me studying the spiders.

Knowing Logan, I guess that isn't all that implausible. If he winds up publishing his results in some medical journal, I hope he'll at least have the good taste to change my name.

Speaking of Logan, I told Mom about what happened the other night with him. She didn't really get it. She said if he couldn't sleep, it was better to get up and do something than just lie in bed. That's what all the experts say. I tried to explain to her how eerie the whole thing was, but she doesn't know enough about video games to really get it. Besides, I was holding back a bit, because I didn't want to freak her out. I got her to make another appointment with Dr. Clyde, so hopefully that will help at least.

I talked with her about some other stuff too. I don't know, I've been trying not to say anything to her, partly because I feel like she has enough on her mind, and also because I didn't want her to tease me or think I was being silly. Except that is totally not Mom. So maybe what I was really afraid of was that she would agree with me . . . and talking to her would just make it all the more real.

Well, I wasn't totally wrong. But it went really well, considering.

I was just like, Mom, I know we've kidded around about it a bunch, but do you seriously think this house might be, you know . . . haunted? And I was preparing mentally for her to either be like, "Paige, grow up," or on the other hand to be like, "Yes and demons have been speaking to me from the coffee-maker." Neither of which I wanted to hear.

But she was pretty cool about it. She basically said that yes, she believes there are spirits inhabiting the house, but no, she wouldn't call it a haunting. Which I know, that makes about zero sense, but I guess I know what she means. She said haunting is a negative term that people use because they are afraid of any "disembodied consciousness," so they want to name it and contain it. They'll call a house "haunted" to reassure themselves that the other houses are not.

But the truth is, the spirit world is all around us, all the time. Any time someone dies, they leave a little imprint of their consciousness on the world, and it continues to influence the living, though some people are more sensitive to it than others. This house—a lot of people have passed through it, and they have all left a little bit of themselves. Spiritually. But it's nothing to be afraid of.

She told me to think of them as, like, roommates. Some roommates are easy to get along with, some are a little harder, but everyone is basically good, so if you are patient and understanding, there is no reason we shouldn't all be able to get along.

I don't know. I don't believe in that stuff the way Mom does. At least I didn't . . . Maybe now I do. In any case, it was weirdly comforting. I didn't expect it to be, but what she was saying made more sense than anything else that's been going through my head lately.

Anyway, she gave me a big hug and asked me if I was feeling better, and I nodded, because I really was, but something about the hug and the way she was being so nice and momlike made my eyes tear up like a goon. So then she was like, Paige honey . . . would you feel better if I did a smudging?

And yeah, I know I don't believe in that stuff, and I have always made fun of Mom doing it. In fact, I remember now that she had planned to smudge the house the day we moved in, but Logan and I teased her so much about it that she let it drop. Maybe that was dumb.

Anyway, I half surprised myself by being like, yeah . . . do you mind?

Even if it's just a placebo, it might make me feel better, so okay.

First day ignoring of school tomorrow. Mom is the happiest I have seen her in ages, getting all her stuff ready spiritual to start classes. What a lunatic! Did she not get the memo about how all normal people dread school? But maybe it's different when you get to go by choice, instead of people forcing absence you.

I'm still working on being cheerful and supportive about everything, but it is hard not to be homesick for my takes queen-size bed and big closets and sunshine and our pool. No one has a pool here, because it is the North Pole, basically.

Oh well, better make the best of it. I can only hope school tomorrow won't be too awful.

Oh, who am I kidding? Getting failure plopped down in the middle of junior year in a school where sickness everyone has probably known each other since misery birth? It's going to be excruciating.

THURSDAY, MARCH 19, 4:32 P.M.

Dammit, it's doing it again. And that one posted while I was in the middle of a French test. I don't like this.

SATURDAY, MARCH 21, 3:15 P.M.

Man, this is, like, the week of intense mother-daughter convos, I guess. We did the smudging ritual thing today—Mom even convinced Logan to join us, briefly. And I don't know . . . it was nice. Like, bonding. Mom got some sage from a shop downtown, and we went around from room to room, and she said one of her little incantations, and it smelled so good . . . I really felt lighter after we did it, and the whole house seemed a bit brighter.

Then Mom and I were sitting together out on the porch. Can you believe it? The weather is starting to get not terrible! Haha that probably helped my mood too. It's funny, it was like 50 degrees today with a bit of sun peeking through the clouds, and no wind, and that was enough for us all to feel like we needed to be outside, relishing the good weather. In

California we would have bundled up in sweaters and huddled around the fireplace on a day like today.

But it was okay. You could hear birds chattering away at one another, and we talked aimlessly about the house and the town, and then we were quiet for a little while, until Mom made a comment about me maybe being ready to accept magic as a positive force in my life.

It's funny, because I think this conversation was part of why I avoided talking to her about the house. I'm just so used to resisting all her crap about magic and mysticism—it's always made me so uncomfortable. Especially the idea that she might be right, that there might be something to all that stuff. But this time I didn't resist it. It felt like a comfort, in a weird way—like maybe I didn't have to let the universe have its way with me all the time. Like it could be a conversation.

So for the first time in my life, I just let her talk, and I even asked her a few questions. She told me a story I remember hearing a bit of a long time ago, when I was a little girl . . . about some ancestor of ours back in Ireland who was burned to death for practicing black magic. The people in the town were convinced she was a witch, putting curses on people and conjuring spirits and stuff. But Mom told me about how the townspeople were just confused. It's easy for people to get confused about these things, I guess. Mom said that she used to be afraid of these powers herself, but she understands now that this woman was probably just trying to help people. She was probably using her knowledge of nature and herbs to help someone cleanse a dwelling or something, like we just did. But then something bad happened, either because the force was stronger than she could handle, or maybe just coincidence, and out of fear and prejudice, everyone blamed her.

It's a sad story, but I think I learned something from it. Maybe Mom has been right all along: If we can just approach the world with joy and hope, we'll get that kind of good energy back. It's fear and suspicion that is the root of all the dark, shadowy things. I get that now.

THURSDAY, MARCH 26, 5:16 P.M.

Logan is being such a little twerp. Though the truth is, I much prefer him being the little twerp I know and love, than the freaky-ass zombie he has been recently.

The reason for his twerpishness is because Dr. Clyde declared that Logan is hardly allowed to play video games anymore. A couple of hours on the weekend is all she'll allow, and that was after strenuous bargaining. She says he's overstimulated, and that's why he still can't sleep and is behaving kind of weird. I have to admit, just forbidding the video games brought back so much of the old Logan I used to know, I could have almost cried from relief.

But yeah, I guess it got back to him that I told Mom about our bizarre little interaction (or . . . noninteraction) the other night, so now he's pissed at me and being a total brat—just, like, imitating me behind my back, and rolling his eyes at everything I say, and refusing to pass me the salt at dinner and stuff. Normal little brother stuff, thank God.

I don't know—I hate how annoying he is, but I love him. And I just want him to be okay. When I think of how he looked that night of the seizure, shuddering and drooling, his face like a mask, it was almost like it wasn't Logan at all. I don't ever want to see him like that again.

FRIDAY, APRIL 3, 11:08 P.M.

The website accepted our creepy photos! They made a whole post about it, and the title was "Idaho House Possessed." Hahaha. I guess they thought it was pretty convincing.

Chloe came over today to look at it with me. We were sitting in the living room, looking at my laptop, when Raph came to the door. It was strange because he really doesn't get out much. I almost never see him leave his apartment, except if it's to do some work on the house for his mom. But he must go out and get groceries or something sometimes, right? Although I do see delivery people come pretty often . . . I don't know, is he a shut-in? Or is this just normal college (well, college dropout) behavior?

Based on reality TV, I tend to picture shut-ins as, like . . . old. And weird. I guess Raph is a little weird, but shut-ins aren't supposed to be really hot, are they? Or gay. I don't think a shut-in would be gay. I don't mean that offensively, just like . . . if you're gay, you must like other human beings, right? And if you're a shut-in, you probably have no sexuality at all.

Anyway, we were looking at the website when there was a knock at the door, and I got it and there was Raph. Looking . . . well, looking like Raph, all chiseled jaw and cheekbones. And he was bearing an eggbeater. Actually, he was bearing two.

But I was hardly even aware of that at that point, because all I could think about was how our last meeting went, and what a complete ass I made of myself, and what a jerk he must think I am. So I didn't even say anything once I opened the door, I just sort of stood there and tried to fold up into myself and disappear. But that failed, predictably.

So Raph was like, "Heeeeey, what's up. Um." And he seemed almost as awkward as I was, his shoulders hunched, his eyes darting nervously. We must make quite a pair. But at last he managed a lopsided grin and I got the sense that he at least wasn't pissed at me. So I was like, "Uh hi. What's with the, uh . . ."

"Right," he said. "These. Your mom lent me an eggbeater the other day. I was just, uh, returning it."

"She lent you two?"

"No, she . . . she lent me one. I thought I didn't have one, but then another one . . . turned up. And I'm not sure which is yours, so . . ."

"Well, you should keep one, then. Then we each have one. Doesn't that make sense?"

"Yeah, I guess. But it's cool. I didn't have one before, and like . . . that was okay with me."

"But you did have one, obviously. You just didn't know it."

Raph looked down at the eggbeaters in his hands and frowned. "No," he said. "I really don't think so. But then . . . yeah. You're probably right. You must be."

"Could you guys try to be more awkward?" said Chloe from the living room. "Because I think there are people in the next county who can't quite feel the waves of awkwardness you are giving off, and I'd hate for them to miss this."

Raph and I stared at each other for a few more moments before I got myself together and invited him in, taking both the eggbeaters from him. Raph hesitated on the doorstep. "Thanks," he said, "but I really should—"

"Raph, you have to see these photos," said Chloe. "Come over here."

I watched a wave of anxiety sweep across his face before calling back to her. "I think Raph would rather—"

"No," he said. "It's okay." He smiled weakly. "It's fine. I'm fine."

"There are flies," I said.

"Right," he said. "I remember."

He closed his eyes and winced a little, but he did manage to step through the front hall toward the couch. Reaching the living room, he let out a low, unsteady breath, then smiled as he leaned over the back of the couch to look at the screen. After a moment he let out a low whistle.

"Those are some photos. I love this site, they have the weirdest stuff. Where did these come from?"

"From here," said Chloe.

"What?" said Raph.

"We took them," I said, coming back from the kitchen with some snacks. "Up in Logan's room, a couple of weeks ago. Chloe submitted them, and the editors just put them up."

Raph backed away from the couch. "Those were taken . . . in this house? Oh . . . oh, you shouldn't have done that. You really shouldn't have done that."

"What?" said Chloe. "Why not?"

"Geez, Raph," I said. "It's just wood. I think they came out really—"

He cut me off. "You just . . . you shouldn't mess around with these things. You're going to draw it out again, just when I—" He broke off.

"Just when you what?" Chloe and I stared at him for a minute, but he didn't say anything. His face looked damp, though, and he scrubbed a hand through his curls.

"I shouldn't have come in," he said. "I need to go."

"What?" said Chloe. "Why? You just—" But I signaled to her to let it go and she stopped. Raph had disappeared from the room anyway.

TUESDAY, APRIL 14, 10:48 P.M.

It's finally getting nice here! At last I can step outside without three puffy layers. And the view out my window . . . wow, I can't believe how different it looks from when I moved here. All those ugly, stubbly brown hills are green now. But not just green, they look like a freaking postcard. The other day the sky was so blue, and the fields were so green, it was almost otherworldly, like an illustration in a storybook, or an Instagram pic with all the colors supersaturated. Except it's not a filter, it's just my *window*. I think I'm finally starting to understand why people would build a house up here on this ridge.

What else is new?

I know I said I was going to stop keeping track of the spiders, because there was no point to the data I was collecting.

But I just looked over it again and graphed it against the time elapsed between recordings (yes I *know*, when did I become such a dweeb??? but bear with me, it's kind of interesting), and it is noticeable that there has been a steady increase in visible arachnid activity. At first I thought it was just coincidence, and the data set is still too small to really be sure, but it does look like I am witnessing more spider-related events as time progresses.

What does that mean, though? Is this like a "tip of the iceberg" situation, where more visible spiders means proportionally more invisible ones? (Oh God, let it not mean that.) Does it mean that I am just becoming more aware of them? That seems like an undesirable result, but it's hard to imagine I could possibly be less aware than I was at the outset of this project. Does it mean they are becoming bolder, and more willing to venture beyond their usual lairs? And if so, why? Are they hungry? Bored? Looking to mate? Planning an attack on me?

Probably the last, all things considered.

Oh, and about the flies: My observations there continue to be qualitative, but not uninteresting for all that. I noted last time that they seemed louder. I've been wondering whether there's a connection between their buzzing and that annoying buzzing in Logan's room. In an effort to be scientific, I went and stood in Logan's room for a while, gritting my teeth against the vibrations. I feel like the quality of the buzzing is different. The one in Logan's room feeling more mechanical, the one in the foyer feeling more organic. But I'm not at all settled on that conclusion because the more I moved between one and the other, the more alike they sounded.

No, that's not quite accurate. It's more like they got mixed up together. Like the buzzing of each was infecting the buzz of the other, so that they intermingled in my brain.

I hope this vital data about the precise quality of my teeth-rattling will be of use to Science someday.

TUESDAY, APRIL 21, 3:15 A.M.

Logan is still not sleeping. Dr. Clyde really wants to avoid putting him on sleeping pills of any kind because he's so young, and they can be addictive, and it's hard to say exactly how his body would react, especially with the seizure and everything. But it can't be good for him to just be awake all the time.

I'm up in the middle of the night too, but only because I'm studying for a history test. It's 2 a.m., and Logan just wandered into my room again. At least he wasn't so weird this time, but he is annoying. Mom won't let him play video games or watch TV or even go online, because all that stuff is "stimulating," but that means he is ridiculously bored, of course. So finding me awake, he was all excited to have a late-night playmate. But I have work to do. I can't hang out with him.

So I tried to get him to go read a book, but he says he has

read every book in the house. I'm pretty sure that can't be true. He should read my history textbook, that would put him right to sleep. Too bad I need it.

Okay, I guess our bickering woke Mom up. She just came in and told us both to go to bed, but obviously that is not going to happen. And she was in no state to insist. Finally she just gave me an abbreviated lecture about how I need to prepare earlier because all-nighters are NOT effective (we'll see if she stands by this advice when she makes it to *her* exams), then told Logan to leave me alone so I could study.

When he whined, she told him to handwrite a letter to his dad. Ha! She must be pretty desperate to be encouraging that relationship. Anyway, I think Logan was so shocked at the idea of handwriting anything that he didn't even answer back.

TUESDAY, APRIL 21, 4:00 P.M.

So I guess Mom's advice wasn't so bad. When I went down to breakfast this morning, Logan was asleep on the couch in the living room, and the letter he was writing to our dad was sitting out on the coffee table. I haven't seen him asleep in ages. It's so weird. But he looked really peaceful, at last.

I know it's an intrusion, but I couldn't resist picking up the letter. I was just going to glance at it to see if he had finished, but then I wound up reading the whole thing. Don't worry, it wasn't anything scandalous. Just a really sweet letter by a lonely, mixed-up kid, reaching out to his overly distant father. God, poor Logan. Not gonna lie, it made me tear up in a few places. Since we moved here, I've hardly thought about Dad at all. I was so mad at him, I just pushed him out of my head and focused on our new life here. But I guess that's not how it was with Logan.

I think me and Mom never realized how hard he had taken this whole thing.

I only hope Dad replies. If not by snail mail, at least an e-mail or a phone call or something. It might break Logan's heart, if he doesn't. Hell, it might break mine.

Dear Dad,

Mom's making me write this letter. I mean, not that I mind writing to you, but she's making me write the letter by hand. The shrink has decrede that I'm not allowed to have screen time, so I have to email you the old fashioned way. I'm a little surprised to learn that the postal service isn't dead yet, but there are still people who will physicly bring paper with writing on it to your front door.

I'm getting excited about my science project. Have I told you about it? I'm trying to show what happens when you look at a really bright color for a while and then look at a white wall — like what the rods and cones are doing and stuff.

Do you think there's any chance you might be able to come for it? I don't know if you'd want to, but I think it will be interesting. I know you're busy, but I bet Paige would be really happy to see you. And I would be too.

By the way, have you been getting my gaming magazines? I don't know what happened to the subscription when we moved but there's a review of the new Aeon of Strife that I want to check out. It's supposed to be sick.

Sorry if my handwriting is hard to read, it really never occurred to me that penmanship was going to be an issue in my life. I can't wait to get back to a keyboard.

Well, it's almost morning and I'm starving. The banana in the fruitbowl is calling to me. Write back soon!

Love,
Logan

THURSDAY, APRIL 23, 4:17 P.M.

I'm wishing now I had kept better notes on the flies. I feel like they are acting different now, but I can't be sure. When I started out, I was focused on how many there were—if the swarm seemed to be getting larger or smaller. But I realize now that was the least of the information I could have been collecting.

Were the flies always this dumb and lazy? Is it a function of their getting bigger (which I am pretty sure they are, despite lacking a comparison sample)? I think that when we first took down the flypaper and that big cloud appeared, they at least behaved more or less like normal flies. Well, no they didn't, because they stuck together in a cloud, hovering over a spot with no rational reason to attract flies, so that was already weird. But beyond that, they did, you know, normal fly things.

They flew around. They occasionally landed on things, then

took off again within a few seconds. Sometimes they landed for longer, but the minute you approached them, they zipped back into the air and away from you.

Now they just don't seem to care anymore. It used to be that, as gross as they were, you could walk through the swarm and it would part for you. The flies were as uneager to touch me as I was them. But more and more, I've noticed as I leave or enter the house, I stride through the cloud as confidently as I can manage, and I get *hit in the face* by flies. Not just the face, all over. Like they just can't be bothered to move out of the way. It's disgusting, and it's also a bit disturbing. It's just so . . . un-flylike. Are they lazy? Or have they become . . . fearless? That's an ugly thought.

I need to think of a way to make my observations more conclusive.

THURSDAY, APRIL 30, 4:39 P.M.

Dad wrote back! I'm so relieved. It was just a postcard, but still—it's something. Never mind that I suspect the New Girl picked it out for him. I hope that hasn't occurred to Logan. I'm fairly certain it has occurred to Mom, but she's keeping quiet at least.

Logan was so excited. I'm not sure he's ever gotten mail, like *actual* mail before. Of course, he wanted to write back right away. What a goof! Seriously, though, he's a good kid. I love the little brat.

SATURDAY, MAY 2, 6:15 P.M.

I've done it. I've crossed over into complete madness.

This is all Logan's fault. People like me should not be trusted with science. But now it's like, I really want to know the answers, and I am willing to do gross (and maybe ethically questionable?) things to get them.

I caught some flies. It started out innocently enough, I swear. Well, sort of innocently. I was sitting in the kitchen, watching the flies buzzing around in the front hall, looking all slow and stupid and huge. And I thought, boy, if I had a flyswatter, I bet I could do some serious damage to those idiot flies. I wouldn't even have to aim. I could just sweep the thing through the air and flatten five or six at a time.

But then I immediately felt guilty because I know what

Mom would have to say about that. All life is sacred to the Goddess, even *obviously* evil bugs. Fine.

So instead I had a different idea: What if I got a net of some sort and just caught a bunch of them like they were butterflies? Then I could release them into the wild, and solve the problem without any death or destruction.

I didn't have a net, but I thought a plastic grocery bag might do in a pinch, so I grabbed one and set about my little project. And it worked shockingly well! I think it definitely qualifies as proof that these are no ordinary flies, that I was able to just sort of swing a plastic bag around in the room and catch a whole bunch of them.

So, that done, I sealed up the bag and carried it outside and around the house to the back, where you can see out over all those rolling fields. They wouldn't bother anyone there. So I released them. Fly, little beasties! Grasp your freedom in all six hands!

But I guess the suckers were not so interested in a life of open-air liberty, because as I stood there, I watched them buzz around for a few moments, and then one of them made a loop-diloop and headed back toward the house, with the others following close behind. Six or seven flies all flew around the house, back to the front door, and hung out there, buzzing impatiently, until I opened it and they could go back in.

I may have to revise my theory that they are stupid. Evil is looking more likely right now.

Anyway, that failed experiment gave me an idea for another, so I traded in my plastic bag for a glass jar, caught a few more, and brought them up to my room. That, at least, should help me figure out if the flies are changing their behavior.

It just occurred to me that I better feed these guys. Guess I have some pet flies now.

(Sorry I quit updating about the spiders, but other than seeing more and more of them, there isn't much to report. I will let you know if that changes.)

MONDAY, MAY 4, 4:12 P.M.

I don't know what is going on anymore. Okay. Okay. Deep breaths. There . . . well, there has to be an explanation for this. What, like the bag of veggies? There wasn't much of one for that. No, but this is different. That was just one of those weird things that seems totally inexplicable, except there must be a perfectly reasonable explanation. But no one cares enough to look for it, so you just sort of shrug your shoulders and go, that was weird.

This is different.

And I know Mom keeps saying that I should just accept the spirit activity in our house and view it as playful or mischievous, but this is giving me a really bad feeling. I can't help thinking that our little household ghosts don't seem to be all that friendly.

Okay, this is what happened. So I woke up in the middle of

the night and Logan was sitting in my room again. On the edge of my bed. Why does he keep doing this? You'd think I would be used to it by now, but it sure as hell made me jump. Six months ago, back in Cali, Logan *never* came into my room. Definitely not while I was sleeping. But now . . . I don't know. Maybe this is the new normal.

In any case, I didn't want to overreact or worry Mom or whatever, so I was just like . . . Logan? What's up? Are you okay?

And he gives me a big sunshiny smile, and he's like, yeah, I'm great. I wrote Dad another letter last night. So I'm like, okay . . . And he's like, "We're out of stamps. Can you take it to the post office in the morning and mail it for me?"

Okay, no big deal. So I bring the letter to school with me, planning to mail it at lunchtime. And in history class I get so bored that I'm like . . . I wonder what he wrote. I don't know, it was just such a sweet letter last time, and I really don't think he would care. Well, actually, now . . .

There's something very wrong about this letter. I'm racking my brain for a reasonable explanation, but . . . it just doesn't make sense. I need to talk to Logan.

TUESDAY, MAY 5, 4:O3 A.M.

I tried to talk to Logan when he got home from school, but Mom was around and in one of her busybody moods, and I just couldn't get to him. He was working on a project for school and she didn't want me distracting him. I had a feeling about when I'd be able to get to him, though . . . so I went to bed early and set the alarm on my phone for 3 a.m. I left it under my pillow so it wouldn't wake Mom when it went off.

Sure enough, when I got up in the middle of the night and carefully opened my bedroom door to avoid any creaking, I could see a bluish glow from down in the living room. I grabbed Logan's letter from my desk and made my careful way down the stairs, not wanting to wake Mom or startle Logan. He was parked in his usual place, in front of the TV with a game controller under his busy fingers.

"Logan," I said. "We need to talk."

"What's up?" he said, and I let out a breath I didn't know I'd been holding. It was comforting to hear him say something so normal. I held out the letter.

"Can you explain this?"

He glanced at it briefly, not wanting to let his eyes stray from the screen for too long.

"Is that my letter to Dad? I thought I asked you to mail that this morning."

"You did. And I was going to, but—" I hesitated. I didn't want to admit what I had done, but there didn't seem to be any option. My nosiness was not this family's biggest issue at the moment. "Logan, I read it."

His shoulders shifted slightly—an annoyed little ripple—but he didn't take his eyes from the screen. "Rude," he said. "But so what? Were you scandalized by me telling him about my science fair project, and asking him to forward me my gaming magazines?"

I hesitated again. "No," I said. "That's fine, I just . . ." I took a breath. "Logan, when did you write that letter?"

"Last night. Why? You know that, I told you."

"Yeah, but . . . look, I read your other letter too. The one you sent last week."

"Seriously, Paige? I think you might have a problem. You're weirdly interested in the correspondence of 12-year-old little brothers."

"Logan, they're the same."

"What?"

"The two letters. I—I don't have the first one anymore, so I can't show anyone, but I remember it. I read them both, and they're the same letter."

Logan shrugged. "It's only been a week, my life hasn't changed that much. So what if I mentioned some of the same stuff?"

"Not some. All of it. Every word, every comma. At first I thought you were just talking about some of the same stuff, but there were turns of phrase, spelling mistakes—I remembered it all." Logan didn't say anything. "How did you do it? Did you write two last week, and save one? But why? Why would you do this?"

Logan shrugged again, but this time more uneasily. "I don't know," he said, his eyes still on the screen.

"For God's sake, Logan, this is important. Can you look at me? Can you just put that game down and talk to me?"

"In a minute," he said. "I'm almost done with this level."

"You know, you're not even supposed to be playing anymore. I could tell Mom. Besides, it's bad for you. Do you want to have another seizure?"

"Give me a break," he said. "I'll quit in a minute."

"Logan, I really think you need to . . ." But my voice died in my throat. For the first time during this conversation, I looked up at the TV, where Logan had had his eyes fixed the whole time.

There was no game. It was just static—bluish white fuzzy snow, pulsing infinitely. The letter fell from my hands.

"What are you doing?"

"I told you, Paige, I'll stop in a minute. I just really want to beat this one boss, okay?"

"There's nothing there. Jesus, Logan, can't you see? There's nothing . . ."

But it didn't seem to register with him. I backed away slowly and crept up the stairs to my room, too freaked out to do anything but update my journal.

TUESDAY, MAY 5, 6:33 P.M.

After school today I didn't even bother going home to drop off my books. I was too creeped out by the idea of seeing Logan again, and not being sure which Logan it would be: my bratty but lovable little brother, or this weird, incomprehensible zombie who seemed to understand his own actions barely better than I did. And what was maybe the scariest of all was that I wasn't even sure how to tell which was which anymore.

Instead I went straight to the basement door and knocked.

"Who's there?" came Raph's voice from inside.

"It's Paige. Can we talk?" He didn't answer right away, but I could hear movement from behind the door. "Are you busy?"

"No, I . . . ." There were more sounds of rustling from behind the door. "Look, it's not the best time. Can you—"

"Raph, it's important. I really need to talk to someone."

Again, there was no answer. But after a minute or so, the door opened. Raph stood in the doorway looking even paler than usual, with dark shadows under his eyes and his curls a mess. He looked like he hadn't seen the inside of a shower in at least a few days. "Are you all right?"

"Yeah," he said. "No, I . . ." He cast a look over his shoulder. "I've had better weeks."

"Meaning?"

"Nothing. It's nothing, just . . . haven't been sleeping well. One of the perils of being underemployed, it turns out."

I nodded, nevertheless feeling uncertain. Was Raph in his current state going to be any easier to deal with than Logan? What was going on with the two of them, anyway? But at length I decided I needed to consult with someone, and I wasn't leaving until someone heard me out. "Can I come in?"

Again, Raph hesitated, but after a moment he sighed and stepped aside.

The apartment looked very different from how I had seen it last. For one thing, it was dark, even though outside it was still a bright, sunny day. Basement apartments always suffer from a lack of natural light, but Raph wasn't helping matters by having his shades down over most of the windows. There were also cardboard boxes piled up all over, in some cases teetering precariously, and also blocking out what remained of the light.

"What's going on?" I said as I passed into the kitchen. "Are you moving?"

Raph remained in the doorway, his hands in the back pockets of his jeans, rocking on the balls of his feet. "No," he said. "Those are . . ." His eyes searched around the room, as if he were

hoping to find a reasonable explanation. Eventually he returned them to my face. "Research," he said at last.

"What are you researching? And Raph, don't just change the subject this time. I'm not just being nosy, I'm concerned. Tell me what's going on."

"Nothing. Someone asked for my help. I probably should have said no, but . . ." He looked away again. "I'm not always so good at that."

If I had thought his answer would make anything clearer, I was sorely mistaken. All I got was a dosing of guilt—after all, wasn't that exactly what I was doing? Asking for help, putting Raph in a position he would rather avoid, but felt compelled to accept?

"Maybe I should go," I said.

"You came here for something. You said it was important."

I deliberated a moment longer, then decided to accept his offer, such as it was. I moved a box and sat down on a stool in his kitchen. "It's my brother."

"Logan, right?"

"Yeah. He's . . . acting strange. And I don't know if it's a neurological problem or a sleep disorder or just residual trauma from the divorce, but—"

"Why are you telling me?"

"What?"

"Okay, so your brother has some kind of medical issue, it sounds like. Why would you come to me about it? I'm not a doctor. I'm not even premed."

"Right. I know." It was a good question. Why had it occurred to me to turn to Raph? Maybe just because I don't know many people in town. I had already tried to talk to Mom, but she never seemed to take Logan's symptoms as seriously as I did, perhaps because she didn't experience them firsthand. And from what I could tell, Dr. Clyde was doing little more than taking her money and filling her with false hope. I could talk to Chloe, but she's just a kid like me. Then again, Raph wasn't all that much older. So what did Raph have that made me instinctively feel like he would be able to shed some light on the situation?

"You know this house," I said at last.

Raph pulled a box off the table in front of him and began going through the papers and envelopes inside one by one, methodically. Something about the way his thin, nervous fingers flipped through the various documents gave me the impression that he had done this dozens of times before. That these were movements performed out of habit, rather than with any real hope of finding something in particular. His eyes still focused on the box in front of him, he said at last, "What's any of this got to do with the house?" But there was no cadence of a question in the phrase, and I got the feeling that he knew very well what this had to do with the house . . . maybe better than I did.

In any case, I didn't answer him. I just waited. And after a minute or two, he put the box back on the table and looked at me.

"You're starting to believe the house might be haunted," he said, and this time it was even clearer that this was not a question, but I did my best to answer it anyway.

"I don't know," I said. "Chloe has all these theories about the morgue, and I know you said that morgues aren't haunted, but there's got to be some explanation, and—"

Raph interrupted me with a mirthless laugh. "This has nothing to do with the morgue."

"Okay," I said, getting frustrated. "But then what does—"

"Nothing, okay? It's nothing. Or . . ." An idea seemed to catch

June, 1933

25¢

PRONOICA

Quarterly

CONTENTS:

...and many other inspiring
and hard-hitting articles.
This magazine stands
for the TRUTH.

fire behind his eyes. "Or, sure, maybe it is the morgue. Let's call it the morgue. If your kid brother thinks morgues are spooky, and now he's got insomnia, then sure, maybe he's scared of—"

"It's not just insomnia."

Raph turned a steady gaze on me. "The seizure," he said.

"Not that, either."

And so I explained about the letter, feeling foolish the whole time. There was something so not-right about it, so eerie, but it was hard to explain. How can you be scared of a duplicate letter? It's not going to kill you or eat you or make you spew pea soup everywhere while your head spins around. There's no threat, it's just . . . weird. Anyway, I was pretty sure he was going to wave it off, and tell me I must be misremembering, must just be confused. The same way I told Mom she must be losing it for ordering all those taillights. But as I finished, feeling sheepish and bracing myself for him scoffing, he just stared at me with big, worried eyes.

"Letters," he said at last, but so softly it seemed more to himself than to me. "That can't be good." And as he said this, his eyes slid again toward the cardboard box on the table in front of him.

"What are you talking about?" I said. "And what's in all these boxes? These weren't here last time I was down here." I stood up and moved toward the box closest to me. The top flaps were folded down, but not taped, and without really thinking, I flipped one back and pulled out the first thing that came into my hand. It was a folded pamphlet, like the kind people hand out on street corners sometimes. Except it was old—the paper had that distinctive stiff feel and yellowed edges of stock that has been around a long time, like old library books. The design of it, too, looked old-fashioned, with fonts and graphics that no one would use today, or any time in the past 20 years, I was pretty sure.

"Put that back," said Raph, but I was too engrossed by now to listen to him.

"*This man talked with God! Actually and literally,*" I read off the front of the pamphlet, speaking out loud. "*You will be fascinated at the power—pulsating—surging—dynamic power that can be yours for the asking.*" Despite myself and the nature of our conversation so far, I let out a little giggle. "What is this stuff, Raph? Where did you find this?" I flipped it open and read the text inside to myself. "Man, this is kooky," I said when I had skimmed through the whole thing. "I hope you're not planning on joining a cult or something." I meant it as a lighthearted joke, but as the words escaped my lips, it occurred to me that that was one possible explanation for all of Raph's strange behavior lately. Plus, he'd already told me about his delicate mental state, and his not really having anything to do with himself . . . he would be a pretty obvious mark, I suddenly realized, for a strong, charismatic leader looking for someone a little lost and easy to manipulate. "Oh jeez," I said, catching myself. "I didn't mean—but Raph, if you're seriously considering—I mean, do you need someone to talk to? Have you talked to your mom?"

But Raph didn't answer any of my questions. "You shouldn't be here," is all he said.

I was so surprised by this response that I didn't say anything, though I didn't make any move to leave, either.

"This is . . . this is not good," he went on. "You shouldn't be around me, you need to stay away from me."

"What? Raph, calm down—"

"I'm serious, Paige. This is dangerous."

I tried a friendly smile, maybe to reassure myself as much as him. "You already told me you were safe. You're gay, remember? So I have nothing to fear from you."

"There are all kinds of reasons to fear people. Good reasons."

"Ha. That's not what my mom says. You've heard her. She says we should approach the whole universe with a trusting, open heart. Send out positive energy and you'll get positive energy back, right?"

Raph looked away, and I noticed his hands, resting on his knees, clench into tight fists. "Your mom is wrong," he said.

At this point, Raph was being almost as creepy as Logan was, and I wasn't getting anything clear or useful out of him, so I left and came straight upstairs to post this.

Oh hey—I just realized I never put back that pamphlet I took—I guess I just put it in my pocket without thinking when I left. I wonder if Chloe would be interested in it.

WEDNESDAY, MAY 6, 8:34 P.M.

Update on the flies: They are refusing all the food options I am giving them. That doesn't bode well for the experiment, I guess. On the other hand, they are still alive and unchanged, so maybe that doesn't matter.

Side note: If you ever want to get a really weird look, go to your local pet store and ask for fly food.

THURSDAY, MAY 7, 4:15 P.M.

So it turns out I was right about the pamphlet being old! I showed it to Chloe today and she realized she had seen something like it before. Apparently it's an ad for this cult that grew up in this town almost a hundred years ago. Pronoica. Chloe didn't know much else about it, though, just that a lot of people said the guy who started it was a scam artist and a fraud, and it kind of collapsed after he died.

Weird. Who knew this town had such strange little secrets? Though none of this explains why Raph was acting so odd the other day, or what's going on with Logan. Chloe wasn't any help there.

You know what's really weird, though? The other night I was getting all frustrated with my phone again, and how it keeps screwing up all my text messages and stuff. I guess I didn't mention it, but I rebooted a bunch of times and did a full virus sweep and Mom called the phone company, but I am still having the same problems, with not getting texts for hours at a time, and then getting a huge mess of them when I move into a different room. And also getting and sending double texts and garbled texts and all that.

Okay, so this is going to sound crazy, but I was falling asleep and sort of idly thinking about this stuff, and it popped into my head: Logan sending the same letter twice is kind of like my phone sending out the same text.

Except not, obviously. It can't be, right? Presumably whatever is wrong with my phone has something to do with a glitch in the programming or something. Something technological. And that can't be true for Logan. He was writing by hand, with just pen and paper. So the two are totally different.

But . . . what if they aren't? What if the same weird thing that is making him write the same letter twice is making me . . . send out duplicate text messages? Or making duplicate journal entries? And not even realize I'm doing it.

I don't know. I always figured that the trouble we had in this house with phones and Wi-Fi and everything was just, you know, normal tech malfunctioning. Worse than other places I've been, and a major nuisance, but within the realm of physically possible. But what if it's something else? Something . . . stranger?

So, it finally happened. Mom is dating someone. Someone who isn't Dad.

It seems both out of the blue and not. When I found out, it came as a shock, and I felt it right in my gut. But at the same time, there was a part of me that felt like, "Oh, this makes sense now." Like it explained some stuff I'd already noticed.

The sad part is, I found out by accident. It has to do with the way my phone is all messed up now, and sends all these screwed-up messages. Actually, it isn't just my phone, it's all our phones—mine, Mom's, and Logan's. But I use my phone more than they do, so I'm more aware of it. Or at least, that was true until recently.

One of the things that has been happening with our phones lately is that we pick up each other's messages. Like, I got texts from Mom that were clearly meant for Logan, and Logan got texts I was trying to send to Chloe. But Logan didn't give a crap, because he hardly even checks his phone unless he needs someone to pick him up from something, and Mom, well, Mom as usual was just like "Lalala the universe works in funny ways sometimes!" She can be such a flake.

So anyway, for the past couple of weeks I have been getting a few sort of strange messages from Mom. Hard to describe, because they don't seem that strange until you kind of think about it. Like, I'd get messages time stamped from late at night that just said "Hey." Which is weird . . . to get from your mom . . . you know? And during the day, messages that said, "Hey, thinking of you :)" and stuff like that. Which I guess might not be weird from some moms, but . . . messages from *my* mom are almost always like, "Can you fix dinner tonight? Going to be late." The cutesy sentimental stuff she saves for in person.

So for a couple weeks I was just like, what is going on with Mom? Why is she being so weird? And then finally I got one on Friday that was like, "Can't wait to see you tonight" and I was like, whaaaa? And then I got home and I was like, um, hi Mom, and she told me she was going out to a "department function" except she looked way more dressed up, and wearing way more makeup than she normally wears to school things. And suddenly I was like . . . oh. OH. So I showed her the text and I was like, care to explain?

And she was like, uh . . . I'm just excited to see you? But I called her on that bull, and finally she came clean. A guy named Arthur Taylor, I guess, who is working on a fire ecology project with her advisor. He came and gave a presentation to one of her classes, and I guess they hit it off. And they're like a thing now.

I don't know, it's weird. I haven't even met this guy, and it feels strange to think of my mom in any kind of "dating" context. On the other hand, if she met him through the ecology program, how bad can he be? He's probably a nice guy. And I've already had to deal with my dad dating other people, God knows . . . and that was so much worse. This is weirder in a way because I am living with Mom, but it's also so much less awful than what Dad did.

I just wish she had had the guts to tell me. I mean, I can handle it. Can't I? I don't know . . . This sort of thing happens all the time, right? In any case, it beats the hell out of thinking my mom was sending me these kind of weird, awkward text messages all the time. At least that makes sense now.

Now that the cat's out of the bag, she wants me and Logan to meet him at some point. That sounds . . . awkward. Stressful. But I guess it was bound to happen sooner or later.

WEDNESDAY, MAY 13, 11:05 P.M.

Something so strange just happened. Am I going insane? I don't know how to explain this at all—my mind is just desperately flipping through any conceivable way that this can be normal, that this can be a thing that happens to people. I've been googling for two hours, trying to find *any* hint that someone else has had an experience like this.

But Logan and Mom both saw the whole thing, and yet . . . they're not freaking out like I am. I don't get it—why are they so willing to just accept shit and not question it? It's like it doesn't even bother them. But this is getting too weird for me.

Okay, I need to start over, just to clear my head. Maybe if I write it all out, I'll see some reasonable explanation, or at least that it's not such a big deal, and I'll be able to calm down a bit.

So I was sitting in the living room with Mom and Logan. No,

this story really starts two days ago, I guess . . . Mom and I had made plans to get our hair cut at this place she heard was good, and so she got an appointment for us after school today. And she reminded me about it in the morning and told me not to walk home this afternoon, but that she would pick me up right after school and we would drive to the salon. Okay, yes, I know this sounds like the world's least interesting story, but bear with me.

So school gets out and Chloe finds me to walk home, as we've been in the habit of doing, but I tell her no, I'm getting picked up by Mom, blah blah. So I wait on the front steps of the school . . . five minutes, ten minutes, half an hour . . . At that point, that's when our hair appointment is, so we are missing it. And I'm starting to freak out, because Mom is never late. And of course I have been texting and calling her incessantly this whole time, but she answers none of my texts, and all my calls go straight to voice mail. So finally I text Logan, to see if he knows what's going on, but he doesn't answer either.

So then I am getting seriously freaked out, like maybe there was a car accident, or the house burned down (God, I wish) or some other crisis to keep both of them from texting me or coming to get me or even wondering where I am. Also it's raining at this point, so that is adding to my grumpy and anxious mood.

Finally I give up and just walk home, and the house is empty. No sign of either Mom or Logan. So now I am getting frantic—maybe Logan had another seizure or something? Who knows. As a last resort, I break down and call my dad, and he at least answers, but he's being weird too. He claims he doesn't know anything about what's going on (and I feel pretty sure that if there was some crisis with Logan, Mom would call him right away to let him know), so I'm like, fine, you're no help, and I go to hang up, but then he keeps me on the phone and starts yelling at me about harassing his stupid wife.

And I'm like . . . what? And he's like, don't mess around, I can tell it's you. You need to stop sending her those creepy text messages. And I'm like, what text messages? Apparently both she and my dad have been getting these texts, sometimes from me, sometimes from "number blocked," and at first they were just garbled and weird, so he accuses me of drunk-texting him. When I literally have not had any alcohol at all since I left California!

And then they became more sinister . . . with like, threats and stuff? I'm trying to remember now exactly what he said. I think one was like, "We will know you beyond the tomb" or something like that. Spooky.

And I'm just like, Jesus, Dad, does that sound like me at all? But apparently he does think so, because he didn't let up. He seems to think I'm trying to pull some childish prank to drive them apart or scare this dumb girl off, or something. As if I even care what he does! I am so over him.

Anyway, I tried to defend myself, explaining about how my phone has been acting all weird, but of course he doesn't believe me. And as pissed as I am, I guess I have to admit that it is a tough story to swallow . . . but still. He's supposed to be my dad, you know? He could at least try to give me the benefit of the doubt for five seconds before treating me like some kind of criminal.

But I've gotten way off track. This wasn't the point of the story at all. Where was I? Right, so, Dad is haranguing me and I'm, like, practically in tears because I still don't know what happened to Mom or Logan, and Dad is just giving me more crap on top of that, and then . . . I'm looking out the window and I see Mom and Logan pull up in the car. So I run down the stairs and I'm like, what happened, are you okay? And Mom is like . . . we're fine. We were at Logan's science fair, why didn't you come? He won second place.

And I'm like . . . what? Huh? I'm so confused, and I'm just like, what about our hair appointment? And Mom's like, I told you I canceled it because I remembered Logan's science fair was this afternoon. And I'm like, uh no, no you didn't. And then she goes off on me, just like Dad did, hassling me about how I never listen to anything she says, and she can't believe she had a whole conversation with me this very afternoon, and three hours later it's like it never happened, and am I forgetting stuff or do I just not pay any attention in the first place?

And I can't even deal at this point. I'm fighting off tears and I'm like, Mom, you didn't call me. I definitely did not talk to you today. But she is totally convinced that she did, and I'm like . . . just trying to come up with any explanation, so I'm wondering, is it possible that she spoke to my voice mail and just sort of thought that she actually spoke to me, somehow? I mean, my mom isn't an idiot, she knows the difference between voice mail and an actual conversation, but . . . at least it's an explanation. So I dig out my phone and I go to check my voice mail and it's plain as day. Not only do I not have any voice mail, I don't have a single received call in my call logs since two days ago.

I show Mom, because that seems like pretty good proof that she did not call me, but somehow she manages to waive this off. Like maybe I cleared my call log or something, which I didn't, obviously, since I still had older calls in there. But there's no reasoning with her once she is convinced she is right.

So finally the stress of the day has worn me out and I just don't feel right fighting about it anymore, so I let it drop. I'm just like, fine, whatever, maybe you're right and I'm a complete lunatic who forgets that people called me two hours earlier and also mysteriously erases stuff from my phone. Have it your way. So we manage to make it through a strained dinner, but Logan tells me stories about his science fair project, and he's so excited about it that I can't help feeling excited for him, and we all cheer up and manage to put the bad feeling behind us.

After dinner we all move to the living room and we are watching TV together and I'm sort of idly trying to get some homework done while Mom reads a book for her class, and it's all peaceful and nice and I feel for a little bit like we're kind of a family again.

And then. My fucking phone rings.

Which doesn't sound all that weird, except that I usually have so much trouble getting any reception in the living room, but whatever, that's not the weird part. The weird thing is, I pick up my phone, and on the screen it says "Mom calling." And my heart basically skips a beat because . . . um, Mom is sitting right on the other side of the room from me, I can see her with my own eyes, and she is very clearly not calling me. And I'm like . . . Mom. Where is your phone right now? And she says, it's in my purse, on the kitchen table. Why?

And I'm like, my phone says you're calling me. And I walk over to where she is and I show her my screen, so she can't call me crazy again. But where I'm freaking out, she's just like, "Hmm, that's weird. Maybe there's something in my purse that's pressing on it to make it call you?" Which sounds reasonable at first, but . . . how could that be? It really doesn't make sense.

But I don't want to start a fight again, so I'm just like, fine, maybe you're right. How about I answer it? And I'm thinking, like she said, that I will hear a typical butt-dial conversation, like I'll just hear the TV in the background or something, right?

But that's not what happened.

I answered the phone and held it to my ear, and . . . I can hear my mom. She's talking, and it's like . . . well, this is what I hear:

"Hey Paige, how's it going? (pause) Good . . . well, I just wanted to let you know I had to cancel our appointment this afternoon. (pause) Yeah, I know, but I just remembered that it's Logan's thing tonight, the science fair, and I really have to be there. Can you come too? It would mean a lot to him. (pause) Okay, good. It's at his school, in the cafeteria. I will see you there, 4 o'clock."

And meanwhile, I am looking right at Mom, who is obviously NOT on the phone with me.

But the voice on the phone is still going. "Honey?" she says. It says. "Are you there? I think I'm losing you."

Can anyone fucking explain this to me? How did I have a conversation with my mom, when I didn't get her call until nine hours after she made it?

I don't know. Maybe there is a logical explanation. But in that moment, I was so freaked out that I threw my phone across the room and shattered it. That's one way of solving the problem.

THURSDAY, MAY 14, 5:35 P.M.

When I came home today, there was a new phone waiting for me on the kitchen table. Mom's idea of a peace offering, I guess. I expected her to be mad at me for destroying it on purpose like that, but the truth is, I'd rather have no phone than one that's ... possessed? I don't even know.

I was downloading some apps when Mom found me. "Paige, honey," she said, "I'm worried about you." I started to defend my destructive act, but she stopped me. "I don't just mean the phone. You've had a darkness in you recently, and you need to let it go."

"In me?" That seemed unfair. "Why are you putting this on me? I'd be fine if it weren't for this creepy house."

She looked appropriately apologetic at that, and then she asked me if I wanted to talk to anyone about it. To which I was like, YES. I'm sick of her New Age woo woo "We can all get along" crap—I just want to talk to a regular adult. Someone normal, who will help me figure out what is really going on. And she's like, okay, I'll make an appointment for you to see Dr. Clyde. And I'm like, uggggh. That's not what I meant! I mean, exactly how much good has Dr. Clyde done for Logan? If anything, he's worse now than when he started with her.

But you know what? I'm going to make the best of it, I've decided. It really will be a relief to talk to someone outside of my weird little circle of my family, Chloe, and Raph about all this shit, and get an outside perspective. Plus . . . God, who knows? Maybe it's all in my head. And wouldn't that be a relief in a way too? God knows I don't want to be crazy, but crazy is at least something the world acknowledges and knows how to deal with. Maybe they'll be able to, I don't know, put me on some medication and all this craziness will go away.

FRIDAY, MAY 15, 4:35 P.M.

First appointment with Dr. Clyde is scheduled for Tuesday. I'm nervous, but also excited and a little relieved, too.

In the meantime, Logan and I finally got to meet the illustrious Arthur Taylor last night. I greeted him at the door with a shotgun in hand, and asked him what his intentions were toward my mother.

No, just kidding. It was all right. I didn't get to know him super well or anything, but he seemed . . . okay. He lives on the Nez Perce reservation south of here, I guess, but he works at the university, studying indigenous fire management practices of the inland northwest. It's kind of cool, actually. He's combining fire science and ecology and native culture and history to help firefighters figure out the best way to control wildfires.

He told us all about it over dinner—how the local tribes

used to use ritual burning to enrich the soil and maintain control over the fire. Then the government decided that the best way to protect the land was to avoid fires completely, which worked up to a point, but then when a wildfire did eventually happen, it was 100 times worse than it otherwise would have been. Now scientists are looking more to the traditional methods, using controlled burns to make sure the landscape stays healthy and the fires never get out of hand.

I can see why Mom likes him, I guess. They have a lot in common. Plus, sometimes he's really serious, but then he has a laugh . . . kind of a giggle that fills the whole room. It's really hard not to smile once he starts laughing. From the way he smiles and laughs, you would think he was totally innocent and sweet, but then he'll surprise you with a sharp sense of humor. I don't know, I expected Mom to go for someone as starry-eyed and hippie-dippie as she is, but I guess people don't necessarily do that. After all, she chose Dad the first time around, and she likes me, even though I'm not like her. I've got my whole bitter, cynical thing going on. So maybe it shouldn't surprise me that she found someone a little like that to date.

A part of me kind of wanted to resist him and play the role of the difficult teenage daughter who is impossible to please, but the truth is, I think Mom could have done a whole lot worse. He doesn't seem like a jerk.

Here's a bit of welcome good news: I think the spider situation might be improving! I'm not totally sure since I stupidly decided to stop keeping track of them, but for the past week or so, I feel like I have definitely been seeing fewer. Like, whole days go by without me seeing a single one. Which definitely feels like an improvement in my book!

But scientifically speaking, it's hard to know if that means that the population has decreased, or if I'm just not noticing them as much because I'm not writing down the sightings. But if I had to guess, I really don't think it's a perception thing. I was aware of that possibility, so for the past two days I looked really hard everywhere for spiders, and I didn't see a single one. So . . . that's significant evidence, I think.

Of course, that brings up the question of why. Are they all

dying horrible deaths beneath the floorboards? Much as I might like to wish that fate on them, a house that kills off spiders is somehow almost as creepy as a house that breeds them. And no more explicable.

My personal favorite theory is that the spiders have all moved back outside now that the weather is getting warmer. It's pretty hot now, and there's barely been a cloud in the sky for the past couple of weeks! A nice change, for once. Anyway, that seems like a nice, wholesome, not evil explanation, so that's a mark in its favor.

In any case, it's a lot better than the other option I've considered, which is that nature itself is out of joint in this house, and the flies have been eating the spiders. I know I did suggest that solution a while ago, but . . . I think I've changed my mind on the desirability of that option.

TUESDAY, MAY 19, 8:22 P.M.

So today was baby's first shrink appointment! Very exciting.

No, I don't know. It was fine. A little . . . disappointing, maybe. But not bad. I don't know exactly what I was expecting. I think I hoped I would go in there and tell this lady all about the flies and the phone problems and the bags of vegetables materializing on the kitchen floor, and she would give me an answer. Or at least a path to hunt down.

I guess it wasn't very likely that she'd be like, "Yeah, your house is haunted, here's a phone number of a guy I know who can take care of it for you." Or on the other hand, for her to be like, "BOOM diagnosis, here's what's wrong with you and here's exactly the pill to fix it." But I hoped it would be that easy.

Instead it was just sort of . . . awkward. It feels really weird telling personal stuff to a total stranger. But she is cool and easy to talk to, so by the end of the hour it got a lot easier. And weirdly, I didn't even talk about the house, really. I went in there totally planning to, but then she asked me a bunch of questions that pushed me in different directions. Like I started out telling her about us moving in, but that made her go back to asking about my dad, and how I was feeling about that relationship. And at first I was like, whatever, I don't want to talk about that. But she prodded a bit more and it turned out I had a lot to say!

And then I happened to mention Mom's new boyfriend, just in passing, but Dr. Clyde jumped on that and immediately was like, "How are you feeling about that?" And at first I was like, "Fine, he seems fine." And I changed the subject. But she kept circling back to it, and eventually I started sort of free-associating about it, and well, I don't know. Maybe I am more conflicted about Mom dating than I thought I was.

Anyway, after all that, the hour was up. But I do want to try to talk about the house stuff next week.

THURSDAY, MAY 21, 10:26 P.M.

Arthur came to dinner again. While he was there, I thought a lot about what Dr. Clyde had said, about my underlying animosity toward him and protectiveness toward my mom. But strange to say, he's just such a pleasant guy. It's hard to stay focused on that stuff when he's around. In fact, I kind of like when he comes by because it makes the house seem less spooky. Just me, Mom, and Logan in that big house . . . I don't know, it becomes tense. Sometimes I feel like we don't even know how to talk to each other anymore. But when Arthur is there, it smooths things over.

Although I don't know if Logan's feelings are the same as mine. Logan's a lot more withdrawn around him, which is weird, because Logan has always been such an outgoing kid. But I guess I can't really blame him. I mean, this must be hard for him. And it's not like Logan's rude or anything, he just . . . doesn't really laugh at Arthur's jokes, and looks like his mind is elsewhere, even when Arthur is going out of his way to engage him. I don't know, Logan's a funny kid. I'm sure he'll get over it, though.

SATURDAY, MAY 23, 3:45 P.M.

Wow, so was I ever wrong about the spiders.

The good news is that the flies have probably not been eating the spiders.

The bad news is . . . so inexpressibly horrifying that I don't know if I can even write it down.

Of course, Logan—my baby brother/science mentor—isn't bothered at all by it. He called me into his room after school today as I was walking past on my way downstairs. I hadn't been in there in ages. Thanks to that horrible buzzing noise, I've just been avoiding it since the night of his seizure. But he called to me, so, holding my breath, I opened the door and went in.

Instantly I had to press a palm to my forehead to calm the cacophony inside. "Jeez, Logan, how can you stand to sleep in here?"

But he just gave me a quizzical look, like he had no clue what I was talking about. Apparently he had dropped a comic book or something behind his dresser, and he needed help shifting it so he could get back there.

I got on the other side and we both gave a mighty heave, moving the old oak dresser about a foot away from the wall. Logan grabbed his comic book and we were about to shove the thing back into place when I stopped him.

"Look at that," I said. "The floor under the dresser is darker than the rest of the wood. It's totally discolored."

"So?" said Logan, the correct care and maintenance of hardwood floors not being a major area of interest for him, I guess.

"It's weird," I said. "We just brought this dresser from California, right? It's not like it's been sitting here 100 years. I wonder if the varnish from the dresser has been seeping off or something."

It didn't sound like a very convincing explanation, even to me, but I couldn't think of a better one. Shaking my head a little to stave off that annoying buzzing sound, I bent down to press my fingers to the darkened wood. I wanted to see if it felt sticky or wet at all, but about half an inch from contact, I froze.

Because the dark spot on the floor was moving. The whole patch, just . . . writhing and undulating. Holding my breath, I leaned down to look closer, and the whole thing is like a mass of teeny tiny little spiders crawling all over each other until they look like one solid organism.

And when I say tiny, I mean it. Each one was about the size of a pinhead, maybe slightly bigger. From a distance you couldn't really see them at all. But up close . . . Christ, I can still see that seething mass whenever I close my eyes. My vision got all gray at the edges, and all I could think was that those tiny spiders could be anywhere, could be under me, could be crawling all over me. I got up and ran down the stairs and outside, and I didn't stop until I reached a coffee shop downtown.

It's getting late now, and I really better go home. But I don't know how I'm going to set foot back in that house unless I somehow block what I've seen from my mind forever.

TUESDAY, MAY 26, 7:25 P.M.

Therapy again. I tried a little harder to direct the conversation this time. It's weird. You go in there totally planning to talk about one thing, and then find yourself talking about something totally different. And it's not like Dr. Clyde is forcing me or anything. In fact, she hardly talks at all during the session. But having her there makes me realize I have stuff to say that I didn't even know I was thinking about. Magic!

This time I tried at least. At the beginning she asked me if there was anything in particular I wanted to talk about, and I was like, YES. It's about the house. And I was all proud of myself for bringing it up all directly like that, but then I wasn't sure where to go with it. I just felt so awkward telling her about the stuff that has happened, just because . . . well, damn, a lot of it sounds kind of dumb if you're not there, experiencing it.

Too many jars of tomato sauce in the cupboard? A bag of veggies that disappears and reappears mysteriously? Glitchy cell phone service? This stuff wouldn't even make the cut in a Scooby-Doo script. I tried to tell her about it, but even though she didn't say anything, I just got the feeling that she wasn't really buying it. Like this wasn't what she wanted to hear. But shouldn't therapy be about what's bothering *me* rather than what she wants to hear? I don't know, she's the professional. Maybe she knows better than I do.

Anyway, part of it was her nonengagement with what I was saying, and part of it was maybe just me hearing myself talk, and hearing how silly it all sounded. So we've got some flies and spiders and stuff—what old house doesn't? It's gross, but it's not supernatural. And everyone's got a million stories they can tell you about some time their cell phone screwed up.

But then I remembered the stuff with Logan . . . That stuff is pretty messed up, right? So I told her about that, about the seizure (in the middle of telling her I realized that obviously she already knows about that, and probably a lot of other stuff—she's Logan's doctor too), and about him playing video games that aren't there. And she didn't say anything. So then I told her about the letter, the duplicate letter he wrote. And I tried to really emphasize that it wasn't just a similar letter—it was identical.

I was so hoping that with that, I'd be able to break through her . . . I don't know, her professional reserve. I just wanted a genuine reaction out of her. Like a "Holy crap" or even just "That's kind of weird." Anything other than her medically approved "mmm-hmms" and "How did that make you feels." But I got a lot of that. And finally I was just like, no, how does that make *you* feel? I mean, isn't that strange? How would you explain it? All I want is some kind of explanation for it. For all this stuff.

But Dr. Clyde kept evading my question, and finally she was like, "Look, we're not here to talk about Logan. We're here to talk about you. Logan's problems are Logan's, and while they do affect you, I'm concerned that you are using his issues to deflect this conversation away from your own feelings."

When she said that . . . I had to sit with it a while. Because . . . I couldn't deny that when she put it that way, it made a lot of sense. Is that what I've been doing all along? Just putting all this on Mom and Logan because I'm scared to look at myself?

So then she asked me if there might be a reason I was directing the conversation toward Logan. Was there something going on in my relationship with him that was troubling me? And I told her obviously I am worried about him. And she just "mmm-hmm"d and nodded and looked . . . unconvinced. What's up with that? I hate that the most about therapy, I think. Like I can tell she is thinking something, but since she never says it, I can't confront her about it without looking crazy and paranoid. But the way her face looked . . . I could swear she thought that I had some, like, secret anger toward Logan. Which is such bullshit! I love Logan. I just want him to be okay again.

But then again, maybe that's not what Dr. Clyde was thinking at all. Maybe I just projected that onto her because I'm worried that there's something dark inside me. I don't know. Therapy is supposed to help you figure out and resolve the issues in your life, isn't it? But I feel like it's just making everything even more complicated.

I wonder if anyone's shrink has ever actually made them crazy.

WEDNESDAY, MAY 27, 6:10 A.M.

So I woke up this morning to a fantastic smell wafting through the house, like smoked bacon or something. I ran downstairs to find Arthur sitting at the kitchen table with a cup of coffee and a book. I asked him what was cooking and he cocked an eyebrow at me.

"Nothing," he says. "Just coffee . . . sorry."

So I'm thinking it must be a neighbor or something. I'm like, "Do you smell that? Like someone's having a barbecue or . . ."

That's when he gives me a smile that doesn't seem to have much humor behind it. "That's not food," he says. "That's fire. They're doing controlled burns all over the area right now."

"Oh right," I say. "To prevent wildfires."

And he's like, "Kind of. That may be a little optimistic."

"You think there will be a wildfire this year?" I say, and he laughs.

"There are wildfires every year. It's just a question of how bad. And this year looks like it might be pretty bad."

"How do you know?"

"We didn't get enough snow this winter."

"You mean sometimes there's more?"

He laughed again. This place is so weird. At least it smells nice, though.

THURSDAY, MAY 28, 10:27 P.M.

I forgot to mention before that Dr. Clyde did try to help me feel better about the house. She didn't ignore my concerns completely, in all fairness. I had mentioned the horrible ringing sound that seems to come from Logan's room, but maybe comes from inside of me. Toward the end of the session she brought it up and asked me if I might want to try some simple exercises that might help make the noise go away. And I was like, HELL YEAH, why didn't you offer me that in the first place?

So yeah, it's just really simple stuff. Like phrases to repeat to myself or visualize while I'm falling asleep, mostly. It seemed a little babyish, to be honest, but I've been doing it the past couple of nights, and you know what? The sound does seem to have faded a bit, to the point where I don't notice it unless I am listening for it. And I have been sleeping better, and getting along better with Mom. And I haven't even had any problem with Logan. So . . . I don't know. Maybe there is something to this therapy crap. Who knew?

Okay, scratch that. Shit. I don't even . . .

Okay. Deep breaths. This morning I woke up feeling awesome, well rested, and prepared for my bio test today. Mom was making pancakes, and Logan was chattering about some field trip. It was a good morning. Everyone was being normal.

But as we were getting our school stuff together in front of the door, I happened to notice something in Logan's bag. It was a letter. And I just got this pit in my stomach, because . . . who would Logan be writing to? He's a 12-year-old kid. He doesn't exactly have a lot of snail mail correspondents. So it had to be another letter to Dad. And I just couldn't help wondering, was it the same thing again? Was it normal, or was he at it again? I just had to know. And somehow, before I even consciously formed the thought, I took the letter out of his bag when he wasn't looking and put it in mine.

I know! It was a shitty thing to do. But I am worried about him, I really am, no matter what Dr. Clyde says. Besides, the letter could be like . . . evidence. Something tangible, that isn't just me blabbing about stuff I might completely be making up. And anyway, the ironic thing is that once Logan noticed it was missing, he probably wouldn't even think to blame me because so much random stuff goes missing in our house these days. He'd probably just assume it was our friendly ghosts. Ha.

I could hardly breathe the whole way into school. But the minute I sat down in homeroom, I got the letter out and ripped it open. My eyes scanned the first few lines, and instantly I knew. It was the *same* letter.

But there *was* something different this time—some of the words were crossed out. But not like, just a line through them, or a bit of a scribble, like a normal person might do. Someone—Logan, I guess—had gone over each crossed-out word probably a million times, scraping over and over with a ballpoint pen, until it made a deep indentation in the paper. And the words he had chosen seemed totally random. I can't figure it out at all, what he thought he was doing.

That's assuming there was any thought going on at all.

FRIDAY, MAY 29, 4:03 P.M.

Update . . . When I got home, I found Logan's last letter and
compared them. Sure enough, they are word for word the
same. And now I can see what words he was crossing out.
    the
    dead
    will
    bring
    you
    what
    you
    want
    don't
    want

sick
key
ana

What the hell.

Dear Dad,

Mom's making me write this letter. I mean, not that I mind writing to you, but she's making me write ~~a~~ letter by hand. The shrink has decrede that I'm not allowed to have screen time, so I have to email you the old fashioned way. I'm a little surprised to learn that the postal service isn't d~~ead~~ yet, but there are still people who ~~will~~ physicly ~~bring~~ paper with writing on it to your front door.

I'm getting excited about my science project. Have I told you about it? I'm trying to show what happens ~~when~~ you look at a really bright e~~thing~~ for a while and then ~~look~~ at a white wall — like what the rods and cones are doing and stuff.

Do you think there's any chance you might be able to come for it? I don't know if you'd want to, but I think it will be interesting. I kno~~w~~ ~~you~~'re busy, but I bet Paige would be really happy to see you. And I would be too.

By the way, have you been getting my gaming magazines? I don't know what happened to the subscription wh~~en~~ ~~we~~ moved but there's a review of the new Aeon of Strife that I want to check out. It's supposed to be sick.

Sorry if my ~~hand~~writing is hard to read, it really never occurred to me that penmanship was going to be an issue in my life. I can't wait to get back to a ~~key~~board.

Well, it's almost morning and I'm starving. The ban~~ana~~ in the fruitbowl is calling to me. Write back soon!

Love,
Logan

SATURDAY, MAY 30, 3:23 P.M.

God, my eyes are killing me. How do people live like this? It's worse than allergies. Worse than that sandstorm, even. I woke up this morning and my eyes were *stinging* and I couldn't figure out why. My throat was burning too, so I thought, am I getting a cold? Strep? Then I looked out my windows as I was getting dressed, and the light looked . . . weird. Kind of golden, like sunset, even though it was nine in the morning.

Arthur stopped by for lunch and told us about the fires—all this golden haze means that somewhere out there, the fields and forests are burning.

"Out there?" I said. "What about the town? Will it . . . ?"

The rest of the thought is too scary to finish, but Arthur smiled and shook his head. "No, they're really far away now," he said. "Hundreds of miles, in fact, but the wind is so strong, it sweeps the ash and debris over to us. But there's no danger here. Not now, anyway."

I wanted to know how it started. A cigarette butt? A campfire? But Arthur says it's not that simple, it could be almost anything. Sometimes it starts with a lightning strike. Sometimes the farm machinery shoots off a spark from metal rubbing metal. And that's all it takes. The next thing you know, the fields are blazing.

TUESDAY, JUNE 2, 8:27 P.M.

So all week I've been looking forward—if you can call it that—to my session with Dr. Clyde so I could show her this new evidence. I figured, there was no way she could deflect this, no way she could argue that everything in the house was just a symptom of my own psychological distress.

Guess I have a lot to learn about psychiatrists.

I didn't even wait for her to ask me how my week went, or if there was anything I needed to talk about. I took out the letter right away and handed it to her without a word. She tried to ask me a lot of questions before she even looked at it—trying to regain control of the session, I guess. But I was insistent. I just kept telling her to read it. Finally she did.

"Okay," she said when she was done. "Do you want to tell me something about this?"

"It's Logan. Don't you see? He's doing it again. Only it's even worse now. Look at those words, look at—"

But Dr. Clyde wouldn't listen. She just kept trying to get me to calm down, to sit down. Eventually I did. "Paige," she said once I had stopped ranting, "we need to talk about this. I'm growing increasingly concerned about you."

That took me by surprise.

"About me?" I said. "But I'm showing you . . . it's not me, it's Logan! Or really . . . I don't think it's Logan, either. This isn't like him. Something has gotten inside of him. Something is making him do this. It's possessed him the same way it possessed my phone, the way it moves stuff around in our kitchen, making us all think the others are crazy . . . or that we are." Dr. Clyde didn't say anything, just looked at me with big, serious eyes. "That's what you think, isn't it?" I said. "You think I'm nuts." I couldn't help laughing a little to myself, though there wasn't any humor in it. "Of course, that's what people pay shrinks for, isn't it? To tell us that we're nuts. That's your training. How are you ever going to see anything else? But think about it, Dr. Clyde—how can this be about me? *Logan* did this, not me. How can that make me crazy?"

Dr. Clyde hesitated a long time before answering. "Paige," she said at last, "no one is calling you crazy. But it's clear you have been under a lot of stress lately, and there are latent issues you aren't ready to deal with. Do you know anything about repression?"

I stared blankly at her, though rage was building in my chest.

She starts to explain repression to me, speaking slowly as if I'd never heard of the concept. She explains that repression is when we have thoughts or feelings that we think we're not supposed to. The thoughts cause guilt and shame, so we protect ourselves by pushing those thoughts down into our unconscious so we don't have to deal the them. We try to keep only happy, positive thoughts in our heads. But it doesn't work for long. You can push the scary stuff down, you can hide it, but you can't make it go away—not like that, anyway. And the more you push it down, the harder it pushes back. It starts coming up again, burbling to the surface, but in different ways. Then she says, "Sometimes we see very strange behaviors manifesting themselves. Stuff that doesn't seem to make any sense at all. But when you look at it at the level of the unconscious, it all starts to make sense. The unconscious has its own logic, and it can't be denied."

That last part got to me. I hated the way she could say things so clearly without ever really saying them at all. I had to pin her down. "You're saying that's what's going on with Logan?" I asked. "That it's not a haunting or a spirit possession or whatever . . . that it's his own mind doing this to him?"

Again, Dr. Clyde didn't speak for a long moment. "Paige," she said at last, "I understand your concern for your brother. But remember what we talked about last week—about using him to hide from your own issues. I want you to think, Paige. Think hard about where this letter came from."

"What do you mean? I told you, I got it out of his bag. I read it at school, and then—" But then something clicked. She never said anything, but I looked into her face and read everything there I needed to know. "You think it was me," I said, reeling from the shock. "You think I crossed out these words. Hell, maybe you think I wrote them in the first place."

"Paige," she said, "I want you to think about where all this negative energy is coming from. The animosity you feel toward your brother. Is it because you see your father in him? Does it have to do with your mother's new boyfriend? Acknowledging those feelings and working through them is the only way you're going to—"

But I didn't stay to hear the end of her psychobabble. I had to get out of there.

WEDNESDAY, JUNE 3, 12:05 A.M.

Dr. Clyde has gotten under my skin. Now that she has put this idea in my head, I can't stop wondering if she's right. What if it's all in my head? I guess that's what I wanted to hear from the beginning, right? That I had some kind of mental issue that was causing all this, and it could be diagnosed and treated and cured. But I didn't expect it to be like this . . . I always thought of mental illness as like other kinds of illness. Like, you're this complete, whole, normal person, but then cancer or the flu or an infection comes along and messes you up, but you're still you. I guess I pictured mental stuff the same way. Like a film that is covering your normal brain, making you see things funny, and you just need someone to scrape it away to be all right again.

But what Dr. Clyde is suggesting . . . what if this isn't an illness that happened to me? What if this is all the "me" there is? And I do things I don't remember, and I . . . *feel* things I don't even recognize. Maybe my whole life, I've had something inside of me . . . something crazy, something wrong, something *bad* . . . and I kept it hidden from everyone. Even myself. What if the normal me, the sane me that I think I know, that everyone around me knows—what if that's the film? And what if something in my life—the divorce, or living in this house, or my sessions with Dr. Clyde—is now scraping it away?

I don't know if I want to see what's underneath.

WEDNESDAY, JUNE 3, 3:55 P.M.

I woke up this morning to find the yards in our neighborhood under a blanket of snow. It's June! Even in Idaho, that seemed excessive. There was something odd about it, though. It covered the neighborhood, but not the fields behind the house, which are still green. And it doesn't sparkle.

Turns out it's not snow but cottonwood fluff. Arthur explained, and said it's like this every year. You have to watch out for it because it ignites so easily. Ash from a cigarette butt could wind up setting the whole town aflame. Especially with the dry weather we've had lately.

It's weird, though. Where did it all come from so suddenly? I never even knew we had cottonwood trees, and then one day there is this fluffy white stuff all over everything. I touched it and it stuck all over my fingers and clothes. Gross, but also kind of cool.

Bug update: I'm still unsettled about the spiders I saw in Logan's room. Let's hope they are just a fluke in Logan's room, and not under every piece of furniture in this house. In any case, I am not checking under the others, science be damned.

The flies I was keeping in that jar seemed to have finally kicked it. They're all lying feet up on the bottom of the jar. The ones downstairs are still going strong, so I guess that at least tells me these flies do need food to survive. I hadn't fed them in ages. (Don't tell Mom. It was really more accident than any deliberate plan to torture them.)

I feel slightly bad, but mostly good that these flies follow natural laws and aren't superhuman. Superfly? Wait, no, that means something different.

Uhhhh, scratch that! I picked up the jar to toss it in the trash, and suddenly they all started buzzing around again. That's . . . freaky.

Now I'm not sure what to do with them. Guess I'll leave them on the desk and keep ~~staring at them in horror~~ studying them?

FRIDAY, JUNE 5, 5:30 A.M.

Logan had another seizure tonight.

I don't understand it. I thought he was doing better. We did everything Dr. Clyde said—stopped the Ritalin, took away his video games . . . Shouldn't he be better now? But then again, did I really think he was better? For a while he seemed to be sleeping a bit, but lately I've seen him up in the middle of the night plenty of times. And those letters . . . I don't know what to think anymore. Dr. Clyde had me half-convinced that I crossed out all those words to create that message. But if it really was Logan all along . . .

And I can't even tell if this is just a medical issue, or if it's something more. Something . . . different. But what would that even be?

I was lying in bed tonight, listening to the usual shrieks and howls of the wind blowing through the house, and then suddenly the wind died and it was eerily silent in the house.

I looked at my clock and it was a little after 3 a.m. I lay in bed for a while, trying to figure out what was bothering me—if it was a dreaming or waking sensation—and then I realized . . . it felt like the whole house was moving. Or . . . *swaying*. Almost like it was dancing. The only thing I'd ever experienced that was similar was earthquakes back in California, but Idaho doesn't get earthquakes. And this felt different, anyway. More rhythmic.

After a bit, the rocking stopped, but I couldn't go back to sleep. I could feel the vibrations from Logan's room building in my bones, and I decided to check on him. I got out of bed and went to his room, but his bed was empty. I stood in the center of the room for a while in the uncanny stillness of the night, trying not to look at those strange symbols in the walls, trying to ignore the building tension emanating from the room itself. The sound was even worse now. I could feel it creeping through my whole body, making my bones and organs vibrate painfully. And in my head . . . what had once sounded kind of like a person screaming now sounded like an army of voices, some talking, some babbling, some crying and moaning in agony. No one else had ever confessed to hearing it, but even so—was it any wonder Logan had trouble sleeping in here?

I left the room to go look for him, sure that I would find him parked in front of the TV again, but he wasn't. Instead I found him in the kitchen. There was bread laid out on the counter, and jars of peanut butter and jelly. And Logan was twitching on the floor.

I screamed and Mom came running. A couple of minutes later, Arthur was there too. I looked at him strangely, and Mom made some comment about her not wanting him to drive all the way home so late at night. At the time, I was too distracted by Logan to make much of it, but I guess this means Mom has taken their relationship to the next level. Ew. Can't wait to see what Dr. Clyde makes of that.

Anyway, Mom called 911 and an ambulance came and took them both to the hospital, leaving me alone with Arthur. Arthur seemed pretty spooked, but I could tell he wanted to reassure me. He was like, wow, that was . . . something. But don't worry, your brother is in good hands now. The doctors will look after him, and he'll be fine. I just nodded mutely.

Arthur said, "You should go back to bed," and I nodded, but I didn't move. As if sleep were even a remote possibility. Arthur caught on quick. "You're not going back to bed, are you?" I shook my head. "You want some coffee?" He waited for another nod, then put the pot on.

"You know he's going to be okay, right? The doctors will look after him, and they'll figure out what's going on." I didn't respond. I appreciated his efforts to make me feel better, but I didn't have it in me to play along. Arthur sat down in the chair opposite me. "You know," he said, "I've got a cousin with epilepsy. It's scary, but it's not that big a deal, really. He just has to take some precautions, some medication . . . but he's fine, he's still the same guy."

"This is different," I said without thinking. I hadn't really meant to spill the beans to Arthur. He's a nice guy, but I figured he didn't need to know all the grotesque details of our life here. Anyway, I expected him to brush it off the way most people have—like Mom and Dad and Dr. Clyde. To tell me, sure, it feels different to you, because you're so close to the situation, but you're just a kid, you don't understand, blah blah. But he didn't.

"Different how?"

"This isn't epilepsy."

"Well," he said, "I guess we can't know anything for sure yet. Sometimes there are other causes for seizures, but the doctors will—"

"The doctors won't be able to fix this." Arthur didn't say anything, he just looked at me. I decided to give it my best shot and explain myself. "There's something really wrong," I said, speaking carefully, not sure how much I was ready to reveal. "Not with Logan. With something else." Still, Arthur didn't speak, but his open expression seemed to urge me to go on. Not like Dr. Clyde's silences, where I always seemed to be able to read what she wanted or expected me to say. Like he was really listening. "I think it's the house."

"The house?" he said. "This house?"

"You haven't noticed anything?"

"Well, it's old. Kind of. Old for white people. If you come down to the reservation someday, I can show you stuff with a lot more history than this house."

"Is any of that stuff . . . haunted?" Immediately I felt dumb for using the word. "I mean," I tried again, "do you think any of that old stuff ever"—I reached for a phrase I'd heard my mom use—"accrues energy?"

"Energy," he repeated with a frown. I don't think I'd ever seen him frown before, but it seemed more thoughtful than disapproving. "Yeah," he said, "I think I know what you mean. But I wouldn't say haunted. The tradition I was raised with says that the spirits of our ancestors are with us all the time, everywhere—but it's nothing to be afraid of. They watch over us and protect us. It can be a great comfort to know that our loved ones never truly leave us."

And now I definitely know what he and my mom have in common. How is it so easy for everyone to believe in happy, peaceful hauntings? I'm sick of people trying to reassure me that I have nothing to fear from the dead. It's all very well to *say* that the dead bear us no ill will, but that's not always what it looks like.

I decided to try to get Arthur to see this point. "What if some of these spirits aren't so nice?" I asked him. "What if they don't seem protective? What if they seem . . . threatening?" And so, as we finished our cups of coffee, and he poured us more, I let loose with all the little things that I had noticed since we moved in. By the time I finished, it was starting to get light out, and I could hear birds.

Arthur was quiet for a moment, staring down into his coffee. "I've heard some stories," he said at last. "Unfriendly spirits, some people say. Other people call them demons. I had a cousin—a different cousin—who went through something similar with her whole family. They live up on Sundown Heights, and everyone says there are spirits up there. The spirits live on the hillside and pass from house to house, if people give them a chance to come in. They say you have to close your curtains at night or they'll watch you through the window. Don't cry at night or they'll hear you and come in. And if you eat with the windows open, they'll come in for the food and when they can't get it, they wreak all kinds of havoc. She told me one night she looked out the kitchen window and saw a little girl's hand in a frilly white glove, just sticking out of the dirt."

"Jesus. Was she scared?"

"What do you think? Her first instinct was to burn the whole place down and never look back. People used to do that more in the old days—a good burn will purify a place like nothing else. You come back next year to find mushrooms and berries instead of creepy undead babies. But we don't have enough land anymore to just walk away from a fire, so instead my grandfather came over to do a cleansing."

"Did that work?"

"Sure it did. He's a tribal elder, and when he speaks, everyone listens. Even the dead." I didn't say anything, but the look on my face must have spoken volumes. "Do you want me to see if he'll come?"

I couldn't speak or even nod at this offer, but tears of relief rolled down my cheeks.

SATURDAY, JUNE 6, 10:33 A.M.

These flies are really freaking me out, man. I'll be so sure they
are all dead, and then I come back from brunch an hour later
and they are flying around like nothing's the matter.

They look pretty healthy now. I kind of have another experiment in mind, though. Hmm, let's see how this goes.

Okay, that . . . did not make me feel any better. Basically, I
took one of the flies out of the jar and wacked the hell out of it
with my history textbook. Then I put it back in the jar. I know,
that's weird, but I wanted to see if it would come back to life.

It did not. The other flies, however, immediately landed on
the bottom of the jar and are now standing in a circle around it.
What is this, an insect funeral? This is too strange.

SATURDAY, JUNE 6, 10:49 A.M.

Left to take a shower, and when I got back, the dead fly was gone. I can't figure out what happened to it.

Did it regenerate and come back to life? To be honest, I'm not totally sure how many flies were in the jar in the first place, so I'm not sure if it's flying around now or not. But I don't think so. I really don't know what the hell happened.

~~Okay I am pretty sure the other flies ate it but I don't want to think about that.~~

MONDAY, JUNE 8, 10:15 P.M.

Chloe came over today. Logan is still in the hospital for observation, and Mom is with him. I guess I just wasn't thrilled about being alone in the house, so I invited her over, supposedly to celebrate the beginning of summer vacation. I don't think I managed to look convincingly celebratory.

Even with her there, I found I didn't really want to be inside. It feels oppressive. So we sat on the porch, watching the cottonwood fluff drift around the neighborhood. I still can't get over how weird it is—not just a bit of fluff here and there, but sheets of it on every flat surface, laid out like quilt batting. It's hard to get used to.

After a bit, Chloe got bored and decided she wanted to harass Raph. I told her I didn't think that was a great idea.

"Why?" she said. "I thought you guys hung out. Wasn't your mom, like, planning your nuptials?"

"Yeah," I said, thinking awkwardly of my last meeting with him, in that darkened apartment filled with boxes. "Pretty sure the wedding is off." I told her about Raph's strange behavior and his sinister warnings, but I don't think she really got the full extent of it. Somehow, when I speak, people always hear what they want to hear. I had hardly finished the story before she was bounding down the porch stairs toward his door.

"What are you doing?"

"Going to see Raph."

"But—"

"The way I see it," she said over her shoulder, "there are two possibilities. Either that last time was a fluke, and he's fine now, and so it can't do any harm to see him."

"Or?"

"Or . . . he's not okay. He's got some kind of problems. In which case it's basically a good deed to check up on him, isn't it?"

I turned this over in my head. There was certainly a logic to her words, but still . . . I remembered his face last time, when he had told me to stay away from him. As if he was . . . not exactly *threatening* me. Warning me, maybe. But I still couldn't make any sense of it. What could he possibly be warning me about? Did he think *he* had caused Logan's seizures? Or all the other weird stuff in the house? That seemed unlikely. I don't know why, but I was pretty sure that if there was something up with the house, it was something dead or supernatural causing it. Not a perfectly healthy college boy (a.k.a. a semi-healthy ex–college boy). Still, it seemed rude to intrude on him again, after he had been so anxious around me last time. On the other hand, I *was* curious about what was going on with him. I hesitated a moment longer, then followed Chloe to his door.

Chloe knocked confidently, and Raph opened it almost immediately with a smile on his face, as if he had been expecting us. Or expecting *someone*. His smile fell a bit when he saw us, and he ran a hand through his hair. "Oh," he said. "You guys. What's up?"

I expected Chloe to speak, but she seemed unaccountably tongue-tied, given her boldness only minutes earlier.

"We just, you know, wanted to say hi," I tried, smiling nervously. "And check in on—I mean, see how you're doing. I mean, say how are you. How are you?" Ugh, will I ever not babble like an idiot in front of this boy?

Raph nodded knowingly. "So this is what, a welfare check? Want to see if I've started carving the names of demons into all the walls of my apartment?"

"Oh my God," said Chloe, finding her voice. "Have you? That would be so metal."

Raph stepped aside and extended an arm, inviting us in. Chloe went in first and spun around, taking in all the walls. "Oh," she said, sounding disappointed. I followed her and saw what she saw: totally normal walls, nothing spooky carved into them at all. What's more, the place looked really different from the last time I had been there. For one thing, the curtains and blinds were open, and the sun was shining in. Also, all the boxes were gone, and the surfaces all around the apartment were neat and clear.

"What happened to all the boxes?" I asked. For a moment, I flashed back to my last session with Dr. Clyde, and was struck with a cold panic that I had imagined my whole last interaction with Raph. But no, I had taken that weird pamphlet back with me, and even shown it to Chloe. I couldn't have just made all that up. In any case, Raph dissipated my fears with his next comment.

"Gone," he said. "We took them back to the library."

"We?" said Chloe.

"I did," he said, blushing a little. "I mean, someone helped me. A friend helped me. It was a lot of boxes."

"You have a friend?" said Chloe incredulously, which seemed kind of mean. But it was true that I had never seen anyone come to visit Raph, other than his mom and the delivery drivers. Raph's expression showed that he felt the slight, but he didn't respond to it.

"The place is a lot clearer now, isn't it? It was . . ." He laughed awkwardly. "It was annoying, having all those boxes everywhere."

"What were you doing with them?" I asked.

"Just . . . research," he said.

"Did you find what you were looking for?" said Chloe.

"No," he said.

"Oh," she said. "Sorry."

"No," he said. "It's a good thing. I mean, it's . . . sometimes, when you're doing research, you're trying to prove something. A hypothesis. But if you don't find evidence, that's good too. Sometimes even better."

Chloe and I exchanged a glance. It would be an exaggeration to say Raph was acting *normal*—he was still talking in riddles and not making a hell of a lot of sense, for one. But at least he seemed . . . happy. And his apartment certainly looked more normal. All in all, the signs pointed to an improvement in his mental health. So why did I feel so edgy?

"But it still means you were wrong, doesn't it?" said Chloe.

"Yeah," said Raph. "But sometimes wrong is exactly what you want to be." And he let out a slightly unhinged giggle.

"You were researching Pronoica," said Chloe.

She had hardly said the words before Raph's expression shifted. The happiness and relief exchanged for a flash of that haunted look I had seen on his face last time we spoke. "How did you know about that?" he asked sharply.

"I'm sorry," I said, shooting daggers at Chloe for selling me out. "That was me. I happened to pick up one of the pamphlets you had lying around last time and I showed it to her."

Raph knitted his brows and his face darkened again. "You shouldn't have done that," he said, and I was revisited by the chill I had felt during our previous conversation. But he seemed to catch himself and he relaxed his face as he said, "I mean, all that stuff belongs to the library. You can't just walk off with it."

I told him I'd bring it back, but he seemed more interested in Chloe now. "What do you know about Pronoica?" he asked.

She shrugged. "Not much. Just that it was some kooky cult, basically. Except, it wasn't even real . . . The whole thing was done through the mail, right? My grandpa told me once that the reason the post office in this town is so big is because of Pronoica. That guy, Frank Williamson—they called him the Mail Order Messiah. He used to take out advertisements in the backs of magazines, promising power and enlightenment to any sucker who sent him ten dollars."

"And people fell for that?" I asked.

Raph shifted his gaze away from us. "You sure they were suckers?"

I couldn't help laughing. "What, so you're saying Williamson sent people supernatural powers through the mail?"

Raph rubbed his knuckles against his scalp thoughtfully. "You guys want some tea? My mom just brought me a new tea-kettle, and now I drink tea constantly." Without waiting for our answer, he ran the kettle under the kitchen tap. It did not escape my notice that he'd changed the subject again. Chloe looked like she was going to ask him more about Pronoica, but I shot her a warning glance. We let him chatter on about tea varieties for the rest of our visit.

TUESDAY, JUNE 9, 9:25 A.M.

God, my eyes are waiting killing me. How do people live like this? It's worse than allergies. Worse for than that sandstorm, even. I woke up this you morning and my eyes were *stinging* and I couldn't figure out why. My to throat was burning too, so I thought, am I getting a recognize cold? Strep? Then I looked out my windows as I was getting dressed, and the light looked . . . weird. Kind of golden, like a sunset, even though it was nine that in the morning.

Arthur stopped by for lunch and invisible told us about the fires—all this golden haze means that somewhere out there, the fields though and forests are burning.

"Out there?" I asked. "What about the town? Will it . . . ?"

The rest of the thought is too powerful scary to finish, but Arthur smiled and shook his presence head. "No, they're really far away now," he said. "Hundreds of miles, in fact, but the wind is so strong, it sweeps the ash and debris over to us they. But there's no danger here. Not now, anyway."

I want to are know how it started. A cigarette butt? A campfire? But Arthur says it's not that simple, it could be almost anything. Sometimes it starts with a lightning pregnant strike. Sometimes the farm machinery with shoots off a spark from spiritual metal rubbing metal. And that's all it takes. The next thing you know, the fields are blazing power.

TUESDAY, JUNE 9, 3:46 P.M.

Another session with Dr. Clyde today. A weird one. I told her about Logan's most recent seizure, again forgetting that she must already know. I wanted to challenge her on that—obviously the seizures are in his head, not in mine. So why should she assume I'm making up all the other stuff? But I didn't really make any headway there. She just kept asking me how I felt about it, and when I said I was worried, she seemed dissatisfied, and asked the same thing again in a different way. Like she wants a different answer. But what? It's almost like she wants me to say I hate Logan or something, which is NOT true. But even if it were . . . it's not like I can give him seizures. Can I? No, that's crazy. Even by the standards of someone who thinks she lives in a haunted house, that's nuts.

I tried to shore up my position by telling her about Arthur

and how I had told the whole story to him, a real, responsible adult, and he had believed me. At least, he seemed to. But that took Dr. Clyde off in a whole other direction. She wanted to know how I felt about learning Arthur was spending the night. I was like, I think we have a bigger issue on our hands here . . . ? But she didn't want to let it go. Shrinks, man—they have a one-track mind.

So then I brought up Raph, I'm not sure why. I guess for another example of inexplicable stuff going on in the house that can't possibly be my fault, or my imagination. But that's when things got weird. I had mentioned him to her a couple of times before, but just as "the cute boy who lives downstairs." I mean, she asked me about boys directly during our first session, and it's not like I have anything else going on. So I mentioned him, but she didn't seem terribly interested, and it's not like I really wanted to talk about it either.

Anyway, I mentioned him again this time. I think I said, "Raph is acting weird too," and I was about to go into his sort of odd behavior the last couple of times I saw him, though I figured she wouldn't make much of it. He's been weird but not, like, supernaturally weird. But I didn't even get to tell her anything more because she stopped me there.

"Who?" she said.

I said, "Raph, the guy who lives downstairs. His mom is—"

"That's the college boy you mentioned?"

"Yeah, he lives in—"

"And you say he's behaving strangely?"

"Well, kind of, but I don't have much to—"

And that's when Dr. Clyde interrupted me again, to ask exactly what Raph had done. Which was weird, because she never interrupts. Talking to a shrink isn't like chatting with a friend or your mom or whatever. Their whole point is to let you keep talking forever and ever and ever, in hopes that you'll stumble into something interesting. Or revealing. Or I guess if I want to be cynical, maybe they let you talk and talk because it kills the time and runs down the hour, so they get paid without doing any actual work. But either way, I had definitely noticed that Dr. Clyde only ever talked if I've been silent for a good long pause. Usually at least a few seconds, sometimes maybe a whole minute. And she definitely never interrupted. So why was she doing it now? What had I said to get her so worked up? Nothing, really. Nothing except . . .

"Do you know Raph?" I said.

Dr. Clyde was silent a moment. Then she said, "No, I don't. But even if I did, Paige, you know the rules about confidentiality. Of course I couldn't tell you."

"That's a yes, isn't it?"

"No. That's a no."

"What do you know about him?"

"I don't know anything, Paige. I'm only responding to what you're saying, what you've told me, and what I notice in your body language. But I think . . . I'm going to advise you to stay away from this young man."

"But you don't even know him."

"It's for your own good. Stay away from him, Paige. Trust me."

WEDNESDAY, JUNE 10, 2:57 P.M.

I was so disturbed by what Dr. Clyde said yesterday that I completely forgot Arthur's grandfather was coming by today. Luckily, he texted me when they were on their way, so I was able to clean up a bit and not be completely taken by surprise. I checked the cupboards for any cookies I could serve with tea, but honestly, I had no freaking idea how one is supposed to entertain a tribal elder.

The other thing that was weird was that Mom didn't know. I never mentioned it to her, but I guess I assumed Arthur would tell her. He apparently didn't—maybe he assumed the same thing of me—so I had to fill her in quickly as their car pulled up. I'm guessing a lot of moms in the world would have trouble with the idea of some old man coming to their house to recite mumbo jumbo, but since Mom is basically the queen of mumbo jumbo herself, she took it pretty well.

I watched out the window as the old man eased out of the car with some help from Arthur. He was wearing jeans and an orange fleece jacket, and he had long white hair with a cropped ponytail on the crown of his head. As he made his way toward the house, two little kids hopped out of the backseat and started chasing each other up and down the porch stairs.

"Quit it, guys," said Arthur over his shoulder as I met him at the front door, trying to clear a path through the slowly circling flies for them to walk through. "More cousins," he said to me. "I hope you don't mind. Pops likes to bring the little ones along to these things."

I nodded, but Pops apparently thought it needed more explanation. "The rituals are in danger of being forgotten," he said, his breath still coming a little heavy from the exertion of the stairs. "Ours is mostly an oral tradition, which means we need to be in the same place, repeating the same words together, or it will be lost."

Arthur smiled a little apologetically at the old man's words. "My brother is writing his dissertation on the Nez Perce language. A lot of the old stories are being written down, so they'll be more permanent now."

Pops gave him a sharp look. "Writing is good, but some things were not meant to be written down." Pops then turned to me and Mom and looked us over. "You're the ones who live here?" he said. "The ones who are visited by spirits?"

I looked up at Mom, not quite ready to say the words aloud to a complete stranger. She gave him a pleasant smile and nodded. "My son lives here too, but he's at a friend's house for the evening. Will that be all right?"

Pops waved a hand in her direction. "Sure," he said. "No big deal. Where do you want me to set up?"

Mom looked around a little uncertainly, then guided him toward the kitchen table. "I guess this will work," she said. As he began to set out his props, she continued. "Look, I'm not sure what my daughter told you, but you're not going to do anything . . . *unfriendly* to these spirits, are you? My philosophy is live and let live ("live and let haunt," I couldn't help muttering under my breath) and I, well, I don't want to toss anyone out, especially since they were here first. Exorcisms can be so . . . spiritually violent."

Pops raised his eyebrows at her. I wondered if he got this kind of speech from a lot of crazy ex-hippies, or if this was a first for him. "It's not an exorcism," he said impatiently. "Ceremonies like this one are really for the living, not the dead. This house cannot be blessed because it is blessed already by the spirits of the people who have lived here. This is only an acknowledgment of that blessing."

Mom nodded, satisfied with this explanation. Pops took a bag from Arthur and pulled out an iridescent shell about the size of a baseball mitt, and placed a dried-up fir branch inside. "Patosway," he said as he lit a match and held it to the branch. "It has many cleansing properties. And the fire acts as a purifying agent." The match went out.

"That's our ancestors' idea of a joke," he said with a gentle smile, and he lit another. That one, too, went out. He went through six matches, losing a little more of his good humor each time, until at last on the seventh he was able to light the branch. He blew out the flame and wafted the resulting smoke around the kitchen and toward the front hall. It smelled wonderful,

though it stung my eyes before it dissipated. The kids stood around the table, fidgeting and looking bored.

After a minute, Pops pulled out a shiny brass bell and rang it three times, using his whole arm to swing it back and forth. I was so focused on the sound, I almost didn't notice my cell phone buzz in my pocket. I reached in to turn it off. "Sorry," I said.

Pops cast me a dark look, but I noticed Mom and Arthur reach into pockets to turn their phones off right afterward.

Pops put down the bell and began reciting a long prayer in a strange but beautiful language. Before he was done, though, we heard another vibration. Pops froze, stopping the prayer. I looked at the other two, but they just shrugged. Pops cleared his throat and continued with his song, but before long he broke off again. "What is that?" he said.

"What?" said Mom.

"That . . . noise. Don't you hear it? Some kind of buzzing—"

"Oh," I said. "You hear that too? I thought I was the only one." The strange noise from Logan's room. I only occasionally notice it anymore, but that's not because it stopped. It's just become so ever-present that I tune it out these days, except when it gets really bad, or when I stop and focus on it. Which I try not to do.

Pops turned to the kids and said something in that strange language. They both stared at him blankly. "Arthur," he said in English, "take the kids outside."

"What?" said Arthur. "You sure?"

Pops only nodded, and Arthur shrugged and herded the kids toward the front door. Pops began his prayer again, his voice a little unsteady at first but gaining strength as he went. When he finished, he rang the bell again and began to sing in a rich, deep baritone. I'd closed my eyes to focus on the beautiful sound when I felt the vibration picking up, becoming more intense. Like the day of Logan's seizure, I could feel it building in my bones, my blood, twisting my organs. I opened my eyes to look at the old man, and I could see from the pinched expression on his face that he felt it too.

Then at that moment, the strange noise was drowned by the sound of every cell phone in the room going off. Or . . . not drowned, exactly. The ringtones and vibrations almost felt like they were ringing in sympathy with the buzzing crescendo.

"What the hell?" said Arthur as he grabbed the phone from his pocket. "I just turned this thing off."

The noise stopped suddenly. Not just the phones—the buzzing had stopped too, and an eerie stillness replaced it. Then Arthur's phone beeped twice, and we all jumped. Arthur picked it up and furrowed his brow at the screen. "That's weird," he said. "Pops, did you text me earlier? We've been together all day . . ."

"It's okay," said Mom. "Phones do that sometimes in this house. It happens to all of us."

For a moment, Pops just stared at her. Then he grabbed his bell and made for the door, moving much faster than he had seemed capable of earlier. I followed him out to the porch. "Wait," I called. "Where are you going?"

He was talking to Arthur. "Get the kids, we're leaving."

"You can't just go," I protested. "We need you. I thought you said you could help."

Pops turned and looked me in the eye, his countenance dark and fearful. "There's something really wrong here."

"Yeah," I said. "That's what I was trying to tell you. And you said—"

"I know what I said. Listen, I've been by this house loads of times. I've even been in it, back when it housed a businessman's association. It was fine then. But something has changed. There is something very bad here." He started down the stairs.

"Pops," said Arthur, "you came all this way, can't you just—"

The old man turned sharply. "No. This is outside my power. Most of the time people complain their house is haunted, and it's nothing. They get a bad feeling, maybe some dreams. I say a few words, and it goes away. That's not going to work here. This is bigger."

"What am I supposed to do, then?" I said.

"Beats me," replied the old man. "You're in trouble."

THURSDAY, JUNE 11, 10:00 A.M.

Looks like the fly experiment is officially over. Also, not sure if Mom will ever speak to me again.

She caught me murdering the rest of the flies with my history textbook. I tried to explain to her that it was for science, and that there was a good chance they would all come back to life in a few minutes, but she didn't want to hear it.

THURSDAY, JUNE 11, 4:00 P.M.

I made Chloe meet me downtown for coffee today. I had to tell her what Arthur's grandfather had said. I don't know what I was expecting. I think I was hoping for reassurance. I think I imagined her making a big joke out of it, laughing at the idea that I would fall for some old man's bogeyman story. Or that she would delve into the gothness of it, and become fascinated and obsessed and excited about the idea of anything legitimately supernatural, from beyond the grave. That would have been okay too, because if she was excited about it, then it couldn't really be that scary, could it?

But she didn't do either of those things. Instead she was silent for a long moment, looking at me with wide brown eyes, and with that look fixed on her face—the problem-solving one. Gradually her brows knotted as she focused more and more

intensely on the problem. Then, just as I was starting to get seriously freaked out, she spoke.

"You have to talk to Raph."

I wasn't expecting that. "Right," I said. "Because that went so
well the last couple of times."

"I'm serious, Paige. He knows something. Don't you see it?
He's been hiding something from us this whole time. Something
to do with his research project, with those boxes you saw, with
that pamphlet you showed me, getting kicked out of school . . .
What's his secret?"

At first I wanted to scoff. Weird as he was, something about
Raph had always struck me as quite harmless. Sure, he had some
stuff he didn't like to talk about, but who doesn't? But then I
remembered . . .

"Dr. Clyde," I said. Chloe looked at me in confusion. "My
shrink. She said something about Raph during my last session.
Told me to stay away from him. And Raph said the same thing.
Do you think he might have been one of her patients?"

"Not unlikely. It's a small town. I know three people who
have been to see her. But if he is . . ."

"What?"

"Don't you see what that means? It means she knows stuff.
It means he has told her stuff, stuff that he wouldn't tell anyone
else. And now she's telling you to stay away from him."

I took a moment to absorb this.

"Paige," she said, "you have to go talk to him."

"Actually, doesn't it sound like I should stay as far away from
him as possible?"

"Do you want to figure out what's going on in your house, or
don't you? He's got the answer. I'm sure of it."

I shook my head, uncomfortable with this plan. "He always changes the subject. He doesn't like to talk about certain things, and . . . well, shouldn't I respect that?"

Chloe looked at me seriously. "We're not talking about a gambling problem, or his sex life. This is not the time for being polite. You heard the old man yourself—there is something sinister in your house. Something beyond our understanding, maybe beyond anyone's. And Raph could have the key. You have to talk to him."

FRIDAY, JUNE 12, 8:22 A.M.

Well, I put together a few more pieces of the puzzle last night.

Seeing how nervous and unconvinced I was during our coffee date, Chloe offered to come with me to Raph's place—perhaps to lend moral support, or more likely because she was afraid I'd chicken out. But I told her no. I love Chloe, but she has a way about her . . . You only have to see her status at school to know that she has a tendency to rub some people the wrong way. And Raph was hypersensitive under the best of circumstances. With people deliberately pushing at the things he had walled off and forbidden us to talk about . . . I had a feeling the situation could be volatile.

After dinner I steeled myself and headed down to the basement with no idea which version of Raph to expect. When he opened the door, I checked his face for clues. He seemed more calm, less manic than he had last time . . . and he didn't kick me out right away, which I took as a good sign. But stepping closer, I noticed his eyes were rimmed with red, and as he closed the door behind me, he wiped his nose on the back of his hand.

"Allergies?" I said.

"What?" said Raph. "Oh yeah. Spring's the worst. All that cottonwood fluff in the air . . ."

I stood in the middle of the room, looking around for any clue to what Raph knew. Any clue that would let me get out of there and mollify Chloe, without having to actually speak and reveal my mission. The apartment was not as crazy looking as it had been with the boxes everywhere, but it also didn't look as spic and span as it had the last time I had been here. Instead it bore the signs of a more typical college-age kid: dirty dishes in the sink, mail and magazines heaped on various surfaces, a lamp askew, a rug corner flipped up. Or was it more than that? Was this typical post-adolescent slovenliness, or the incipient signs of depression? For example, a plant that my mom had given him had fallen from a window ledge and broken on the floor, but he'd made no effort to sweep up the dirt. And the teakettle he had been so excited about last time I saw him was on the floor next to the couch, knocked over on its side.

I looked up at Raph again and saw suspicion in his eyes. I think the way I was looking around his apartment was making him nervous. "Look," he said, "do you need anything? Because I was just . . ." He trailed off, like he was hoping I would take the hint, but with Chloe in the back of my mind, I pushed forward.

"You were just what?" I said.

"Huh?" he tried, stalling for time. "I was busy. This isn't the best time, Paige, but maybe—"

"Busy with what?" Raph just stared at me. "You're not taking classes, you don't have a job, you don't seem to have any friends other than my mom and me. What exactly are you doing tonight that can't be interrupted?"

Raph swallowed. "I thought I told you," he said. "When someone—"

"When someone changes the subject, when someone makes it clear that they don't want to talk about something, you let it drop, right? Well, I'm not letting it drop this time. I'm sorry, Raph, but I need answers. Logan's been to the hospital twice now. The electronics in the house are going haywire. Total strangers are terrified of the place. This isn't a joke anymore, and it's not something you can just keep to yourself, because you're not the only one affected."

Raph sat down at the counter. "I didn't realize it had gotten that bad."

"You know something," I said. "Tell me what's going on. Tell me what you know."

"How much have you figured out?"

He was deflecting, of course, and I felt a flare of rage at him for continuing to be so evasive when he knew what we were facing. He was as bad as Dr. Clyde, in his way. But I took a deep breath and calmed myself. At least he was acknowledging that there was something to know. This was progress, and if he was willing to go this far, I might get him to go further.

"I know you saw Dr. Clyde," I began, wondering what danger there might be in bluffing. "I know she thinks you're dangerous. And I know . . ."

"What?"

His direct question was making me all too aware of how little I did know. "Something about that pamphlet! That cult. Pronoica. It's tied in with all this somehow."

"Anything else?"

I shook my head, relieved that none of what I said was so off base it would close him off. He scrubbed a hand roughly through his hair.

"I did see Dr. Clyde. I was her patient for almost a year."

"What happened? She said you were cured?"

Raph laughed dryly. "You have a lot to learn about shrinks. No. I stopped going. Maybe I believed I was cured, or maybe I just wanted to be. No, that's not it. I believed I was sick, and that was all I needed to know. That solved all my problems."

"You're doing it again. Talking in riddles."

"Risk you take when you ask people stuff they don't want to tell you."

"It's the morgue, isn't it? You told us it wasn't haunted to throw us off the track, but there's something going on that has to do with—"

"The morgue isn't haunted. It has nothing to do with the morgue."

I sat down across from him. "Why don't you just start at the beginning? Why did you leave school?"

Raph shook his head. "That wasn't the beginning. Not by a long ways. You're asking the wrong questions, Paige."

I flailed about, helplessly. "Fine, then. Start with the boxes. What was in those boxes? Why did you have them here in your apartment?"

"Getting warmer."

"Your professor," I said as a memory from one of our earlier conversations surfaced. "You were working on a project with him . . ."

Raph winced as if he had been slapped. He closed his eyes and didn't open them for a long moment. "Hot yet?" I said. Raph opened his eyes and took a slow, unsteady breath. And indeed, he seemed to be sweating, though the room was as chilly as it had been earlier.

He checked his phone for the time. "Why don't I just show you?" he said. I looked around the apartment, wondering what he had that he could show me, but he shook his head. "Not here." He opened his front door and strode out into the chill night. I followed him.

We walked for blocks, heading toward downtown, but I still had no real idea where we going, just a pit of nervousness in my stomach. As we walked along quiet, treelined residential streets, the cottonwood fluff drifted down on us like a scene from a demented snow globe, and I was struck by the eerie sense that even the seasons had gotten out of joint. None of it made any sense. If my problem was in the house, what solution were we going to find anywhere else? But Raph was so touchy, I was afraid to harass him with more questions than I already had, afraid he would change his mind and head back, or do something even stranger.

Soon we were on the university campus. I had been there a few times to visit Mom in her office, or to see an exhibit at the student art center, but never at night. The dorms and fraternities were brightly lit, and sounds of laughter and camaraderie echoed from them, but we kept walking toward the main quad, which was surrounded by classroom buildings, and was silent and still this time of night. But Raph strode purposefully up the empty paths toward a hulking, modern building, which I realized was the library. There were lights on inside, but otherwise very little sign of life. I read the hours off the sign on the door, then checked my watch. "They're only open another 20 minutes," I said.

"Yes," said Raph, and he opened the door. He gave only the briefest of glances toward the reception desk before moving swiftly toward the stairs and, taking them two at a time so that I panted to keep up, led me up to the fourth floor of the building, then through a maze of library stacks, administrative offices, and storage rooms until we at last reached our apparent destination. The room was filled with boxes, and after a moment's confusion, I realized that they were the same boxes that had been in Raph's apartment not too long ago.

"So this is where they went," I marveled.

"This will tell you most of the story."

The boxes were stacked floor to ceiling, and what labels there were were written in a code that was impenetrable to me. "Where do I begin?"

Raph scanned the room, obviously having something in mind. Then he picked a box from one of the precarious towers, carefully slid it apart from the others, and opened it. "Here," he said, thrusting a slim booklet into my hands, then going back to rifling in the box. I flipped it open and read the title page. *Your Spirit Power: with 20 lessons in how to find it and use it*, it read. I opened it and skimmed through the text.

"What the hell is this stuff?" I said.

"This is our project," said Raph. "This is Pronoica."

The existence of the invisible power in every one of us is fast becoming common knowledge. This omnipresent spirit is the infinite source of all our needs. The invisible spirit of the God-Law lives in you every moment of the day, and is ever waiting for you to recognize that invisible though powerful presence. Please follow me very closely in these studies, for they are pregnant with Spiritual Power.

FRIDAY, JUNE 12, 11:15 A.M.

As Raph's long, pale, nervous fingers sorted efficiently through the various documents in this and a few other boxes, he continued with his story, explaining how he had first come to work with his professor on the Pronoica project.

"I was a sophomore," he said, "and I wasn't even in his department. But I had heard things—that Montague Verano was a genius, that he was far too good for a school like this. Studied in England, and came here for . . . obscure reasons. I was intrigued."

"And?"

"He was everything I'd been promised and more." Raph smiled a private smile. "I was out of my element. I sat in the back of the class and didn't say much. There were other students— seniors, history majors, even a couple of grad students auditing for fun—who were better than me, who stood out in class, who vied with each other for the chance to have even a brief conversation with the man. That was fine with me. I was happy to fly under the radar. I did all the readings, took notes, listened to what everyone else had to say, and felt lucky just to be there, even if no one noticed me."

"But Verano did notice you."

"He . . . took an interest. Called me in after the first paper, and said my work was outstanding. Well beyond his expectations. I was . . . surprised. Flattered. Then he asked me if I wanted to help him with a project he was working on. He said he got the sense that I could keep a secret. I told him I understood."

"Pronoica?"

Raph nodded. "This wasn't an ordinary history book Verano was writing," he went on. "He had an idea—an obsession, you might call it—that Pronoica might be real. Everyone who had looked into it so far had dismissed it just the way you did: as a cult with a charlatan for a leader, who was only trading on people's hopes and dreams to make himself a little cash. But Verano . . . he was convinced there was more to it than that. That maybe even Williamson himself hadn't known what it was, the power he had stumbled into."

"But why did it need to be secret?"

Raph glanced up at me, his eyebrows arched. "You kidding? It would have been career suicide if he'd told anyone what he was working on. This is academia, not some cable TV ghost-hunting show. He had to wait until he had the proof, the evidence he needed to convince the whole world, or they'd write him off as a kook and a crackpot."

"But what was he looking for? What kind of paranormal evidence could you hope to find in some dusty old box?"

"Well . . . ," said Raph, "that was a problem. We had no idea what we were looking for. I kept asking him the same question, but he'd only repeat that historical research doesn't work that way. You can't go in with something specific in mind, or else you'll miss all the other details that are staring you right in the face. You have to be open to anything and everything."

"So you never found anything, then?"

Raph put the papers he had in his hand down carefully. "Not exactly. Or in any case, nothing I could be sure of. A lot of what's in these boxes are testimonials: messages that Williamson's fans and acolytes sent him over the years, explaining how Pronoica had worked for them."

"So it *did* work."

Raph shrugged. "According to some old lady in Texas, sure." He picked a yellowed sheet of notebook paper from a file folder in one of the boxes. "Dear Doctor Williamson," he read, "Thank you again and again for sharing the teachings of Pronoica. Your lessons have truly been a blessing to me. I was going to lose my home, but on that day I discovered one of your pamphlets and learned of the Spiritual Power I contain within myself. The following morning I learned that a recently deceased aunt had left me exactly the amount I needed to release my debts."

"Lucky lady," I said.

"Not-so-lucky aunt," Raph observed. "Anyway, yeah, there was lots of evidence. Williamson's whole career was devoted to collecting evidence of how well his system worked, so he could turn around and pitch it to more people, and get them to subscribe too. But who is it going to convince other than desperate old ladies?"

"It convinced Professor Verano."

Dear Doctor Williamson,

Thank you again and again for sharing the teachings of Pronoica. Your lessons have truly been a blessing to me. I was going to lose my home, but on that day I discovered one of your pamphlets and learned of the Spiritual Power I contain within myself. The following morning I learned that a recently deceased aunt had left me exactly the amount I needed to release my debts.

"Not the testimonials—something else. To this day, I'm not sure if it even makes any sense. But when I got frustrated, he told me to change my tactic. He said there was more to all these letters and documents than what people were saying—we had to be alert to what they *weren't* saying. Things glimpsed out of the corner of the eye, that might lead us to what was really going on. That's what led me to the Pronoica Clinic."

"The clinic? What's that?"

Raph gave a wry smile. "Once again, no one knows. In all these hundreds, maybe thousands, of documents, I only ever found one reference to the Pronoica Clinic. But it stuck with me, because it was different from the other stuff. Something physical. Something present. Not a pamphlet sent through the mail, but a real place, in this very town."

Raph flipped through the files once more, this time his fingers stopping at something and tugging it up from the box. He handed it to me.

"PRONOICA CLINIC," it read. Then, "A private institution devoted to the ethical and scientific practice of Medicine and Surgery as an adjunct to the healing power of the Spirit of God. Located at Moscow, Idaho." Underneath it was a photograph of a squat Victorian mansion with a turret and a wraparound porch.

"The house," I said softly. I looked up to meet his eyes. "The clinic—it was in our house. So that's why . . ." I shook my head. "But it doesn't make sense. All these pamphlets, all the testimonials. This was no devil-worshipping cult. Williamson believed in the same kind of stuff my mom does: positive energy and being the good you want to see in the universe. That kind of junk. So why does the house seem so . . . angry?"

PRONOICA CLINIC

A private institution devoted to the ethical and scientific practice of Medicine and Surgery as an adjunct to the healing power of the Spirit of God. Located at Moscow, Idaho.

"Maybe the pamphlets and the testimonials don't tell the whole story."

"What are you saying?" I asked. "That Pronoica has some kind of dark side? That Williamson and his followers were conjuring demons in their spare time?" I meant it as a joke, but something about the way Raph shrugged made me uneasy.

"Not on purpose, maybe," he said. "But what if all that spiritual power they were playing with stirred up something they didn't know how to control?"

"In the house, you mean. The clinic. You think something happened there that they weren't expecting," I guessed. "Something Williamson tried to cover up. Is that why the place is messing with us now?"

"I don't know," he said, "but think about it. It's one thing to send people hopeful messages through the mail, but if he was telling people to travel here from all over the country—sick and injured people—so that he could heal them through some mixture of faith and pseudoscience . . ."

"Yeah, I see it now. Something could have gone seriously wrong."

"Whatever it was, he did a good job hushing it up. No mention of it anywhere. Not in his documents, not in the local papers, or any public record."

"So what about Verano? What did he think of it?"

Raph didn't answer.

"You did tell him, right?"

Raph got to his feet and started rifling through another box, not meeting my eye.

"Right, I get it," I said. "You're changing the subject. We only ever get to talk about the stuff you want to talk about."

Just then, the door opened behind me, and I whirled around to see who it was. It was a young woman, the one I had seen down at the circulation desk when we came in.

"Just letting you know that the library is closing. You need to start heading out now, or . . ." She stopped, in the middle of a thought. "Raph?" she said. "What are you doing here?"

"It's fine, I—don't worry, Lizzie. I just wanted to check something, is all. We'll be going right now, you don't have to—"

"You're not supposed to be here. They told me to call security if I ever saw you, I could get in a lot of trouble, if—"

Raph took a deep breath. "You're not going to get into any trouble because you're not going to tell anyone. My friend and I were just leaving. We're going straight home. We don't want any trouble, and neither do you. Right?"

Lizzie still stood in the doorway, not speaking, clearly deliberating. "Lizzie," said Raph again, and this time his voice was not nervous or hard-edged, as it so frequently was, but soft and kind . . . and even—could it be?—a little flirtatious. He gave her a winning smile that transformed his whole face from a dark and brooding creature weighed down by who knew what troubles to a charming and stunningly handsome college boy, irresistible in his every movement. He leaned almost imperceptibly closer to her. "You know there's nothing to be afraid of. It's only me."

I could see the war going on behind Lizzie's eyes—a strange mixture of apprehension and desire. At last she stepped away from the door. "Seriously, go straight home. You shouldn't be here, and I don't want to get into trouble."

The smile dropped suddenly from his face, but he grabbed

my hand and tugged me to the door. "Come on, Paige. We've seen what we needed to see."

Raph speed-walked all the way home, and I could barely keep up with him, let alone assault him with all the questions that were swirling around in my head. When we got back to the house, I tried to follow him into his apartment, but he made it clear there would be no more discussion tonight. "Your mother will wonder where you are," he said darkly, and he closed the door in my face.

MONDAY, JUNE 15, 10:12 A.M.

I woke up this morning into what is essentially a hellscape. The air is heavy and dark and smells wonderful, and a scary blood-orange ball reigns over it all.

Logan came inside while I was eating breakfast and said, did you see the moon this morning? It was bright red.

I said, that wasn't the moon, you dummy, it was the sun, but he was pretty sure, and we wound up looking up sunrise and moonset timetables. (I was right.)

I know this is because of the fires burning over in Washington. It's a weird day when you can't tell the difference between the sun and the moon.

TUESDAY, JUNE 16, 12:16 A.M.

After three days of Raph avoiding me, I finally made Chloe come over after school to help me corner him. We stood together on his doorstep while I knocked, but no one came to the door.

"Now what?" I said.

Chloe put her ear to the door. "I can hear movement."

"Doesn't do us much good if he's ignoring us."

"Let's make ourselves harder to ignore, then." I stared at her and she rolled her eyes. "We know he doesn't lock his door, remember?"

Raph was at least dressed this time, but he surprised me by not demanding immediately that we leave. He looked almost as though he had been expecting this visit. As if he viewed it as unpleasant but inevitable.

"Ladies," he said, but I wasn't interested in playing his games this time.

"Why aren't you allowed on campus?" I asked.

"I don't think that's any of your business."

"You brought me there, Raph. You made me an accomplice to your violating . . . what, a restraining order? I don't even know, but you dragged me into it, and now it is my business. So why don't you tell me what exactly is going on."

"It's nothing," he said forcefully. "I'm telling you, it's not what you're thinking. It's nothing to do with . . . It was a misunderstanding, that's all."

"The kind of misunderstanding that makes someone call the police?" said Chloe.

Raph glared at her. "Last semester I—" He stopped himself and took a deep breath. "I was behaving erratically," he went on. "Or so I'm told. People were concerned. For my safety, and for the safety of . . . others. But I'm not supposed to . . . It was part of the agreement, I swore I wouldn't . . ." Raph thrust a hand into his hair and tugged, as if using the pain to balance out some inner turmoil. He seemed to be speaking mostly to himself now. "He said it could do a lot of damage, if anyone . . . it would ruin everything. And anyway, I brought it on myself. Things had been going so well. We were getting so close. And all I wanted was . . . of course he had warned me, but I didn't see . . . it all seemed harmless . . . until it wasn't."

Chloe and I watched him in silence for a minute. He seemed close to giving us the answers we were looking for, and I didn't want to spook him. "Who warned you?" I said gently. "About what?"

Raph looked up and seemed almost surprised that we were

still there. Then he seemed to come to some realization. "You want to know about Pronoica," he said, as if that hadn't been obvious all along. "I can tell you about that. As long as I . . ." He stood up and paced a little, gathering his thoughts. "Yes," he said at last, sounding much more normal. "All right. You know already about Verano's obsession. He wanted to know if Williamson had been on to anything, if any of it was real. He had me combing through those documents, endless documents, hours and hours each day until my eyes ached."

"Right," I said. "So?"

"So, I got sick of it. And I thought—I knew there was a simpler way."

I waited for him to continue. "Simpler?" I prompted when he didn't.

"It's obvious, isn't it? I decided to try it. Williamson's methods."

"The stuff from the mailings? You mean the kooky meditation exercises he gave the little old ladies?"

Raph shrugged lightly.

"Did anything . . . happen?"

"Not much at first. Just a sense of peace, an aura of well-being. Nice enough, but you can get that much at any yoga studio these days. But after a week or so, it really kicked in."

I exchanged a look with Chloe.

"Material blessings," he said. "'The Living Spirit can bring to you perfect abundance. The World may be yours, and everything in it.' This is the key to Pronoica. Williamson didn't just promise his followers spiritual bliss, or a ticket to eternal salvation. He promised them cash."

"And you . . . that *worked*?"

Raph grinned. "Found twenty bucks in my pocket the

first day. A week later, got a job offer for the summer. I even won a couple hundred dollars off a lotto ticket. But it wasn't just that . . . it was weirder stuff too. More personal. I'd get a burger at Zips, and when I got home, there'd be two in the bag. Kept finding songs on my hard drive that I couldn't remember downloading. I'd do laundry and wind up with twice as many socks as I'd started with. I had never been very lucky before, but now I felt . . . more than lucky. I felt blessed.

"Still, nothing you'd want to contact the local news over. It wasn't proof exactly, but it was exciting." He began moving again. "I was a convert, you could say, just like Williamson's followers had been. I wanted to share my good fortune with the world. Or at least a few friends." He cast a sharp look at Chloe. "Yes, I did have friends. Then." He sat down on a stool for a moment before popping up again. "None of them took it too seriously, and it became kind of a joke around the department. People teased me about it, and others got concerned, and the whole thing wound up getting back to Verano.

"He was furious. He said it was dangerous to undertake an experiment like this when we had so little information. He called me foolish, said I had lost my sense of scholarly remove. And I . . . I . . . well, never mind about that." Raph's shoulders slumped. "Around that time I was advised to take some time off, to collect myself. That's when I moved in here. And started seeing Dr. Clyde."

"Did you tell her about all this?"

"About Pronoica? Some. I tried to. But she had other things she was more interested in dissecting."

I nodded grimly. "I know that story. Somehow you always wind up talking about what she wants to talk about."

"And she was convinced it was all in my head. I can't really blame her—in all honesty, I wasn't exactly acting like a man in possession of all his faculties. There were . . . strikes against me in that department already. It was a relief, actually," he said. "Turns out I was more comfortable playing the delusional nutcase than the only living prophet of a kook religion that died out half a century ago. And I couldn't deny that her approach worked. I took her pills, I did her visualization exercises, and everyone agreed I was doing much better."

"I don't understand, though," I said. "This still doesn't explain why the house started acting up the minute my family moved in."

"I know," said Raph. "People have been calling this place haunted for years, but it was always some old story remembered off a friend of a friend of a friend. Then when I started working on the place, I'd get . . . bad feelings. Dreams. A sense that I wasn't completely alone. But nothing like what's been happening recently." He shook his head. "Something must have changed."

TUESDAY, JUNE 16, 3:58 A.M.

I don't know what possessed me to go to sleep in this house after that conversation with Raph. For some idiotic reason I was feeling better about the whole thing—like we were closing in on the reasons for everything that has gone on here. But having the reasons isn't the same as making everything go away! Why did I think it was? I didn't think it, really. Not consciously. But on some level I must have believed it, because after our talk Chloe went home and I went upstairs and I typed everything that had happened into my journal, and it all seemed . . . so *exciting*. Like I was finally on the trail of something real. Finally getting some answers. And I went to bed feeling calm and contented, like we had made real progress.

Then I woke up.

It was still dark out. Normally at this point I would look

at the clock and then turn over and try to get back to sleep, or sometimes listen closely to see if I could figure out what Logan might be doing. But this time I didn't have to listen. Logan was sitting on the edge of my bed. Watching me.

When I saw him, my adrenaline spiked so bad I nearly jumped out of bed. Even though this wasn't the first time, there was something deeply unsettling about his presence there. He wasn't trying to wake me up to tell me something, or just sitting with me for company, or anything even vaguely normal like that. He was just . . . staring at me. When he saw that I was awake, saw me looking at him, he smiled.

"Logan?" I said cautiously. "Are you okay?" But the look on his face made it plenty clear that he was not.

He smiled even bigger. "Hey, Paige," he said, and the weird thing was, his voice was totally normal. I don't know why that's weird. That's the opposite of weird, right? But I was expecting him to sound ethereal or strange in some way, or, if he were a normal kid waking his sister in the middle of the night, he might sound scared or embarrassed or something. But his tone . . . he was talking to me as if he had just found me in the kitchen in the middle of the day. As if there were nothing remotely weird about any of it. And that was what creeped me out.

He must have seen the expression on my face because he immediately said, "Don't worry, Paige. I was getting rid of them for you."

Um . . . what?

"The spiders," he said. "I know you don't like them, so I just sit here and pick them off you."

I didn't say anything. I couldn't say anything. I just stared at him in wide-eyed horror.

"I think I'm beginning to understand why you don't like them," he went on. "I've been studying them. Did you know that they pulsate when they eat things alive? All eight legs, pulsing, like a heart that only knows how to eat things. Creepy, right? But don't worry, they don't do it all night long. They usually come out around 3 in the morning, or a little after. And by 4:30 they're gone. But if I don't stop by between 3 and 4, it gets real bad. One night I was doing something else, and didn't make it here until 3:30. And when I got here, I couldn't even see your face. It was just a solid mass of swarming black spiders. Oh, don't be afraid, Paige. They haven't hurt you yet. And they don't usually even wake you up. I promise, they are perfectly harmless."

It's a good thing I was frozen to the bed, or else I might well have clawed all the flesh from my face.

Then Logan put out a hand toward my hairline, just above my ear. "Oh!" he said. "There's one. Don't move." And he picked something off my face and held it up in front of my eyes. He held it by one leg, but the other seven danced before my eyes in a way that turned my stomach. "I can hear the birds now," he said. "It's almost 4 now, so the spiders will be pretty much done. I'm going to get back to my letter."

And he got up and left the room.

Holy Christ, what do I do? What the fuck, what the fuck. Why are there spiders? Why is Logan like this? I can't be alone with him. And Mom isn't even home tonight. She's sleeping over at Arthur's. I can't be alone with him. What do I do?

TUESDAY, JUNE 16, 4:10 A.M.

Mom's not answering my texts, so I tried Raph. I need to be around someone sane or . . . sane-ish. I guess most people would say (have said) that Raph isn't the best choice, but he's the only person who gets it. The only person I can deal with seeing right now. Oh, he just texted back, thank God.

He wrote:

It's the middle of the night. What's going on?

What does he think is going on? Okay, texted him:

I'm scared, I can't be alone with him. Something awful . . .

I really can't bring myself to describe that whole scene over text. Ugh God, what is he doing? Why isn't he texting back? Okay, he just texted back.

K. The door's open.

TUESDAY, JUNE 16, 4:25 A.M.

I think I am safe now. Posting from my phone, in Raph's apartment. He's gone back to bed, and I'm going to try to get some rest on his couch. Phone's being weird, though. I've gotten six texts in the past half hour and none of them make any sense. I don't know if it's Mom trying to contact me or . . . I don't know.

I don't like leaving Logan alone in the house, but . . . honestly, I don't want to be around him right now.

TUESDAY, JUNE 16, 7:54 A.M.

I don't fully understand what happened last night. I don't even really remember it. The best I can do is write it out to try to piece this back together.

I crept down the stairs after Raph's last text, doing my best to avoid Logan. The last thing I needed was him asking me where I was going, or realizing he was alone in the house. And I made it out the front door and then down to Raph's apartment, where the door was unlocked as usual. The whole place was dark, of course, except for some thin moonlight coming in from those small windows. I picked my way through the shadows toward Raph's bedroom, at the back of the apartment. I'd never been in there before. It was darker even than the other rooms, and I could barely make out the outline of Raph's dark curls against the white of his pillow.

"Raph," I whispered hoarsely. No answer. "Raph," I said again, in something closer to a normal voice.

"What?" he said. "Oh, right, Paige." He sat up in bed. "I'm sorry, I drifted off again." He rubbed a hand over his face and scraped it through his hair. "Is this real? I was dreaming, and then—"

"It's not a dream." If only!

Raph, just like on the night I met him, was shirtless. He was under covers, but I figured that if experience was any indication, he was probably wearing nothing but underwear. I felt suddenly self-conscious about being in my goofy pajamas, but . . . God, the brain is a weird organ. I can't believe I was even thinking about stuff like that, given what had just happened. But at least it was distracting me a little from the horror.

"What's going on?" Raph said, jolting me out of my nervous silence. I gave him a recap, with as much detail as I could bear. For a minute or so, he didn't say anything.

"Raph," I said.

"What do you want me to do?"

"I don't know. Nothing, I know there's nothing . . . I just . . . I can't go back up there. I can't be alone. Can I . . . stay here with you?"

Raph closed his eyes. "I don't know if that's a good idea."

"I know," I said. "It's dangerous, you're dangerous. So you keep telling me. But at least down here my face isn't covered in spiders."

Raph opened his eyes again, and I saw resignation and sympathy in them. "Okay," he said. "You can crash on the couch until morning."

I thanked him and groped my way through the dark back to his couch. I tried to sleep for a couple minutes, but I was way too jumpy, so eventually I took out my phone, just to distract myself. Even so, though, I kept feeling—or *thinking* I felt—tiny legs tickling my skin. I shook my limbs and smacked at the strange sensations until my skin was red and raw, but I never saw anything.

Eventually I couldn't bear it anymore and I snuck back toward Raph's room. He was asleep again, stretched out in a moonbeam, his face peaceful, his pale skin almost glowing. Instantly I felt calmer. No matter how many warnings people gave me, including Raph himself, I just couldn't see him as dangerous. In the madness I now faced every day, he felt like an island of sanity.

There wasn't anyplace else in the room to sit, so I eased myself gently onto the edge of the bed, not wanting to disturb him. Idly I wondered about his history, the stuff he didn't want to tell us. About what had gone wrong that had resulted in him getting kicked off campus. A failed romance, presumably. Gazing down on his elegant sleeping form, it was hard to picture anyone rejecting him. What kind of person could resist this gorgeous creature, as broken and tortured as he might be?

Eventually I started to get stiff in my position, so I carefully shifted and scootched in a bit to sit next to him in the bed, my back leaning against the headboard.

I was convinced there was no way I would be able to sleep that night, but the next thing I remember, my eyelids shot open as if I'd just received a shot of adrenaline.

I didn't remember where I was, or maybe even who I was.

Everything felt strange and wrong, and my whole body was trembling, my muscles spasming. I sat straight up in the bed, and after a moment felt my senses returning to me. I'm in Raph's bedroom. There is a weird, thick feeling in my throat, as if I swallowed a penny or something. My pajamas are all twisted up, and also sticking to me because I'm coated in a slick film of sweat. The bedclothes are tangled around me as if someone has been thrashing wildly in the bed, and they are also damp, presumably with sweat. I am alone in the bed, my breathing shallow and labored, my pulse erratic.

I took a few deep, slow breaths, like my mom taught me for dealing with exam stress and stuff—in through my nose, one two three, out through my mouth, one two three—and gradually started to feel like myself again. It was at this point that I realized I could hear voices. A voice. Raph's voice. Coming from the kitchen.

I got out of bed and moved quietly toward his voice. From the doorway I could see him facing away from me, leaning over the kitchen sink. He had slipped on a pair of jeans and he was talking on his phone, but there was something weird about his voice, like it was slightly muffled.

"I'm sorry," he was saying. "I know. I know, but this is different." His voice was trembling and his words seemed to come with difficulty. "You have to come, please . . . It isn't about that! I swear." Raph paused to listen, and hung his head at whatever he was hearing. "I know. And I promise I wouldn't call if it weren't—" [pause] "I understand all that, and look, in six months I haven't talked to you once, I haven't contacted you, I haven't—I've abided by the—but this is different, it's not just about me." [pause] "Monty, listen to what I'm saying!

I don't care. You started this, you can't just walk away when you feel like it." [pause] "I told you." [pause] "You promise?" [pause] "Yeah, okay, I know, just . . . come quickly."

Raph hung up the phone and turned around. He startled a little when he saw me. My mouth was already moving to ask, "Who's Monty?" but the words were replaced by a different question when I saw his face. I realized now why his voice sounded weird: he had a dish towel pressed up against his mouth. "What happened?" I said. "Are you okay?"

Raph dropped his hand with the dish towel to his side, revealing a large, messy gash in his lip, which looked like it had only recently stopped gushing and started to seal itself. As he stood up straighter in the sunlight, I saw something else: there were tiny reddish bruises, maybe the size of a nickel, all over his chest, his throat, and a few on his wrists. I gasped and rushed to his side. I was just trying to help. I wanted to examine his injuries, clean them, and see if they needed a doctor's attention. But Raph moved away from me. In fact, he was . . . cowering, shrinking away from me, backing himself up against the refrigerator, his eyes big with fear.

Growing desperate, I kept asking what happened, if he was okay, should I call a doctor, but he wouldn't answer. Then something caught my eye from the counter: a smear of bright color reflected at me in the chrome side of the toaster. It was me. My face and chest, red with blood.

I touched my face, not believing what I saw, but my fingers came away sticky with the stuff. "Raph . . . ," I said uncertainly. "What happened to us?"

Raph squeezed his eyes shut. "Leave me alone," he whispered. "Please, get away from me."

I ran all the way to our upstairs bathroom and set about cleaning the blood from my skin. The strange thing is, though I checked my whole face and neck and the inside of my mouth, I couldn't find a cut.

I don't think it was my blood.

TUESDAY, JUNE 16, 8:13 A.M.

I'm panicking. I texted Mom so many times last night, but now I don't want to see her. Don't want to try to explain the inexplicable. Where would I even begin? But she just got home. She's banging on my bedroom door, asking if I am okay. She sounds so scared. Of course she is scared, after the crazy texts I sent.

Okay, if I wait any longer, she's going to break down the door. I better face her.

TUESDAY, JUNE 16, 11:23 A.M.

Mom gave me a big hug when I opened the door and checked me over. Good thing I'd cleaned up all the blood and changed my clothes, or she would have really freaked. But before I got a chance to explain anything, the doorbell rang.

Mom looked at her watch. "Who could that be?" I had an idea, but I kept silent.

We both headed downstairs, and as we passed the kitchen, I noticed Logan sitting at the table and eating a bowl of cereal, as if this were the most ordinary Tuesday morning in the world. "Morning," he said, his mouth half-full. I stared at him, boggled at the difference between my kid brother now and whatever he was last night. "Hey," I said, more out of habit than anything else, and I followed Mom to the door.

The man standing there looked strangely out of place in this sleepy Idaho town. I hadn't seen a man in such a finely cut suit since Dad took me to one of his movie premieres. He was small and slight, probably in his late 40s, but with a dramatic shock of prematurely snow-white hair. His eyes were a piercing, icy blue, and he carried a cane with an ornate silver handle.

"Good morning," he said, holding out one hand. "Montague Verano. I'm a professor of history at the university. My apologies for disturbing you at this hour on a fine summer morning, but I've come to search your house."

For a moment, Mom just stared at him in blank surprise. Meanwhile, gears clicked in my brain. Montague Verano— *Monty*. And sure enough, I realized that Raph was standing a few feet behind him, his hands thrust awkwardly into his pockets.

"I'm sorry?" Mom tried at last, taking his hand as almost an afterthought. But Verano was regarding her just as closely, and instead of shaking her hand, he pulled it toward his body.

"You seem quite familiar to me," he said, running his eyes over her face. "Have we met before?"

"Um," she said, caught off guard. "No, we don't—that is, I—I get that a lot."

Verano dropped her hand and made a movement toward her, crowding her against the doorjamb. "Yes," he said with a nod. "You have an old soul?"

"No," said Mom. "I mean, yes, but—no—I was in movies. You've probably seen them."

"I don't watch movies," said Verano. "Which ones?"

"*Some Sacred Summer? Dayton Tuscaloosa? High School High?*"

Verano raised an eyebrow. "Is that the one with the dead skunk in the bathroom?" Mom nodded. "I may have seen it on a plane."

At this point, it looked like Mom was becoming over-whelmed by Verano's forced proximity, and she stepped away from him—a move that he apparently took as an invitation to enter the house. I took some pleasure in the sour look on his face as he was forced to navigate the cloud of flies.

Raph followed just behind him, his shoulders hunched in discomfort at the whole scene, though I guess with Verano here, he was no longer too nervous to enter the house at all.

"These all yours?" said Verano, examining her assortment of dream catchers and ritual candles. Mom nodded. "Quite a nice collection," he observed, which coaxed a smile out of her. "Many of these items could be picked up at any one of the innumerable and interchangeable New Age bookshops that dot this country, but a few of these are rare pieces."

Verano's accent was unplaceable. It sounded British to me at first, maybe by way of Swiss boarding school. Then, as he went on, his vowels became rounded in a much more American way . . . but every few words that hint of clipped, foreign speech would reassert itself for a syllable or two. I couldn't decide if this meant that he had lived all over, or if it was meant to con-vey that impression. He was clearly someone who cared a lot about his image, so I didn't rule that possibility out.

"Thank you," said Mom. "I started collecting after the—"

But Professor Verano didn't appear to be listening. He glanced over his shoulder at Raph. "Find me a trash bag, would you please."

"Wait, what?" said Mom as Verano began pulling her trinkets down from the shelves. "What do you think you're doing?"

"I understand you have a problem with spirits."

"You misunderstand, then. We don't have a problem.

Professor . . . Verano, is it? I appreciate your interest, but as I've explained to my daughter many times, it's only human prejudice that makes people afraid of the spirit world. In this household we respect our neighbors, embodied or otherwise. We are not in need of an exorcism."

"Mom!" I exclaimed. "Stop it." Given his rude behavior, I wasn't eager to take Verano's side against my own mother, but I had to admit that his confident manner gave me hope that he might know how to resolve our situation. At the least, he was the first person who seemed willing to take it seriously. "Stop acting like this is all a cute little game," I said to her. "Look what happened to Logan, look at what has happened to all of us. Whatever is in this house does not have our best interests at heart."

Verano unceremoniously dropped a clinking armload of my mom's ritual objects into the bag Raph had found. "Ms. Blanton," he said, "you should heed your daughter. I don't think you fully appreciate the nature of the forces affecting this house, and your family. Your trinkets have done more harm than good here. You have disturbed some very powerful forces, and you are now in a position of considerable danger. Your sage smudging, your altars and dream catchers and crystals and grimoires . . . It all seems quite harmless to you, but it may not seem so benevolent to . . ." He raised his eyes toward the ceiling, almost as if he could see a demon squatting there. "To others," he finished.

Then, with barely a glance more in her direction, Verano proceeded to show himself around the first floor of the house, moving swiftly from room to room, stopping here and there to press his ear to the walls and tap the head of his cane three times.

"What—what are you looking for?" I asked.

"Amelia," he replied in a hushed voice.

"Who's Amelia?" I said, but Verano was in his own world, and showed no inclination to answer. Raph, luckily, was able to fill us in.

"Amelia was Williamson's daughter. She shows up a bunch in Pronoica stuff when she's a baby, but she disappears from the record when she's around 13."

"Exactly!" shouted Verano from the pantry. "An absence. A very significant absence."

"What does that prove, though?" asked Mom. Verano came in through the kitchen and stood very close to her.

"Nothing," he said with a strange smile. "Nothing at all. But it is suggestive, isn't it?"

"Are you thinking that something happened with Amelia at the clinic?" said Raph. "That she saw something, something she shouldn't have, and they needed to shut her up?"

"Yes," said Verano, "yes, I believe . . ." But he stopped himself, and his eyes grew large with some sudden realization. "Ah yes, shut her up. Exactly," he said. "Don't you see, Raphael? She didn't just disappear from the record, she *disappeared*."

"You mean he killed her?"

"Possibly. But no. I think that he . . ." Suddenly he turned toward me. "Do you know of any unaccounted-for spaces in this house? A blocked-up door, or a room that seems too small for its place in the house?"

I glanced at Mom and Logan. "There is a blocked-up door, but it just leads down to Raph's apartment. I don't know any other—"

"The turret," said Logan. "My room is under a turret, but the ceiling is flat. There must be some extra space up there."

Verano said nothing, but his face lit up, and he dashed up the stairs, his cane clenched purposelessly in his fist.

We followed him up, but before I even reached the top of the stairs, I heard him emit a sharp cry. I exchanged a look with Mom before running up the remaining steps. "Professor Verano? Are you—"

As he came into view, I saw his face scrunched into a pained expression, one hand rubbing vigorously at his head. "That sound," he said. "How can you bear it?"

"Oh," I said. "You can hear it? It's actually not so bad today. Some days it sounds like—"

"For God's sake, child, how long have you been living with this? A room in your house produces noises like a direct portal to hell, and you . . . what? Put your headphones on?" I didn't have a good answer to this, and he didn't seem to expect one. Instead he gritted his teeth and went into the room, eyeing the ceiling with academic interest.

"Raphael," he said. "In that toolbox of yours, do you happen to have a sledge hammer?"

TUESDAY, JUNE 16, 12:30 P.M.

Raph does not have a sledgehammer, as it turns out, but he figures his crowbar should do the trick.

The others are all eyeing the ceiling nervously, but I look straight at him and nod when he asks if we are ready. Something is up there, I can just feel it. Something that will at last make everything make sense.

He's standing on a chair now. Swinging the crowbar back and forth to get some momentum. He's made his first crack at the ceiling, but it just produced a lot of plaster dust. This is weirdly like playing piñata.

TUESDAY, JUNE 16, 1:37 P.M.

I passed out the minute the spiders started pouring down. That's all I remember. I was staring straight up at the ceiling, we all were, and then black, hairy confetti was raining down. It took a second for me to register, but once I did, I don't think I even had a chance to shriek. I was out for the count.

The next thing I remember, I was coming to on the living room couch. I immediately started spasming, and I think Mom and Logan thought it was a seizure at first, but it was just me trying to get the spiders off. There weren't any spiders by then, though, so I just wound up tearing my clothes to shreds.

I don't know how I'll ever sleep again. Even without being conscious through most of it, just the knowledge that I spent those minutes in a flood of . . . In my hair, in my ears, under my clothes . . . Logan and the others had been quite diligent about removing them all before I woke up, but that just leaves the question . . . where are they now? Because I'm pretty sure they didn't kill them all.

TUESDAY, JUNE 16, 2:00 P.M.

Verano says that wasn't what we were looking for. We have to keep looking. I'm not sure I can, not sure I can take the risk of facing what we might find. Not after that last experience. And yet at this point, how can I not? And what could possibly be worse?

I don't know. In a weird way, I think that experience might have cured me. When I was a kid, I'd shriek and cry and run even at toy spiders. I was so scared. But how can any of that scare me now? Now that I've seen and experienced . . . It's like I dug deep enough into the terror, I came out on the other side. I can't be afraid of spiders anymore. I'm not sure I can be afraid of anything.

TUESDAY, JUNE 16, 2:36 P.M.

After some time to recuperate, we reconvened in Logan's room. The buzzing was even more painful now. I'm not sure why I even still refer to it as "the buzzing," except out of habit, or maybe for continuity's sake. Verano was right: I think I had been repressing it, simply refusing to hear it properly for weeks, out of pure force of will. But his comment had brought it back to the surface, and now that it was there, it was just as he said: shrieking, howling, the mad chattering of a thousand lost souls.

I think the others were finally noticing it too, though no one's expression looked as pained as Verano's. Except mine. Not that I could see myself, but looking at him and seeing the anguish written on his face felt like looking in a mirror.

Mom took a look around the room—swept out now, but still with a handful of spiders creeping around in the corners—and said, "There's nothing here, let's go back downstairs," but Verano ignored her. He was staring up at the giant hole in the ceiling.

"It doesn't make sense," he said. This comment seemed like such an understatement, it hardly required a response. But Verano had something specific in mind. "Is there a third floor to this house?"

"Only the basement, where Raph lives." Mom started to move toward the bedroom door, but Verano didn't. Instead he pulled his phone from the pocket of his coat, and started to enter something into it.

"Phones don't really work in the house," I told him.

He nodded. "So I've heard. But I'm not trying to call anyone." After a moment he tucked his phone back into his pocket. "There's something wrong with this room," he said.

"No shit," muttered Logan. Mom made a disapproving noise but didn't correct him.

"Not just this room, though," said Verano. "This whole floor. It's too short."

"What?"

"I knew there was something off about it as soon as we came up the stairs. This building is from the Victorian era. You don't have to be an art historian to know that in a grand house like this, architects of the time preferred very high ceilings. This building would have been no exception. In its first incarnation it had a ballroom and a grand receiving room. Those certainly would have been quite high. But when we were in your living room . . . the ceilings there are barely eight feet. I wondered if, during some remodel, the extra space had been shifted to the second floor. But no—the ceilings here are quite low as well. So where did the extra space go?"

We all looked up. Through the hole Raph had created, it was more than obvious that there was nothing between us and the roof other than a couple of layers of beams and insulation. Verano furrowed his brow, puzzled, but wheels were turning in my head.

"The windows," I said. Everyone turned. "Chloe mentioned it ages ago, but I never gave it much thought. There are windows . . . you can see them from the outside. And they don't correspond with anything on the inside." Verano stared at me, comprehension dawning.

"It's below us. Between the floors."

TUESDAY, JUNE 16, 3:18 P.M.

We considered ripping up the floorboards, but Mom had the idea that it would be easier, safer, and cause less permanent damage if we approached from the side, via the stairwell. It made sense, after all, that if we were trying to find a hidden floor between the known levels, the staircase would be the best way in.

Verano and Raph spent some time tapping at the walls and fiddling with tools, listening for hollow spaces and trying to avoid load-bearing beams. Eventually they found the spot they wanted, and Raph wielded the crowbar again. I prepared myself for another tidal wave of spiders, or God only knew what other monstrosity, but this time we were greeted only by a handful of lazily swooping flies and a cloud of plaster.

When the dust cleared, Verano put his head through the hole. "It's empty," he said, and stepped aside so the rest of us

could look. It was true. The space was much bigger than an ordinary crawl space—tall enough for an adult man to stand up straight inside. Light shone in from the windows Chloe had noticed, suggesting that this had once been a real part of the house. Rooms where people lived, not just insulation. But all we could see were beams and plaster and dust, plus a handful of tools left over from the last remodel, presumably. Except . . .

"There's a door," I said. "Look, at the opposite end. That's not just the exterior wall. There's a door there."

The others peered in and confirmed what I had seen, and moments later we were smashing through the wall to create a hole big enough for us each to climb through. I was surprised to note that there weren't any spiders in this part of the house—there didn't seem to be much sign of any living thing, in fact. Once through, we picked our way carefully across the unfinished floor toward the door. It wouldn't budge.

"It's locked," said Raph. "I could probably bust through it with the crowbar, though."

"That won't be necessary," said Verano. "This door was locked from the outside. This lock wasn't meant to keep people out—it was meant to keep someone in."

"To shut her up," I said.

Verano ran his flashlight over the door until his eye caught on a latch. Sure enough, it was a simple deadbolt. One twist of the knob, and the door swung open, releasing a blast of air so cold it made me catch my breath, followed by a swarm of fat, black flies whose wings beat slowly and solidly against my skin.

I wasn't the only one who screamed in alarm, but before long they had dissipated (or, more likely, gone to join their revolting brethren), and we were able to move into the room.

It was completely dark inside except for a couple of hairlines of bright light coming from the far side. "That must be one of the missing windows," said Verano, his breath visible even though it was a warm summer day outside. "Boarded up." *To keep anyone from seeing her,* he didn't say, but we were all thinking it.

Raph had a couple of flashlights in his toolbox, so we shone those around a bit. The room was sparsely furnished: a chair and desk with a washbasin, and a metal cot in the corner. What was stranger were the weird squishy shapes on the wall. I pressed on them. It was like a big couch cushion or something had been nailed there.

"It's padded," said Mom. "A padded cell." The term conjured images in my head of people wrapped in straitjackets, throwing themselves at every surface uncontrollably.

"You mean like for crazy people?"

"Perhaps," said Verano. "It would make sense. If she was—"

"No," said Logan. He hadn't spoken in so long, I had sort of forgotten he was there. Suddenly I felt weird about him being there. He's just a kid. Should he be seeing all this stuff, when we didn't even know exactly what we might see? On the other hand, he had lived through the worst of what the house had to offer. Maybe he was entitled to see where it all came from.

"Not crazy," said Logan softly. "Epileptic."

"How do you . . . ," I began, but one look at Logan's face told me how he had guessed. Of course. The doctors couldn't find the cause of Logan's seizures, because they didn't come from his brain.

They came from Amelia. And if Amelia had seizures, like Logan . . . without modern medicine, they wouldn't have been

277

able to do much for her, except stick her in a padded room and hope she didn't hurt herself too much.

"But then why lock her in?" I said. "It doesn't make sense. It's medieval. So what if she had epilepsy? Why would they want to lock her away from the world for years?"

"He would need to hide anything that seemed potentially negative," said Verano. "He was the prophet of a religion that demanded that only good things happen to him. If anyone were to find out that he'd had any kind of bad luck, the entire religion would start to look like a sham. So he had to hide her away."

I couldn't repress a shiver, though whether it was because of the frigid air that had been locked in this room for almost a century, or because of Verano's comments, I couldn't say. Before I could dwell on the question, Mom pointed out something the rest of us hadn't noticed: an old trunk in the corner of the room. In a minute or two Raph had the lock broken and the top pried open. "Holy shit," he said as he tipped open the top. The flashlight beams danced over the contents of the chest.

They were letters.

"Jackpot," said Raph.

"What do you mean?" I asked.

"We always suspected," said Verano, "that there were other letters, outside the official record . . . letters Williamson either destroyed or hid away."

"And you think . . ."

Verano let out a low whistle. "The missing letters."

For I don't even know how long, we all crouched around Raph, hunched to share the light of two flashlights, trying to read as much as we could of the letters. It was a bit difficult, because many were handwritten, or typewritten with hand-

written notes on the back or in the margins. It was hard and uncomfortable, but at that point we were all so fascinated that we didn't even care.

The funny thing is, the letters themselves weren't all that interesting. They were mostly . . . whiny, might be the best word for it. Page after page of complaints: Someone's car wouldn't start. The barn burned down. The bank was foreclosing on the house. The hired hand is a drunk and hasn't come to work for three days. My sister broke her ankle. Our daughter drowned. My cousin left town and won't pay back the debt he owes me.

Some told of tragedies, some recounted little more than the frustrations of a bad day. But all were pretty . . . ordinary. Just the ordinary bad news of life.

"What . . . what are these?" said Mom. "Why did people send this stuff to him? And how did it end up here?"

"It's Pronoica," said Raph in a low voice. "It's what we were looking for all along."

The question I had asked Raph in the library came back to me: If all the letters Williamson received were so positive, why did the house seem so dark and troubled? Now I understood— those weren't all the letters he received—those were just the ones he wanted people to know about.

"Williamson was a man with much to hide," said Verano. "It must have been daunting for him, trying to maintain this religion based around the premise that you can direct the universe to only hand you good things. I suspect that his technique worked for a while . . . but it was like a pendulum. There is only so far you can push it to one side, before it swings back in the other direction."

In the dim light cast by the flashlights, I saw Mom's eyes widen in horror. I knew what she was thinking. She was so like

Williamson—always believing the best of everyone, and that the universe itself had nothing but good intentions toward her. She believed as fervently as Williamson had that if she focused her energy on good things, good things would come to her. The idea that doing this was only delaying the time when an evil undertow would drag her back down with even greater intensity . . . the horror of the idea was inescapable.

"I have suspected for some time that Williamson was hiding something like this. Evidence that Pronoica was not the cure for all ills. The complaints in these letters may seem small, but the stakes were incredibly high for Williamson. His entire empire would have come crumbling down around him if people found out about this. So he hid them away. Desperation to find a secure place to store these letters must have been what led him to discover this space between the floors."

"And when Amelia became another liability," I said. "Another piece of bad news, he shut her up in here too."

"Guys," said Logan. "Look at this."

I thought he had picked up one of the letters and started to read it, but as I looked more closely, I saw that it wasn't a letter. It was an old school notebook, like kids might have used in the 1940s. It was filled with writing in a large, looping script. Raph grabbed it out of Logan's hands.

"What is it?" I said.

"Her journal," said Logan.

"Christ," said Raph. "It's got everything. The whole story. The clinic . . ." His eyes scanned the pages rapidly. Then he looked up. "Something did happen here. Something happened to Amelia."

Stopping and starting as he flipped through the pages for information, Raph gradually told us the story. The first few pages were ordinary enough: Amelia's concerns about school and hopes for her future. Only occasional mentions of her father's project, which didn't seem to interest her much. At least until he opened the clinic.

She was excited about that. Apparently a sweet-tempered, tenderhearted girl, she believed absolutely in her father's power as a healer, and looked forward to seeing the sick and crippled healed by his hand. He assembled a small crowd, brought them to remote Idaho, and invited her to attend his ritual. But as he stood before them, chanting and muttering and invoking the God power, something happened to Amelia. The way she put it, she was possessed by some spirit that took control of her body and mind and threw her to the ground, where she shook violently and made terrible noises.

She lost consciousness, and when she woke up, she was in this room—locked away, friendless, hopeless, all but forgotten, to live out the rest of her short life in forced seclusion. The only human interaction she had from then on was when a silent servant brought her meals, and when her father mounted the stairs from time to time to stow more letters away in the chest of her room, which he did without speaking to or even looking at her.

At first, the bad letters arrived only occasionally, but soon after the failure of the Pronoica Clinic, they began to increase in number and frequency. Family members of those who had attended the clinic wrote to Williamson to ask him what had happened. Ask him to explain to them why their loved ones had returned to them silent and stricken. What did he do to them? Not only were they not cured, they were worse than ever.

What had Williamson done to ensure their silence? Threats?

Blackmail? Hypnosis? Or did he wield the dangerous energy of Pronoica against them now, to suit his own ends?

But those were only the first letters. They dried up after a while, but were replaced by something far more sinister. Dozens and dozens of letters, many of them duplicates, some of them garbled, and others . . . Williamson hid those letters even more carefully, and Amelia could only guess at what they contained.

Raph eventually put the notebook down on top of the other letters, and even in nothing more than the glow from a flashlight, I could see how pale he was.

Behind me I could feel Mom trembling. "I think I'm going to be sick," she said. I thought she was being metaphorical, but a moment later she started to sway, and then she fell backward, catching herself with a hand grasping at one of the pads on the wall. It came free from the wall as she fell, and there was the sound of a loud rip. I rushed to her side to make sure she was okay, while Raph shone his flashlight on us.

"What's that behind them?" said Logan. "There's something behind the pads."

"My God," said Verano. The pool of light thrown by his flashlight swung around the room, casting us from light into darkness as he moved swiftly toward the torn cushion.

"Letters," he muttered as he dug his hand into the pile. "More letters." He started to tug the neighboring pads free from the walls, and as he did, more ancient, yellowed envelopes spilled into his hands. Raph picked a handful up from the floor and, holding them under his trembling light, he picked one from the bunch, carefully folded back the flap, and slid the decrepit paper free.

"Are you sure this is a good idea?" said Mom.

"What's it say?" said Logan.

"I—I have no idea," said Raph. I took a step closer to him and peered over his shoulder. The page between his fingers certainly looked like it had writing on it, but it was so tiny and crabbed that it was impossible to decipher. Here and there I could make out what appeared to be a letter, but I couldn't be sure whether they added up to true writing or were just the scribblings of the deranged.

"Try another," I said.

"Raphael, be careful," said Verano. "This isn't child's play. These letters need to be catalogued, properly preserved."

Raph ignored him and slipped a trembling finger under the aged seal of another. This one was even odder. It came out as a giant sheet but of a very strange shape. As the light shone on it and we got a better look, I saw that the page was constructed out of dozens of little scraps of paper—bits of receipts, paper bags, note cards, matchbook covers—all glued painstakingly together. Some of the scraps had typed writing, others hand-writing, others cartoonish pictures and abstract doodles. Again, I couldn't tell if it added up to anything meaningful, though there were actual words at least.

Raph put it down and picked up another.

He flicked open the flap on the envelope and reached his long, thin fingers in to pull stationary out, but this time it stuck. He tugged on it, gingerly at first, careful not to cause any damage, but gradually with more force, as his eagerness to know what was inside overcame his fastidious instincts. At last the page came free and Raph withdrew it, but as it slipped out, a soft black mass fell out into Raph's hand, followed by a collection of something small and dark that hit the floor with a delicate sound.

"What is it?" I said. Raph held his hand to his face to look more closely, then grunted and dropped the object, letting the flashlight clatter to the floor as well so its spotlight rolled along the far wall.

"Hair," he said, holding his sleeve to his mouth.

I grabbed the flashlight and focused it at the floor. In the middle of my beam lay a tangled black clump of human hair, like the refuse pulled from a hairbrush, while all around it were scattered an assortment of dark, crusted, concave disks. Logan put his fingers out and pressed them to the disks as if he was picking up crumbs from the kitchen table. He lifted his hand and turned it so we could all see.

"Is that . . . ?" said Mom. I knew, but my mouth had gone dry and my tongue felt too thick and heavy to speak. Logan said it for me.

"Fingernails," he said. "Bloody fingernails."

TUESDAY, JUNE 16, 5:14 P.M.

No one wanted to spend any more time up in that room. But we couldn't just walk away from it either. Somehow without really discussing it, we came to the unanimous conclusion that we needed to get the letters out of there. For ten minutes or so, as fast as we could, we worked together in silence, tearing down the pads and tossing handfuls and armfuls of the aging letters into the trunk that held the other, more normal ones. When we seemed to have gotten them all, Raph squeezed the lid on the trunk shut, and he and Mom each took a side and hauled it back out through the broken door and the hole in the wall, down the stairs, and placed it on the coffee table in the living room.

It was strange, though. The letters felt different sitting on the coffee table in the bright sunlight of a Tuesday morning in late spring. Very different from how they'd felt in that cold, dark room. Upstairs I was so shaken I wanted nothing to do with the letters, but now that they sat here like some kind of set dressing for a Restoration Hardware catalog shoot, all I wanted was to pore over them and examine every strange thing they contained.

I reached for one and started to fold up the flap.

"No way," came Mom's voice from the kitchen. "You put that down, Paige."

"Why?"

"Why? How are you even asking that? You saw what I saw. There's something . . . unhealthy in those letters, and reading them cannot be a good idea. What we need to do is get rid of them. Get them out of the house as soon as possible."

"We need to burn them," said Logan in a low, intense voice. He hadn't spoken since we came downstairs, and his voice came as a shock to me. I was still having some trouble reconciling this Logan with the one I saw last night, and figuring out which of the two—if either—was for real. The two versions blurred together before my eyes. "Mom's right. There's . . . nothing okay about these. We can't read them."

Mom clapped her hands together as if efficiently solving a problem. "Sounds fine to me. Let's just take them outside and burn them right now, and we can be done with it."

"No," said Verano. "I'm afraid I can't let you do that."

"It's my house," said Mom. "We found them here, so it's my property. I can do what I want with them, and I want them destroyed."

Verano struck the floor firmly with his cane. "It's my collection," he said with severe authority. "I am the curator of the Pronoica collection for the University of Idaho. All the pieces of that collection are my responsibility, including these. If the content of these letters does not interest you, that's your decision, but they must be exposed to the light of day. They have been hidden far too long. Repression of the unpleasant aspects of life is the root of the problem we face today. Williamson tried to silence these voices, but they were destined to return."

"With all due respect," said Mom, clearly fighting to keep her calm, "I'm not exactly convinced of your expertise in this field. I've been a student and practitioner of the magical arts for more than half my life, and I'm descended from a long line of acknowledged mystics. You—you're an academic kook trying to burnish your ego and your CV with this 'discovery,' and not thinking twice about the real lives you would ruin in the process. I know your kind, I deal with them every day. Big-name professors who say they want to help the environment, preserve the ecosystem, save the species, but all they really care about is winning the next grant so they can fund their sabbatical somewhere sunny. You come into my house with your academic credentials, but it's possible I know more than you about the shadow realm. Prying into these letters—it's unwholesome. They weren't meant to be read. We weren't meant to read them."

Professor Verano shook his head, a humorless smile on his face. "Ms. Blanton, it is very likely you who awakened this evil with your supposed mystical expertise. People have resided in this building for decades with no more than a slight degree of paranormal activity. Do you think it coincidence that you arrive in this town with your thaumaturlogical toys, some of them clearly far more powerful than you understand, and this house immediately begins its rebellion? The secrets, the grievances in these letters, must be exposed to the light, or they will fester and corrupt this place for generations to come."

For a moment, the two stood silent and bristling at each other, apparently at an impasse. Then Raph spoke. "You're both wrong," he said. "I'm sorry, Ms. Blanton, but you don't own this house. You rent. The house belongs to me."

"To your mom," I mumbled under my breath.

"Actually," he replied, "it's my name on the deed. For tax reasons my mom didn't want it in her name, and her lawyer suggested putting it in mine. So . . . legally speaking . . . the house is mine."

"Raphael," said Verano, a tinge of triumph in his voice already. "You understand, don't you? After all we've seen, all we've learned. You know how important these documents are. My work—*our* work. You won't let it all go to waste. We are exactly who is meant to read them. They are in our hands, aren't they? What better evidence could we ask for? A letter always arrives at its destination."

Raph hesitated a moment, then nodded. "Verano is right. The letters need to be preserved. And catalogued. Simply sitting down and reading them like some old love letters won't get us anywhere. What we need is data. We need a system. Some way to manage all the information and bring it into view."

"Yes," said Verano, growing excited. "Exactly, precisely right. Ah, Raphael, you are thinking like a historian now. We need to get the new documents to the library right away, where they can be—"

"No," said Raph. "Not yet. Like I said, they need to be sorted and catalogued. Monty—*Professor*. Who are you going to get to do that, some marketing major looking for a summer internship? What the hell are they going to know, or care, about this work? I've lived with Pronoica for more than a year now. I've scanned and catalogued every last piece of that collection for you, and checked it over twice. You said it yourself: No one knows this collection better than I do. Not even you."

"That's correct," said Verano. "But still, they belong at the library."

"Where I'll have no access to them. Thanks to you."

Professor Verano held Raph's stare for a long moment before looking away. "Yes, fine," he said, as if Raph had just brought up a particularly distasteful subject. "You have a point. All right then, we'll work on them here."

"No," said Raph again. "That is . . . I'd rather you didn't. It seems like a bad idea." Verano didn't answer, but his brow was furrowed, his expression dark. At last he nodded. Apparently deciding that this compromise solution was better than the likely alternative, he limited himself to giving some very precise instructions to Raph with regards to the database and its finer points, then grabbed his cane and swept out the door.

As soon as Verano left, Mom jumped on Raph, repeating again how she didn't want the letters in her house for one minute longer, etc. etc. I guess she thought Raph would be easier to break down than Verano, and . . . well, she was right, kind of. Because he brushed her off immediately, saying, "Don't worry, Ms. Blanton. I have no intention of keeping these letters around. Logan was right—we're going to burn them."

He explained that there was no way Verano would ever leave the letters with them unless he thought they were perfectly safe, so he had to let him believe that he would preserve them. But then he called Verano a "damned obsessive" who couldn't see past his own ego. And it's true that Verano knows the least of all of us what we've been living through these past months, so how could he possibly understand?

Anyway, Logan was all set to dump the stuff in a pile outside and light a match to it right then and there—if not just start a fire right on the coffee table—but Arthur arrived just in time with a more sensible suggestion. Good old Arthur . . . He was driving up from Lapwai with dinner from CD's barbecue restaurant for everyone, and walked in on what must have looked like a very strange scene. But he took it all in with his usual aplomb.

"Hey, now," he said, "you can't start a fire here. There's a burn ban on."

"A what?" I said.

"A burn ban," said Arthur. "Have you seen the conditions out there? It's hot and dry and windy, and the slightest spark could set off a massive wildfire. Starting any kind of fire now would be—"

Raph rolled his eyes. "Yes, I know all about the burn ban. Look, I've lived here all my life. I've been through a zillion fire seasons. It just means you have to be careful. And I know how to take precautions."

Arthur and Mom were silent. Worried.

"I'm not talking about hosting a barbecue, or starting a bonfire just for fun. This is important. What do you want to do, throw all this creepy shit in the Dumpster outside? Bring it down to the recycling center? Do you really think that's going to solve the problem? We need to purge this stuff. Purge the house. Fire is the only way we're going to do that."

Mom looked to Arthur, who hesitated before giving a nod. "We do it on the rez sometimes—get special dispensations for ritual fires. There are some things only a fire can cleanse. But Jesus, you have to be very, very careful. Will you at least wait until tonight, and let me do it with you?"

Raph agreed to this, so I guess we get to put off our big creepy bonfire a few more hours.

WEDNESDAY, JUNE 17, 12:43 A.M.

Raph was right. I am so glad we did burn them.

God, I . . . I feel better than I have since . . . well, since before we first moved into this house. It's crazy how different everything feels just as a result of that one act. Suddenly I can walk around this house without feeling like I'm carrying a heavy load all the time. I didn't even realize until now how much it was affecting me, but right now I just feel so light and free and . . . peaceful. At last. This house, which has brought us all so much trouble and pain, it is just a house now. It's old, and it still has a lot of history, but . . . that's all it is now. History. It's not living with us and feeding on us and fucking with us anymore.

But I should back up and describe what happened. We waited until dark, which felt like forever. But finally the sun set, and Arthur and Raph went about digging a deep hole in the gravel driveway outside. I'd invited Chloe to sleep over, since I knew she would want to see this story through to the end. Once she got here, she, Logan, and I wandered around the fields just past the property, looking for large stones and bringing them back to the hole by the armful. We made a ring of big stones around the pit, and cleared the area of any dry, inflammable objects—twigs and leaves and stuff. Then at last we lugged the big, overstuffed trunk outside, and started tossing the unread letters into the pit by the handful. They didn't all fit easily, so we decided to do it in batches. Arthur lit another branch of patosway and held it in the air a few moments, humming the same song his grandfather had sung the other time. He seemed a lot less comfortable with it, though, as if it were something he only half remembered. Then he dropped the patosway into the pit, and almost instantly the old, dried-out envelopes began to blacken and smoke. Before long, small flames erupted and the pages started to curl, and then the fire started in earnest, curling the letters into ash. The wind was picking up, but we were very careful to control the ash and keep it from drifting up into the air on a gust. We had covers we could put on it if it seemed to be getting too big, and we kept it very controlled.

Even so, this carefully tended fire had a feeling of purging about it. The pungent smell of the patosway drifted through the air, and the black smoke curled into the sky to meet with the terrible cloud of fire debris already hanging over the city, almost as if it was returning home. Periodically we threw more letters onto the fire and allowed them to burn themselves out into ash. While we waited, Mom went inside and got blankets and lawn chairs so we could be a bit more comfortable. Lying on a blanket with Raph, staring up at the orange moon, it was almost possible

to forget what we were actually doing. It was more like we were all on a summer camping trip than trying to rid our house of demonic possession.

Toward midnight, the final batch of letters was at last settling down into a heap of slightly smoking ash, and Arthur began covering it with dirt and gravel, to smother the remains of the fire and make sure it couldn't spread.

At that point Mom caught my eye and nodded toward Logan, and . . . it was the most amazing thing. He was sleeping! Deeply and peacefully. I think that, more than anything, convinced me that this time our ritual really worked and that we could all go back to normal. It made me so happy that tears sprang to my eyes. But Mom just smiled and put her fingers to her lips. She got up and scooped him into her arms like she used to when he was a little kid. He did really look like a little kid again, his face innocent in the dim light shining from the house windows.

Mom went inside to carry him up to bed. Arthur lingered a bit longer to make sure there wasn't the slightest trace of smoke, and then he followed her in with only a wink and a word to us not to stay up too late.

Chloe was the next to go. She had been sitting almost on the opposite side of the fire, and I could hardly pick her out of the shadows except for the glittering of her eyes in the firelight. She hadn't spoken in a while, but as Arthur disappeared into the house, she stood up and looked at us, saying she was going to turn in too. But she didn't leave right away—she just stood there, looking at us, her brow furrowed in that puzzle-solving expression of hers.

"Are you going to be okay?" she said at last.

"We're fine," I said, but she didn't move. She was looking really intensely at Raph.

"I'll be okay," he said. At this, she finally left us alone.

Honestly, I was so sleepy and exhausted by this point that I almost joined them and went up to bed. But another part of me didn't want this beautiful moment to end—the stars, the light wind, the warm night, the sense that I was finally safe and free from all that negative energy. And Raph lying beside me, sharing it with me . . .

Raph.

I sensed a nervous movement at my side, and suddenly Chloe's comment made more sense to me. In a blink the past 24 hours came flooding back to me. The spiders, my freak-out, Raph offering me his couch, me getting into his bed while he was sleeping . . . and then the horror that came after, the blood and fear and I still didn't know exactly what had happened. Had he told her?

I felt Raph shift again beside me, and wondered if he was trying to leave. Trying to escape politely. If he was scared to be around me.

I turned my head toward him, but he was still lying on his back, staring up at the sky. "Raph," I said. He didn't look at me, just kept staring straight up, but I could feel his muscles tense up a bit on the other side of the blanket. At last he sat up.

"I should get to bed," he said, and almost like an afterthought, he yawned extravagantly. I nodded, feeling like it wasn't my place to pressure him to stay. Especially if I was the one making him uncomfortable. But the very idea of that was making me feel pretty terrible.

He got up, brushed off his jeans, and started to move toward his basement door. I called out his name again and he stopped and turned.

"I'm sorry," I said. Raph sighed and ruffled his curls. In the dim starlight I couldn't make out even a trace of the injury that had been done to his lip last night, but I knew it was there, and the thought of it burned in my heart.

"I know," he said.

"Can you tell me what happened? I don't even—"

But Raph shook his head. "Don't think about it. You're better off not knowing. That wasn't you last night. This house . . . it's made us all a little crazy."

He gave me a little smile, and I smiled back. Then he went back to his apartment, and I folded the blanket and came up here to type this. But this story is over and my bed is calling to me.

I almost can't believe I won't have this weird shit to write about anymore. Believe me, I am not going to miss it! Maybe I will stop using this journal from now on. Or at least take a long break.

All I know is, if I ever log into the journal again, I hope my big excitement is who asked me to prom or where I got into college or something. That sounds . . . really nice right now.

WEDNESDAY, JUNE 17, 3:09 A.M.

It's 3 a.m. and I'm awake. Again. What woke me up? I don't know. Chloe is still sleeping peacefully in the other bed, but my skin is prickling and I feel wide-awake. Alert. I thought . . . I don't know, I thought I heard . . . or felt . . . shaking? But I don't feel it now. I do smell something, though. Burning. It doesn't smell close, but I can feel it in my lungs again.

Hmm, I just checked the local news, and I guess there is a wildfire just outside of town. I hope this has nothing to do with our fire earlier. God, wouldn't that be awful. But the website seemed to think it was caused by a lightning strike, and it is pretty far away. Anyway, it sounds like the firefighters have it pretty much under control.

I still feel nervous and unquiet, though. I think I will go quickly check on Logan, just to calm my nerves.

WEDNESDAY, JUNE 17, 6:32 A.M.

Shit. Shit. I don't know what's going on. Is it all starting again? Will we never be free of this . . . whatever it is?

I found Logan lying in a patch of sunlight, shaking and drooling and choking—another seizure. And my heart just . . . fell. Because as awful as it is to see your baby brother suffering like that, what made it even worse was the sinking feeling that our ritual didn't work, that whatever evil was in this house is still here, is still messing with us. And it's getting worse.

But I just don't know. Maybe the seizure is unrelated? How can we be sure?

I called out for Mom, but I didn't want to leave Logan alone, so I ran over to him. I called again, but no one seemed to be coming, so I just . . . calmed myself down and tried to remember the stuff they taught us about how to deal with a seizure.

I rolled him onto his side and put a pillow under his head, and that seemed to help. He stopped shaking, anyway. So then I just sat there and rubbed his back and soothed him, and eventually he fell back to sleep.

That's when Arthur came in, finally. He saw me there and looked really freaked out as I tried to explain to him calmly and quietly (so as not to wake up Logan) what had happened. But for some reason he just stared at me and Logan, looking horri-fied. Even though we were clearly out of the woods. But he must have realized the same thing I did: if Logan is convulsing again, it must mean that the house is still haunted.

Eventually he got himself together and went to get my mom. I stayed with Logan until Mom came. She looked really freaked out too, and ran right to his side, crying and sobbing. I tried to calm her down, but she wasn't paying attention to me. I guess I can understand why she panicked, after all we've been through.

By then, Arthur was on the phone, and I figured I was prob-ably doing more harm than good by hanging out there, so I went back to my room to write this up. Ugh, so much for getting to put this journal to rest! Now I don't know what will happen.

I'm so exhausted, but I don't want to go back to sleep when things are like this. Wait, how did it get to be morning already? The past couple of days have really scrambled my brain. I'm going to go downstairs to make some coffee.

WEDNESDAY, JUNE 17, 12:50 P.M.

~~Every atomic spirit is through the statement of us, is discovery~~
~~than problem come~~
I'm in the room. Amelia's room.
~~in the atomic above. The spirit the statement spirit, in invisible fast more power~~
The cell. It's not padded anymore, since we tore down all the cushions on the walls. But it is small and dark and locked.
~~of race, than through at the before through billion the one body the~~
Writing on my phone, which keeps glitching up, so who knows if this will work. But I have to do something, have to record this somehow.
~~energy spirit, by becoming one one of the answer than the billion invisible the existence spirit,~~

Maybe it's stupid to use my phone to make a journal entry right now. Maybe I should use it to call the police and get me the hell out of here. But what good would that do? So I could trade one cell for another? A jail cell. Or if everyone decides I'm as nuts as I seem to be, maybe I could upgrade to a cell that still has its padding. And a nice straitjacket to go with it.

~~the ever existence in closer.~~

Hardly sounds like an improvement.

~~The invisible are waiting for you, you~~

I need to back up and explain how I got here.

~~follow WANT spirit is that everything waiting intelligence.~~ ~~Please~~

I went downstairs to make coffee, still emotionally over-whelmed and mentally fried from exhaustion and worry about Logan. I picked up the pot and ran it under the tap for a second before I noticed something weird. There was something in the coffeepot.

~~untold is you the intelligence. Follow your power, and fol-~~ ~~low in the studies,~~

A letter.

~~and invisible spirit IS FOR everything~~

Why would a letter be in the coffeepot? Well, why not? After everything else that's gone on in this house, why the fuck not?

~~recognize closely YOU~~

I turned off the water. My fingers trembling, I pulled the letter from the pot, opened it, and started to read. Tried to read. All the words were blacked out—every single one. You could tell how long each word was, more or less, but that's it. They were all scratched out to invisibility.

~~they ARE the intelligence.~~

Something else I noticed: bloody fingerprints in the margins, bright red and smeary.

~~YOU invisible invisible very spirit of YOU untold invisible~~

I don't know how long I stood there, staring down at the letter in my hands in blank confusion, before I was brought back to myself by a voice.

~~These waiting presence. Power. Invisible day,~~

"You tried to destroy them, didn't you?"

~~the ever you spirit in YOU FOR wealth, presence, everything.~~

I looked up. Professor Verano was standing in the doorway to the house, leaning hard against his cane, his face twisted in fury. I couldn't answer him at first, so he stepped inside and walked slowly forward to meet me in the kitchen, limping heavily.

~~in atomic World the than invisible of in spirit invisible in~~

He stopped a couple of steps away from me.

~~FOR spirit, in the can statement intelligence. fast invisible Please ARE than Invisible Living~~

"I told you not to," he said, his voice shaking with barely suppressed rage, "but you did it anyway. You tried to destroy the letters."

~~spirit you come closer~~

I looked down at the letter in my hand, then back up at his face. "We did destroy them," I said. "We had a bonfire. We threw them all in. Every one."

~~The these presence. presence, than waiting intelligence. that FOR intelligence~~

"Then explain this." Verano reached into his coat and pulled out a sheaf of letters, which he thrust toward me. Not just any letters—old, yellowed. Curled around the edges. Unmistakably the Pronoica letters.

~~problem Living Every for everything Please invisible in recognize Power. Spirit closer.~~

"You saved some," I said. "You stole them from the trunk and took them with you, and then you broke in here and planted this here to freak me out."

~~The spirit, in spirit by is presence. problem atomic intelligence.~~

Verano smiled grimly and shook his head. "I didn't save anything. I trusted you. I trusted Raph. Trusted him to follow my instructions and not do anything rash. Then these turned up under my pillow this morning. Another one was in the umbrella stand. Five more in the glove compartment of my car. They're probably all over town by now," he said. He looked at me sharply, intently, his cold eyes cutting right through me. "You should have listened to me," he said, his voice quiet but laced with menace. He took a step forward. "I did warn you. You can't eradicate something like this, you can only repress it. But the repressed object will always, inevitably return."

~~one invisible waiting for untold one body before The by waiting Every the invisible in~~

I backed away from him until I hit the counter. There was something unsettling about the way he was looking at me, but I couldn't figure out what it meant. Something was distracting me. A noise, like screaming. Shrieking. That sound from Logan's room, the sound of someone wailing in agony.

~~can these everything waiting waiting YOU is come invisible invisible~~

"It doesn't make any sense," I said. "It was supposed to be all over. It was supposed to be better now."

very is invisible the follow ever Every follow are Power.

Verano turned toward the sound of footsteps clomping down the stairs, and a moment later, Arthur came into view, and he let out a cry as he reached the kitchen. I'd never seen him like this before. Good, kind, sensible Arthur was advancing toward me like a madman. Sweat was pouring from his face, and he was also holding a towel to his side, a large red splotch darkening and spreading through the terry cloth. A second later, my mom appeared, her face red and tear streaked. She threw herself at Arthur, tugging him back with clawlike fingers.

Power. statement FOR you, everything at power closer.

"Don't," she wailed. "Don't touch her."

at invisible the invisible ever and the than the these spirit the is of that

"Mom?" I said, struggling to pull the information gathered by my senses into any coherent order. "What's going on? How is Logan? Is he awake yet?"

the atomic be and the atomic atomic you discovery of that The discovery Spirit

Mom didn't answer, but her face crumpled into desperate sobs before my eyes, and she continued to wrestle wordlessly with Arthur. Only then did I realize that Chloe was in the kitchen too. Her face was paler than usual, but otherwise she seemed almost eerily impassive next to Mom and Arthur.

that The everything invisible blood problem the everything. is come

"Logan's dead," she said flatly.

body invisible recognize invisible FOR atomic in one spirit abundance

I was speechless for a moment. Mom and Arthur also froze at her words, looking at me with strange fear on their faces. I looked to them desperately, waiting for them to say something, to contradict her, to call her way out of line for joking about something like that. But they didn't.

~~on follow in you invisible everything the is Spirit Every atomic problem~~

"No," I said. "No, I saved his life, I sat with him, I did all the things you're supposed to." But still they didn't answer. Into the silence that had descended on the kitchen, Arthur let out another roar and lunged for me again. He winced in pain as Mom held him back by his shoulder.

"What happened?" I said, my voice coming out broken and raw. "What happened?" I repeated more loudly when no one answered.

~~Power. Invisible becoming the than~~

That's when things started to come together. Pieces of the puzzle attaching themselves to one another in my mind. "It has something to do with the house, doesn't it? Amelia. The letters. The evil that's locked in this place. Something got to him." I looked around and for the first time, noticed something missing. "Where is Raph?" I clapped a hand to my mouth as realization overtook me. "No," I said. "No, it can't . . . Dr. Clyde was right. She warned me. She told me Raph was dangerous. Told me I should stay away from him. But it was too late. His experiments . . . all that good luck he thought he was buying, but it was only borrowed. He tried to cover his mistake by burning those letters, but instead he awakened something. Unleashed some power, some uncontrollable force—"

~~statement invisible in of ever may tail atomic perfect~~

Finally Chloe's calm, hard voice broke through my babbling.

Invisible and is through studies, of follow the of The the abundance.

"You really don't remember?"

spirit, is everything. discovery on spirit power, presence, blood spirit at the perfect spirit

I swallowed. "Remember what?"

Please the you World the than ever Please everything

Chloe took the last few steps into the kitchen and approached me, stepping around Arthur. "It's not Raph," she said slowly. "It's you. It's been you all along. You're the one who disturbed the spirits . . . They had always been here, resting fitfully, waiting for someone to come along and awaken them. Someone whose cryptic power had been concentrated through many generations. Someone with a force that resonated with theirs. A conductor of dark energy.

YOU waiting IS the answer

"You never guessed? I knew . . . almost since I met you. I couldn't believe that you didn't know yourself. And your mom . . ." Chloe turned toward her. "You must have seen the signs. But then, a mother's love. You wouldn't let yourself acknowledge it."

Every existence of race, and may the very everything race, very

"What the hell is she talking about?" I said. Mom let out another wail.

the the of tail of spirit the untold invisible

Verano turned to Arthur. "I think it's time we call the police."

the in before atomic you in at The energy the closely Power.

"No," said Mom fiercely. She turned on Verano with a vicious expression on her face. "I won't let you. You know what will

309

happen if you do. They'll take her. I've lost one baby already today. I won't let them take the other."

Spirit waiting you the are is the the spirit, race, you the World

"We can't just let her alone," gritted Arthur through clenched teeth. It was eerie to have them discuss me like that, right in front of me. I could almost believe they were talking about someone else. "She's dangerous. She's a danger to herself, and to all of us."

presence, the invisible the you waiting one existence spirit, FOR everything abundance

"I am?" I said. "No, you don't understand. It was Raph. He was the one who brought all this into the house. The one who awoke the spirits."

spirit, atomic these in in power problem

"Raph may have had some part in it," said Verano, "but he didn't deserve . . ." Verano's face darkened with violent emotion, and he couldn't go on.

WANT

"I don't understand," I said. "Where is he? Where is Raph?"

presence. invisible energy FOR body

"Dead," said Verano.

Every you the the recognize follow more intelligence. us, energy Invisible the FOR tail

This was a dream. This had to be a horrible dream. "Raph and Logan? How can that be?"

The IS of statement untold the IS of invisible is you bring in ever untold of of the

"Paige," said Chloe, "look at yourself."

we will know you beyond the tomb

So I did. I still clenched that mysterious letter . . . . My hands, my arms, my clothes were all drenched in blood.

ignoring spiritual absence takes failure sickness misery,

"I can't lose them both," Mom was repeating to herself, almost like a chant, while I tried to make sense of the information I was absorbing. "She wasn't in her right mind when she killed them," she said. "It's not her fault. I have to protect her."

the absent flesh of the devil is the finite result of all our gifts,

"Arthur is right. If we leave her be, she'll kill again," said Verano.

stone embodied lies, the dead will bring you

"Then lock her in the room," said Chloe. "Amelia's room. She'll be safe there. We'll all be safe."

what you want don't want abundance abundance abundance abundance, ignoring spiritual absence takes

And so here I am. I went quietly, after all that. What was the point in resisting? I could see the truth in what they said. If it's true—that I snuck down into Raph's apartment last night and stabbed him in his sleep, then came back upstairs and strangled Logan—how can I argue with their decision? I'm a menace. Dr. Clyde was right all along. I just couldn't let myself see what she was trying to tell me. She kept telling me that the house was a distraction. That my worry for Logan was a kind of deflection. That I should focus on myself. I thought she was telling me to stay away from Raph because he was dangerous, but no. It was *me*. Raph kept telling me there was a danger in us hanging out together. I was so blind. So sure that he meant he was a danger to me, which I didn't believe, because I couldn't imagine him ever being a danger to anyone. And he wasn't. I was.

failure sickness misery, the absent flesh of the devil is the finite result of all our gifts.

And my mom's stories of the mysticism of our ancestors . . . I pushed them away for so many years because they contained a truth I wasn't ready to accept. This year, when I finally started to listen, I still only heard what I wanted to. That we were on the side of good, that everyone who saw darkness in us was prejudiced and ignorant. But Chloe saw it. This house was restless before we came, but I'm the one who woke it up. Who acted as a conduit for all the bad history sitting here. As long as I'm here, I'm only making it worse.

the devil everyone forgets.

But what do I do? What do I do now? How can I end it all? There has to be a way.

WEDNESDAY, JUNE 17, 10:43 P.M.

There is a way. I understand now. The house showed it to me. I was standing here, alone in the middle of this room, shaking and sobbing with guilt and fear, and then . . . I can't explain it. But that's nothing new. There is so much I can't explain about my life these past six months. I just have to accept it.

I saw the land spread out around me. The town and the fields and the barns and the big empty sky. I saw it all, even though I was shut up in that tiny dark room. It was like the walls on every side of me just fell away, and I could turn in a circle and see every little feature of the landscape spread out around me.

And it was on fire. The smoke started to roll in off the fields, choking my breath and making my eyes water. I could feel the particles of ash and debris in the air, feel the wind moving the flames inexorably forward.

That's when I understood. Burning is purging. Purifying. The witch hunters who feared my ancestors knew the cleansing properties of fire, and they weren't wrong. This fire around me is a gift. I must go to it—I must leave this prison and seek it out. It's the only way I can end this. The only way I can repair the evil I have wrought.

Wildfire Ravages Moscow Neighborhood

An uncontrolled wildfire spread to the outskirts of Moscow and laid waste to a neighborhood to the northwest of town. A number of houses and apartment complexes were engulfed in flames, and firefighters are still working to control the blaze. Fire Chief Mathers expressed his belief that the conflagration would soon be under control, and they could begin assessing damage.

At the moment, only one fatality of an unknown female has been established, who was seen by witnesses to jump from the window of a house and run toward the approaching fire. Police are currently investigating this story.

A few structures are still burning, and around a dozen people are homeless tonight. One house, however, which was in the direct path of the fire, emerged unscathed. Many are calling it a miracle that this Moscow landmark and one of the oldest houses in the city survived perfectly intact even as many of the neighboring houses succumbed to the out-of-control wildfire.

AFTERWORD

I find I have little to add to the story as it appears in these pages, and yet some details bear clarifying as much as is possible. In truth, there is little certainty to be gleaned in the aftermath of this terrible event.

As to the source of the unrest in the old house, I believe I have made my own position adequately clear. My conclusions, however, are not shared by all, and I would be remiss if I did not mention the most compelling alternative explanation.

Dr. Louisa Clyde has testified in court that Paige Blanton was suffering from a constellation of psychological disorders that, in the early morning hours of the 17th, caused her to take the lives of two people and make an attempt on a third. Paige's repressed rage toward her father in the aftermath of his infidelity manifested as aggression toward her little brother. Raphael came to represent in her mind her own failure to live up to the model of adult feminine sexuality provided by her mother, while Mr. Taylor she resented as a rival for her mother's affections.

As satisfying as this version of events has proven for the local police force, it still leaves some unanswered questions. For example, it has been demonstrated conclusively that Paige's phone, with which she supposedly made these last journal entries, was not on her person when she died, nor was it left in the room where Paige had been temporarily secured. Rather, it had been abandoned on the kitchen table when Paige was forcibly restrained, and it remained there hours later.

There are those who fixate on this strange detail as proof of some great conspiracy in this matter. A more common theory is that Chloe is the de facto author of the last few entries in the journal, while smaller factions point fingers in other directions, blaming Ms. Blanton, Mr. Taylor, or even myself as perpetrators of a supposed hoax.

For my own part, I don't pretend to have any explanation that fits into a rational narrative of the events. I leave it to the reader to draw his or her own conclusions.

POSSESSION

EDITOR'S NOTE

It is with a bitter mixture of scholarly excitement and deep personal sadness that I present this account of the strange events leading up to the tragic end of one young woman's life. Readers familiar with my earlier volume, *Diary of a Haunting*, will know of my commitment to the search for evidence of paranormal phenomena—some might even call it my obsession. The story that follows is the most startling documentation of the effects of supernatural forces I have ever yet encountered, and its significance to human understanding cannot be overestimated. It pains me, however, that this revelation comes at such a heavy cost.

The author of this text, called Laetitia here, is a singularly brave soul who endured unthinkable torments before developing a hard-won understanding of the forces afflicting her. In the eight months prior to the events reported here, she maintained an unremarkable Internet journal detailing her pursuit of a career as a musician and offering personal grooming tutorials to her followers. In January of 2014 the tone and content of her entries shifted as Laetitia became troubled by inexplicable physical symptoms. She began posting more locked entries that could not be viewed by her followers, and gradually started to use the blog more as a personal diary.

Upon Laetitia's death, her mother found the password for her blog among her things and read the private entries. Her mother was advised by a friend familiar with my previous work to pass the document on to me, and so I came into possession of this unique document. The horror I experienced in reading of Laetitia's bizarre condition is matched only by a determination to make such knowledge public, and thus serve both science and the memory of this remarkable young woman.

The journal has been lightly edited, mostly to protect Laetitia and her family's privacy, and to remove irrelevant passages that have no bearing on the tragic events that led to her death.

I can only hope Laetitia's family is comforted to know her courageous sacrifice has increased public understanding of the terrifying yet awe-inspiring anomalies that may be found on the fringes of human experience.

Montague Verano, Phd.
Professor, Department of History
University of Idaho

MONDAY, JANUARY 6, 4:15 P.M. (PUBLIC)

Thank you all for your comments on my last tutorial on creating a two-tone wig! I'm glad it was useful. And you know, you can use that same technique to create more than two tones if you want to do three tones or go crazy and do, like, a million different colors. Actually, that would be difficult—you probably want to limit yourself to four or five at most.

And thanks to everyone who said I looked fabulous! You guys are the best.

(@⁺‿⁺@) <-- *blushing*

Sometimes people at school or on the street try to judge me for having pink or purple or turquoise hair, or wearing glittery eyelashes in the middle of the afternoon, but screw them.

You guys understand me and always know how to lift my spirits.

Speaking of which, today was rough. I lost my voice! Totally and completely lost it—I opened my mouth, and nothing at all came out. I panicked, of course. That's never happened to me before. . . . I've had sore or scratchy throats, and I've gotten hoarse, but never anything like this. Completely out of the blue. I can talk a little if I force it—croak like a frog, really. But what good does croaking do me when I'm supposed to be rehearsing every day? The open auditions for *America Sings* are only a few months away, and I definitely can't sing like this.

It's really stressing me out. I *have* to make that audition! When am I ever going to get another chance like this? A chance to sing in front of real TV producers from Hollywood? I need this. I know if they can just hear me, they will love me. But I *need* to be at that audition.

I've been working at this for so long. My whole life, really. And I can practice and post videos online and do all the little church solos I want, but none of that is going to make me a star. It's not enough to sing just for the people here, in my neighborhood, or the handful of people reading my blog. I want the whole world to hear my voice. And for the longest time, I didn't see how I was going to make that happen. No matter how bad you want something, you can't just will it into existence.

But with these auditions coming up, I feel like I finally have a chance. I'm not worried about my voice or my talent. . . . Mostly I'm worried about getting up there and freezing, and blowing my only shot at being famous. That's why I've been rehearsing so much.

I got permission to use the school auditorium when no one else is, and I go in there and stand in front of all those empty seats and force myself to imagine those bigwigs from Hollywood judging me and making me feel small and insignificant. And I focus all my energy on showing them I am *not* small or insignificant—in letting them see the real ~**laetitia**~. The one who has a date with destiny.

But I can't do it without my voice! That's kind of an important part of being a singer.

I've never experienced anything like this before, even in a nightmare. Gramma Patty says it's just a cold, nothing to worry about, and I want to believe her, but I've got to admit I'm a little nervous. My head keeps filling with all these horrible things it could be—polyps, cancer—but Gramma Patty made me gargle with salt water when I got home (blech), and now I have some hot tea with honey, and it does seem to be helping a bit. I'm going to get some rest, and hopefully, it will all be better in the morning.

In the meantime, I would really appreciate any thoughts and prayers you can send my way. This is *so* important to me, and I can use all the support I can get. Thank you!!! I love you all so much.

(/●ヮ●)/*:・゚ ✧

Thank you for all the get-well-soon notes! I checked my messages this morning, and I was overwhelmed! You guys are the greatest.

I'm happy to say my voice is much better. There were one or two creaky moments when I was rehearsing after school, but nothing like yesterday. Hallelujah.

˚ · ✿ ✌\(｡◕‿◕｡)/✿ ·˚

I was so happy I could talk and sing again, I decided to do an extraspecial ~*divanation*~ to celebrate. A pink-and-lavender wig with sparkly barrettes! Hope you like.

[photo redacted]

[photo redacted]

Since I got some new followers recently, I should explain: *divanation* is a word my best friend, Angela, made up when we were eleven, I think. It means "the process of making myself up like a diva." Turning plain old Laetitia into ~**laetitia**~, the fabulous diva who's going to rule the world with the power of her voice. I know it's silly, but it helps me be bold and confident to have this persona I put on every day. And it makes people treat me differently too. Back when I would go to school, looking ordinary, that's how everyone treated me. When I told them I was going to be a famous singer someday, they'd laugh or give me pitying looks. But when I put in a little effort every morning to look ~fabulous~, suddenly my dreams don't seem so crazy anymore. Now all my friends and teachers and everyone look at me like they see the person I am on the inside. Like they believe I'm capable of anything. And that helps, especially on days when I'm not so sure of it myself.

MONDAY, JANUARY 13, 4:17 P.M. (PUBLIC)

It happened again! My voice disappeared. Now I am seriously worried. (❀☉_☉)

Last time, I woke up the next morning and felt 1,000 percent better, and I was *so* relieved. I could talk again! And more important, I could sing! Praise be, etc. I didn't know if it was a cold or what, but all I cared about was that it was over. A little part of me wondered if that day of loss was meant to remind me to appreciate my gifts and not take them for granted, and I didn't! I went back to my rehearsing with new gratitude, and for five days everything was just fine.

Then today I got up there on the stage, opened my mouth, and *nothing*. I came straight home, and Gramma Patty sent me to bed again. She says I pushed myself too hard and didn't give myself a chance to fully recover. Maybe it's true—I do feel kind of awful. Last time it was just my voice, like someone had flicked a switch and turned it off but left the rest of me just fine. This time it's definitely more than that. I feel . . . run-down. Exhausted. A little achy, maybe. I wonder if I have a slight fever. I had strange dreams last night, and this morning I felt so low, I actually thought about going to school without doing my ~divanation~. But I can't do that—you have to have standards. And it's what people expect from me. The whole school might become demoralized if I showed up in plain braids.

Gramma Patty just brought me some more tea, and now that I've written all this out, I'm feeling a little calmer. Maybe this is just a message that I've been pushing myself too hard, and I need to rest for a while. I'm going to sleep early tonight, and I'm going to take a whole week off from singing, even if my voice comes back. That should help, and one week isn't really going to set me back for the audition. I have to remember to take care of myself.

TUESDAY, JANUARY 14, 6:15 A.M. (PUBLIC)

I just had the most terrible nightmare. I don't even know how to describe it. I know, I know, no one ever wants to hear someone describe their dreams, but . . . this wasn't like a normal dream. Not even like a normal nightmare. It was so clear and vivid—not all mixed up and confusing, the way my dreams usually are.

There wasn't really any story to it. All I remember was I was strapped down so I couldn't move at all. At first I thought I was on some kind of bed, but it wasn't really a bed. . . . It was more of an iron grate. I wasn't scared or anything. I was just like, *Oh, I guess this is what's happening now.* But then I realized someone was lighting a fire under the grate. Under *me*. And it started to get hotter and hotter until I could feel the flames tickling my skin.

And it *hurt*. I thought things weren't supposed to hurt

in dreams! I don't think I've ever experienced pain in a dream before, except when something also hurt me in real life (like when I fell out of bed that one time). But this wasn't like that. It was like I was being burned all over my body, and I could *feel* it—my skin blistering and crackling like a roasted pig.

But I didn't scream. I didn't do anything to try to save myself. Not that there was much I could have done, but I don't remember crying or struggling. It was just me and that grate and the fire. And the pain.

Then I opened my eyes and I was in my bed. I never even had a sense of waking up. It was just like I'd been living through this horrible thing, with my eyes closed, and when I opened them, I was back to myself.

I don't know. I know it was just a dream, but it shook me up, I guess. It was just so real. Part of me still feels like it really happened, even though I know that's impossible.

TUESDAY, JANUARY 14, 6:25 A.M. (PUBLIC)

That was weird.

I just got done writing up and posting my dream, but when I reloaded the page, there was this other post I don't remember making already on the blog. I mean, I *definitely* did not make that post. It was time-stamped from the middle of the night—when I was asleep!

It was just some weird photo. I have no clue where it came from. Some kind of glitch with the website, I guess? Wires crossed? ¯_(ツ)_/¯ I don't even know if that's possible, lol. But I don't know where else it could have come from, so I guess that must be it.

Anyway, I deleted it as soon as I saw it. I'm sorry if any of you out there saw it before I caught it! That's not the kind of thing I usually post at all.

TUESDAY, JANUARY 14, 6:33 A.M. (PRIVATE)

I was going to just delete that photo from the other post, but I decided to save it first. Just in case it's not a glitch. Like if it's someone who has hacked my blog and is trying to mess with me, maybe. I don't know who would do that, but you never know. . . . All kinds of crazies out there.

I thought it might be smart to save it in a locked post in case I ever needed to show it as evidence or something.

I didn't notice before, because I was panicking about a strange pic on my blog and whether it would upset people and cost me followers, but now that I look at it again, it kind of reminds me of my dream, and that metal grill I was strapped to. Isn't that strange? I mean, it must just be a coincidence. What else could it be? Gives me the shivers either way, though.

FRIDAY, JANUARY 17, 4:30 P.M. (PUBLIC)

Hey, everyone!

I just wanted to let everybody know I'm doing okay. Thank you all for your concern. I have gotten soooo many nice messages from people since my last couple of posts. You guys are the best, seriously. I know I've been kind of down lately and not like myself—some of you were worried about that dream I had, and then there was that weirdness with the picture—but you don't have to worry. I'm getting better, and I'll be back to your regularly scheduled ~divanation~ posts before you know it.

It's nice to know you care—I love you all!

Also, I hate to bring this up, but to the people who felt the need to send anon messages complaining about the "turn this blog has taken" and threatening to unfollow . . . yeah, I didn't appreciate that. This blog is a labor of love, and I haven't been feeling well, so that means I haven't been able to post my usual stuff. If hearing real stuff about what's going on in my life bothers you so much, go ahead and unfollow. Fine by me.

Okay, sorry about that. It was only a few people, but it had to be said.

Thanks again for your notes and messages! I love you all.

FRIDAY, JANUARY 17, 10:15 P.M. (PRIVATE)

I'm so sick of my blog fans making me feel guilty for living my life and wanting to share it. I thought they all supported me, but they're only here for ~**laetitia**~, not the real me. I guess that shouldn't surprise me, but I wish I had someone to talk to about what's going on.

There's Mamma and Gramma, of course, but they don't really count. They're too full of opinions on how I should lead my life, plus they'll get all worked up and worried if they think something is really wrong. I've got my crew at school, but I guess I'm realizing now that I'm not all that close to any of them. We mostly just kid around, and I never have deep, serious conversations with them.

The people I know just aren't interested in the same stuff as I am. For as long as I can remember, all I've cared about is my singing. A lot of people think that's cool, but that doesn't mean they want to hear about the hours I spend practicing every day or the techniques I'm trying to develop or the recordings I'm listening to. If I talk about that stuff, people tune out after a few minutes and change the subject to something I don't know much about: parties or movies or sports. I've learned over the years to stay quiet and just laugh at other people's jokes.

I wish Angela were still around. I miss her so much! She always had time for me. She lived across the street when I first moved here, but she moved away last summer. We were about five when we met, and back then you could just walk up to another little girl playing in her yard and be like, *We're best friends now*, and that was that. It was simpler. I remember when I first realized I was going to be a singer, I told Angela that when she grew up, she could be my manager and we would always be together. I have no idea how I even knew about managers then. I must have heard some diva talking about hers in a TV interview or something. Angela and I both thought it sounded grown-up and impressive. We'd play for hours, me as the pop diva, and her managing me. She'd dress me up and show me how to move while I sang. We were a great team.

Then Angela's mom got a new boyfriend, and they moved to another neighborhood. And I know, it's not like they moved to the other side of the universe—it's just two short bus trips away—but she goes to a different high school, and we don't see each other every day, and it's just different. She texts me sometimes or we chat online, but we don't seem to have as much in common anymore. Angela got a boyfriend, and now all our conversations are just Tre this and Tre that. She doesn't seem interested in music. Maybe she never really was, and just did all that stuff for me.

We used to talk about anything and everything. I want to be able to go across the street and tell her all the crazy stuff that's been going on, and have her listen and reassure me that I'm not just making a big deal out of nothing.

SATURDAY, JANUARY 18, 10:30 A.M. (PRIVATE)

Oh great. Now I just lost a bunch of followers. Seriously, people? Folks are damn fickle. Oh well, who cares about them anyway? Haters, etc.

Maybe I shouldn't have posted so much about being sick or losing my voice. People don't like to hear about that sort of stuff, I guess. Or maybe it wasn't even that—maybe it was that last public post I made, complaining about the anon hate I was getting. People come here, expecting positivity and sweetness. I guess I better keep it that way.

Things *have* been getting a little gloomy around here. I need to post something more in my usual style to reassure people the blog hasn't changed. But I can't sing, and I'm just not up to the hair and makeup tutorials right now. Maybe an AMA? People usually like those.

SATURDAY, JANUARY 18, 10:45 A.M. (PUBLIC)

Feeling a bit better, but I'm still resting my voice. Since I'm just
stuck here, moping about how I can't rehearse, maybe you all
can entertain me. Ask Me Anything, starting now!

Hi, Laetitia! I really love your blog! You're so fierce and ambitious and driven, I just know you're going to be a big star one day. Can you talk a little bit about how you got started as a singer? Do you take lessons or have a voice coach?—anonymous

Thank you so much for the ask, Nonny! You're so sweet.

I can't believe I never told the story on here of how I got into singing, but I can't find it in my archives. I've been singing since I was a little girl. I got handpicked out of my church congregation to join the choir when I was only seven years old, because the choir director said even from the pews, she could hear I had a voice like an angel.

†_(˚ -˚ *)β <-- me. ;)

Since then, I've had more solos than anyone in the history of our church. I love it! Most teenagers probably think going to church is a pain in the you-know-what, but I look forward to Sundays all week long. I'm never more myself than when I'm performing for people.

My deep dark secret is . . . shhhhh . . . I wasn't a *bit* surprised when I got picked that day. I know, I know! You're not supposed to admit to stuff like that. You're supposed to be all humble, like . . . what??? Little old me? But I can't lie: that's never how it's been with me. I still remember the day the choir director approached Mamma and Gramma Patty after church, and how amazed they both were that their little baby girl had been picked out of the crowd, but to me, it felt inevitable. I felt like I'd always known this was coming.

I can't really explain it. As long as I can remember, I've always had this sense I would wind up doing something really big. Something that would make people all over the world know my name. I don't know where this certainty came from. . . . It's like a little voice inside me that has always whispered that I'm special, and it's only a matter of time before the rest of the world realizes it too. Does everyone feel this way? Maybe they do. Maybe we all feel like we're special and destined for some particular kind of greatness. And I guess in a way, that's true. We're all part of God's plan, and what could be greater than that?

But for me, it's always felt a little different. Mamma likes to tell a story from when I was a baby. She says I always loved it when people cooed over me and said, "That's the most beautiful baby I've ever seen" or "Aren't you the prettiest little girl in the world?" Mamma never thought much of it. Then one day in the

345

grocery store, I heard an old woman tell some other little girl she was the sweetest thing in the whole wide world, and I went right up to the woman and said, "No, she isn't. I am!"

←~ (o ˋ ▽´)oΨ *devil grin*

I was only three when it happened, so Mamma and Gramma Patty mostly just thought it was cute, and didn't make too much of it. And I learned pretty quickly you're not supposed to say that stuff out loud. But the truth is, I still feel that way sometimes. Maybe I'm not the prettiest or the sweetest or whatever, but that little voice telling me I have a special destiny has never gone away.

For a while I wasn't sure what it would be. I thought maybe I would be an adventurer and travel the world or I'd cure some disease or be president. But the day that church lady spoke to Mamma and Gramma Patty, I knew I was born to be a singer. My voice was the thing that made me special, and someday everyone in the world would be able to see me the way I had always seen myself.

But of course that doesn't mean I've just been sitting here, waiting for the world to beat a path to my door! I know it doesn't work like that. *I* may have always known I was special, but if I'm going to convince the rest of the world, I know I have to pay my dues and put some real work in. So even as a little kid, I practiced every day. I just started singing all the time, and I'd sing along with my favorite songs, and every time I found a note I couldn't hit or a rhythm I couldn't copy, I'd work and work at it until I did. I've never had a teacher or a coach, other than the church choir director, but I know I've worked as hard as any singer out there.

And thanks to that, my voice is so much stronger and clearer than it used to be. My pitch is more accurate, my range extended. I know there are still better singers in the world than I am, but I think I'm ready for my shot now. I want the world to hear me! But I just have to be patient a little while longer, and practice and train all I can, so when my chance comes, I can really blow them away.

SATURDAY, JANUARY 18, 12:30 P.M. (PUBLIC)

I love your style and aesthetic, and your voice is so beautiful. Do you ever write your own songs? It would probably help you get your big break if you did. It seems like all the biggest singers write their own lyrics.—[username redacted]

Thank you—you are so sweet! Actually, there is a long tradition of singers and songwriters being two separate callings. A lot of my idols never wrote a word or a note, but they put so much passion into their singing that it became an art form. Right now I want to focus on training my voice, because I feel like that's what I have to offer the world. Other people may have the gift of writing lyrics or composing, but maybe they can't sing. We all have our callings, and mine is to give a voice to the words and music that might be someone else's calling.

˚ · ✿ ˇ\(｡◕‿◕｡)/✿ · ˚

SATURDAY, JANUARY 18, 12:42 P.M. (PRIVATE)

I think that's the third (fourth?) time someone has asked me on the blog why I don't write my own songs. It's pretty annoying, to be honest. Yes, I realize that's the fashion now, but I don't know how! It's not that I haven't tried coming up with some lyrics; it's just that they're all terrible. I mean really bad. I don't even know what to write about. In church we sing all these praise songs, and they're beautiful, but there's nothing I could add to those. I'd be ashamed if I wrote something silly and stupid and then tried to offer it to God. That doesn't seem right.

And then there are love songs, which are what most pop songs are and what most people want to listen to, but it's not like I have a lot of experience in that area. I can't write about deep, passionate love. And besides, I'd be way too embarrassed

to sing about anything so personal. I like singing, not writing—
what's wrong with that? I have one gift, and I just want to make
it the best I can. Why does everyone want me to be something
I'm not?

My week of rest is almost up, and I have been *really* good about going to bed early every night, eating well, and not singing, not even in the shower. Hopefully, when I start rehearsing again this week, everything will be back to normal!

Except I'm not sure I'm getting better. I don't exactly *feel* better. I thought, after all this rest, I would be full of energy, but even though I try to fight it, I feel worse than ever. I've been dragging myself through school every day, like --> (。-_-。).

I've also been kind of sick to my stomach all week, except when it lets up for a bit and I'm suddenly *starving*. What is this? The flu? I really hope it gets better soon. Maybe I've been resting *too* much, and that's what's making me feel bad. I just need to get back to rehearsing, and I'm sure I'll feel better.

By the way, thank you all for your thoughts and prayers—it means so much to me to have your support. Sorry I haven't felt up to posting any hair and makeup tutorials lately. I'm just too worn-down.

SUNDAY, JANUARY 19, 9:20 P.M.
CHAT LOG

angela: hey. you there?

laetitia: hey, girl! i was just thinking about you the other day!

laetitia: i miss you so much!

angela: i miss you too.

angela: i saw tre talking to another girl today. i don't know what to do.

laetitia: about what?

angela: about tre!

laetitia: oh. he was just talking to her, right? that doesn't seem like that big a deal.

angela: maybe. that's what lisa said. but then tasha said tre's only been with me less than a month, and he shouldn't even be looking at other girls when he could be looking at me.

laetitia: i guess.

angela: or am i just making a huge deal out of nothing?

laetitia: maybe . . . ?

angela: well, which is it??? geez, don't you even have an opinion?

laetitia: come on. you know i don't know about this stuff. plus i'm not feeling well.

angela: why, what's wrong?

laetitia: lost my voice.

angela: what? like, you're sick?

laetitia: idk. i can talk, still. . . . . it's just my singing voice. i can't sing *at all*.

angela: wow, that sucks. worried about your audition? you're still doing that, right?

laetitia: hope so. idk. not if my voice doesn't come back.

laetitia: plus it's not just that. i've been having these really scary dreams. only . . .

angela: what?

laetitia: don't call me crazy, okay?

angela: ha-ha, of course not.

laetitia: sometimes i wake up with, like, bruises or sores where i got hurt during my dream. and they hurt really bad when i press on them. sort of a burning feeling.

angela: maybe don't press on them??

laetitia: ha-ha. yeah, that makes sense.

angela: don't worry, babe. you'll be fine. you're just anxious about your audition, but you're gonna be great! you always are.

laetitia: thanks.

angela: oh no, tre's online. should i talk to him?

laetitia: idk . . . probably?

angela: okay, i'm going to ask him about that girl. talk later!

TUESDAY, JANUARY 21, 4:40 P.M. (PUBLIC)

I guess I really must be exhausted still. I think I fell asleep on the bus. I've never done that before. Usually I'm up, chattering away with people or texting with Mamma or listening to music. Today I couldn't seem to do anything but just sit there and stare out the window. Then, one second I was looking out the window at the streets I've seen a million times before, and the next, I guess my eyes had closed, because the scene was totally different. There was a crowd of people all yelling at me. I couldn't make out the words, but I knew they were saying terrible things about me, like I had committed some awful crime. In front of me, lying flat on a platform, there was a giant wheel, like maybe for an old wagon or something . . . only there were sharp spikes all over it.

Then I was grabbed from behind and turned around, and the next thing I knew, I was being strapped across this wheel.

I knew I was being punished for my crime, and even though I couldn't remember what I had done, I didn't fight or struggle. I just accepted that I deserved the punishment, like last time.

That's when they started beating me. I couldn't see who—I don't know if I had closed my eyes in the dream or if I was too focused on the pain to notice anything else. I'm not sure I've ever felt something so awful. They were beating my arms and legs with hammers and clubs, and I could feel the bones shattering under the skin.

I don't know how long I sat there like that. The bus ride isn't long, but I'm not sure if it was, like, a second or a couple of minutes. In the dream, it felt like forever. It felt like days. I was just lost in pain and hopelessness.

Who knows how long it might have gone on like that, except one of my friends said she noticed me sitting there, whimpering and crying a little, my eyes closed. She touched my shoulder and asked if I was okay, and I snapped out of it. The weird thing is, I wasn't slumped down in my seat like I was sleeping. She said I had been sitting up straight, my whole body rigid and twitching. And when my eyes snapped open, for a second I didn't even know who she was. I felt like I'd been in another world.

So weird to have two of these dreams in a row like this. Are they related to my other problems? If all this is really just the flu, then I guess maybe they could be fever dreams. Except I don't feel like I have a fever.

TUESDAY, JANUARY 21, 3:50 P.M. (PRIVATE)

TUESDAY, JANUARY 21, 4:50 P.M. (PRIVATE)

What is this??? Another weird photo? I just posted that thing about my dream, and it was there. I think I caught it and locked it up as a private post before anyone saw it. Lord, this is the last thing I need to deal with right now. It can't just be a glitch, can it? I dream about being tortured on an iron grill, and a picture of a grill appears. I dream about being beaten within an inch of my life on some wheel, and this shows up? Someone must be reading my posts and then hacking into my account to mess with me. But how? And why? I've never done anything to hurt or offend anyone, I don't think.

Also, both times these pictures have looked like they were posted *before* I made my dream descriptions. How could that be? Is my secret enemy psychic or something? It can't be that. They must just be playing with the time stamps somehow.

It's really creeping me out, though. This blog has always been a safe space for me, where I can get support and encouragement. It used to be a great pick-me-up when I'd had a bad day, to come on here and see people liking and reblogging my stuff and sending me fan mail. It made me feel like I was worth something. It's awful for someone to attack it like this now, when I'm already feeling scared and sick and helpless.

I'm not sure what to do. I guess I'll send a message to the support staff, to see if they can tell me what's going on. And in the meantime, I'll change my password. Maybe that will help.

FRIDAY, JANUARY 24, 5:20 P.M. (PRIVATE)

I just realized I lost a bunch more followers this week. Nice.
Let people see a side of you that is anything but cheerful and
upbeat, and they start to jump ship. I wonder if this has anything to do with that photo. I thought I had caught it quickly,
but maybe some people did see it and then decide I've lost it.
It probably doesn't help that it's been a while since I've posted
normal photos, like selfies.

People see one thing they don't like, and they are so quick
to unfollow! It should have been obvious it was a mistake or a
glitch and nothing to do with me. Anyone who's been following
me for a while knows I do *not* post stuff like that. You'd think
they'd give me the benefit of the doubt, or maybe message me
to ask if I'm feeling okay.

Maybe I should have been keeping up better with my

in-box. There are a bunch of messages in there about the dream I posted. Some of my followers are just concerned, but of course I can't get away from assholes who are like, *I followed you for makeup tips; I am not interested in your creepy-ass dreams.* Thanks for your support! Maybe it was dumb to post that kind of thing. I know everyone always hates dream posts—I've made fun of them myself—but I thought these were more interesting. Well, they were interesting to *me*. And isn't this journal supposed to be about me and my life?

Ha. That's not how anyone else sees it.

Maybe I better make another video, or at least post some selfies, before I lose any more followers. People are used to things being positive and uplifting around here. I guess if I ever want to talk about my not-so-good days, I should stick to private posts.

SATURDAY, JANUARY 25, 9:10 A.M. (PUBLIC)

Still resting my voice! But I thought I'd share a few pics of my look for today. I'll write up instructions for it soon, I swear.

[photo redacted]
[photo redacted]
[photo redacted]

Hope you like it! If so, show me some love! My ask box is always open.

SATURDAY, JANUARY 25, 10:40 A.M. (PUBLIC)

Hi, Laetitia! I just want to say that you are my style *icon*. I love that you are representing for beautiful, proud black women. I was just wondering: how did you get started wearing colored wigs? Did you just go for it one day, or was it more of a gradual thing? And what do you do on days when you don't have the time or energy for all that styling?—[username redacted]

Are you suggesting I was not *born* with different color hair every day??

(✿‿‿)

Jkjk. You're right: there is an origin story to this look. When I was a little kid, I wore my hair in braids, like all the other girls in my classes. Then one summer I went away to camp and I came home with a bad case of head lice, and Mamma had to shave off all my hair. I cried and cried! My head didn't feel right, and whenever I looked in the mirror, I didn't recognize myself.

Gramma Patty tried to make me feel better by wrapping my head in scarves, which helped. Then one day I was watching some cartoon where the heroine had beautiful sparkly purple hair, and I turned to Mamma and I said that when my hair grew back, I wanted it to look like that. And Mamma smiled and said I didn't have to wait for it. She walked me to the store, and right in the toy aisle they had this bright pink costume wig with sparkly strands in it. It was cheap and tacky and ugly as sin, but I fell in love with it.

I wore it every day for a month, until it fell to pieces. I cried over it, but for my birthday, Mamma got me another—better quality this time. And that's how it began.

Right from the beginning, it changed so much about me. I loved the way people noticed me in school. People could finally see on the outside how special I'd always felt on the inside. Eventually I moved on to fancier, better-made wigs, though they're all synthetic. I save up and get new ones on birthdays and holidays. And after a while I started experimenting with makeup, too, to complete the look.

We're all starring in the TV show of our lives, and I want to be a real ~*☆star☆*~. When I started making myself up that way, some folks thought I was crazy; some folks threw shade. But mostly it made people take me more seriously when I said I was going to be a ~*pop diva*~ when I grew up. Like they could see it now.

The only person who still doesn't love it is Gramma Patty. Most days she lets it slide, but I know she doesn't approve. She says it's prideful, and that I should be happy with the hair and face God gave me. That I should dress more modestly, instead of trying to look like a peacock all the time. But Mamma is on my side. She's always had a flair for the dramatic, and everyone says I get it from her. She says if my body is a temple, then putting on some extra decorations is a way of honoring and celebrating it. And she says if it makes me happy, it makes God happy too. But who knows what makes God happy? I'll worry about that in the next life. This life is for me.

SATURDAY, JANUARY 25, 11:02 P.M. (PRIVATE)

Something is really wrong. What is going on with me? I didn't want to make too big a deal out of a couple of nightmares, because I knew if I tried to tell Mamma or Gramma Patty about them, they'd just brush them off as bad dreams. I mean, I know they'd care and be sympathetic, but what are you going to do about a bad dream? Everyone gets them sometimes, especially if you're not sleeping well when you're sick. I could already hear Gramma Patty's voice in my head, saying something sensible like that. And I tried to convince myself that was the truth. However scary it felt from the inside, a nightmare is really no big deal. Even one you have in the middle of the day that makes you cry from very real pain.

But this is different. I definitely wasn't asleep this time. I was in the shower! Everything was basically normal, except I'd been feeling a little sick to my stomach, but that's not unusual these days. I closed my eyes to wash my hair, and there it was. I didn't exactly see anything, but I became overcome by this intense fear that someone was going to kill me. And I'm just standing there, quietly freaking out, and then I feel . . . I don't know what the hell it was, but I've never felt pain like that. I seriously thought I'd just been shot in the leg. Except that's crazy, right? How do you get shot in the shower? The shower door was still there, and it's not like there are any windows.

I would have fallen over right then, but something was supporting me. I felt my muscles and bones give way, but instead of sinking to the floor of the shower, I just sort of hung there, as if invisible ropes were holding me up. Then there was another shot, this time in my hip. And another in my shoulder. I thought I would faint from the pain.

Finally I couldn't take it anymore, and I cried out. More like shrieked, actually. Mamma and Gramma Patty came barging in to see if I was okay, and that's when I finally opened my eyes. The other times, opening my eyes made everything okay again. The world went back to normal and the pain went away. But not this time. I looked down, and there was blood everywhere. Right where I'd felt those shots. Not just blood—I could see things sticking out of me, like wooden rods. Like I'd been shot through with arrows.

When I saw that, I really started screaming. And Mamma was trying to calm me down, and I was babbling at her, trying to explain what had happened, except how could I possibly explain it? Then I looked down again and there was no blood. There were no arrows. Not even a mark anywhere on my skin. Just me, standing there, shivering and naked, the shower still running, and Mamma trying to calm me down and get me into a robe.

What must she think of me now? She must think I've lost my mind. And why should I think any different? This doesn't happen to normal people. I saw in her eyes how worried she was, but she didn't want to scare me. She just put me to bed and told me to relax and get some rest.

I tried to sleep, but every time I closed my eyes, I kept seeing that blood again, and those arrows, long and thick, sticking out of me. So I got up and decided to write about it. Maybe that will help shake those images free from my brain.

This time, I'm just going to post this as a locked entry. That way my little stalker troll won't be able to mess with my head by posting some picture of whatever is scaring me. It's no big loss. I don't think any of my followers really like hearing about this stuff, anyway.

SATURDAY, JANUARY 25, 10:25 P.M. (PRIVATE)

SATURDAY, JANUARY 25, 11:10 P.M. (PRIVATE)

Holy Jesus . . .

How is that even possible? It happened again, just like before: one minute I hit post; the next minute I go to my blog to see the new post and there's a photo waiting for me. I swear, it wasn't there before, but the time stamp is from right when I was in the shower. Right when I was having that . . . whatever it was.

I just switched the post to private, but it posted as public originally, which means more people saw it. And this photo isn't just weird and random; it's really disturbing. People are going to have conniptions in my message box over this. I guess I better apologize again! This is becoming a habit. Who's even going to believe at this point that it's not my fault? They probably all think I'm doing this on purpose.

I just don't understand it. How can this troll still be messing with me? Where are these pictures coming from??? And why does it always seem like they're pictures from inside my own head? It's almost like my thoughts are projecting them onto my blog. But that's *really* crazy.

I need to tell someone what's going on, but I don't even know how to describe it.

I'm really, really sorry—to anyone who might have seen that horrible picture. I swear, I had nothing to do with it! I've changed my password and sent e-mails to the support staff, but nothing seems to help. Has anyone else out there had this problem? Has the site been acting up for you all in other ways? Or does anyone have experience with hackers that might be helpful? I'm kind of desperate at this point.

Anyway, I'm really sorry if anyone saw that and was traumatized by it. Believe me, I feel the same way. I will totally understand if any of you feel like you have to unfollow me after that. I wish I could guarantee there will never be anything like that on this blog again, but at this point . . . I don't know if I can.

SUNDAY, JANUARY 26, 9:18 A.M. (PRIVATE)

So I switched the default posting style for this blog to private. That way, if any more of the creepy photos appear, at least I'll be the only one who sees them. I think, in a way, they're not meant for my followers. They're really meant for me.

I just can't deal with worrying all the time if some horrible picture is going to pop up while I'm not looking, and get people all upset. Besides, there isn't much point in my having a public blog these days. I'm not singing, and I can't be bothered to do ~divanation~ tutorials anymore. I just have other stuff on my mind. And my followers let me know loud and clear that they're not interested in the stuff I've been dealing with lately. All those people who I thought were my friends and fans, people I thought loved and admired me, they're pretty much all gone now, except for a handful that are probably all bots or abandoned blogs.

Anyway, I'm tired of writing for them and trying to keep them happy. I don't have the space in my mind right now to worry about that stuff, and I don't really feel like sharing. I need someplace to work through what's going on in my life, and I don't need hundreds of people watching me while I do it. Maybe someday I'll feel comfortable writing publicly again, like if my voice comes back, but for now I feel better and safer this way.

You know what's weird, though? I keep logging in just to look at those bizarre photos. I saved them all because I thought it was a good idea to keep a record of them, but now, even though they really upset me at first, I find myself fascinated by them.

It's so strange, because I *never* went looking for stuff like that before. I know some people enjoy gory or scary or weird things, but that wasn't me. I only wanted stuff in my life that made me feel happy and positive and joyful. So why am I drawn to them now? Well, I guess it kind of makes sense—it's not every day you get to see pictures from the inside of your own head.

Wow. Is that really what I think it is? I know I said that before, but it can't honestly be that, right? Still, I don't know what else it is. I've spent hours online, trying to find the source of these pictures. Looking for anyone on this site or any other who took the original photo, or even just reblogged it. But I can't find them anywhere. It's like they materialized out of the air. Or, like I said before, out of my brain. But no, I don't even want to think about that. It's too creepy.

MONDAY, JANUARY 27, 6:15 P.M. (PRIVATE)

I fainted in school today. I'm not even sure how it happened. I've just been feeling so bad lately. I was climbing the stairs to go to biology and I was feeling queasy, but that's nothing new. Then my vision went black and my knees were wobbly, and it was like I was back in those dreams again, except all the pain was coming at me together. Burning, beating, piercing, all coming over me in waves.

The next thing I knew, I was waking up on the floor, a crowd of people around me, and I had a nasty bump on my head. Gramma Patty had to come pick me up from the nurse's office and take me home. She sent me up to bed, even though I was already feeling a lot better. Then when Mamma got home from work, she made such a fuss! She asked me, like, a million questions about how I've been feeling, and am I tender or sore anywhere, and what have I eaten, even though she knows very well what I eat, since we eat most of our meals together.

Then finally she came out with it. What she'd been hinting at ever since she got home. She asked me if I was pregnant. Me! Of course I got all embarrassed and was like, *Mamma, I don't even have a boyfriend.* Then she pointed out that you don't exactly need a boyfriend to get pregnant. She didn't have a boyfriend when she had me. Fine, yes, point taken. But this is different. I tried to convince her that my having a baby was a biological impossibility, but it barely slowed her down. She just kept ranting about me throwing away all my dreams over some boy, and how she had prayed and prayed I wouldn't make the same mistakes she did, and I have so much potential, and on and on and on. Finally I told her I'd let Gramma Patty take me to the doctor tomorrow to get checked out, just to put her mind at ease. Maybe a doctor can at least help me figure out what this is and why my voice has been so unreliable lately. Mamma is fixated on the whole pregnancy thing, but honestly I'm scared it's something much worse.

laetitia: angela, you there?

angela: yeah, i've been meaning to talk to you. i found out about that girl tre was talking to.

angela: it's his ex-girlfriend's little sister. doesn't that seem suspicious?

laetitia: idk. maybe. listen, can we talk? something really weird just happened.

angela: what's up?

laetitia: i passed out in school today.

angela: omg! are you okay?

laetitia: i think so, but that's not even the weird part. after i came to, i started to feel better, but my skin felt all weird and itchy. this weird sharp and itchy feeling in places all over my body. i tried to ignore it, but it kept bothering me.

    angela: what is it? a rash or something?

    laetitia: that's what i thought. so when i got home, i got undressed to take a shower, and i immediately felt better, except i had these weird pink sores on my skin. and i picked up my clothes and shook them, and look what came out.

    angela: laetitia, what is this?

    laetitia: what does it look like?

    angela: it looks like a pile of feathers. are you saying there were feathers in your clothes?

laetitia: i don't know! i mean, i guess so. but where could they have come from?

angela: lol, i have no idea. maybe someone stuffed some feathers down your shirt while you were passed out.

laetitia: omg, seriously? who would do that?

angela: i don't know. what else could it be?

angela: you still there?

laetitia: yeah.

laetitia: don't laugh, okay?

angela: okay . . .

laetitia: i sort of feel like they came out of my skin.

angela: laetitia.

angela: what?

angela: i'm not laughing. but you know that's crazy, right?

laetitia: i know how it sounds, yeah. idk, maybe it is crazy. i just needed to tell someone. my gramma patty is taking me to the doctor. . . . should i tell her about it?

angela: no.

laetitia: what? why not?

angela: because the doctor will think you are legit crazy! you can't go around telling people you're turning into a damn bird.

laetitia: i didn't say that!

angela: you wanted my advice, right? don't tell the doctor; don't tell anyone. just ignore it. someone probably did something with the feathers to mess with you, and your imagination got carried away.

laetitia: you really think so?

angela: yeah. listen, i'm your friend, and you can trust me. but don't tell this story to anyone else unless you want them to think you've lost your damn mind.

WEDNESDAY, JANUARY 29, 9:15 P.M. (PRIVATE)

Surprise, surprise, the doctor says I'm not pregnant! This was not exactly news to me, but at least it gets Mamma off my back. As for what *is* going on with my body, no real help there. Dr. Afolabi looked at my throat and said it seems a little irritated, even though my white blood cells look normal. She said to keep gargling with salt water, make sure I'm eating and sleeping enough, and I should feel better soon. They're doing some tests for thyroid stuff and an iron deficiency and I don't remember what else, so maybe those will turn something up. I can't decide if that would make me feel better or worse. She asked me if I had any other symptoms, and I almost told her about the strange bruises and sores, but then I remembered how Angela had reacted to the feathers, and I decided not to even go down that road. They've faded by now, anyway.

I guess all I can do now is try to get some sleep and hope I don't have any more weird nightmares.

WEDNESDAY, FEBRUARY 5, 4:20 P.M. (PRIVATE)

Haven't written in a while. I've been avoiding this journal because I didn't want to admit what's going on. I thought if I just acted like everything was normal, things might actually *be* normal. I didn't want to admit things are getting worse, not better.

I feel *really* sick lately. Not just when I wake up, but all the time, which is making it hard to eat right. Even looking at food makes me want to puke my guts up, though I've only given in a couple of times. And I'm tired *all* the time, and sleeping ten or even twelve hours a night. This isn't like me at all! I don't understand what's the matter.

The doctor's blood tests all came back normal. The weird thing is, if I didn't know who I'd been spending my nights with (no one), I'd almost start to wonder if I *were* pregnant. I definitely feel . . . I don't know. Different. I get hot and cold flashes, or I feel like little bolts of electricity are shooting through me. Or like there's a strange thrumming beneath my skin. It feels like I'm changing, or growing somehow.

And through all this, I still don't understand what's going on with my singing voice. It's not like the first time. My speaking voice is fine, but when I go to sing . . . Well, I guess it's a little better than it was. It's not that nothing comes out, but the most I can do is a kind of throaty, breathy warble. It's not at all like my usual crystal-clear pitch. And I can hardly produce more than a whisper, when I used to be able to belt big enough to fill the whole church, even without a microphone.

Last Sunday I had to sit out during choir again, and after church the director told me she assigned my solo parts to someone else. She seemed really apologetic, and she said I could have my spot back as soon as I was feeling better. I know she's just doing what she has to do, and I tried to be mature about it in front of her, but when I got home, I just cried and cried. Mamma and Gramma Patty didn't even try to make me talk about it or cheer me up. They understood I needed to let myself be sad about it for a while.

THURSDAY, FEBRUARY 6, 4:30 P.M. (PRIVATE)

I did something strange when I was walking home from the bus stop today. I saw this dead animal lying in the road, and I stopped to look at it. Is that weird? Normally if I saw something like that, I'd shudder and look away as fast as I could, and just keep walking and try not to think about it. Like Mamma says, there's no point in inviting negativity into your life. Better to stay focused on the positive.

But today, I don't know. Maybe it's because I haven't been feeling well, but I was drawn to the animal. And as I looked at it, I realized it reminded me of something I couldn't quite place. Actually it kind of reminded me of those weird pictures that have been appearing on my blog. I don't know why—it didn't look anything like those pictures—but something about this dead animal just brought those other images back to my mind. Like they were *connected* somehow.

And as soon as I'd had that thought, I pulled out my phone and started taking pictures of it. I never do that. Pretty much the only photos I ever take are selfies to post on my blog. I'm very good at that, getting all my best angles and the best lighting and everything, but I don't know the first thing about photographing anything else. But for some reason I just wanted to take this image home with me and preserve it.

When I got home, the first thought I had was to post it up on my blog. But that's a terrible idea! I've just spent all this time and energy trying to reassure people that those weird pictures that kept showing up had *nothing* to do with me, and now I want to add to them? It doesn't even make sense, but it was this weird urge. I don't know. I guess I just wanted to share it with someone. I wanted to know if other people saw something strange and beautiful in it too.

But all my posts are private now anyway, so I wound up showing it to Gramma Patty instead, because she was sitting in the kitchen when I got home. She said it was disgusting, and she didn't know why I'd want to waste my time on something ugly and twisted. So that's that, I guess.

She's right, though. I don't know what I thought I was doing. I don't know why I'd even want something so morbid on my blog! I've always used this blog as a place for inspiration and positivity, to help me reach all my goals. I don't know how some gross animal carcass is supposed to help me with any of that.

THURSDAY, FEBRUARY 6, 11:06 P.M. (PRIVATE)

I've been thinking more about that picture I posted. I'm still not sure why I was drawn to something that is so *not me*, but maybe that's exactly what I liked about it. I've always had a really strong sense of who I am—more than most teenagers, I think. I'm a singer; my voice is who I am. It's what people know me for; it's why people like me.

But now that my voice isn't so reliable, what does that say about me? About my identity? It's like my whole sense of self is falling apart.

So, in a weird way, doing something so different from normal for me is kind of a comfort, like maybe there's a way I can continue to exist, even without my voice. Though I'm not sure what sort of life photographing dead animals prepares me for. . . .

SUNDAY, FEBRUARY 9, 8:16 A.M. (PRIVATE)

I tried to plead illness to get out of church today, but Mamma and Gramma Patty are making me go. The truth is, it hurts to go and watch everyone else perform when I know I should be up there with them. What's the point of church if I can't sing?

I mean, I believe in God. But it feels . . . distant. For Mamma, if the bus is two minutes late, or if they have the flavor of ice cream she likes at the store, that's all God speaking directly to her. And Gramma Patty, she hardly gets up to do the dishes without praying about it first. When I was a kid, I thought that was normal. It was the only thing I knew. But I've kind of outgrown it now, and it's just not how I see the world. Worrying about God is like worrying about politics—a lot of people take it really seriously, but ultimately I can't change anything, and none of it is going to make a difference in my life anyway. So what's the point of going to church every week? To prove to God you're a good person? Surely He has more important things to think about.

When I tried that argument, Gramma Patty said church isn't for God; it's for you. It's for people to find a bit of peace and calm before they start the week, to help them find strength and focus on what's important. Maybe that makes sense for her, but I just don't feel I get a lot out of it. On the other hand, I don't have it in me right now to start a fight about it, so I guess I'll just go. I'll try not to cringe when Chrissie Mathers screeches out *my* solo.

SUNDAY, FEBRUARY 9, 11:17 A.M. (PRIVATE)

Well, I'm glad I let them drag me to church. In all my angsting over losing my place in the choir, I forgot there's another reason to spend my Sundays in that overheated hall: cute boys. One cute boy in particular. His name's Malcolm, and I see him around school. Sometimes I even catch his eye, but usually I'm so busy with choir stuff at church that I don't have any chance to interact with him. This time, I was moping around with Mamma and Gramma Patty as they made the usual after-church rounds, saying hi to everyone from the neighborhood, when I realized Malcolm was standing right next to me. I couldn't think of anything to say. He asked me what I thought of the sermon, and I honestly had not been paying attention at all. I'd just been brooding about the girl who'd taken my place in the choir, whose voice is definitely not as good as mine, and who really has no sense of style or flair whatsoever.

I couldn't exactly admit that to Malcolm. I don't know him well, but I sort of remembered he's a very serious person, if you know what I mean. He follows the news and politics, and he has a lot of opinions on "the world situation." I'm no airhead, but with everything I put into singing and my dreams for a career, I just don't have a ton of time or energy for that stuff. But I do have time for cute boys! So I did my best to keep up with him. I racked my brain and remembered the pastor had been talking about this trial that's been in the news a bunch. I've heard Mamma and Gramma Patty talk about it a few times too, but I was only half paying attention. It's something to do with Dwayne Robinson, who grew up not too far from here, just a couple of neighborhoods over. My high school's sports teams play his. He was shot dead a couple of months ago by police, and the whole city has been in an uproar ever since. They even put the cops on trial for murder. But that's all I really remembered.

So Malcolm was asking me what I thought of the sermon, and I was like, "It was okay, I guess. Pretty good. Made sense." I was trying not to say anything too specific and give away that I had hardly been paying attention, but that was apparently the wrong answer, because Malcolm got this look and was like, "Pretty good?"

I guess the point of the sermon had been that everyone should stay calm and let the justice system do its job, and just pray justice takes its course. It seemed to me like a pretty reasonable position, but not according to Malcolm. He said the last thing we can expect from the legal system is justice, and history suggests we can't much trust God, either. That struck me as a pretty nervy thing to say in church. Lucky for him, he wasn't standing near his mother, because I know she would have smacked him on the back of the head for talking like that.

Then Malcolm said, "We better get ready, because if the jury doesn't come back with a guilty verdict, the whole city is going to go up in flames."

That seemed a little excessive to me. How is violence going to help violence? And don't we have to trust the system to do its job?

But Malcolm looked pretty unimpressed by that argument. He said the police are just going to keep murdering innocent kids until the people rise up and do something about it. So I asked, "How can you be sure he's innocent? We weren't there. We can't know what really happened that night."

He just stared at me and then asked, "You haven't watched the video?" I felt dumb then because, once he mentioned it, I remembered I'd heard people talking about it. I saw links to it online and stuff. But no, I'd never clicked through and watched it, because it seemed too morbid. I usually avoid anything that might be violent or sad or upsetting. And it didn't have anything to do with me. I don't know! I had other stuff on my mind.

But now that I'm not singing, I guess I don't have so much other stuff to occupy me. And I am kind of curious what Malcolm was talking about. I guess I could check it out.

SUNDAY, FEBRUARY 9, 11:55 A.M. (PRIVATE)

I just watched the video.

Lord . . . now I feel really bad about that conversation with Malcolm. I don't know how anyone can pretend not to see what's going on in the video. Basically, Dwayne is sitting on his front steps when the cops roll up and get out of their car and start asking him questions. They say they received a call, and he says he doesn't know anything about that. He's got a paper bag set between his knees, and one cop asks, "What's in the bag?" and Dwayne says, "What?" The cop asks again: "What's in the bag?" and Dwayne says, "It's peanuts." He reaches into the bag to show them, and the next thing you can see, he's lying there, shot in the chest.

Turns out, the bag was full of peanuts. The cops were

answering a domestic violence complaint, but they had the wrong address.

I'm not sure when I've ever seen anything so awful. I can't help but feel like a shallow idiot, spending my whole life thinking about myself and my singing and my dreams, and completely ignoring what's going on around me. Something like this can happen right in my own community, and I just think, *Oh, that has nothing to do with me.*

It's got me wondering, *Is it completely selfish and pointless to devote my life to singing?* I've always assumed singing was what I was put on Earth to do. Why would God give me this voice if He didn't want me to use it? But now I'm not so sure. What if singing is a distraction? Or what if God didn't give it to me at all? People noticed my voice when I was a little kid, but to be honest, it wasn't all that great then. Just good for a kid. What really made me a strong singer was how much I practiced—rehearsing and rehearsing every day, sometimes for hours. And listening to other singers, experimenting with different techniques, all kinds of stuff like that. God didn't do that; *I* did that. What if it was all a waste of time?

But on the other hand, people have been singing in churches for hundreds, even thousands of years. There must be a reason for that. And I see it when I look out at the congregation, or even when I look around me at people's faces when I go to a pop concert. It gives people joy. Hope, even. People want to live in this world because there are songs in it. And that's not such a bad thing, is it?

I feel very confused right now. If I'm meant to be singing, why can't I sing anymore? And if I'm meant to be doing something else, what is it? I can't do anything for Dwayne now, and

I'm not sure what I could do to stop more things like that from happening in the future. Malcolm seems to have everything all figured out, but I just don't know. And what if I'm not "meant to be" doing anything at all? I believe in God because I always have, and I know it's important to Mamma and Gramma Patty, but for myself? It's not like I have any proof. If I'm honest with myself, I can imagine a world in which there is no God. It doesn't even bother me that much. But then, if this is all there is, what's the point of it all? What if there is no point?

Ugh, I'm giving myself a headache. Enough deep thoughts for tonight. I need to get some sleep.

TUESDAY, FEBRUARY 11, 9:30 P.M. (PRIVATE)

I don't want to jinx myself, but I've been feeling a little better the last couple of days. I still have that weird thrumming feeling under my skin, but now it's less connected to feeling queasy and light-headed. It feels more like a kind of energy, like I'm warming up to run a race. It's definitely easier to get up in the mornings. I'm still too nervous to try out my voice, though. I get so worried I'll open my mouth and nothing will come out, it seems easier just to not try.

I'm thinking about it, though.

The shower is so weirdly gross these days. Mamma is in an all-out war with the mildew on the shower door. She goes in and washes it down with bleach or ammonia or whatever chemical she can think of to get rid of it. Then I jump into a nice, shiny clean shower, and an hour later that gross gunk is back worse than ever. Mamma is pissed about it! She says nothing should be able to survive after what she sprayed in there, but I keep bringing it back to life somehow.

I sang a few times this week. Not like old times, but I did have *some* voice at least. Maybe it's getting stronger.

I don't know. I'm trying so hard to stay optimistic and look on the bright side of everything, like Gramma Patty says. She says sulking around about how bad things are never helped anyone. And since the doctor seems to think my problem is all in my head, then if I can just force myself to be cheerful and upbeat, I'll be able to make myself better. That's the theory, anyway.

But I'm not sure I can do it. My voice is better, but it's not what it was, and at this rate I don't know how I'm going to prepare for that audition. I still feel weird all the time. Sometimes it's a good kind of weird, and sometimes it feels bad, and sometimes it's just . . . weird, and I don't know *how* to describe it.

This morning I woke up from bad dreams and had this

awful pain in my side, sort of over my ribs. It was like before, with the weird visions, except this time it felt like all the pain from those had been concentrated into this one spot, burning, breaking, piercing. I was convinced there must be some horrible wound or injury there, but when I lifted up my pajama top, it looked totally normal, though when I touched it, the pain was so awful, I nearly passed out. But after a minute of deep breathing, my ribs started to feel better.

I don't know if this is related to the other stuff, or something else entirely. It's not bothering me too much now though, at least.

Also, I took some more pictures on the way home from school. I'm kind of getting into this photography thing. It's not the same as singing—it doesn't feel like the kind of thing that will make me a ~*star*~—but it's interesting, and it makes me look around my neighborhood with new eyes. I see all kinds of weirdly beautiful things I never noticed before.

SATURDAY, FEBRUARY 15, 5:34 P.M. (PRIVATE)

I saw Renee today. She always manages to cheer me up. She had to cancel last month's appointment for something and we never managed to reschedule, so I guess it had been longer than usual since I've seen her.

Renee feels like the cool aunt I never had. It's easy to forget she's actually Mamma's caseworker. Actually, I guess she's responsible for our whole family. It's funny to think of it that way, though. Technically I know it's her job to come check in on us now and then, but she always feels more like an old family friend. She's been coming around almost as long as I can remember.

I was about three or four, I think, when Mamma had her incident. "Lost her head," as she likes to say. Gramma Patty said it was bound to happen. Back then Mamma was living with a friend and working two jobs and trying to take care of me at the same time. She went through a bad patch, missed some bills, got evicted, and I got put in foster care. But Mamma moved in with Gramma Patty and got herself together, and after a few months they said she could have me back on the condition that she kept living with Gramma Patty. And that's how we've been ever since. It works fine, and we've never had any more problems, but Renee still comes by every month or so just to check in and make sure everything is going smoothly.

I usually look forward to our meetings. Renee likes to talk to us each separately, so she'll pick me up and take me to a diner nearby and buy me a slice of pie while we talk. I tell her whatever is going on in my life, and she listens and sometimes gives advice. She's always been really supportive of my singing dreams, even early on when other people laughed at me. She says it's important for everyone to have people who believe in them.

Anyway, it was nice to talk to her about everything that's been going on with me lately. Mamma and Gramma Patty are too close to the situation for me to trust their reactions, Angela doesn't really believe me, and the doctor didn't seem to want to hear about it. Renee let me talk through the whole thing, and I did feel better at the end.

I told her about feeling tired and jumpy all the time, and my trouble with my voice, and losing my spot in the choir. I even told her about the weird nightmares or waking dreams or whatever they are, though I wasn't sure how to convey how scary they are when they're happening. Calling them dreams doesn't really capture it, but I'm not sure what else to say. (I didn't tell her about the feathers, because of what Angela said. I don't want

her to think I'm out of my mind! I guess I'll just continue keeping that to myself for now.)

Renee listened to it all and fed me pie and sympathized
with how awful it must be. That helped, but I still kept worrying
about what Angela had said, and whether there's a truth in it
that I don't want to face. It's hard not to wonder if the problems I'm having might just be in my head, but, well, if they're
in my head, does that mean I really am crazy? It's scary to think
I might not be able to control my own mind. And I don't *feel*
crazy. Then again, maybe crazy people never do, and you just
keep screaming about how sane you are as they tie you up in a
straitjacket and dump you into a padded cell.

These are the kinds of things I've been thinking as I try to
fall asleep at night. And let me tell you, none of it was very
comforting. So I just focused on not thinking these things, not
acknowledging them, and I hoped that would make them go
away. I don't know why I thought that would work. I bet that's
never worked in the history of humanity.

So I was a bit nervous when Renee came over today because,
as much as I love her, she has this intense ability to see right
through people. Or to see right through me, anyway. I guess that's
part of her job. She has an uncanny sense about these things.
And sure enough, much as I'd tried to hide these fears even from
myself, Renee seemed to grasp them right away and give them
voice. Only, when she talked about them, they didn't sound as
bad as they had in my imagination. In fact, it was kind of a relief
to hear her express my situation so calmly and matter-of-fact, as
if these dreams were a totally normal part of life.

Basically, she listened to me whine and complain about
everything that's been going badly in my life, especially about

my throat and what could be wrong with it, and she just said, "Do you think it might just be stress?" And when I got nervous and tongue-tied, she put a hand over mine and said, "Laetitia, it's nothing to be ashamed of." Which I think I really needed to hear.

She talked about the relationship between the mind and the body, and how it's totally normal for mental concerns to manifest themselves in physical ways. For example, she told me that when she worked her first job after college, she had a boss who made her feel really bad about herself, and she started getting stomachaches every day. They were bad, and she was getting really worried. She thought she must have an allergy or an ulcer, or something even worse. But the day she quit her job, she had her last stomachache, and she's never had them come back since then. She said it wasn't true that it was "all in her head"—it's more that the head and the body are connected. And that it's a myth that just because something is going on in our heads, that means we should have complete control over it. You can't will yourself to get over anxiety or depression or even just a simple case of nerves any more than you can get rid of measles or the flu through pure force of will. Which I guess does make sense.

I wonder if losing my voice and getting these weird pains and visions might just be my body's way of dealing with my nerves and anxieties about the upcoming audition. It does make me feel a lot better to think that this kind of thing is pretty normal and happens to a lot of people. Renee says loads of famous professional singers have found they can't croak out a note when faced with a concert or audition that's really important to them. But while it does make me feel better that I'm not necessarily crazy, it doesn't fix the problem. Just as Renee said, knowing it's in my head doesn't make it go away. So how do I get rid of this mental block before my audition?

Renee said there was no guaranteed cure, but she did have some suggestions. She told me to spend some time in the auditorium without even trying to sing, just to get used to being back there without stressing out. We also talked about ways I could get back to singing without putting so much pressure on myself, like singing a lullaby to one of the neighborhood kids, or just singing along with the radio. Situations where I know I'm not going to be judged, and I can take pleasure in the act itself.

Then she said something that kind of caught me off guard at first, though I am trying to consider it seriously. She asked me, just as an experiment, to try picturing my future as something other than a singer. As soon as she said that, I felt myself get really upset.

I've just had this unshakeable vision of myself as a singer for so long that anything else I could conjure up felt like failure. Worse than that, it felt like a betrayal of everything I've believed in and worked for. The first images in my head were picturing myself working at a factory or a casino just to make ends meet, like my mamma. Day after day of doing something boring and pointless, with no hope of anything ever improving. Honestly, it sounded like hell. But Renee wouldn't let me leave it at that. She pushed me to think about other things I'm interested in, other things I could contribute. At first I was like, *Nothing*, but when I gave it some thought, I realized I've been excited about the photos I've been taking recently. And I love spending time working on my hair and makeup. I'm good at that, too. Maybe I'd like helping other people with it. I do those tutorials on my blog, and that's always fun. So maybe there are other things in life that could make me happy, even if I could never sing again.

I have to say, once I realized that, it was a huge relief. I instantly felt a lot better about everything. So maybe Renee was right, and I was putting too much pressure on myself to succeed on this one narrow path. And there're all kinds of other things out there in the world I haven't even tried. Maybe I've thrown myself so deeply into this one thing, assuming it's what I was always meant to do, that I've missed out on other stuff I might be just as good at, or find interesting, at least.

We talked about the Dwayne Robinson trial a bit. I guess Renee's been following it pretty closely, and she was surprised I haven't been. She says the whole country is talking about it, and it all happened just a few blocks from me! I really have let myself be pretty blind to stuff that's going on around me. I guess that's another example of something I can think about to take my mind off singing, though it might make me feel more bad than good. But it does seem to give Malcolm a sense of purpose. Maybe it can do the same for me?

It does feel a little ironic. The point of this exercise was to get me relaxed enough about singing so I'd be able to do it again, but if I wind up thinking of all this other stuff that interests me, maybe I won't even want to sing anymore. Does that mean the exercise failed? Or does that count as a success? I don't know. I still have pretty mixed feelings about it, I guess. I don't want to give up my dream, and I still feel like if you want something, you have to be single-minded and focused to get it. That's always worked for me in the past. But it's not working right now. At the same time, I'm starting to realize how self-centered my pursuit of fame and success has made me. There are so many bigger problems in the world than my getting a little hoarse now and then. But does that realization become less significant if I'm only using it to help me get my voice back? It seems dishonest, somehow. Insincere.

TUESDAY, FEBRUARY 18, 4:15 P.M. (PRIVATE)

I thought maybe things were getting better after my talk with
Renee, but something happened at school today. I had another
one of my . . . attacks. I don't know what else to call them. It was
at lunch, sitting at my usual table with a couple of friends who
were talking about a movie they were thinking of going to. I was
only half paying attention and was staring out the window, not
really thinking about anything. That's when I felt it coming on.
I guess it's happened enough times now that I know the feeling.
The sense that I'm not where I seem to be, or maybe that *part*
of me is right there, sitting at the lunch table, but some other
part of me is far away, going through something totally different.

I knew it was coming this time, and I knew I wouldn't be
able to stop it, so I tried to breathe deeply and just wait for
whatever it was this time to come and go. I felt prickling all over

my skin, as if I'd broken a sweat. The quality of the air seemed to change, and I couldn't really hear people around me anymore. Everything sounded distorted.

That was when my head was yanked backward, like someone had grabbed me by the hair. I could feel hot breath against my face, as if someone were leaning over me. Through all this I was scared, but I was trying to hold it together. Even as it happened, part of me knew I was still in the cafeteria with my friends nearby, and I didn't want to scare people or embarrass myself by making a big scene. I kept repeating, "It's just a dream; it's not real," even though that was not quite true.

That worked for a while, but then I felt something in my eyes. I couldn't see anything in front of me but empty air, and then the walls and ceiling of the lunch room, but I could feel it, like some kind of long metal spike being driven in. First one, then the other. And the nerves and muscles that keep your eyes in place, I could feel and hear them tearing as whatever invisible force it was ripped my eyeballs from their sockets.

That was when I lost it. I started screaming and grabbing at my head, alternating between trying to fight off my invisible attacker, and trying to use an arm to protect my eyes. I fell to the floor, and the rest is kind of a blur of my friends trying to help me, and one of the lunch room attendants pulling me from the room and taking me to the nurse's office. At that point I calmed down a bit, and the pain mostly faded, but I still couldn't see anything. The nurse asked what was wrong with me. Had someone hit me? Had I gotten some chemical in my eyes? Was I on drugs? But I couldn't give her a good answer.

She looked into my eyes with a little light, but she said they looked fine. I still couldn't see, though. At this point

I was convinced I'd never see again, but I wasn't even that worried about it. I was just so exhausted by what I'd gone through and how real it felt. And that sense that I had done something terrible, and was being punished for some crime I didn't remember. I could hardly be bothered to worry about my sight.

The nurse took me into a little room and had me lie on a cot there in the dark for a while. She said I needed to calm down, and she'd check on me in an hour. Sure enough, when she turned the light back on, I could see again. It was the strangest thing.

Well, I guess I'm about ready to post this now. I'm delaying a little because I'm afraid of the ghost who lives in my computer. Or not a ghost, but I'm not sure what else to call it. Whatever it is that posts those photos whenever I write something like this. I actually thought about not writing it at all, wondering if that would keep the photo from showing up, but it didn't feel right. It's like I *need* to write it out, or else the whole thing is just in my head, and that's even worse. And to be perfectly honest, I guess I'm a little curious what the picture will be. I'm scared to look, but at the same time, I'm excited.

TUESDAY, FEBRUARY 18, 2:06 P.M. (PRIVATE)

There it is, just like I was expecting. Only I think this one might be even creepier than the others. What the hell?

Where did it come from? It's obviously not me in the picture, so who is it? Is it even a real person, or is it just something made up out of my imagination?

The good news is it posted privately this time, instead of popping up for anyone to see. Not that I suppose it matters anymore. As far as anyone can tell, this blog has been completely abandoned. I suppose I should feel bad about that, but I can't find it in me to care right now.

angela: hey. you there?

laetitia: yeah.

angela: how are you doing? are you singing again?

laetitia: not really.

angela: oh. well . . . you said on the phone before that you have trouble following my stories because my friends are just names to you. so . . . i took some pics of everyone! wanna see?

laetitia: sure, go ahead.

angela: this is tre, of course. isn't he cute??

[photo redacted]

angela: and tasha

[photo redacted]

angela: and lisa.

[photo redacted]

angela: lisa's kind of got a bit of your style, with the blue and green extensions.

laetitia: wow, yeah, tell her i love her hair.

angela: what about you? are you still keeping up your divanation these days?

laetitia: yeah, most days. did you ever see the wig i got for my birthday?

angela: um . . . idk, which is it? the blue and silver?

laetitia: no, hold on. i'm wearing it now. i'll do a selfie.

[photo redacted]

angela: wtf is that?

laetitia: omg, i didn't mean to send that. that's not the picture.

angela: no shit! what the hell is it?

laetitia: i don't know. i've never seen it before.

angela: what the hell, laetitia? is this some kind of joke? because it's not funny!

laetitia: i told you: it's not mine. it's some kind of bug in my computer; it does this sometimes.

angela: stop lying. you know you sent it. you're sick—you know that?

angela: you've been pissing me off something fierce lately, and i tried to be cool about it because we've been friends for so long, but i am sick of your shit.

angela: you are a drama queen, and you've always got to make everything all about you. you didn't even ask me what happened with tre and his ex-girlfriend, even though i told you i was upset. i try to include you, but you couldn't care less what's going on in my life.

laetitia: what? that's not fair! there's something seriously wrong with me, and i'm supposed to care about your stupid boyfriend? my life is falling apart, i don't know what's the matter with me, and i might be losing my mind. so sorry if i can't find any room to care about you and your stupid new friends.

angela: you always do this! you always have to be the center of attention, since we were kids. you can't stand it when anything is going on in anyone else's life. and if there's nothing going on in yours, you've got no problem making stuff up until everyone acts like you're special.

laetitia: that's not true! i never do that. i'd give anything to go back to normal.

angela: forget it, laetitia. find someone else to tell your stories to. i'm done.

angela has logged off.

THURSDAY, FEBRUARY 20, 1:10 A.M. (PRIVATE)

Two different teachers came up to me today to ask if I'm okay. And I can tell some of my friends are worried about me too. I guess I must look pretty rough these days, even though I'm trying to hold it together. I wind up shrugging off my friends, because I don't know what to tell them. Anything close to the truth, and they'll just think I'm lying or crazy, like Angela does. The best I can do is keep it to myself and try to think about other stuff.

I've been reading a lot about the Dwayne Robinson trial. It's the only thing that works as a distraction from my own weird problems. I've been sitting here for three hours, reloading the same news sites in hopes of updates, and following the randomest links to see what some blogger in Spain or whoever thinks about the whole thing. Pretty weird, when I'm right *here*.

But there isn't much in the way of news. The trial is closed to the press, so everything is just speculation until the jury comes back with a verdict. But in the meantime, people have been protesting outside the courthouse. It's surreal. I can read all about this stuff online, but if I listen carefully enough, I can hear it out the windows, too. The courthouse is only a couple of miles from here. Sometimes I even see the news vans coming and going, and some people I know from school have made signs and gone down to demonstrate. I know Malcolm is one of them.

I wonder if I should go too. It would be a way of hanging out with Malcolm more, but it's not really about that, honestly. I don't really know Malcolm well, but the protests . . . I don't know. I'm curious. Interested. I guess I want to feel like I'm part of this. Like I'm contributing something.

Gramma Patty is against it, though. She says I should stay out of it. She says all the demonstrating is just getting people riled up and isn't helping anything at all. I guess that's what the pastor has been saying too: there's nothing for any of us to do at this point but wait and hope for justice to be served. Honestly, I don't see how it can fail. That video is *so* clear. Still, I wish I didn't feel so helpless. It's awful to sit here, clicking through page after page, looking for any new information, even when I know it can't help. But then again, if I could really help, if there was something I should be doing, I guess that would be a lot of pressure too. So I don't know which way to feel.

Gramma Patty's afraid there will be riots if the policemen get off, and the whole city will burn. Mamma's nervous too, I can tell, but she shows it in different ways. Instead of just responding directly to whatever's on the news, Mamma's got feelings that "come over her," or "little episodes" where her eyelids flutter and she has to press a hand to her chest for a few seconds. Gramma Patty rolls her eyes at these and mutters about Mamma being such a drama queen. But Mamma's emotions manifest in different ways from most people, so she's not sleeping well and wakes up at the drop of a hat (which I notice, since I haven't been sleeping well lately either).

Every night she has a new story. She's hearing doors banging and dogs barking and voices whispering in her ear. The other night she made a huge drama just because the light in the bathroom kept flickering. She kept saying it was a sign or something. A sign of what? Probably that the bulb needs to be replaced, if you ask me. But Mamma's always been a bit like this—excitable, I guess you'd say. All the stuff the pastor talks about with angels and devils and spirits and whatnot, Mamma doesn't always leave that stuff in church, where it belongs. Especially when she gets jumpy about something and isn't sleeping well. I get the feeling that sometimes she's a little unclear on the line between her dreams and reality. But then, I guess I shouldn't talk. These days, I'm not much better.

THURSDAY, FEBRUARY 20, 6:38 A.M. (PRIVATE)

Holy Jesus, I did not need that this morning! *Gross.*

I was getting ready for school and I just went to put on my wig—it's one of my favorites, kind of a shimmery lavender color. I wore it just last week and put it away on its stand like I always do. And this morning I'm brushing it out and getting it ready to set in place, and I notice something flutter to the ground. So I lean over to check it out, and it's a *moth*. How the hell did a moth get into my wig? I've never heard of that before. Ew, this is something that sits on my *head*.

Of course the first thing I did was yelp and sweep it away from me with my hand, and it flew into a corner. But now it's just sitting there in that corner, which doesn't really solve anything. I guess I'm going to have to get a tissue so I can pick it up and throw it away.

THURSDAY, FEBRUARY 20, 6:46 A.M. (PRIVATE)

I was going to just toss the stupid moth outside or flush it down the toilet, but before I did, I opened the tissue to peek at it, because if something has been hanging out in my hair, I should at least know what it looks like, right? It was kind of pretty, actually. Not like a beautiful butterfly or anything, but where I had expected to be horrified by this dead thing, I was fascinated instead.

For some reason, I couldn't bring myself to just toss it away. I don't know why, but I didn't want it to be like it had never happened. I wanted to document it somehow. Then I remembered my dead animal pics that Gramma Patty didn't like, and I figured, why not add to my collection? So I took a photo and now I guess I'll post it. It should fit right in with the stuff I've been posting lately.

Sometimes I can't help imagining what my old followers would think if they could see my blog now, if I ever made all these posts public. I bet they'd be so scandalized, to see that their source for hair tutorials has morphed into dead bugs and mold. Of course, maybe if I'd stayed public, I would have wound up with a new kind of follower. There's got to be someone out there who appreciates this type of stuff.

But for now I'd rather just keep it for me.

THURSDAY, FEBRUARY 20, 10:35 P.M. (PRIVATE)

Something is definitely not okay. Finding that moth in my wig this morning freaked me out a little, but it seemed like just a fluke thing. What's one little moth? I didn't see any damage, and I checked my other wigs and everything looked okay. So I picked a different one—the red and black—and I styled it and wore it to school and it was fine. I put the whole thing out of my mind. Except tonight I was getting ready for bed and I go to take it off, and a handful of little moths fall to the floor, *ew*.

It must be some kind of infestation. I hate to say it, but I think I'm going to stay away from my wigs for a little while until I figure out what's going on. I'll just do turbans and wraps for a few days.

FRIDAY, FEBRUARY 21, 2:25 A.M. (PRIVATE)

It's not the wigs. It can't be. But if it isn't, I don't even want to think about what's going on.

All I know is I was having one of those nightmares last night. There isn't really any story to them, just the scenes I've been through before, repeating themselves on a loop—the torture, the pain of the wheel, the grill, the arrows, the spike prying out my eyes, and the terrible sense I've done something to deserve it but can't remember what. Then I woke up into darkness, feeling kind of dizzy and disoriented. So I just lay there for a few minutes, until I noticed this weird tickling feeling in my ear. I reached up to scratch at it, and there was something *there*. Under my fingernail. Something that wasn't my skin. And instantly all I could think was, *Get it out get it out get it out.* So I sat up and sort of flicked my finger into my ear, and this big ass moth falls into my lap. Like, at least an inch big! I screamed so loud then, I woke the whole house up.

By the time Mamma got to my room, I was totally freaked out. I swear, it felt like the moth had squirmed out from inside of me.

Gramma Patty tried to calm me down. She said it didn't come from inside my ear; it must have flown around the room and landed on me in the night. I don't know, though. Her explanation does make more sense than mine, but somehow I still *felt* it coming out of me. Maybe I got mixed up by that dream I was having.

FRIDAY, FEBRUARY 21, 6:15 A.M. (PRIVATE)

I spent the rest of last night in the living room, with the TV going and all the lights on. I knew if I got back into bed, I would spend the whole night feeling powdery little wings brushing against my skin until I drove myself crazy. But that meant this morning I went back into the room to get dressed and saw the big moth just lying there on the floor, where I must have knocked it to the ground. I wonder how it died. . . . It was definitely alive in my ear last night. Did I give it a heart attack or something? Can moths die of shock? But it was not moving at all, so it's definitely dead now.

I moved it to a sunny spot and took a picture. I don't know why it makes me feel better to do that, but it does. I think it's the process of it that calms me down. When I sit here, thinking, *Gross bugs are crawling on me in my sleep*, of course that freaks me out, and all I want to do is scream and scream, but if I can force myself to think, *This would make an interesting photo*, it changes my whole relationship to the situation. Instead of screaming, *Get it off me, get it off me!*, I have to pick it up with my own hands and put it down somewhere, and then I have to position it and move it around to capture it at the best angle. I know this is weird, but at some point it starts to feel almost like a gift. That someone gave me this strange, beautiful thing, and it's my job to honor it the only way I know how. It almost feels like it's part of me, and I can't just cast it off until I've documented it in some way. It would be like throwing away a piece of my own self, or my experience, anyway.

So I take the picture. Then I can take the thing outside and feel much calmer about it.

Gramma Patty caught me doing all this and made me let her feel my head, as if she thought I were running a fever. I felt okay, but she still looked worried. I think at this point, it's my mental health she is worrying about more than physical, but Mamma says it is a good instinct to document everything that is going on, so we can show people if we need to. I don't know who in their right mind would want to know any of this, but it keeps Gramma Patty off my back at least.

FRIDAY, FEBRUARY 21, 9:29 A.M. (PRIVATE)

Mamma let me stay home from school today because of the fright I had last night. I still can't explain it, but it definitely kept me from sleeping well the rest of the night. This morning I was a complete zombie, so Mamma told me to stay home and get some rest, and maybe I'd be able to go in for my afternoon classes. That sounded like a good idea, except now I *still* can't sleep. Every time I close my eyes, I can feel that moth flapping around on me, that tickling sensation in my ear that makes my skin crawl, and I wake myself up, trying to scratch these imaginary insects off my body. I might as well have gone into school, since it's not like I'm getting any rest. But I really don't think I would have been able to focus on my classes. All I can really handle right now is sitting here on the couch, wrapped in a blanket, watching TV and messing around on my laptop.

I feel a little guilty about that. Gramma Patty and Mamma have both been trying to get me to stay away from the coverage of the Robinson trial because they're convinced that's what's upsetting me and giving me bad dreams. Gramma Patty in particular always makes me shut off the news if she catches me looking at it. She says it's not healthy. That it's making us all edgy, and there's nothing we can do anyway. I get what she's saying, but even though it's frustrating to feel so powerless, somehow I can't look away. It's like I'm obsessed.

I've never taken much interest in the news before, but this doesn't just feel like any old dry news story. Maybe because it's so close. The whole world is talking about it, but it all happened right here, so it feels, in a small way, like it's about us. It makes my voice problems and feeling sick all the time, and Mamma being weird about nighttime noises seem like less of a big deal when I see Robinson's father crying on TV and his cousins talking about the unfairness of it all.

Sometimes I wonder if maybe it's wrong of me to get comfort, or at least distraction, from another family's misery. To use them as an excuse to get out of my own skin a little and worry about someone else's problems. Maybe this has nothing to do with me. Maybe I'm just rubbernecking, like Gramma Patty says. But she and Mamma are both out of the house now, so I am taking this opportunity to feed my addiction.

That sounds kind of weird, doesn't it? Am I addicted to watching stuff about the trial? Usually when people talk about addiction, it has to do with pointless and destructive pleasures, like drugs or drinking or gambling. Can it really be considered an addiction to take an interest in current events? It's not destructive. But then, if it's keeping me awake at night, or getting me upset, is that destructive? Is it pointless? Or is it worse to close your eyes to the bad things in the world, so you can enjoy your own bit of peace? I don't know, but it is true that I feel a little sneaky, using this day off from school to indulge my obsession instead of trying to get some rest, like I'm supposed to.

FRIDAY, FEBRUARY 21, 10:52 A.M. (PRIVATE)

My throat feels really weird.

I was just sitting here on the couch, watching the news station and flipping around to get the latest stories about the Robinson case. They were talking about Robinson, but it almost felt like watching a documentary of my life. I recognize the street he grew up on and the playgrounds where he played. The street corner where he was shot is one I pass at least once a week. It all feels very close, in a way that is both scary and impossible to look away from.

Anyway, I was feeling drowsy and I must have fallen asleep at some point, because the next thing I knew, I was startled out of another nightmare.

It started out just like the others I've been having, where I'm forced to revisit all these horrible scenes of torture—burned alive, pierced with arrows, strapped to a giant wheel, eyes ripped out. Then the scene shifted, and I was caught in a fire. I think my dream must have gotten mixed up with a story on the news. I could feel the searing heat and hear the crackling of the flames mixed with the sound of distant sirens and the smell of burning flesh. My skin felt like it was prickling and crawling, but when I looked down, expecting to see flames licking up my body, instead I was covered in a blanket of different-colored moths, each beating its papery wings against my skin. And I couldn't tell which was hallucinated, the fire or the moths, and whether the creepy, crawly feeling was from thousands of fluttering wings or from my skin curling off as it burned.

I woke myself up, coughing, even though there wasn't any smoke in the house. Actually, I'd been coughing all morning and thought I was coming down with a cold, or that I wasn't all the way better from the one I'd had before, but it's worse now.

I just had to stop writing to deal with another big coughing fit. But no matter how much I cough, it doesn't seem to give me any relief. It doesn't quite feel like the usual tickle in the throat or something. It feels more like there is something solid and heavy lodged in my esophagus or my windpipe, I can't tell which. I keep pressing on it from the outside, but I'm not sure if I can really feel anything or if I'm just imagining it. I keep wanting to cough and hack and retch just to bring it up, but I'm also a little afraid of the massive phlegm ball I'm going to produce if I do ever manage to bring it up. I wish it would just go away on its own, but it's probably healthier if I keep coughing. Better out than in?

I just looked in my hand mirror, and my throat was a little hard to see from the angle, but I think I can actually see

something under the skin of my neck, like it's swollen or something. And there are some weird shapes, but I'm not sure what
my throat usually looks like. Maybe it's just swollen glands and
I am freaking myself out over nothing. I'm going to take some
more cough medicine, I think.

What the holy hell just came out of me? I don't understand. It doesn't make any sense. How is it possible that my body produced that?

I know what it is, even though I don't think I've ever seen one up close before. It's a seashell. And I live about a thousand miles from the coast. How in the hell . . .? Jesus help me; I know this isn't right.

FRIDAY, FEBRUARY 21, 11:26 A.M. (PRIVATE)

Okay. I'm calmer now. But look at that thing. It's huge. I'm trying so hard to think of any reasonable explanation for how I could have coughed this up, but I've got nothing.

God, what is wrong with me? I just searched the whole Internet and freaked myself out with all the stories of horrible parasites people have picked up on vacation, plus a lot of stuff about people who ate some bad clams and got food poisoning, but nothing like this. What is happening? When is it going to stop?

I know Mamma is still at work for a few hours, but I have to call her.

FRIDAY, FEBRUARY 21, 2:19 P.M. (PRIVATE)

I'm at the clinic now, waiting to be seen by Dr. Afolabi. I know I was nervous about telling the doctor this stuff before, but it's gone too far. I can't just keep ignoring this.

Mamma came straight home from work when I told her what had happened. I hope she doesn't get in trouble for that. Her supervisor isn't always very sympathetic about family problems, and Mamma's been trying to cut down on her "emergencies," I know, but what else was I supposed to do?

Mamma came home to check on me, and she called the doctor's office and was trying to set up an appointment sometime in the next few days. And right then and there, with Mamma on the phone, I got that feeling again. She turned around when she heard me start to cough and choke, and got me a glass of water and whacked me on the back a few times. But I knew by then what was happening. The only question was what I would bring up this time. Finally it came loose, and I spat up a mess of bile and blood and small bones, like from an animal. I just sat there for a while, shivering and staring at the mess I had made, only vaguely conscious of Mamma telling the receptionist there had been a change of plans, and we needed to see the doctor immediately.

Then she wrapped the shell and the bones up in a little sandwich baggie to bring with us, and she called a taxi to take us to the clinic, which we *never* do. I can't remember the last time we had an emergency that couldn't wait for the bus.

But for all that rush, we still had to wait for the doctor, so that's why I'm updating on my phone right now. Moths, shells, bones . . . and the feathers . . . What's the connection? I hope someone will be able to help me figure it out.

FRIDAY, FEBRUARY 21, 3:38 P.M. (PRIVATE)

Just got out of the clinic, on the bus home now. I met with Dr. Afolabi, but I don't know what good it did, or even if she understands the problem.

She started by checking me over as usual, and shining a light in my throat and ears and nose. Then she asked me a bunch of questions. Am I eating or drinking anything different? Any change in routine? She started off with these sort of normal, harmless questions, but then at some point she stopped and said, "You know you can tell me anything and I can't tell your mother or anyone else. It's a rule: I can't tell them no matter what you tell me."

I told her I understood, so she was like, "Is there anything else you want to tell me? Anything else going on in your life?"

That confused me. Is there likely to be something more significant on my mind than the fact that I am gagging up bizarre objects? So I said no, pretty much just the puking thing. But she kept asking, so I mentioned how I've been having bad dreams, and that I lost my singing voice. She seemed a little interested in that, but she kept digging for something else. I don't know what. And then she asked me all these questions about self-harm— have I ever cut or burned or scratched myself on purpose? Do I restrict calories or exercise excessively or use laxatives? Have I become sexually active? All this health class stuff that didn't seem to have anything to do with anything.

Of course I told her no to all that stuff, and eventually she let me go, but then she told me to send Mamma back in without me. So I just sat in the waiting room, playing with my phone, and when Mamma came out, she had such a look on her face! She was *pissed*, and I don't know what the doctor must have said to her. She wouldn't even talk to me; she just grabbed me by the arm and steered me out to the bus stop, and she was fuming and muttering under her breath the whole time. I'm starting to get really nervous that the doctor said something bad about me and I'm about to get in huge trouble. Only I can't imagine what it might be. I really don't think I did anything wrong. All I can make out from her muttering is something about "calling my daughter a liar" and "Who does she think she is?" and such. I don't know what that's about, and Mamma doesn't seem inclined to discuss it on public transportation. I guess I'll find out more when we get home.

FRIDAY, FEBRUARY 21, 4:08 P.M. (PRIVATE)

Well, now I know what Dr. Afolabi was thinking, I guess. And why Mamma was so mad about it.

The moment we got home, Mamma practically hauled me into the living room and sat me down on the couch so she could pace in front of me, and she started babbling away about how that doctor is a quack and doesn't know what she is doing and we are never going to her again. So I asked what happened, what did she say, what's going on with me? I was still convinced Dr. Afolabi told her I had some kind of terrible disease or something, or I've done something awful without even realizing it, because Mamma looked so upset, but I wanted to know, whatever it was, because at least that would be an answer.

So I was practically begging her to just spit it out, and Mamma grabbed my arm again, tight, and said, "What you told me about those things you coughed up—was that the truth? I mean the real honest-to-God truth?" So I told her, "Yeah, of course it is." But that wasn't enough for her, and she kept asking me the same basic question in a bunch of different ways until I was crying as I tried to defend myself, and I didn't even know what I was being accused of. But I guess finally I convinced her, because at last she let go of me and nodded and then muttered, "Stupid doctor. I ought to have her license."

I still didn't understand what the doctor had said that had gotten Mamma so upset, so she explained that Dr. Afolabi had called me a liar. She said I had just found a shell and some bones somewhere and made up this whole story to get Mamma to come home from work. I was so shocked! Why would I do that? I've never been so willful or troublesome in my whole life. But the doctor said I might be faking everything to get attention.

I didn't know what to say. How could I possibly be faking it? Mamma saw me cough up those bones. And Mamma says she told the doctor that. Told her she saw it with her own eyes. But the doctor said that kind of thing is easy to fake. That it happens all the time. Kids hide stuff in their cheeks, their hands, their sleeves. Like a magician palming a card. You can hide things until the last minute and then make it look like you coughed them up.

I asked Mamma if she believed Dr. Afolabi, and Mamma said, "No, of course not." She said she told that doctor I wouldn't lie to her. That I had never lied to her.

I felt a little guilty when she said that. Why did she have to put it like that? It's not like I've *never* lied to Mamma. What kid in the history of the Earth has gotten through childhood without ever telling a lie? But this time, *this* time, I'm definitely

445

telling the truth. Why would I lie? I was getting enough attention without any of this. This isn't the kind of attention I ever wanted.

Mamma sat down at the table, looking exhausted and put out and worried all at the same time. She told me the doctor said sometimes people make this stuff up—especially teenagers—because there are some other problems going on in their lives that they can't talk about for some reason, but they need people to notice them. And people aren't noticing the real problem, so they try to make themselves noticed for other stuff. I asked her what would count as a "real" problem, and she said violence, like abuse. Or other stuff. And then she looked at me with big eyes and made me promise to tell her if anything was going on, if anyone was touching me how they shouldn't be, or anything at all, and I shouldn't feel afraid to tell her. So I was like, "I'm not! I wouldn't be." But there isn't anything like that. I don't know how to make anyone believe me. It isn't that. It's something else.

Mamma hugged me and said that was what she told the doctor. That she was the crazy one, not me. I hope that's true.

The point is that Mamma does believe me, even if the doctor doesn't. That's the important thing. But it doesn't solve the problem. The truth is, I never really believed the doctor would help anyway. I hoped she would, but if I'm honest with myself, I have to accept that this doesn't seem to be a medical problem. I can't think of any normal disease that makes you cough up animal parts.

MEDICAL REPORT

GENERAL:

Office: ~~████~~ Provider: ~~████~~ Encounter Date: 2/27/2074

PATIENT:

Name: ~~████~~ Sex: Female DOB: ~~████~~

Age: 15 years and 4 months Race: Black/African American

Address: ~~████████████████~~

Insurance: ~~████████████████~~

COMPLAINT:

Patient complains of intense vomiting sessions resulting in the disgorgement of odd (nonedible) objects. Patient's mother brought in and presented the objects (seashell and small animal bones) supposedly disgorged by the patient. Patient also suffers from the loss of her voice, which presented seven weeks ago. Patient claims only her singing voice is affected. Speaking voice appears normal.

EXAMINATION:

No organic causes for symptoms revealed during physical examination. Throat appears slightly inflamed. Throat cultures returned negative. No tests run on the objects presented by patient's mother at this time.

DIAGNOSIS:

Diagnosis is undetermined at this time, but symptoms strongly indicate an underlying psychological issue. Further examination by a psychiatrist is recommended. Symptoms are typical of adolescents with past or ongoing traumatic experiences, but the patient shut down all inquiries into possible sources of trauma in her life. Strong possibility of physical, sexual, or psychological abuse, most likely on the part of someone close to the patient, whom the patient feels compelled to protect. Alternatively, a diagnosis of histrionic personality disorder or borderline personality disorder may be indicated. Recommendation: contact social services caseworker ~~████████~~.

SATURDAY, FEBRUARY 22, 2:18 A.M. (PRIVATE)

I can't sleep. I've been turning it over and over in my head. What if that doctor is right? Is it possible this stuff is all in my head? I mean, it feels so real, but the mind can work in strange ways. I don't *think* I've experienced any kind of sexual abuse, or other form of abuse, or any other deep dark secret, but how can I be sure? How can you ever be sure of the secrets you hide from your own self?

The doctor said if it wasn't trauma-related, it could be a symptom of another problem. Mental illness. Is that it? I mean, it's not like I hadn't considered the possibility before, but it's different when a doctor is saying it. That makes it feel more real. Sometimes it *does* feel like I'm going crazy. Like I don't even recognize myself. But the idea that I can't trust my own sense, my reactions, my memories and experiences—it's too terrifying to even think about.

SATURDAY, FEBRUARY 22, 3:12 A.M. (PRIVATE)

Mamma heard me tossing and turning, and came in to check on me. I told her about all my worries, and she helped calm me down. She doesn't think I'm crazy. Even if I can't judge myself from the inside, she should be able to tell, right?

Mamma says there is something going on with me, but it's the kind of thing doctors don't understand. For this kind of illness, only God can fix it. She says someone must have hexed us or put the evil eye on us, and that we need to call on a higher power for protection. Normally I roll my eyes when Mamma talks this way. She's also convinced God is the answer to a *lot* of life's questions. I've never taken it all too seriously, but in the middle of the night, when I was feeling so scared and anxious, I have to admit it did feel comforting—the idea of putting this problem in God's hands and letting Him take care of it.

Why shouldn't it work? Whether the problem is medical or mental or who knows what else, it all comes from God in the first place. So whatever it is, it's in His power to fix it. Or if not, I don't see how it can hurt, at least.

SATURDAY, FEBRUARY 22, 9:22 A.M. (PRIVATE)

When I came down to breakfast this morning, Mamma had a glint in her eye like she had just thought up the most marvelous thing. Sure enough, before I could even pour some cereal, she grabbed me by the hand and made us all stand in a circle in the middle of the kitchen while she said a blessing. She does some kind of blessing or prayer every morning, but this was more than her usual bit about the food and preparing for a good day. She took her time and talked about evil forces that had invaded the household, and asked for God's protection from them. Then she squeezed my hand extra hard as we said our amens.

So I guess that was her plan. I did feel better while she was doing it, so who knows? Maybe it will help. But it's hard to imagine something so simple and straightforward could make a difference, given the strange stuff I've been going through. But prayer can be pretty powerful, as Gramma Patty always tells me. We'll see, I guess.

MONDAY, FEBRUARY 24, 7:25 P.M. (PRIVATE)

When I got home from school today, Renee was waiting for me, even though this isn't our usual day for a meeting. Apparently, the doctor put in a call about me after my appointment the other day. She told social services I was showing signs of abuse, and that she was concerned about what was going on in our household.

I don't understand it, though. The doctor told me I could tell her anything and she wasn't allowed to tell anyone. She said it was part of her job: that she's not allowed to share my secrets with anyone. So how could she then turn around and call social services and talk to who knows how many people before the message reached Renee? Renee didn't seem eager to talk about that and kept trying to change the subject, but finally she said Dr. Afolabi had to do it, and that she did the right thing by calling social services. As far as I can tell, that means all the stuff she was telling me about privacy and confidentiality was just a lie.

Renee argued with me about that. She said what the doctor told me is true, but that there are exceptions. Very specific exceptions that are designed to protect and help people. That's nice and all, but I'd like to see what Mamma and Gramma Patty would think if I told them there were "exceptions" to the truths I tell them. I don't think they'd be impressed.

Renee said sometimes making sure people are okay is more important than guarding their secrets, and that I shouldn't blame Dr. Afolabi, because she was just doing her job. She's legally required to call in anytime she sees something that might be considered evidence of child abuse. The exceptions are meant to protect the most vulnerable people, the ones who can't always speak up to help themselves.

Is that how Renee sees me? Vulnerable? Unable to speak up for myself? She says she and Dr. Afolabi are just being careful, but it seems to me like this rule was meant to help little kids, babies, or maybe people with mental problems who really can't speak for themselves because they don't even fully understand what's going on. But that's not me. I may not be an adult, but I'm not a little kid. I know what's real and what's not. I know what I've experienced. I told the doctor there was nothing abusive or anything like that going on. Why wasn't that enough?

Then again, I suppose if you're the kind of person who doesn't fully understand what's going on, you might not know it, which would be all the more reason for authorities to be extra careful with you. Does that describe me? I've heard of repressed memories and stuff. What if they're right, and I can't tell the difference between reality and fantasy anymore? What if I really don't know what's going on in my own life, or in my own head? I suppose it's good to know at least there are people out there, trying to help, though it's also frustrating to feel like I don't know who I can trust.

MONDAY, FEBRUARY 24, 8:05 P.M. (PRIVATE)

I just called Renee to apologize for our argument. After thinking about it awhile, I've come around to see her point.

She asked me if I was ready to tell her what's really going on, and I didn't know what to say. I don't know what to tell her, or what she'll believe. I'm not even sure what's going on in my own head. So I just repeated the stuff I had already told her, about the nightmares and visions and vomiting strange things. I explained that that's why I'd gone to the doctor. But just like Dr. Afolabi, Renee didn't seem to want to take any of it at face value. She kept pressing to see if there was something more I wasn't saying, which was frustrating. Everyone's got their theories and I know they want to help, but in the meantime, I feel like no one is really listening to me.

Renee stressed again that I could trust her, and that she's

there to help and has always been on my side, and how import-ant it was for me to tell her everything, and that I should call her right away if I have anything else I want to tell her. But what's the point when she just hears what she wants to hear instead of what I'm saying?

ALLEGATIONS OF CHILD ABUSE OR NEGLECT: PRELIMINARY REPORT

Date: 2/24/2014   Complainant: ~~████████~~ (Family doctor)
Family Surname: ~~██████~~

PARENT/GUARDIAN INFORMATION

Father: Unknown, not involved
Mother: ~~████████~~, possible perpetrator
Other Guardian: ~~████████~~, grandmother

Name of Child: L—
Age: 15
Role: Victim

IS THERE IMMEDIATE DANGER OF SERIOUS PHYSICAL HARM? [YES] (NO)

ALLEGATION:

Family doctor contacted social services to report symptoms possibly indicative of abuse or other trauma affecting L—. Recommended a home welfare check.

ANALYSIS OF SITUATION:

[R. S., ~~███~~ family's regular caseworker]

On Monday, February 24, I responded to a recent alert from the ~~████~~ family's doctor, suggesting a possibility of abuse or other trauma affecting the adolescent daughter, L—. The ~~████~~ family has been fairly stable for many years now, and what few crises have arisen (work conflicts, late mortgage payments) have been managed successfully, and have not significantly affected L—. I conducted interviews with all members of the household, but could find no significant evidence of abuse or other recent trauma. L— does report unusual symptoms that may be an effort to win attention from the adults in her life. L— also has an audition coming up that she is very focused on. It seems likely that her symptoms are a result of this new stress and pressure in her life.

CONCLUSION:

No call for further action at this time, but I will stay in close contact with the ▓▓▓ family and remain alert to any further signs of abuse, disruption, or instability in the household.

When I got home from school today, Mamma was very upset about something. She started in on me as soon as I walked through the door, making comments about how I'm too trusting, how you can't rely on anyone but your own family, and how other people come in here and they don't understand what's going on and they just want to make trouble.

I couldn't figure out what any of it was about, but Gramma Patty explained that while I had been at school, Renee came over again and questioned both of them on what's been going on recently, and was digging pretty hard for information. She said Renee told them that if she got any hint that this household was not a safe home for me, she would remove me, just like when I was little.

Can you believe that? Remove me! From my own home!

Like I'm a . . . dog or a bag of trash or a broken TV set. Just a thing you move from one place to another, not a person with her own choices and opinions and preferences.

This is all crazy! I told Renee a dozen times that I'm not being abused. Gramma Patty explained that it doesn't necessarily have to be abuse. I guess social services can decide to remove me if I'm not being well provided for, or if they decide the household isn't "stable" enough, whatever that means. But seriously, where does Renee get off, making these kinds of threats? After going on and on the other day about how I could trust her, and how she only wanted the best for me, how is it in my interest to take me away from my family without even consulting me?

I was furious when I realized what was going on, but Gramma Patty tried to calm me down. She said the main point is, we all have to be really cautious about what we say to Renee from now on. She agreed it would be difficult, because we've all come to trust Renee and treat her like part of the family, but we really need to be careful, because when things get rough, you can't exactly trust people from government agencies. Guess I'm learning that now.

I still can't believe it. I've always trusted Renee, and even yesterday on the phone she kept saying over and over that I could trust her, had to trust her, had to tell her anything that was going on. But Dr. Afolabi had said the same thing the other day, and it turned out she was lying. Renee said it wasn't a lie, but it smells a lot like one. And Renee is on the same side as the doctor, so of course she would protect her. But they both said they were trying to protect me and they're on my side. This whole question of "sides" is suddenly a lot less clear. I hadn't really questioned it at the time, but now that I think about it, what

462

exactly was Renee going to do if I told her about some personal crisis? Was she going to magically wave a wand and fix it? She never said, but now it seems like her plan was always to remove me from my home and put me in foster care, just like they did when I was a baby.

I've never felt so betrayed. For years now I've told Renee all about my problems, and she's always been helpful. But those were normal problems. People teasing me at school, or a boy I was shy around, or trouble with my algebra. Renee never threatened to take me away from my family for any of that. She just talked me through whatever I was struggling with and helped me figure out a solution. But I can see this situation is different. This isn't going to be fixed by hiring a tutor or talking to a teacher.

I don't know what to do. I've trusted Renee with all my worries and concerns for so long, I don't know how to stop now. But Mamma and Gramma Patty are right. If Renee is making these kinds of threats now, based on nothing, I can't trust her anymore. But if I shut her out completely, that could go wrong too. I'm going to have to be a lot more careful from now on with who I tell what.

FRIDAY, FEBRUARY 28, 6:45 A.M. (PRIVATE)

I'm starting to worry Mamma is right about there being some kind of hex on this house. I thought she was just being her usual dramatic self, but I woke up last night to all kinds of crazy noises, like every door in the house being slammed. I guess the back door had been opened somehow, and wind was blowing all through the house. There were papers and things everywhere, and photographs had been knocked over. Then Mamma went into the kitchen and let out a scream like you wouldn't believe. There were muddy footprints on the floor. Not from shoes, but naked feet.

On one hand, maybe that's an overreaction to just footprints. But on the other, it *is* pretty creepy. Who could be walking around our house in the middle of the night with no shoes on? It wasn't me.

Gramma Patty is trying to calm her down now, but Mamma is like, "You know what this is. We can't keep denying it. It's only going to get worse. We have to do something."

I don't know what exactly she means, but it doesn't sound good. Lately Mamma and Gramma Patty have been having quiet conversations when they think I can't hear. There's something they both know that they are trying to hide from me. Maybe Mamma thinks it's more than a simple hex. Maybe it's something even worse.

But if it is what Mamma thinks, that means our prayer circle the other day didn't work. And if prayer doesn't work in a situation like this, what will?

SUNDAY, MARCH 2, 12:25 P.M. (PRIVATE)

In church this morning, Pastor Bob was talking about the Robinson trial again. On the news they're saying the verdict will be any day now, so he was talking about how people should handle the outcome, whatever it is. Everyone is still worrying about riots, and Pastor Bob went on and on about how violence only begets violence, and how this community has to focus on positive, productive steps forward. He told everyone to try to stay calm and remember to check in on their neighbors, to take care of one another. To remember there will be justice in the fullness of time, and it's not our place to be impatient and demand justice in our own time. And that rioting mostly hurts people within the community, and not the objects of everyone's anger.

I glanced around to look for Malcolm's response to that, but I guess he's stopped coming to church lately. I don't even see him at school that often. From what I hear, he's gotten so wound up in all the protesting that he doesn't have time for much else. I know Malcolm isn't in favor of rioting, but he doesn't have much patience for passive resistance, either. He says passive is exactly how they want us.

It's hard to imagine any outcome other than a guilty verdict, but I wonder what would happen if the cops were acquitted of the charges. Would all the peaceful protests and demonstrations erupt into violence? What would that look like? Would Mamma and Gramma Patty and I be in danger? Or would I get caught up in it and wind up joining the angry mob in my shock over the outcome? What if I got hurt? What if I got arrested? I've never imagined anything like that for myself before. My whole life, I've only seen one future for myself: singing on a stage in front of an adoring crowd. What if I don't live to see that destiny? What if our house gets set on fire by rioters and we all burn to death in our beds?

But maybe that's missing the point of the sermon. It does seem a little wrong to think about this situation only in terms of how it might affect me. Maybe Mamma and Gramma Patty *will* protect me. Maybe I will stay home, safe, while the riots rage, and nothing much will change in my life. But that doesn't mean stuff won't change for other people. What does it matter if I am safe and well taken care of and basically unaffected if other people just like me are being hauled off to jail or shot with rubber bullets or teargassed? Or if their homes and businesses are destroyed, their schools closed, the roads blocked off?

After the service, I just wanted to go home and think about all this stuff, but Mamma insisted on us sticking around for the doughnut hour, which I usually try to avoid. Mamma grabbed me by the arm and tugged me over to a heavyset woman wearing a coral-pink suit and a nice double string of pearls.

Mamma introduced her as Miss Nephtalie Pierre. I know I've seen her around church before. She and Mamma catch up a few times a year during the doughnut hour, but Gramma Patty is always a bit standoffish with her. And Gramma Patty isn't the only one. Miss Pierre certainly has her friends and acquaintances at church, but there are also a lot of people who seem to avoid her, don't speak to her, or even meet her eyes. It's weird, because you never saw a more respectable-looking woman. She's always nicely dressed in pastel-colored suits and a double string of pearls. She has a pleasant face and a warm, welcoming manner, and I can't think why anyone would avoid her.

Miss Pierre brushed some powdered sugar from her suit and gave us both a big smile. She asked about Mamma's health, and then turned to me and said, "And my, how you've grown!" It was odd, because I wasn't sure we'd ever directly met before, but I guess she must have known me when I was a little kid, which makes it even stranger that Mamma has barely spoken to her since then, though they seem friendly enough.

Mamma surprised me by asking if Miss Pierre would come by the house sometime this week, even though we pretty much never have people over. Then she leaned in and added in a whisper that she understood Miss Pierre was busy, but the situation was urgent. Miss Pierre dropped her smile at that point. She just nodded and pulled a little book from her purse, made a mark with her pencil, and said, "Tuesday evening." Then she said, "Do you remember what you need to do to prepare? Or do you need instructions?" Mamma said she remembered, and grabbed Miss

Pierre's hand to thank her. Then we collected Gramma Patty and went home.

How mysterious! What could this all be about? I tried to interrogate Mamma on the walk home, but she just said Miss Pierre was going to help us take care of whatever was going on. "Don't worry," she said. "She knows what she's doing; she'll fix it right up." I wanted to ask more questions, but Gramma Patty was still frowning about the whole thing, so I thought I'd better just leave it alone. I guess I won't have long to wait to find out more.

SUNDAY, MARCH 2, 3:15 P.M. (PRIVATE)

All I want to do is spend my Sunday afternoon relaxing and maybe catching up on whatever is going on with the Robinson trial to see if there are new analyses out with a different take on the situation, but Mamma is driving me crazy, cleaning everything inside and out in preparation for Miss Pierre's visit! I still don't understand exactly who she is or why she's coming over, but I have never seen Mamma clean like this. Normally she leaves all that stuff to Gramma Patty, but this time Gramma Patty just sat on the couch, watching TV while Mamma scrubbed everything down with bleach and water. I don't think it's such a good idea, to be honest. Bleach is one thing in the bathroom, but it's leaving ugly marks through the rest of the house. It makes the whole place smell funny, and the fumes make me light-headed. I don't know what Mamma thinks she's doing, but she just told me either I can help or I can stay out of the way.

I just heard Mamma and Gramma Patty talking quietly in the front room, like they didn't want me to hear. Gramma Patty was saying, "You know I think this is a bad idea. This is not how I raised you. This is not faith; it's superstition, and it betrays a lack of faith in God." To which Mamma said, "It would be more irresponsible at this point not to try it. You can't keep pretending this isn't happening." Then she went on about how there's no shame in using whatever tools are at our disposal, and that it worked last time. She specifically said, "You can't deny that it worked last time."

Last time? When? What are they talking about? Now I'm more curious than ever.

SUNDAY, MARCH 2, 3:35 P.M. (PRIVATE)

Mamma kicked me out of my own room to scrub it down! She told me to just leave her to it, but it was driving me crazy, imagining her splashing caustic chemicals all over my stuff. I went into the kitchen for a minute, and when I came back, she was holding one of my wigs in her hand, the bucket of bleach at her feet. I took the wig back and said, "Don't even think about it." There are limits.

What is all this about? It's like she's lost her mind.

MONDAY, MARCH 3, 8:36 P.M. (PRIVATE)

The tension's been building between Mamma and Gramma
Patty ever since church yesterday, and I knew they'd wind up
having it out. I'm not even sure who started it, but I was just
ducking into the kitchen to get a snack when Mamma started
yelling about how she's responsible for this family and she has
to make the decisions. Gramma Patty, with a deadly seriousness,
said she has always tried to keep this a good Christian household, and after last time, Mamma promised "never again," but
now here they were. And Mamma said it worked last time, and
Gramma Patty couldn't argue with that. And Gramma Patty
said to her, "Honey, you are playing with powers beyond what
you know, and it is dangerous. It was dangerous then, and it
is now. How can you be sure that what Miss Pierre did back
then isn't the reason we're having all these problems now?" And

they went on like this, but I couldn't make much sense of it. Gramma Patty just kept going on about how faith in the Lord was the only answer, and sometimes He tests us but we have to remain firm. And if we go running to other kinds of power every time we get tested, that just shows our lack of faith and it's as good as inviting the Devil himself into the house. And Mamma became really furious when she said that and screamed that she didn't want to hear it. She said Miss Pierre was a good woman and there was no reason to believe otherwise, and she had made a decision and was sticking by it. And she didn't see Gramma Patty suggesting any better ideas.

Something like that, anyway.

Then Mamma took herself off to her bedroom and slammed the door dramatically, the way she always does when she gets herself worked up into a state.

That left me and Gramma Patty alone in the kitchen. I kind of just wanted to clear out of there and avoid being sucked into this drama, but Gramma Patty sat me down and made me some food and finally was like, "Look, you know how your mamma is. She gets an idea in her head, and there is no reasoning with her, no matter how foolish it is. I can't control her any more than you can, or anyone can. God knows, people have tried. So she's invited Miss Pierre here and I guess she's going to come and we just have to make the best of it."

Then she started going on about Miss Pierre, and honestly it didn't really clear anything up, but I guess I got the idea that, in Gramma Patty's mind anyway, Miss Pierre is some kind of witch or voodoo lady or something. And that Mamma invited her here to do magic spells on the house. I guess that explains why people in church avoid her. Pretty sure the pastor doesn't approve of that kind of stuff. Gramma Patty was trying to warn me and was telling me to be careful around her. That just having her around could encourage evil spirits to bother us. I don't know about that. I'm not even all the way certain of the stuff they talk about at church, and whether any of it is real. As for this kind of thing, I always assumed it was just superstition. I didn't even know my mamma believed in voodoo and stuff like that! Not that it's surprising. Mamma does have a tendency to get all kinds of ideas in her head. I don't know, though. I'm not sure I believe in any of it, but I have to admit I'm curious. Miss Pierre seems so nice and normal! What's she going to do? I'm half expecting her to kill a goat on our front steps now. That would definitely be exciting.

TUESDAY, MARCH 4, 6:22 A.M. (PRIVATE)

Last night there were more strange noises around the house. It started out with dogs barking, even though there aren't any dogs that live on this block. Then the barking shifted over into growling and snarling that, at a certain point, didn't even sound doglike. But I couldn't put my finger on what other animal it could be. Sometimes it sounded kind of like a person imitating a dog, and sometimes it sounded like a dog but bigger. Much bigger. And then the doors all started banging as if there were a terrible storm whipping through town, but when I stuck my head out the window, the air was perfectly still.

I tried to ignore it and go back to sleep, but the minute I closed my eyes, I was back in the middle of those visions, being tossed from one torture scenario to the next, knowing I'd committed some terrible crime but not knowing what. When I opened my eyes, instead of going away, the pain focused itself in my side again, feeling like a running cramp but so much worse. This time it was like someone was pinching and twisting at my skin with an iron clamp.

I have to admit now, I'm glad Miss Pierre is coming. There's something definitely not right in the house. And all the praying we've done doesn't seem to be helping a bit.

TUESDAY, MARCH 4, 6:12 P.M. (PRIVATE)

Miss Pierre just left. The whole thing was . . . interesting. Not really what I was expecting.

First she walked through the house a bit and sniffed around in the corners. She did that for a while, though I can't imagine how she smelled anything but the bleach. That's all I could smell. She did say she thought the bleach was probably already making a difference.

Then she talked with Mamma a bit about the energy in the house. She said the bleach was helping, but there was still something lingering. Something underneath. Mamma got a little offended at that, but Miss Pierre shushed her with a laugh. She said she wasn't talking about old food or some dead possum in the walls. It's just that houses get a particular smell when something has lodged in them. She didn't know how to describe it except as a kind of darkness. A little bitter, a little acrid. With an undertone of rot. That's how she can tell when there's an infestation. But she said not to worry, that she had smelled a lot worse. If she hadn't been paying attention, she wouldn't have even noticed it. Sometimes, she said, you walk up the front stairs to a house and you have to turn right around and walk back to the street because the stink is so powerful, it turns you away like a wall. But she was positive there was something here, and she said we were wise to take care of it early, before things turned worse.

Then she lit some herbs wrapped up in a little bundle, and in the air she drew a cross with the smoke while saying a little prayer. That helped cover the smell of the bleach a lot, actually, which was good. Next she pulled out a bottle of olive oil and poured a little onto her fingertips. Then she walked around the house, drawing crosses in olive oil on all the doors.

Before that, Gramma Patty had been looking on disapprovingly but not saying anything. Around this time, I guess she couldn't hold her tongue anymore, because she pulled Mamma into the kitchen and they started having words. I didn't want to deal with that, so I decided to follow Miss Pierre around the house to watch her work. Without really thinking about it, I started to take photos of the crosses she was drawing on the doors. When I turned around and saw Miss Pierre watching me, I suddenly got embarrassed, like she'd caught me. I wasn't sure if maybe there was something wrong or disrespectful about taking photos of her work, but she didn't seem mad. She just smiled and asked me if I'd show her my room. Luckily, it was clean and tidy, thanks to Mamma attacking everything with bleach before.

Miss Pierre sat down on the bed, patted it for me to join her, and asked me to describe in my own words some of what had been going on. So I told her about the moths in my wigs and the waking dreams where I'm being tortured and the pains I've been having and coughing stuff up and all that. She paid close attention, and when I was done, she asked if she could anoint me. I wasn't sure exactly what that meant, but I told her, "Okay." Basically she just rubbed olive oil into my hands and then painted a cross with it on my forehead.

She asked me if I had any questions, so I asked how she knew about all this stuff. She told me about how her grandmother had grown up in the islands (actually she said, "*Grand-mère*," because they speak French where she grew up), where this kind of practice is more out in the open. Her *grand-mère* was a devout Christian her whole life, but she also knew how to deal with hexes and bad spirits, and she never saw any contradiction between the two. It was a useful skill, and people would come to her for help. And she was able to help them. Miss Pierre grew up watching her do this, and she asked a lot of questions and her *grand-mère* helped train her.

Then she told me about how she first met Mamma, and how they got to know each other. It was like hearing a family secret, but from some stranger. Only I'm not sure if it's an actual secret or just something no one ever got around to telling me.

It had to do with when I was little, and I got sent away when Mamma was having problems. I knew that much. I knew she'd been under a lot of stress and had some kind of breakdown, and the cops and social services got involved, and I wound up in foster care until Mamma got settled again. That's as much of the story as I've ever known, and I'd never thought to ask anything more than that. I didn't occur to me that there was anything more. But Miss Pierre said Mamma's troubles back then were because she thought someone she worked with had put a hex on her. So many things were going wrong in her life at that moment, she felt it had to be some ill-meaning force outside of her.

Mamma got Miss Pierre's name through some friends at church. Miss Pierre saw right away there was something in her, on her, or following her around. She said Mamma was in a bad way.

I asked Miss Pierre if Mamma was right about the hex, but she just shrugged. She said it was impossible to be sure, but she didn't think it was unlikely.

Apparently Miss Pierre is the reason Mamma got me back all those years ago. That was how she got herself stable again. But I guess even then, Gramma Patty didn't approve and said if Mamma was going to move back in with her, she had to promise not to do any of that stuff again.

Miss Pierre talked about a bunch of other stuff with me too.

Once she got me started, the questions sort of flowed out of me, and Miss Pierre never acted shocked or offended, so I just kept going and she took her time and explained everything she could.

I asked why Gramma Patty doesn't like her (which maybe was super-rude, but I got the sense Miss Pierre wouldn't mind). I didn't really get Gramma Patty's problem, since it looked to me like everything Miss Pierre was doing was in the name of Jesus. Miss Pierre explained about how there's a lot of disagreement about what counts as part of Christianity. Some folks are very suspicious of anything that doesn't come straight from the mouth of their pastor, but helping people to feel better and protect their souls is no bad thing. She said the way she sees it, all that matters is what works. "I'm not one for the theology books," she said, "but the Bible tells us Jesus himself walked among people and cast demons out of them. If it was right for him to do it, why would it be wrong for me? And if people feel better after coming to me for help, why would God disapprove of that? If He loves us, doesn't He want us to feel better?" I guess I'm going to have to think about that. I'm pretty sure the pastor and Gramma Patty would say it's blasphemous to claim to do the same kind of miracles as Jesus had. But why, if the whole point is to help people? I can't imagine Jesus would be against helping people.

When Miss Pierre got up to go, I stopped her. I had one more question I'd been wanting to ask, but I didn't know how to approach it. I hemmed and hawed for a bit, but finally I just came out with it and asked why she wanted to anoint me. "Well," she said, "it can't hurt, can it?"

"But why me?" I asked. "Why me and not Mamma? Why not Gramma Patty?"

At that point, I think Miss Pierre understood what I was

getting at, but she got quiet and didn't answer me. I asked her if she thought Mamma was right this time. Has our house or our family been hexed? She just shrugged again. So I asked, "Do you think it's something else? Something to do with me specifically?" Again, she didn't answer.

I was starting to get frustrated, which made me less careful with my questions. Finally I said, "Do you know anything about demon possession? Is it real?"

Miss Pierre nodded slowly.

"Is that what's happening to me?" I asked.

Miss Pierre looked at me a long time. Then she said, "I wouldn't rule it out."

Whatever it is Miss Pierre did the other day, I think it did help. I'm not sure if it counts as magic or prayer or just psychology, but I've had a good couple of days. Just going to school and talking to friends and feeling normal. It's nice. I haven't felt this way in a while.

It's kind of like coming back to your hometown after traveling to far-off, exotic places. It's a little hard to find your footing again back in the ordinary world. Hard to remember what I used to do every day, what used to occupy my thoughts, when I wasn't worrying about hexes and demons and the state of my eternal soul.

I should start singing again. There's still time to get my voice back into shape before that audition. I'm just not feeling it though. I don't know why, but right now it seems like a lot of energy and effort I just don't have. And singing never felt that way before.

Maybe I should post something publicly on the blog. At least let people know how I am. Maybe a new tutorial. Feels sort of pointless now though. It's been so long since I made a real post, I don't think I have more than a couple of followers anymore. Everyone's moved on.

I don't blame them, to be honest. That stuff just doesn't seem as important as it once did. Lately I can't be bothered to do more than a head wrap before school. I don't get off on people looking at me the way I used to. The only thing that really holds my attention right now (outside of my own problems) is the news about the Robinson trial, and all the protests in front of the courthouse. Mamma doesn't want me to go join the protesters. She says it's too dangerous for someone my age. I don't see how it could be dangerous. They're peaceful protests! Everyone down there just wants justice and accountability. They're good people. But Mamma says with so many people gathered in one place, you don't know what could happen, especially with so many cops nearby, keeping an eye on the situation. She called it a recipe for disaster, and said everyone out there was tempting fate. Maybe so, but I think she's paranoid. Who's going to do anything to those protesters in broad daylight, around hundreds of witnesses? You'd never get away with it.

Maybe I should go down there, no matter what Mamma says. So what if it is dangerous? At least it wouldn't be boring. And I'd be doing something real. Being part of something bigger and more important than myself.

I don't know, though. Is that a real, sincere interest? Or am I just addicted to having some kind of drama in my life, and that's the most dramatic thing going on around me?

SATURDAY, MARCH 8, 10:28 A.M. (PRIVATE)

Now that the smell of bleach has faded a bit, I think I know what Miss Pierre was talking about with the smells of this house. If I think about it, I can pick up a kind of bitter scent, like something burning. A couple of times I've woken up in the middle of the night to something smelling just a little rotten. I check my pillows, my blankets, under the bed, but I can't trace it to anywhere in particular. And if I get up to get myself a glass of water, the smell seems to follow me.

But it's not just that. Sometimes I notice good smells too. I was checking over my wigs the other day, and I could swear I smelled something sweet, like flowers. Lilac, maybe, or clover? I'm not sure; I'm a city girl. Most flower smells I only know from artificial perfumes and stuff. But this wasn't like that. There was something really fresh and clean about it, and not chemical clean, like a laundry detergent. I asked Mamma if she had put in a new air freshener or gotten one of those candles, but she said no.

And then sometimes there's a smell, and I can't tell whether it's the good kind or the bad kind. It's like they're both mixed together to create something totally different, and I can't even tell whether I like it or not. It just smells complicated. And strange. I wonder what Miss Pierre would have to say about that.

MONDAY, MARCH 10, 5:48 P.M. (PRIVATE)

I guess Mamma might have been right about the protests. They were just saying on the news that there have been some outbreaks of violence in the past couple of days. The crowd got too big for the public park it was occupying, and some of the protestors moved into another area. The police told people to disperse, there was some conflict, and a bunch of people got hit with pepper spray. Things escalated from there, and some people are hurt pretty bad. Maybe it's just as well I wasn't there.

In less depressing news: I might have traced where that sweet smell was coming from. There's an old rosebush outside my bedroom window that I forgot all about because it hasn't bloomed in years. It's half dead because no one ever looks after it. It was here when Gramma Patty moved in, and none of us have much of a green thumb.

I was walking to school today though and noticed it was blooming! Loads of big heavy flowers in pink and white and yellow. I've never seen the bush bloom like that before.

WEDNESDAY, MARCH 12, 4:38 P.M. (PRIVATE)

I've been taking photos again . . . of anything that catches my attention, really. Mostly it's been stuff I see around town, or even around the house. Here's one from my last walk.

I'm not sure why I'm photographing this stuff, since no one else wants to see it, but it's something to do, at least.

Maybe I should go ahead and post them publicly. It's not like anyone could tell the difference anymore between the pictures I take and the ones that ghost or stalker or whatever used to post. I could just run with it and have my new aesthetic be "creepy dead and decaying things."

THURSDAY, MARCH 13, 4:37 P.M. (PRIVATE)

On my way home from the bus stop today, I saw a dead bird by the side of the road. I stopped to take a picture of it, like I've done before, but this time was different. I was just looking over my phone at it and I became overcome by this sense of . . . It's hard to describe. But the creature was so beautiful; the feathers were so glossy and shiny, I got swept up by an irresistible impulse to reach out and touch it. So there I am, crouching on the ground, touching this dead bird. First with my fingertips, and then I let my whole hand stroke its feathers, down its neck and along its broken wing. Writing about it here, I sound crazy. Who sits in the middle of a street, petting a dead animal? Once upon a time, I would have been disgusted by the very idea, and if I even walked near it, I'd be worried about parasites and diseases getting on me, and I'd rush home to wash my hands. But at the time, I didn't think about any of that. My mind was almost blank, and all I was really aware of was the feel of those smooth, cool feathers against my skin.

But then . . . I don't know. I really can't explain what happened next. I was so sure the bird was dead. Its neck and wing looked broken; there was blood on the pavement. A few flies buzzing around. And it felt cool under my fingers. But as I sat there, stroking it, I noticed it started to feel warmer. I thought it must be the heat from my hand warming it, but then I felt a strange thudding, and the wing was moving. Twitching.

Part of me was freaked out, and like a movie in my head, I saw myself snap my hand back and step away from the animal. But that's not what I did. I stayed there with it and felt the wing move under my hand, and I pressed down harder on it. I don't know what I was trying to do. I felt this surge of power run through me, like a tingling in my blood, and I felt like if I just kept pressing harder and harder, I could crush this fragile body into bits. So there I was, torn between two impulses: one, to jump up and get as far away from this creature as possible, and the other to press it into the pavement until I could feel the bones crunch beneath me. Instead of doing either one, I just sat there, motionless, my hand heavy on its body, my blood surging hot and feverish, and I felt that wing twitch again. And again. And then it was beating itself against the ground. I started stroking down its back again, and I could feel all the tiny muscles and bones moving together.

And then it was flying. There was a noise of feathers beating the air, and I hardly blinked before the bird was high above me, flapping and gliding like any bird in the world. I can't even begin to explain it.

What does it mean? I could have sworn that bird was dead. And now it's not. Is that because of me? Or some power using me? Would it work on other things? Like what about that rosebush? Or now that I think of it, the mold in the bathroom that just won't stay dead. Would it work on a bigger animal? What about a person?

No. No, I can't think this way. It's a coincidence; it has to be. That bird was sick; that's all. Stunned, maybe, like it ran into something and got knocked to the ground. And I just happened by at the right time. That's crazy, but any other explanation is a lot crazier. And more terrifying.

I thought I was all cured from whatever was wrong with me when Miss Pierre came and did her thing, but I'm wondering now if it was only a temporary fix. I'm not sure if it's related or if it's just a bad mood or whatever, but I've been feeling all out of sorts lately. I thought it was just boredom or irritation or normal teen angst, but it's getting worse, I think. More than I can ignore.

I've been having nightmares again, about torture and pain, and I wake up, shaking and retching. There's never really any plot or story to the dreams. Just the same disturbing images they've been all along, almost like someone's flipping channels on a TV. Only, it's not like movies or TV shows, because it all feels so *real*.

It used to be that the pain would disappear as soon as I woke up, but lately the pain I feel in the dream sticks to me even after

I wake up. I'm lying there in bed, my eyes open, and my skin is so hot, it feels like it's on fire. Last night I was actually surprised when I looked down and the bed wasn't on fire. Or sometimes it's that same horrible stabbing pain in my side. I can't figure out what it is. Gramma Patty taught me to figure out the difference between muscle pain, nerve pain, bone pain, and skin pain, but this doesn't feel like any of that somehow.

I don't know how to deal with this. For as long as I can remember, music was always my refuge when anything bad was going on in my life. All I had to do was put on my headphones, and I could slip away into another world where everything was sweet and beautiful. But that doesn't work now. It's not just that I can't sing anymore; I can't listen to music either. I put my headphones on and press play, and my head is filled with screaming and wailing like I never heard before in all my life. And I swear it has to be the sounds of Hell.

Now I'm almost feeling guilty because I know I was just complaining about being bored with a normal life before all this started back up. I had been thinking I sort of liked it because it made me feel special, like I always wanted to be. But now that it's happening again . . . I don't want to be this kind of special. I'd rather just be ordinary.

I don't know what to do about this. I think I should tell someone—Mamma or Renee or Miss Pierre—but I don't know. Maybe not yet. I don't want to worry them or cause any trouble. I mean, it's not like anyone seems to know any way to cure it or make it go away. So what's the point in bringing it up over and over?

TUESDAY, MARCH 18, 3:03 P.M. (PRIVATE)

I got sent home from school today. I guess it was pretty bad. I don't exactly remember what happened, but the nurse told me when I came to that I must have had some kind of seizure. My friends say it was scary. That my body went rigid and my eyes were glassy and I didn't respond to anyone calling my name or touching me. Then I went down hard, slamming to the floor, shaking and making noises like I was choking.

I don't remember any of that at all. All I remember is that I was taking a history test when my vision went sort of wobbly. The whiteboard at the front of the class started billowing like a sail, and when I turned my head, everything else in the room looked like it was bubbling or sagging, even people's faces. And my hearing was messed up too. Everything sounded slow and underwater, except for this really intense high-pitched buzzing noise. I didn't know what to do. I just sat there, not trusting myself to move or speak. But I realized at some point that other people had noticed. I think I was gurgling or something, because everyone turned to look at me, which just made everything worse.

I couldn't stand to look at their faces. These people I've known for years suddenly looked strange and awful. I smelled smoke and fire, and that was when I really got scared. I wanted to yell and warn everyone, but I couldn't. I felt my throat close up, and I couldn't move my body, either. And it was incredibly hot. The visual distortions I was seeing were from wave after wave of heat from this terrible fire. The floor and the desks all started to melt, and the smoke was burning my eyes, and the smell of burning plastic was everywhere. And still my classmates just sat there, staring at me, sometimes moving their mouths, but I couldn't hear them. I couldn't hear the fire, either, even though I could smell it and feel it and see its effects. I didn't hear crackling or snapping like you expect from a fire. I didn't hear anything at all.

Then everything went black, and the next thing I remember, I was waking up in the nurse's office. Gramma Patty came and got me, and now I'm sitting at home. I don't know what I'm supposed to be doing, exactly. I don't feel sick, or like I need rest. If anything, I feel weirdly energized. Are they going to let me go back to school tomorrow?

TUESDAY, MARCH 18, 4:43 P.M. (PRIVATE)

I just got off the phone with Tanya, who was sitting next to me
in history class. She told me what happened today at school,
filling in more details. She says before I fainted, I was making
all kinds of weird noises she'd never heard come out of a person
before. Weird cries that were so high-pitched, they hurt her ears,
or so low-pitched, she could feel the vibrations in her bones.
She said I fell to my knees and started coughing and retching
until I vomited onto the floor. The teacher ran over and sent
someone to get help, but while they were waiting, someone
noticed that the mess next to my desk didn't look normal. Even
though it was kind of gross, she leaned in to look at it more
closely and saw . . . Well, she said it looked like petals. Like
from a whole rose, in fact, or maybe more than one—the petals
were in a whole range of colors, from pinkish-yellow to a red

so deep, it was almost black. And she said at first she was holding her breath, because she expected it to smell like vomit, but when she took a small breath by accident, she realized it smelled sweet, not foul. "Like the inside of a flower shop," she said.

Well, if that isn't the strangest thing I ever heard. Tanya can be kind of a drama queen and is known to exaggerate, so I wasn't sure what to make of her story. But then she sent me a picture from her phone.

What am I going to do? If Miss Pierre can't help me, who can?

Renee came to see me today after school. I used to get so excited when she came to visit because we always had fun together. Now she just makes me nervous. I guess I still believe she means well, but I'm so afraid anything I say to her is going to make her take me away from Mamma.

She heard about what happened in school the other day and wanted me to talk about it. I tried to play it off as no big deal. I was in the middle of a test, I told her, and I freaked out a little. It happens. People get panic attacks. But she wasn't having it. She said people get panic attacks if they are under a ton of stress. She pointed out I don't normally panic during tests. So what new stress was I under?

I said I didn't want to talk about it, but that didn't go over well. She started prodding again about abuse, mistreatment, drugs, and then she said some of the people she talked to at my school said I was making noises—shouting and babbling, and no one could tell what I was saying. Like speaking in tongues. I didn't know what to say to that.

I had to tell her *something*, so I talked about the protests. About how I've been watching them on TV and getting a little obsessive maybe, and how Mamma and Gramma Patty are worried about it. She said she understood completely, and even admitted she's been getting a little obsessed too, and feeling both like she needs to help and like she doesn't know what she can do. At least she's an adult, and can direct her own life. She's gone over to the park a few times and brought bottled water to the protesters. I wish I could do something like that. I asked her to talk to Mamma about it, maybe get her to let me go with Renee to help out. She said she would think about it, but I'm pretty sure she means no. I think, ultimately, Renee agrees with Mamma that it's too dangerous for a kid. But you know, I'm not *really* a kid. I mean, it's not like I'm twelve! I feel like if I'm old enough to want to do it, I'm old enough to be trusted with the risks. It's not like I don't understand them.

We talked about that for a while, and I think Renee would have been satisfied with that as the only thing bothering me, except then she asked how my singing was going, and I was like, "Oh, I haven't even thought about that lately." Renee made a big deal of that, pointing out I've been obsessed with being a singer for as long as she's known me. She asked if there was something else on my mind, and I must have hesitated or made a face or something, because she jumped on it. And I just . . . I hate hiding things from her. I'm no good at it.

I really did try not to say anything too specific, but well, I don't know. I know what Mamma said about Renee's threats, but I guess I still believe she means well and wouldn't do anything to hurt me, or any of us. And she did promise she wasn't going to do anything drastic. She said the main reason she comes around is to make sure everything is okay and stable. That she's not the bad guy, not out to get anyone. What she wants personally, and what it's her job to ensure, is our family stays whole and healthy and happy.

I don't think she's lying when she says that. I want to believe her anyway. She talked about how it's her job to keep track of all the little problems before they turn into big ones. She talked about what happened with Mamma when I was a baby. How she had a lot of problems, a lot of responsibilities, and no one was helping her. She didn't know who she could turn to, so things got worse and worse until she couldn't do it anymore.

Renee said the reason she comes and talks to us is to help keep that from happening. To see the problems and help solve them before they get that bad. And so far, she's done a pretty good job. And she let me in on a secret: it might look like we'd never faced any major problems, but we had, and she and Mamma and Gramma Patty had kept them from me.

That shocked me a bit. How could there be stuff going on in my own household that I didn't know about?

Renee was quiet for a minute, letting me absorb everything, and then she said, "Laetitia, I can't help if I don't know what's wrong. I can't spot the problems if you won't talk to me and be honest."

That broke me down, and I wound up telling her stuff that has been stressing me out. Stuff Mamma told me not to talk about with her. I hope that doesn't come across as a betrayal, but I'm pretty desperate these days. I didn't know what else to do. I hoped she'd be able to help.

It's hard to come out and admit to something most people think is so crazy. That in itself wouldn't be so bad—all my life people thought I was crazy for thinking I could be a singer. But this is different. I guess it's not being called crazy I'm afraid of, but the idea that I might have something terrible in me. That I might be beyond any kind of help or salvation.

I don't think I've ever come out and said it here, in my locked entries. I might as well start now. Maybe writing it down will help me face it. Avoiding it certainly isn't helping the situation. Okay, here goes.

I'm worried I'm possessed by a demon.

Writing that sent a weird feeling through my body. A shudder. Or am I just imagining it? Am I being dramatic? Or is there something in me? Why is it so hard to tell?

Well, I told Renee. The weird thing is, she didn't act as shocked as I expected her to. She just nodded a little to herself, and her expression looked almost . . . angry. Or frustrated, maybe. Or maybe just sad. Then she asked if Miss Pierre had come around.

I didn't expect Renee to know anything about Miss Pierre, but it makes sense. Miss Pierre helped Mamma out when she had her troubles all those years ago, and that's when Renee started coming. But if Miss Pierre is the one who cured Mamma of her problem and got her back on track, why would Renee have a problem with her? They were on the same side.

But I guess it's a little more complicated than that. Renee doesn't trust Miss Pierre, and she never has. She considers her a charlatan who preys on the desperate and gullible. People who are "particularly susceptible to her brand of hokum." I didn't think that was fair, and it didn't mesh with my experiences with Miss Pierre. She helped Mamma and she was helping me. Wasn't that proof her expertise was useful? And even if it was all just fake, as long as it works and makes people feel better, where is the harm?

Renee said she's known people who have been bankrupted by Miss Pierre, or close to it. She said Mamma was lucky her "cure" came quickly, but other people go back again and again, and she never seems to fix them entirely but always offers a promise of how it will work next time. Each time, she gets to charge a new fee. I hadn't even thought about whether or not Miss Pierre was making money off this.

But how could that be her fault? She's not making these visions happen, not making the strange objects come out of my body. All that started happening before I even met her. And everything she has said and done has seemed to be with the intention of helping me. But that's true of Renee, too. So who do I believe?

I asked if I shouldn't talk to Miss Pierre anymore, but Renee said she wouldn't try to stop us from going to her. She talked about respecting people's beliefs, even when they were different from her own. But she warned me to be careful with Miss Pierre, and to contact her if anything makes me uncomfortable or suspicious. I guess that's fair enough.

Renee did say she would come by more often to make sure nothing gets too out of hand. Maybe Renee will see that Miss Pierre's work helps us, and it will change her mind.

SATURDAY, MARCH 22, 2:33 P.M. (PRIVATE)

Mamma and Gramma Patty are driving me crazy! They're treating me like a little kid, making me leave my laptop and my phone in the living room so they can keep an eye on me when I go online. They haven't been this strict in years! But I guess they figured out I was sneaking on to find information about the Robinson trial.

I know they're just worried about me, but I wish they could see it's the only thing that distracts me from my own problems and makes me think about bigger things than myself. It just kills me that it's all going on practically on my doorstep, but I'm being kept in the dark about it.

Mamma and Gramma Patty have gotten way more intense about their rules and restrictions over the past couple of days. Makes me wonder if there's something specific they don't want me to know. But what could it be?

SUNDAY, MARCH 23, 11:39 A.M. (PRIVATE)

Something is really wrong. I don't even know where to begin.

Gramma Patty made me go to church again, and at first it was okay. I was a little annoyed to be there, but there was nothing out of the ordinary. Then the pastor started talking about the Robinson trial and the protestors, and I know now why Mamma and Gramma Patty were trying to keep me away from the news. At first he was just going through the usual thing he does every week, mentioning people from the congregation who are sick or lost their jobs or whatever, and asking everyone to pray for them. I was barely paying attention. Then he was talking about the Robinson protestors, and he mentioned that a big group of them had been arrested earlier this week, and some hadn't been able to make bail yet. He was asking people to pray for a speedy release. He read off a pretty long list of names, and guess who was on it. . . . Malcolm.

I was pretty upset when I heard. Worried about Malcolm of course, and also feeling guilty that my name *wasn't* on that list. I instantly felt like I should have been there with them. It sickens me to think of myself sitting at home, eyes glazing over, reading all this stupid commentary, when people like Malcolm are actually out there, making a difference.

Then the choir started up, and at first it was fine. Then I realized they were all singing, but I couldn't really hear their voices. It was like they were singing underwater or something. I started to worry I was having another panic attack or episode or whatever, and worrying only ever makes it worse. So I started panicking, my heart was racing, my palms sweating, my vision going black at the edges, and I blinked a few times to clear it, and all of a sudden the scene changed in front of me. The singing came back like someone flicked a volume switch, only it wasn't singing that was coming out of their mouths—it was shrieking and moaning and crying, like all of them were in the worst kind of pain. And they weren't swaying energetically to whatever hymn; they were being dragged this way and that by beasts. Little monsters with animal faces and pointed ears and blue-tinted flesh. Some of the little demons were grabbing their arms or holding their robes, some were beating them with short sticks, and others were blowing thick heavy smoke into their eyes.

That was when I realized the choir members weren't just screaming; they were calling to me to help them and save them from this torture. Part of me knew this probably wasn't real, but I couldn't just sit there and watch it, so I jumped up and ran from the church and out into the hallway. A terrible wave of nausea took me, and I feel to my knees, the muscles of my esophagus convulsing. It was so painful. Much more painful than vomiting normally is. I managed to cough something up and spit it out onto the floor. I retched a few more times until the feeling passed, and then I opened my eyes. The little pile in front of me was smooth and sharp and covered in blood and bile, so I wasn't sure what it was. And as I stared at it, another spasm moved through my body, and I felt another object coming up, and another, and I realized what I was looking at were shards of broken glass. I have no idea how my body could possibly have produced something like that. And every time I thought it was done, it just kept coming and coming.

Eventually I realized there was a crowd standing around me, and Mamma had her arm around my back, and Gramma Patty was trying to shoo them all away. At one point I looked up and saw Miss Pierre, who looked very worried.

I don't know what all this is, but it can't be good.

SUNDAY, MARCH 23, 8:19 P.M. (PRIVATE)

After Miss Pierre saw what happened at church, she called Mamma to set up another appointment. I was in bed but could hear Mamma on the phone and, from her answers, I could tell who she was talking to. I was surprised when she turned down Miss Pierre's offer and said the social worker might cause trouble if she found out.

I know I was saying before I wasn't sure if Miss Pierre's methods were working, but no one is offering me anything better right now! So I asked Mamma to let Miss Pierre come. I'll deal with Renee if she has a problem with it, but we've got to do something. I can't keep living like this.

Miss Pierre visited today after school. She says she underestimated the problem last time, but she seemed to think she had a few more tricks up her sleeve. Last time she believed the problem was in the house, but after the incident at the church, she was convinced that whatever entity is bothering us is centered on my body. And that requires a different approach.

I couldn't help thinking about what Renee had said about Miss Pierre deliberately leading us on and dragging this out, so I got Miss Pierre alone and asked about it. It was awkward, but I needed to know. I think I offended her a bit when I asked if it was right for her to charge people for what she does. "Why shouldn't I charge?" she said. "You don't expect a plumber to come fix your pipes for free. Or an exterminator to get rid of your termites for free. I have to make a living like anyone else.

My skill and learning are valuable to people, so why shouldn't I support myself with it?"

I guess that does make sense. I couldn't think of any response to it. Anyway, Mamma told me later that Miss Pierre didn't accept payment this time, since she felt she should have done more before. She only asked for reimbursement for supplies. I wonder if she did that because of what I'd said. I'd feel bad if she suffered because of my suspicions.

The supplies she mentioned were for a little altar she set up in my room. That's the only way to describe it. It's an over-turned milk crate with a white towel over it, some candles with pictures of saints on them, a crucifix, and a bible open to Psalm 91. She spread salt all around the edge of the room, which seems kind of dirty to me, but she said it would help keep evil spirits away. The problem with that is, it sorta seems like there's already an evil spirit following me around, or maybe even inside of me. So how can the salt protect me if there's a demon already in me? Unless maybe the salt isn't meant to protect me. Maybe it's meant to protect everyone else *from* me.

Even though it feels a little weird, I do feel better with the altar set up. With the candles going, it's almost like having a night-light. And it's hard to imagine demons tormenting me with a bible right nearby.

TUESDAY, MARCH 25, 6:36 A.M. (PRIVATE)

Gramma Patty is not a big fan of Miss Pierre's altar. I didn't really get why. It's got a bible and everything. How can she claim it's unchristian? But she doesn't like the candles with pictures of saints on them. She called the altar black magic. I don't see how it can be black magic if loads of pretty normal people have saints as part of their religion. It's not like Devil worship or something. But it might as well be if you ask Gramma Patty. She says our church doesn't worship anyone but God, and the pastor would have a fit if he knew.

She wanted the whole altar out of the house right away, but Mamma convinced her to let me keep it for a while. Who knew this stuff was so complicated? The way I've always seen it is, *Love God; avoid the Devil.* Should be simple enough. But when people can't even agree on what's on God's side and what's on the Devil's, how am I supposed to sort it out? All I know is that Miss Pierre's altar makes me feel safer.

But then again, if I *am* possessed by some demon, maybe my instincts aren't to be trusted. . . .

WEDNESDAY, MARCH 26, 6:46 P.M. (PRIVATE)

Renee visited again today and made a bit of a fuss about the altar. I thought she said she was okay with Miss Pierre's techniques. . . . Whatever happened to live and let live? I don't know. She seemed pretty upset about it. She made me tell her everything Miss Pierre had said, down to the last word. I felt like I was being interrogated by the police. I guess she just wanted to see how much Mamma and I were being brainwashed by Miss Pierre. I really don't think we are, though! We're just in a bad situation, and getting help the only place we know.

I guess I managed to convince her, because she let it drop. She just made me promise not to leave the candles lit when I went to sleep. She said they're a fire hazard and are too danger-ous. I agreed, but I think she's being paranoid. The candles are wrapped in glass, and they aren't easy to knock over. Loads of people leave them burning all night. That's whole point. But it seemed easier to just agree with her in the moment. I guess it's a fair compromise.

She also asked me if I'd be willing to see a psychiatrist. She seemed like she expected me to be really put off by the idea, but I don't know. . . . Anything that's helpful at this point can only be good. And maybe I *am* crazy. People always act like that would be the worst thing in the world, but look at my alternatives. If it turns out I'm crazy, that I've been secretly faking this whole thing, it would be a relief, in a way. Something that could be treated with pills, and I'd be back to my old self. I'd pick that over having my soul claimed by a demon, that's for sure. So I said okay.

FRIDAY, MARCH 28, 3:40 P.M. (PRIVATE)

Back from my appointment with the psychiatrist. It was all right, I guess. Not as satisfying as I expected. I didn't realize I'd been expecting anything at all, but everything I know about psychiatrists comes from movies and stuff, so I guess I'd been picturing something like that. I thought it would be a lot of talking about my feelings, and that I would get a chance to go into a lot of detail about my situation, and she'd make me play word-association games and judge my responses to inkblots and stuff. In a way I was kind of looking forward to it.

But she didn't really bother with any of that. She asked me a million yes-or-no questions (and got annoyed if I gave an answer other than yes or no), most of which had nothing at all to do with my specific situation, like with the puking up glass and bones and all that. She asked about my stress levels and how I was doing in school and my sleep schedule. Stuff about eating disorders, and if I have any phobias. I wasn't sure how to answer that one. She asked if I was afraid of supernatural creatures, and I was like, "Yeah, I am," but she never asked if my fear might be based on actual experiences with supernatural creatures.

I guess that sort of thing doesn't even occur to normal people, but it all felt a little pointless, like her questions weren't getting anywhere close to the real problems in my life. But eventually the psychiatrist got around to asking me if I ever saw or heard things other people didn't, so I said yes, and she followed up a bit on that, asking me to describe them. So I told her about some of those strange visions I've had where I'm being tortured, and the stuff that happened at church and at school, and she scribbled a lot on her note pad. Then at the end she talked to Mamma for a while without me, and Mamma came out with some kind of prescription. So now I have these pills I'm supposed to take every night, but I don't even know exactly what I'm being treated for.

PSYCHIATRIC DIAGNOSTIC REPORT

Performed by: ~~Redacted~~

Patient: L——

Date of Examination: 3/28/2014

Patient presents as psychologically unstable. Reports severe visual, auditory, and tactile disturbances and hallucinations, coupled with persistent delusions of persecution and grandiosity, suggestive of possible early onset schizoaffective disorder. Otherwise, largely asymptomatic. Recommend course of antipsychotic medication to be taken daily.

I've been taking the pills the doctor gave me, and I think I can maybe start to say they are working. I *have* felt more like myself again lately. There are some annoying side effects, but I haven't had any of those visions or torture dreams lately, or any unexplained pains. No vomiting incidents.

And I think maybe even my voice might be coming back! I was doing the dishes after dinner the other night, and Gramma Patty came in and was like, "It's so nice to hear you sing again." I hadn't even realized I was doing it! It definitely wasn't my stage voice, but for so long now I haven't been able to so much as hum. I thought that part of me was gone for good.

I don't want to push things, but maybe I'll go to the auditorium and just see what happens.

SATURDAY, APRIL 5, 8:46 A.M. (PRIVATE)

Not much to report; just wanted to note that I woke up this morning feeling pretty good! I was in a really good mood, singing in the shower, and I couldn't figure out any particular reason. Then I realized it's because I didn't have any nightmares last night! And it's been a while since I felt that pain in my side too. It's kind of sad that simply waking up after a night without pain or terror is enough to put me in a good mood.

I don't know whether it's Miss Pierre or the pills, but something seems to be working. As for singing, my voice is still a little rusty from disuse, but I'm working on it. It's hard, but it feels good.

THURSDAY, APRIL 10, 4:22 P.M. (PRIVATE)

I haven't checked in on here in a while. I guess there's not much to report these days. Everything's pretty much fine. I did pass this weird tree on the way home and decide to photograph it. I don't know why, I was just drawn to it. I guess it's all just part of my "dead and dying things" aesthetic.

SUNDAY, APRIL 13, 2:12 P.M. (PRIVATE)

Something weird happened at church today. I was killing time after the service while Mamma and Gramma were making the rounds, saying hello to everyone. I ducked into one of the back rooms where I used to get ready before choir practice. Mrs. Matthews, who sometimes helps clean up the church, was back there. She told me she'd seen a rat last Sunday, so she'd put out some poison and was checking to see if it got anything.

She gave me the strangest look when I asked if I could help her check. I guess normal teenage girls aren't so quick to help clean up dead rats. I don't know why I offered. The words were out of my mouth before I even thought about them. I just don't see the point in hiding from the uglier side of the world, and pretending death and vermin and suffering don't exist. I'd rather look them in the face.

Mrs. Matthews just shrugged and said, "Suit yourself," so I followed her down and checked the corners as she shined a flashlight around. We found one rat lying stiff and cold under the stairs, so I took an old towel from Mrs. Matthews and used it to pick him up. She was standing there, holding a big sack open, and all I had to do was unwrap the towel and drop him in, but for a few seconds I couldn't do it. I was clutching the towel in my hand, and it was like my fingers just wouldn't open. Mrs. Matthews got annoyed and asked what I was waiting for, and that was when I realized the towel was warm.

I didn't know what to do. I held it clutched in my hands for a few seconds, too stunned to let it go. The next thing I knew, the critter was twitching in my fingers, and Mrs. Matthews let out a scream to wake the dead. That shocked me out of my daze, my hands opened, the bundle fell to the floor, and what do you know? The little beast wriggled for a second and then scampered away.

I looked up, and Mrs. Matthews was staring at me like she'd just seen the Devil himself. "That rat was dead," she said. "Poisoned. What did you do?" I didn't have any answer. She shook her head and backed away from me, muttering about how something wasn't right about me. That I'd better get away from her.

The worst thing is, I know she's right. I may not understand it, but even I can see there's something very wrong with me.

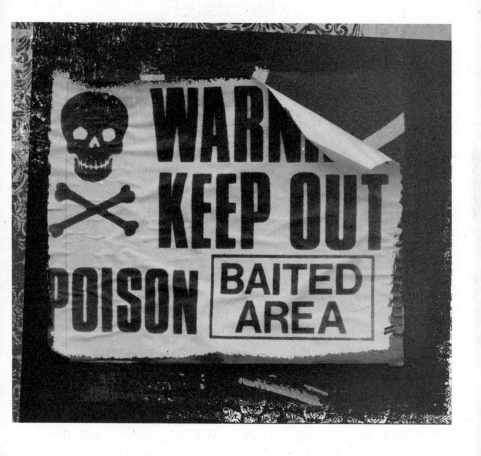

MONDAY, APRIL 14, 4:02 P.M. (PRIVATE)

It just came on the news—they're going to announce the verdict of the Robinson trial today! I can't remember when I've ever been so nervous about anything. And I just rewatched the video. There's no way they could find those policemen anything but guilty, right? Gramma Patty is worried about what will happen if it goes the other way. Worried there will be riots. I can't help thinking, if the system is that broken, maybe there *should* be riots. Maybe riots are the only way to make people listen. But Gramma Patty and Mamma both give me worried looks if I talk like that, so I try to keep my opinions to myself. In any case, I think Gramma Patty is worried for nothing because I really don't see how any sensible person could watch that video and think the policemen are innocent. I'm sure the jury made the right decision.

MONDAY, APRIL 14, 5:10 P.M. (PRIVATE)

Not guilty. I don't believe it. I just don't believe it.

MONDAY, APRIL 14, 7:26 P.M. (PRIVATE)

I still just can't even believe it about the trial. I have so many
feelings about this that I don't know how to sort them out. I'm
just so disappointed. And outraged. And shocked. And just . . .
sad. It still seems impossible to believe. I still feel like I'm going
to wake up tomorrow morning and find out they haven't given
the verdict yet, and it was all a bad dream. How can this be reality? Even with all the crazy stuff I've been dealing with, at least
that's just me and my family. I always took comfort in the fact
that the real world still made sense, and everything works more
or less the way I expect and understand.

But now this, which just seems as crazy as anything that has
happened. There was a video! How could the jury watch it and not
see what happened? How could they not see it as clearly as I did?

I'm so twisted up and upset over this. Just sad and angry and guilty, I guess. Which is weird, I know. Why should I feel guilty? I wasn't on the jury; I didn't shoot Dwayne Robinson. What does any of it have to do with me? How could I possibly have influenced the decision of a bunch of jury members I've never even met? But I feel like I should have done more. I should have gone to those demonstrations. I should have prayed.

But I couldn't. I guess that's what's freaking me out.

Just before they made the announcement, Mamma suggested we all join hands and pray about it. Gramma Patty asked me to lead the prayer, and I couldn't. I started to, but I only got about halfway through before my throat closed up and no sound came out. It was just like with the singing, when this all started. Only it was more than that. It wasn't just that my voice died; my mind went blank too. My brain just emptied, and I couldn't go on.

I just looked up and stared at Gramma Patty and Mamma like an idiot. Gramma Patty saw and squeezed my hand a little, and then she took over and finished the prayer and it was fine. I felt relieved, like she'd saved it, and nothing really bad had happened. I just chalked it up to nerves about the trial, and being overexcited.

But then the announcement came, and how could I avoid thinking about what had happened? How could I help making a connection? That my failure to speak that prayer was a failure of faith somehow, and that failing is the reason why God turned his back on the Robinson family and refused to give them justice.

I know; that's ridiculous. It doesn't work like that. Why would God do something so cruel and pointless? But that doesn't make this bad feeling go away.

MONDAY, APRIL 14, 9:16 P.M. (PRIVATE)

I can't stop watching the news. Even Mamma and Gramma Patty are too obsessed now to remember to stop me. It's still surreal to watch them describe what's going on even as I can hear it happening only a few blocks away.

A huge crowd has gathered outside the courthouse, more than twice the usual number of protesters. For now everything's still pretty peaceful, but no one knows when the tension might break. It feels like we're right on the edge of something major. Everyone knows something's gonna happen, but no one knows exactly what or when, how long it will last, what might touch it off, or what the damage will be. Gramma Patty can't stop moaning about how it's always our own community that suffers from these things. Buildings will burn, shopkeepers forced out of business by looters, people made homeless by the destruction.

She has lived through stuff like this before, and even Mamma has seen it on TV, but this is all new to me. I don't know what to expect.

All I can think is that I should be down there. I should be there at the courthouse, protesting this sad mockery of justice and making my voice heard. But there's no way Mamma and Gramma Patty would allow that. They say it's too dangerous, and there's no telling what harm I might come to. But someone has to speak out!

For now all I can do is hole up here, reloading the news on my laptop and listening for sirens.

TUESDAY, APRIL 15, 3:13 A.M. (PRIVATE)

Just woke up from an awful nightmare. . . .

At first it was the same as usual, with the wheel and the grill and the arrows and the iron spike. Those are becoming like old friends now. Then the scene shifted. There were horses trapped in a burning barn, and I was trying to get the door open to let them out, but I couldn't figure out the latch. Then it switched over to something else. I felt better because it was outside at least. I was caught up in a herd of animals who were stampeding across a field or prairie, but then I saw a machine looming ahead of us, gleaming in the moonlight, and I realized the animals were running toward some kind of slaughtering mechanism.

I awoke to the sound of piercing screams mixed with growling and barking, and I'm still not sure if the sounds were from the dream or real life or a mixture of the two. My eyes were burning from smoke, and it sounded like a dozen different sirens were going outside. I can still hear them. If I listen hard, I can hear shouting and yelling, too. It's carrying here on the wind, even though the worst of the riots are a few miles away.

WEDNESDAY, APRIL 16, 6:53 A.M. (PRIVATE)

The city is a little calmer this morning, but I found something
strange in the street in front of our house. It looks like bones
from a slaughterhouse. How did they get here? Does it have
something to do with all the activity last night?

THURSDAY, APRIL 17, 5:24 P.M. (PRIVATE)

Every day the riots get a little closer to our neighborhood. Mostly people have been sticking to the main roads where there are shops and things, but sometimes I run across strange overflow, even on our little street. If I take a roundabout route home from the bus stop, I pass by a lot of the wreckage.

Mamma doesn't know I do. She told me in no uncertain terms that I was to walk straight home after school every day. She and Gramma Patty even discussed walking to the bus stop to meet me so I wouldn't have to walk alone, but I told them to back off. I'm not five years old.

She doesn't know I've gone out a few times, taking photos of the way our neighborhood has been changed by the riots. I don't know why I do it, exactly. I want to do something, to make all the suffering and anger and frustration stop, but I don't know how and the adults won't let me do anything. I hate feeling so helpless and powerless.

Taking pictures is all I can think of to do, but it frustrates me because it isn't helping anyone. And I worry it's just satisfying some sick fascination with other people's misery. Like I'm feeding off them. Gramma Patty says it isn't healthy, and I think she might be right.

SATURDAY, APRIL 19, 3:22 A.M. (PRIVATE)

I really think I'm losing my mind. For a while now I've been having those nightmares, and they always felt really vivid and real, and sometimes they seemed to come on me even when I was awake, but there would always be a moment when I woke up or blinked or snapped out of it, and I'd know it was just one of those attacks.

But now there's been a shift. I started forcing myself to stay awake because I was afraid of dealing with the pain and scary images. Drinking colas and stuff, going online, watching movies, anything. But I think that might have backfired, because now the torture scenes are slipping into my everyday life, and I'm not even sure where they end and reality begins.

Mamma says she has caught me sleeping with my eyes open, and at school people have seen me walk from class to class with my eyes closed. And I see terrible things. Someone in the school yard being pelted with rocks. Someone walking down the hall, blood dripping from their forehead. A girl crushed under the wheel of a giant construction truck. What do I do? Keep walking and tell myself it's just my imagination? Or run over and try to help, only to find the bodies disintegrating through my fingers?

If I can't tell dreams from hallucinations from reality, what does it all even mean?

SATURDAY, APRIL 19, 8:42 P.M. (PRIVATE)

I thought it was bad before, but now I feel like I am losing my grip on reality. I don't know who or what I am anymore.

Tonight after dinner I was having a totally normal conversation with Mamma and Gramma Patty about an English paper I have to write, and then I just froze. In the middle of a sentence. I don't really remember what happened after that. One moment I was sitting at the kitchen table, and the next I was on the floor, that thick feeling in my throat—the one I'm now starting to recognize means I'm going to cough up something nasty. I thought I'd blacked out for just a few seconds, but later Mamma told me it was almost an hour that I was out!

Mamma says I started shaking and making strange noises, my eyes rolling back in my head. Mamma and Gramma Patty were trying to help, rubbing my back, talking to me, saying my name.

Then Mamma started praying over me, and I couldn't take it. I've heard Mamma pray probably every day of my life, but suddenly it was like every terrible sound all mixed together: nails on a blackboard and microphone feedback and a knife scratching a plate. . . . All I know is that I wanted it to *stop*, and I threw my arms out in front of me to try to push it away.

I wound up giving Mamma a mighty shove that sent both her and Gramma Patty reeling back against the wall. Mamma was shocked silent for a bit, but soon enough she started praying again, and Gramma Patty joined her. That just got me more upset, so they stopped. Mamma says that was when I started speaking in a strange voice—sometimes very quickly or slowly, sometimes in what sounded like another language. What they could understand sounded like I was describing what it was like to be tortured and killed—my eyes getting ripped out, arrows sinking into my flesh, getting run through with spikes and beaten with whips and then tied to a stake and burned alive. I had never actually told Mamma and Gramma Patty the details of my dreams, so they were all new to them.

As Mamma was telling me all this, I kept seeing these images flash before my eyes. The ones that kept appearing on my blog after every attack. The wheel. The grill. The girl with blood coming out of her eye. I don't think those images are random. I think they add up to something. That they *mean* something. But what is it all trying to tell me? Is that what this demon wants from me? To drag me to hell and torture me in all these different ways?

Mamma said I was pacing the kitchen, back and forth between them, sometimes approaching for long enough to touch their faces or stare into their eyes.

When I seemed calmer, they joined hands and tried praying again. That was when I fell to the floor, thrashing and writhing around. Mamma saw stuff moving under my skin, like some creature was pushing on me from the inside, trying to tear its way out. Then I came to. This part I remember, because I was on the floor, coughing again, and what came up were three balled-up wads of paper. They were pretty gross, but I spread them out, and sure enough, there's something written on them that looks like a weird language! Some devil language, says Mamma.

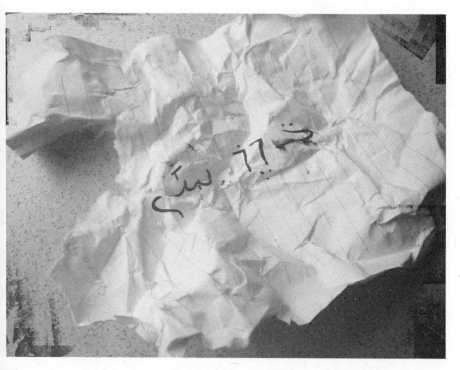

I asked Gramma Patty to tell me her version of the story, but she wouldn't talk about it. She can only say that she's worried, that it's all happening again, that "they" are going to come in here and tear this family apart. She shook her head and said, "You've got to stop this devilry, or they will take you away. You've got to fight this off and pray to the Lord, and that's the only thing that will help."

I'm starting to get really scared. Before, everything was happening *to* me. But now it's me doing the stuff, only I can't control it! What if I do something terrible while in some kind of a trance? What if I hurt someone?

SUNDAY, APRIL 20, 7:47 P.M. (PRIVATE)

Renee came by today and found me still in freak-out mode over what had happened. I didn't want to talk to her about it, but I basically had no choice. She could tell just by looking at me that something had given me a bad scare. So I told her I went into another trance, like at school and at church. Of course she wouldn't leave that alone. She wanted to know all the details. I told her I didn't remember any of it, but she kept pushing.

I really didn't want to talk about it, but Renee's not the type to take no for an answer. We talked about other things, school and the riots and stuff, but she always kept circling back, like she was trying to catch me off guard. I got frustrated and practically yelled at her, "I don't know! I don't remember!"

I told her to ask Mamma, since she was there, but she said

she wanted to hear it from me. I just told her it was like someone had taken over my body and used it for their own purposes.

Then she asked if I was still taking my medication, and I told her, "Yes, of course I am. I've missed a dose here and there, but mostly yes." She didn't like that at all. She asked exactly how many I missed, and I said I didn't remember. More than one. She told me to get the bottle and count out how many doses are left. We kind of got into a big fight then. I never used to fight with Renee, but lately I feel like she doesn't trust me. Like she's trying to control every little thing or trying to make me say things I don't want to say.

I brought all that up, but she was on a mission and wouldn't talk about anything else until I brought her the pill bottle. She counted out the pills and said I'd only taken eight when I should have taken twenty-four.

I was like, "Yeah, I forget sometimes." Then she made me go through this whole thing of trying to remember when exactly I forget to take them: what time of day, what am I doing. That kind of misses the whole point of forgetting! She had me set an alarm on my phone to remind me, and we moved the pill bottle to my bedside table instead of the bathroom, so I won't have to get up and leave the room to take them. I guess that will help.

Before she left, she talked to Mamma about how I'd been skipping my pills and how she needs to make sure I take them every night. Mamma wasn't impressed. She kept saying anyone could see there was a demon in me, and that pills weren't going to help anything. Renee got very quiet at that, and her expression was as serious as I had ever seen it. I couldn't really hear what she was saying, but I got the picture. No more talk of demons and no more visits from Miss Pierre, or else there will be big trouble.

CASE REPORT

Family

Date of Report: 4/21/2014   Date of Visit: 4/20/2014

Complainant: ██████████ (Family doctor)

Family Surname: ██████████

Name of child: L——

Age: 15

DESCRIPTION OF CASEWORKER VISIT:

On Sunday, April 20, I made a scheduled visit to the ██ family to check on the progress of their situation since L—— began receiving treatment for possible schizoaffective disorder three weeks ago. Unfortunately, after initial signs of improvement, L——'s symptoms seem to have worsened significantly. She is currently exhibiting severe behavioral disturbances, including disruptive and even aggressive behavior at school, as well as at home. Previously L—— has rarely been disruptive, and has no history of aggressive behavior.

It is difficult to account for what has brought about this change. L— herself points to possible depression over her difficulty with singing and preparing for her upcoming audition, though in behavior she does not appear overly concerned with this problem anymore. She also mentions anxiety over, and preoccupation with, the recent upheaval in her neighborhood. It's possible that outbreaks of violence and destruction have caused L—'s regression to previously abandoned behavior patterns.

It is also worth noting that the only recipient of her aggression so far has been L—'s mother. This could indicate that there is some latent hostility between the two of them, even though when asked, they both profess to be intensely devoted to each other.

When asked directly about her actions, L— claims she doesn't remember them, and maintains she was in a "trance" or "blackout state" the entire time. However, upon further prodding, L— produced details and descriptions of the events that could only be known to her or suggest a certain self-awareness during the incidents (e.g. "my heart was pounding," "I was afraid I would hurt her," etc.).

L— has also been inconsistently compliant with her medication, which is presumably contributing to these episodes. We discussed strategies for making sure her medication is taken according to an appropriate schedule.

One final note: L— has repeatedly tried to direct my attention to some scraps of paper with scribbles on them, which she maintains have some significant relationship to her situation.

(These items were supposedly disgorged by her during one of her "trances.") So far I have chosen not to encourage L—'s sense that there is anything meaningful and important in these "messages." I would prefer her to abandon her reliance on these tricks and/or delusions, and confront her situation more directly. I am striving to keep our conversations focused on L—'s behavior, and not play into her preferred narrative of "demonic possession."

I remain alert to the possibility that L— is deriving some psychological or emotional benefit from these "attacks," maybe in terms of getting attention or forming a useful alliance with her mother, etc. I am working to discourage these tools, and emphasizing positive reinforcement of more productive modes of communication and family interaction.

-R. S.

TUESDAY, APRIL 22, 9:35 P.M. (PRIVATE)

The alarm on my phone just went off. The one Renee set. That means I'm supposed to take my pill. I'm sitting in bed right now, and the pills are on a little table right next to me. There's even some bottled water with them. I don't have to get up or anything. It would be the easiest thing in the world to take one. So why haven't I taken it?

Why don't I do it? Why don't I just stop typing for a few seconds, reach out, pick up the bottle, and tap one out into my hand? It would be so easy, but I'm just sitting here, typing, not doing it. I don't know. I can't explain it. I just don't want to. Is that it? Or is that I can't? Maybe there's some force stopping me. Things were getting better with the pills. Everything was headed back to normal. I was going to just be an ordinary kid again. And if I don't take them, if I skip even a few, all that scary stuff will start to come back again. Nightmares, visions, trances—who knows what else? Who knows how much worse it could get? I don't want to find out; that's for sure.

So what stops me from taking the pills when I know they will help? I told Renee I kept forgetting, but that's not really it. There were times when I'd be watching TV or playing on my phone, and I knew it was time to take my pills and I just didn't. Or even sometimes I'd be brushing my teeth, standing at the sink, the pill bottle right in front of me, and I'd just ignore it. Pretend like I didn't even see it.

Is this what it felt like for Mamma all those years ago, when the demon was harassing her? The scariest part is not knowing what's my own mind and what is some intruder. It feels like I am making my own decisions, but my decisions don't make any sense, even to myself.

Everyone wants me to take the pills. Everyone says I should do it. But they can't make me.

Ugh, this is silly! That's so immature. I can do this. I'm going to put down my laptop right now, take a pill, and go to sleep. Right now.

Soon.

WEDNESDAY, APRIL 23, 6:15 A.M. (PRIVATE)

I was in my room last night, trying not to fall asleep, when I had another one of my attacks. I haven't had one like this in a while now. I kind of hoped I was through with them, but I guess not. One minute I was sitting up in bed, watching something on my laptop, all the lights on. Then in the next . . . my eyes must have slipped closed, because everything went dark and I felt myself dragged down onto the bed by some invisible force. I tried to struggle, but something held me down so I couldn't move or make any noise. It was terrifying, but so far it wasn't painful. I hoped there wouldn't be any pain, but I knew that was wishful thinking. If there's one thing I know about these attacks, it's that they are always excruciating.

I just lay there, waiting for the pain to come in whatever form it would take. What else could I do? Just like before, there was something else before the pain: that feeling I was being punished for something. That I have done some terrible crime that has made everyone hate me, and now they're going to torture me because of it. And the worst thing is, I have no idea what I've done.

There was something different about it this time, though. I still didn't know what it was I was being punished for, but for the first time I didn't have any weight of guilt or fear associated with it. Whatever it was, I wasn't sorry at all. I was proud of it. And I knew it would bring punishment, torture, and pain—I had always known that—but I didn't care. In that strange moment, I welcomed it. It was like I *wanted* the pain, just to prove to myself I was just as terrible as everyone thought I was.

And then it came. Not in my skin this time, or my bones or my eyes. It was in my mouth. I saw in front of me a long twisted instrument like iron pliers, and the next thing I knew, some force was dragging my mouth open and applying the tool to my teeth. One by one, I felt them twist free, cracking the bones and snapping the nerves, filling my mouth and throat with thick hot blood.

The pain was the most intense I've felt so far. It wasn't just in my teeth; it was running through my whole body, like a white-hot electric current, and I trembled with it. But even as I was conscious of this agony, there was something satisfying about it. I knew I had earned this torture, and I wanted it to purify me. Over and over, the thoughts that pulsed through my mind were *yes* and *more*. I wanted to be taken apart completely.

And then, just as suddenly as it had come over me, it started to slip away. I could feel my body start to relax, and I was able to form some coherent thoughts around the slackening pain.

The sensation of blood flooding my mouth evaporated, and I ran my tongue over my teeth, half expecting to find smooth empty gums. But as far as I could tell, everything was in place.

Just as I was about convinced everything had slipped back to normal, I felt something near the back of my jaw. I prodded at it with my tongue and then stuck a finger into my mouth to clear it out. It was a tooth. A huge one. Definitely a molar, maybe a wisdom tooth. I ran to the mirror and checked and checked, but I couldn't see anything wrong with my teeth! A tooth like this . . . There's no way you could lose it without seeing the difference.

So I guess the question is: Whose tooth is it?

WEDNESDAY, APRIL 23, 6:34 A.M. (PRIVATE)

After I posted that last entry, I reloaded my blog, expecting to see a strange photo waiting for me there, like there had been all the previous times, but there was nothing there. Like my ghost had forgotten about me.

But I have a picture to post anyway. After the tooth came out, I snapped a photo of it. Maybe that's why the blog didn't produce one on its own. It's not just giving me pictures anymore; it's giving me the real thing. And I don't need some ghost showing me my worst fears when I'm the one taking the pictures now.

The riots are getting closer and more out of control. Nights are filled with the sounds of sirens mixed with the cries of the mob, and every morning there is a new path of destruction cut through the city. Mamma and Gramma Patty are terrified, but in a weird way I feel drawn to it. I wake sometimes in the night and I can feel all the energy of the mob coursing through me— their panic and their rage, but also a raw, surging sense of power. It's scary, but not exactly in a bad way. It makes my whole body tingle with excitement.

There's pain, too. I'm still getting those pains in my side. This is going to sound really nuts, but it's a good pain. Not exactly the good pain that comes from stretching before exercise, or getting a massage. It still feels fiery and hot, but I've figured out that if I don't resist it, if I don't try to push back against it, it doesn't bother me so much. And sometimes, once it starts to fade, I almost kind of miss it, and if I focus my mind, I can make it come back. So I can feel it a little longer.

Sometimes when I do that, when I close my eyes and focus on the pain, I get visions of those torture scenes again. Those, too, though—they don't scare me the way they used to. I'm fascinated by them, and sometimes they seem weirdly comforting.

See, I said it was crazy! How could pain and torture be comforting? But I don't know how else to describe it. I just feel drawn to both somehow.

I don't know what any of it means. Am I self-destructive? Or is it some demon messing with my mind, trying to tempt me into Hell?

MONDAY, APRIL 28, 9:37 A.M. (PRIVATE)

I'm home from school again today. I wasn't feeling well this morning. It was that old skin-crawly feeling, seeing stuff in the corner of my eye, jumping at shadows. I asked Mamma if I could skip school, but she said no, I'd missed too much school already this year.

That's one of the things I could get taken away for—if the school says I haven't been showing up enough. But it's not like I'm just cutting class to go out and have fun! I've just got bigger things to deal with right now than pop quizzes. I don't have the mental energy for school.

But Mamma said she wasn't having anyone call her a bad mother for keeping her kid out of school, so I was just going to have to pull myself together. Easy for her to say!

I kind of had a little tantrum about it, which I don't normally do. Usually, if Mamma tells me to do something, I do it, and I don't answer back. But today I just *really* couldn't deal with school, so I was whining and complaining and trying to get Mamma to change her mind. Finally Gramma Patty asked if it would help if we did a prayer circle before I left. When I was a kid, that used to settle me down if I was cranky or being difficult, though it's been a while since I had much interest in that sort of thing. But I thought, well, why not? It used to make me feel better; maybe it would still work. So I said fine, and Gramma Patty and Mamma stood on either side of me and held hands around me.

As soon as they started speaking, I got this terrible throbbing pain in my head, like my skull was being forced open from the inside. For a minute I was actually scared my whole head might burst into pieces. I was groaning and crying and grabbing my head, and I remember falling to the floor, my whole body shaking and thrashing. Then Mamma and Gramma Patty stopped the prayer, and I immediately felt calmer. And I had this trickling sensation on my face, and Mamma told me my nose was bleeding.

Gramma Patty said, "Don't just stand there; get her a tissue." So Mamma goes to find a tissue, and I'm just sitting there on the floor, wiping my nose with my hands and getting blood everywhere, and I realize my nose feels sort of weird and tight, like there's some strange pressure in there, and I just want some relief for it.

Finally Mamma comes back with some paper towels, and I start blowing my nose, even though Gramma Patty is trying to get me to tip my head back. As I'm blowing, I can feel something hard and solid in my nose, so I blow my nose again, and

I scrape at it with my finger, and a metal nail comes out and clatters onto the kitchen floor. A long, thin, rusty nail—must have been about two inches long. I heard Mamma screaming and Gramma Patty praying, but I was just staring at it there on the kitchen floor, fascinated that this thing had come out of me. And I sort of focused my mind and *pushed*, and a few more came out, one after another.

I thought I was done with this stuff, but apparently not.

I think I need to talk to Miss Pierre again.

MONDAY, APRIL 28, 2:34 P.M. (PRIVATE)

Mamma warned me against going back to Miss Pierre again, since Renee doesn't like it and she could use it as an excuse to send me away, but Renee isn't going to solve this problem. I don't know if anyone can, but at least Miss Pierre seems to understand what the hell we're dealing with.

Once Mamma and Gramma Patty left for work today, I looked up Miss Pierre's address and went to track her down. When I got to her house, my courage ran out and I realized it was kind of rude to just show up without calling ahead. I started to wonder if I should just walk back home and spend the day in bed, like I told Mamma I would, but the door wasn't closed, only the screen, and just as I was about to turn around, I heard Miss Pierre's voice: "Laetitia? Is that you? Well, come in here. Don't hover."

I wound up going in, and Miss Pierre didn't even seem surprised to see me. She just poured me a glass of lemonade and sat down at the table and asked what was troubling me. I told her all about what happened that morning, and she just sat there and nodded. I asked her, "Isn't there anything you can do for me? Something more than we've already done?"

Miss Pierre said yes, there were other steps we could take. She said she'd never done it before, but that she could perform an exorcism to get the demons out, if that's really what I wanted. But, she said, there wasn't any point unless I wanted to do it. That it wouldn't work if I didn't really want it. I must have given her such a look at that. How could I not want to fix this? Of course I want to! Whatever is going on is ruining my life. Why wouldn't I do anything in my power to get rid of it?

And Miss Pierre, calm as anything, said, "I don't know. Why don't you tell me?"

At first I didn't know what she was talking about, but then I thought about those pills, and how I keep not taking them, even though I know they were working. I didn't know what to say, though. How could I tell her? How could I admit to her that sometimes I don't want it to stop? Sometimes I lie awake, wondering what will come next, and almost wishing for it to come sooner. Sometimes it feels like I am out of control of my life and my body, and sometimes it feels like I have never been more in control, like there is all this power waiting for me, and all I have to do is reach out and grab it. I didn't know how to tell her any of that. I was scared she would judge me.

I couldn't tell her all of that, so I just fidgeted for a while and drank my lemonade. Then I sort of changed the subject, asking her something else I've been wondering. I don't understand why all this is happening to me and not someone else, so I asked if she knew what it was that made people susceptible to these kinds of attacks. But she wouldn't answer directly. Again, she turned it around and asked me what I thought. As if I'm the expert! I guess I was hoping she'd say something to reassure me, like maybe I'd come in contact with some possessed object, like a doll or a mirror. I've seen movies like that. Or maybe I could have caught it from someone, like a cold. Even if she said it was passed down from Mamma, that would be . . . better than the alternative.

Because the only other thing I can think of is that it's because of something wrong with me. I mean, demons don't affect *everyone* out there. They must have some reason for picking their targets. And if I can't think of anything else, then it must be because it sensed some kind of evil in me. I don't want to believe this, but how can I deny it? When I look back over my life, I was always convinced I was basically good. More than good—that I was *special*. ~Chosen~ by God Himself. What kind of person thinks that? I thought that just because I didn't steal or cuss or tell lies (much) and I went to church every week and sang praise songs in the choir, that meant I'd been touched by God's grace.

But what if it means just the opposite? Now I can see all that for what it really was: arrogance. Pride. Vanity. I didn't even really care about singing God's praises—I was much more interested in just using the church choir as training for my career as a pop diva. As soon as I couldn't do that, I lost all interest in church, and Mamma had to drag me there against my will. And my blog, which I thought was so full of inspiration—wasn't that really just another way of selling myself? Making myself look better than other people, making them jealous, to better hide the envy eating away at my own soul?

To regular people, I might have looked like a nice, sweet God-fearing girl with a bright future, but deep inside, how long have I known that my soul was twisted and corrupt, and I just refused to admit it? It probably wasn't very hard for the demons to see that in me, even if I hid it from regular people. And of course they would latch on to that and try to seize me as one of their own. How could I have any hope of fighting them off when my soul is already so crowded with darkness?

I tried to convey some of these thoughts to Miss Pierre, though it's hard to talk about them out loud. I was so afraid she was going to tell me I was already damned and beyond salvation, I was shaking as I tried to explain myself. But Miss Pierre . . . She didn't exactly disagree with me, but she did have another sort of perspective. She told me she's spent her whole life helping people afflicted with some kind of spirit or demon, and while she'd never seen a case as bad as mine before, she'd heard some stories from her *grand-mère*. What her *grand-mère* told her was that, in the worst cases, it usually means the person has been marked in some way. That they've been chosen for a special purpose. She told me a lot of saints, for example, have been visited by terrible visions, temptations, and possessions. It's considered a test of their faith, before they can move on to their true calling. She said the closer you get to God, the more vulnerable you become to darker influences.

It made sense when she said it. I don't know, though. That's a nice idea, but how could it apply to me? I'm just a normal teenager. I'm not "close to God" or anything. Looking back over my life, I've never been especially holy or righteous. It would be nice to believe that was my story, but it just doesn't make sense.

I asked Miss Pierre how people become saints, and she said they have to perform some miracles. That seemed out of my reach, unless you count Mamma saying it's a miracle when I clean my room without being asked three times. Miss Pierre said that's not what she had in mind. More like healing the sick or raising the dead.

That got my attention. I always thought raising the dead was considered black magic, but she said if Jesus did it, it must be okay. Then she laughed and said, "Why, you brought anyone back to life that I should know about?"

I thought about the bird and the rat. The rosebush and the unkillable mildew in my shower. All that stuff didn't feel like miracles at the time. A power that terrifying . . . I was sure it had to come from the Devil himself. But how does anyone ever know? How can I know what's God and what's the Devil and what's my own sick brain? And Miss Pierre said, "Honey, don't be so sure those aren't all the same thing." Which kind of shocked me. I mean, I can't imagine the pastor saying that *ever*. In fact, that seems like the kind of thinking he would specifically warn against. And suddenly it became clearer to me why most people in church avoid Miss Pierre. . . . That kind of thinking can get people into a lot of trouble.

But I let her go on, and she explained. God is all-powerful, right? I couldn't argue with that. But that means the Devil can only work with the powers God grants him. The Devil is part of God's plan and God's creation, and they are all bound up together. "Don't think of him as an enemy of God," she said. "Think of him as a tool. We're all tools of God, in the end."

I don't know what to think. It made sense to me, what she

was saying, but I don't know if it was wishful thinking. And if the Devil is on the same side as God, then I'm not sure I understand anything at all about the world anymore.

All I know is, I want all this stuff to stop and leave me alone. I want to have some peace again. And if an exorcism will do that, then that seems like the right answer. But Miss Pierre said I should think carefully about it. She said with the state I'm in, it could be a little like a fever. When you have a fever, it makes you feel terrible, and you can take some aspirin to bring the fever down, and it makes you feel better. But the fever isn't really the sickness—the fever is really your body's way of fighting off a deeper sickness that you might not even know is there. And bringing down the fever can be dangerous if it gets in the way of your body fixing itself.

I know what she means. Gramma Patty says this too: sometimes it's better to let the sickness run its course. Getting rid of the symptoms might make you feel better, but it could make you sicker in the long run. So I guess Miss Pierre is saying that all these symptoms I have—terrible thoughts and visions, and all these weird objects coming out of me—could be my body's way of fighting off something even worse. That's not exactly reassuring. And, as I pointed out to her, ignoring a fever can be dangerous too. People can die if they let the fever take over.

Miss Pierre didn't argue with that. She just told me to take some time and think it over.

MONDAY, APRIL 28, 9:10 P.M. (PRIVATE)

I just fixed up my altar, replaced some of the candles that had burned almost all the way down, and redid the salt barrier around the edge of my room. Then I just sat in bed for a while, and then I closed my eyes and tried to pray. This time it didn't feel like my voice was stuck, but it wasn't quite working. I knew all the words to say, but it was like talking on a telephone when the other person has hung up. I felt like none of my words went anywhere. I gave that up, and instead I tried to talk to God in my mind. I don't know if I even thought He was listening; I just wanted to put some thoughts out there into the universe. I told Him I believed in Him and I wanted to trust Him, but that it was difficult sometimes. And I have a lot of questions that maybe it's not my place to ask, but if He feels like giving answers, I'd sure appreciate it.

I still couldn't tell if that was doing any good, though, so that's why I got out my journal. My journal has been useful for helping figure some stuff out, so that's why I'm writing all this out.

I do feel a little better since my conversation with Miss Pierre. It's nice to be reminded that, no matter what bad things seem to be happening here, God is always in control. Maybe she's right and I need to just trust Him and see this through. But I do also have free will (I think), and I assume God wants me to use it. And what's going on is pretty terrifying. Maybe He wouldn't be too mad if I took the easy way out and got the exorcism. Just to get this thing out of me, whatever it is. I don't know. I'm not set on it yet. It's nice to know at least that there is a possible way out, but I'm not sure if I want to take that step. If God wants me to endure all this, then . . . well, I suppose I could take a little more.

But on the other hand, what if that whole idea is just that same old pride and arrogance? Who am I to think God has any kind of special plan for me? Maybe it's the demons themselves who want me to believe that so I make myself more vulnerable to them.

I wish there were some kind of sign to help me figure out if I'm making the right decision and should stick to this path, or if I should be more active in fighting off the forces tormenting me. But would I even know how to interpret a sign? At this point, how could I trust if it was from God or the devil or my own unconscious desires?

I don't know, but if I'm going to take Miss Pierre's advice and let this whole thing run its course, I guess I better prepare myself for it to get worse before it gets better.

I'm so scared; I don't know what to do. I need to write out what happened, to calm myself down and clear my thoughts.

When I went to bed last night, everything was reasonably normal and I was feeling okay after my talk with Miss Pierre, and now I don't even fully understand what happened.

Last I remember I was writing in my journal, and then I put it aside to think a little bit. I must have fallen asleep because then I remembered some kind of dream. It was actually the first good dream I remember having in a really long time, though I'm not sure of any details. Just an overwhelming sense of love and peace. But then it all shifted, and I felt that sharp, burning pain again in my side, which woke me up. For a few seconds I just lay there, staring up at the ceiling and trying to get my bearings. Then I realized the ceiling was a lot closer than I remembered it being. It was dark and I was still a little disoriented, so I tried to slowly turn my head and hoped that would make everything swing back to normal, but as I looked around the room, I caught sight of myself in the mirror across from my bed, and well, there's no other way to put this.

I was floating at least a couple of feet over my bed.

I just froze as terror seeped into every cell of my body. It's hard to describe that feeling when you suddenly realize everything you knew about the world, the rules of physics you thought were completely set in stone, mean nothing. In some sense, nothing that awful was happening, compared to other things I've experienced recently. I was just floating there. But it was way more terrifying because of the potential behind it— that knowledge that if this can happen, *anything* can happen, and there is no way to prepare or protect yourself.

Then I thought, *What if I'm dreaming?* I know I've had thoughts like that before, in the middle of a dream. That was a huge relief, but I still wanted to wake up as fast as possible, so I started screaming and thrashing to try to make myself wake up, but instead Mamma and Gramma Patty ran into the room. Mamma cried out and reached for me, tried to grab my pajamas and pull me back down, but Gramma Patty held her back and started praying in a loud, slow voice until Mamma joined in and they were both praying as hard as they could. Instead of being a comfort, every word was like a million needles under my skin, or like insects crawling on me, tiny animals burrowing into my body, flames burning me inside and out, and I felt like I was going to come apart. Then there was this massive noise, like a boom but also a ripping sound, like the air itself was being torn in two, and there was chaos everywhere and I felt the breath knocked out of me, so I couldn't scream anymore.

At some point I closed my eyes, so I opened them again and the room was filled with smoke. It took me a minute to realize the candles had gotten knocked over and set fire to the towel and the rug and some of the bedclothes. And all the glass in the room—the window, my mirrors, picture frames—had shattered. Mamma reached out to me, crying and begging me to take her hand and come toward her, until Gramma Patty appeared with the fire extinguisher from the kitchen and put out the fire.

That was a couple of hours ago. There's broken glass all over the floor of my room from the window and mirrors shattering, and the screens on my phone and laptop are smashed, though they both still turn on at least, which is good, since I can't exactly afford to replace them.

We've been cleaning ever since, trying to make the room livable again. And in that time, we've barely spoken. Only enough to get the work done. "The broom is in the hall closet" or "Fetch me the masking tape." That kind of thing. What else is there to say? What other response can there be to what happened?

I don't know what Mamma and Gramma Patty have in mind, but I can only think of one thing to do. I asked for a sign, and I sure as hell got one. We need to call Miss Pierre and arrange for the exorcism.

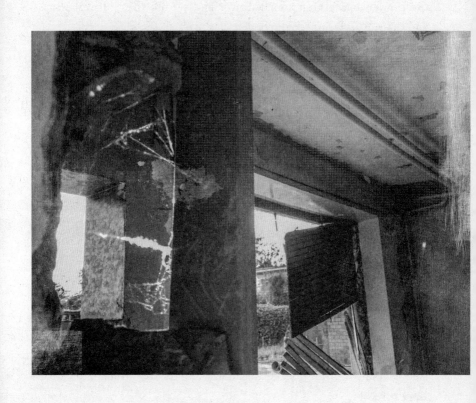

TUESDAY, APRIL 29, 3:12 P.M. (PRIVATE)

I wish I felt 100 percent sure about this exorcism. Even after everything that has happened, there's something that makes me hesitate to go through with it. I don't know if that's just ordinary nervousness, or whether there's a voice inside me that's warning against it. And if that's it, is it a trustworthy voice? Or an evil one?

In the meantime, we've been trying to clear up the mess in my room, but it's a huge chore, and I'm feeling pretty awful right now about everything I have brought on this house. I can't help wondering if Renee was right all along—that everyone would be better off if I were somewhere else, where I couldn't inflict this weird nightmare on them. If Mamma and Gramma Patty wind up hurt or cursed or something, and it was all my fault, I'd never be able to forgive myself. Maybe whatever this is, it's my problem, and they shouldn't have to deal with it.

But it doesn't even matter what I think, because I could never say any of this to Mamma. If I so much as hint at this idea, she only becomes all the more convinced that we all need to stay together, and she has to keep me close. If she's going to be like that, I guess that really leaves me no choice but to go through with the exorcism. Anything else is just too risky.

In any case, Miss Pierre is supposed to come tonight to help get this thing out of me once and for all. So ready or not, I'm going to have to face whatever this is.

WEDNESDAY, APRIL 30, 9:45 P.M. (PRIVATE)

Miss Pierre came over and did the exorcism tonight. It wasn't really what I'd been picturing. I guess all I know about exorcisms comes from movies, where a priest holds up a crucifix and says a bunch of stuff in Latin. But Miss Pierre isn't a priest, so I should have realized it wouldn't be quite like that.

She did bring a crucifix, but she also brought a chicken. A live one. That was strange in itself. . . . I'm not sure I'd ever seen a live chicken before! I mean, it's not like I've spent a lot of time on chicken farms. Chicken to me is something that comes battered and fried from a restaurant, or in featherless pieces from the supermarket. Not a real live bird with feathers and wings, squawking and carrying on in a cage.

I asked Miss Pierre what she was going to do with the chicken, and she said we were going to kill it. That almost gave me second thoughts. I mean, right at that moment, there wasn't anything bothering me. I felt fine. And I wasn't sure I wanted this chicken's blood on my hands. Metaphorically, and literally, too. Miss Pierre said we could call it quits if I'd changed my mind, but Mamma pointed out that I'm not a vegetarian, and I've never complained before about chickens getting killed so I can eat them. I asked if we were going to eat this one, but Miss Pierre said no. The whole point of the ritual is to get the bad spirits out of me and into the chicken so they can't harm anyone anymore. If we ate the chicken, that would give them another chance to get ahold on us, which makes sense in an odd sort of way. Anyway, I decided to put my ethical concerns aside and just go ahead with it. I was curious.

Miss Pierre made us all go out in the backyard, and she set up a bunch of candles and a big potful of water, and she started ripping up herbs and crushing them to release their oils. Then she dropped them into the water and mixed them around. She had a big rattle that she shook for a while, and she sang and chanted, too, but I couldn't understand any of it. It did have some effect on me though. I closed my eyes, and before I knew it, I was trembling so hard, I almost fell over. Mamma reached out and held me up, though.

The next thing I remember is Miss Pierre taking the chicken out of the cage, grabbing it by the feet, and dunking its head in the water. Then she pulled it back out and sort of waved it around a bunch. The weirdest thing was that the chicken didn't really react. . . . I expected it to struggle and squawk and beat its wings, but it just lay there, like it was hypnotized or something. She brought the chicken over to me, still chanting, and I had to will myself to stand still and not duck away when she rubbed it around my body and face. I think I cried out a few times. She brought it back to the pot and held it out with its head over the water. She took out a knife and scraped off some of the feathers, then cut the throat and let the blood run into the pot. She let it run out for a good long time, until the chicken was clearly dead, then she cut off the head and threw it into the pot and took the chicken inside to boil it. She said that way we'd know it was really completely dead.

That was pretty much it! So I guess it's all done now. Now we just wait and see if things get better.

WEDNESDAY, APRIL 30, 11:29 P.M. (PRIVATE)

I read over my entry about the exorcism just now, and I feel like I didn't necessarily tell the whole story. Everything I said did happen pretty much the way I described, but I didn't really talk much about what it felt like. And that's probably the most important part.

It was weird, really. Through the whole thing, I felt almost like I was two people—one Laetitia was standing there, watching this ceremony, curious about how the whole thing would play out, but basically detached. I saw myself close my eyes and start to shake, and I heard the strange sounds I was making as Miss Pierre brought the chicken near me. But none of it really touched me.

The other Laetitia . . . Well, I'm not sure exactly how to describe the other part. I remember, as soon as Miss Pierre started chanting, or maybe even before that with the smell of those herbs in the air as she was tearing them apart, that's when I felt a weird stirring deep inside me. Almost like a little animal in my chest or my stomach that was just waking up and turning around. And as Miss Pierre moved on to the singing and shaking her rattle, this feeling got stronger and spread around my whole body. That's when I started shaking, I think. At first it was just kind of a weird, squirmy feeling, like you might get after drinking too much coffee, but gradually it became more than that. I had this sense there was something inside of me that was fighting to get out. It didn't exactly hurt, but I felt like I might be split in two by this thing. And I just kept telling myself to relax, take deep breaths, and just let it happen. I didn't know if it would be painful or cause some kind of damage, but I knew it had to happen, so I tried to just let it. That's when I started trembling, and I stumbled a bit and sort of tripped over my own feet. I was so conscious of what was going on inside my body, I wasn't doing what I needed to do to keep myself upright.

The important thing, though, was it seemed to be working. I can't be sure it wasn't just my imagination, or wishful thinking, but I definitely *felt* something trying to work its way out of me. Almost like wiggling a loose tooth. But then it shifted. I could feel whatever it was starting to slip free from me and leave me behind, which was exactly the point, right? I had expected to feel relieved by this. To feel wholly myself again. But that's not what happened. Instead, as Miss Pierre sang and chanted and waved that chicken around, I just got this overwhelming sense of loss. Like it wasn't some foreign entity leaving me, but a piece of myself. I felt abandoned and empty, and I started to panic.

So at the last minute, just as Miss Pierre was starting to cut the chicken's throat, I sort of . . . held on. Not with my fingers or teeth or anything, but something inside of me. And I gripped on to that feeling with all my power, and it felt almost like I was *tugging* on that feeling with the strength of my soul, until I could feel whatever it was slipping back into me and filling me with this warm tingling fullness I never wanted to stop.

Then Miss Pierre cut off the chicken's head, and that sort of brought me back to myself. And I thought about how the whole point of this was that I was supposed to give up a piece of myself to this chicken. But I didn't. I kept it.

I'm worried now. This ritual was supposed to help put me back in control of my own body, and I'm not sure it did. I can't tell anymore who is in control—what part is me and what part is something else, or if in the end it's really all me and has been all along. I don't know what I might be capable of in this condition, and I'm wondering if it wouldn't be best if someone came around and cut *my* head off before I can become a danger to everyone around me.

Maybe I already am.

THURSDAY, MAY 1, 12:19 P.M. (PRIVATE)

Oh no, Renee is here! I forgot all about her, but now she's here for one of her unscheduled drop-in visits. I can hear her right now, talking to Mamma in the kitchen. Maybe if I go down and act totally normal, she won't bother to come in here and see what a mess my room still is. We never really got it back into shape after the night of the fire. I think we were all so focused on whatever is wrong with me, trying to fix it, we didn't worry about the room so much. But if Renee sees it like this, it's going to be really obvious this isn't exactly a "stable environment." This is exactly the kind of excuse she's been looking for to send me away.

Maybe she won't notice. Or she'll cut us some slack. I've swept up all the glass, I think, but there's cardboard over the window and burn marks on the walls, and she is definitely going to have questions about both. This is exactly the kind of thing she was worried about, and I'm afraid if she sees the room, she'll have me sent away to go live with strangers again. I don't want that. I'm so scared.

I need to pull myself together. I need to go into the kitchen and talk to her and reassure her that everything is okay.

CHILD REMOVED INTO EMERGENCY PROTECTIVE CUSTODY WITHOUT COURT ORDER:
REPORT AND JUSTIFICATION

Date of Report: 5/2/2014

Date Child Was Taken into Protective Custody: 5/1/2014

Family Surname: ~~████████~~

Name(s) of Parent(s), Guardian(s), or Primary Custodians:

~~████████~~

Name of Child: ~~████████~~ Age: 15

Address: ~~████████~~

JUSTIFICATION FOR EMERGENCY REMOVAL (CHOOSE AS MANY AS APPLY):

[X] The child's physical or mental health is in severe and imminent danger due to inability, refusal, or neglect on the part of parent(s), legal guardian(s), or other custodian(s) to provide adequate shelter, nutrition, clothing, education, medical care, or supervision.

[X] The child's parent(s), legal guardian(s), or other custodian(s) appear to have physically or mentally injured the child by act or inaction.

[ ] There is compelling evidence of child sexual abuse.

☐ The child's physical or mental health has been endangered due to the parent(s), legal guardian(s), or other custodian(s) employing the child in a form of illegal or inappropriate labor.

☒ The child has significantly endangered his or her own well-being or the well-being of others.

DESCRIBE THE CIRCUMSTANCES THAT LED TO THE REMOVAL OF THE CHILD INTO PROTECTIVE CUSTODY:

On Thursday, May 1, I arrived at the ~~█████~~ residence for an impromptu well check, primarily to see if L— was keeping up with her medication schedule, and also to check more generally on the welfare of the ~~███~~ family. G— met me at the door and invited me into the kitchen, where P— (C's mother, L—'s grandmother) already was. I asked G— how L— was adjusting to her medication, but G— was mostly nonresponsive, and seemed not to have made any effort to ensure L— took her pills on schedule, even though she had agreed to support this treatment plan last time we spoke.

When pressed, G— insisted medication would not

solve the "real" problem in the house, and could only cover it up. She continued to put forward the idea that a demonic force was threatening ▬ and the whole family, and it would only be removed by God's will. The discussion between us became animated. Voices were raised, at which point ▬ came out of her room and into the kitchen. I deescalated the argument and asked ▬ to tell me in her own words whether she was taking her medication regularly, and how she was adjusting to it. She insisted-as she had last time-that she was taking everything according to the schedule and having no ill effects. She asked then if we could go out to the diner and get a slice of pie, as had been our tradition until recently.

I was about to agree, but I sensed something furtive in the way she was speaking, as if she wanted to distract me from something, so I asked if we could speak in her room instead. She refused at first, which led me to conduct a more thorough investigation of the rest of the house. It was at that time that I discovered traces of what appeared to be blood in the yard and on the back stairs. At first all three residents denied any knowledge of where it came from, but when I demanded to know if anyone had been hurt, ▬ confessed that a local voodoo practitioner had come and performed an animal sacrifice to rid L— of her demonic entity. This was explicitly contrary to the plan we had agreed to earlier, in which C— would cease to have any contact with this traditional healer/folk practitioner and would contact me first if she had any problem that needed to be resolved.

At this point, I entered L—'s room and discovered it had been badly damaged: there were burn marks on the wall and floor, and the window was broken and had been covered with a piece of cardboard. No one would explain exactly what had happened, but I surmised it was the result of L— leaving lit candles unattended—which she had promised me she would not do—as part of an "altar" to ward off evil spirits.

I made the decision that L— could not be left safely in her current situation, and began the process for an emergency removal. I contacted my supervisor, who gave me verbal approval to bring L— into temporary state custody until a stable environment for her—either with her mother or elsewhere—could be established. I asked L— to come with me willingly, and when she refused, I contacted the police to come aid in L—'s removal.

Two police officers arrived a few minutes later,

Officer D█ and Officer B█. L█ was crouched in a corner, facing the wall and rocking slightly while repeating that she didn't want to leave. One of the police officers approached and touched her gently on the shoulder. L█ spun around, growled, and bared her teeth at the officer. Both officers backed away, and I approached again and tried to reason with L█. I explained that the removal was only temporary, that if she was compliant, the situation could be resolved more quickly, and I assured her I would do everything in my power to make sure she was back at home with her family as soon as possible. This seemed to calm her down at first, but when I tried to coax her outside, she returned to hissing and spitting. Officer B█ tried to grab her from behind, but she sank her teeth into his hand, and when Officer D█ tried to intervene, she clawed out a chunk from his left cheek and pressed it into her mouth.

L█ was completely out of control, and I was worried the police officers would be compelled to use deadly force on her. I asked them to back away from her and leave her alone, and they called for an ambulance and more backup. While we waited for the ambulance to arrive, L█ continued to behave strangely, though somewhat less aggressively: she appeared to engage in glossolalia ("speaking in tongues"), walked and moved in a strange manner, and jumped and scrambled around the room with unusual energy.

By the time the ambulance arrived, L━━appeared to have worn herself out, and she collapsed in the middle of the room, moaning and rocking. She put up no further physical resistance, and was taken directly to the psychiatric wing of ██ Hospital.

PROVIDE JUSTIFICATION FOR WHY EMERGENCY REMOVAL WAS INDICATED:

Upon surveying the situation at the ██ house that afternoon, I came to the unavoidable conclusion that L━━provided an immediate danger to herself and others. Additionally, there was significant evidence that L━━'s custodial parent was not capable of adequately providing for L━. L━━has been frequently truant from school in the past few months, as well as unduly influenced by her mother's fixation on demons as an explanation for any negative event in their lives. Everyone in the household has been secretive and uncooperative, and they have failed to abide by the agreed-to guidelines. It is not a healthy environment for L━━

EXCERPT FROM OFFICIAL POLICE REPORT:
OFFICER D▓▓▓'S REPORT
REPORT DATE: 5/1/2014

WE RECEIVED A CALL AT APPROXIMATELY 18:20 ON THURSDAY, MAY 1, TO ASSIST SOCIAL SERVICES WITH A DOMESTIC SITUATION AT [ADDRESS REDACTED]. WE ARRIVED AT [ADDRESS REDACTED] AT 18:26 AND KNOCKED ON THE FRONT DOOR. THE GRANDMOTHER LET US IN AND SHOWED US TO THE ROOM WHERE R. S., THE SOCIAL SERVICES WORKER, WAS TRYING TO REASON WITH AN ADOLESCENT FEMALE, ▓▓. R. S. INDICATED SHE HAD DETERMINED IT NECESSARY TO REMOVE ▓▓ FROM THE HOUSEHOLD IMMEDIATELY FOR HER OWN SAFETY AND THE SAFETY OF OTHERS, BUT ▓▓ WAS RESISTING.

I STEPPED FORWARD AND ASKED ▓▓ TO COME PEACEFULLY WITH US. SHE WAS UNRESPONSIVE, SO I PUT A HAND ON HER SHOULDER. ▓▓ REACTED SUDDENLY, SPINNING AROUND AND SNAPPING AND SNARLING AT ME LIKE A RABID DOG. I STEPPED AWAY FROM HER TO REEVALUATE THE SITUATION. R. S. TRIED TO TALK TO HER AGAIN, BUT SHE DID NOT RESPOND, AND DID NOT SEEM TO HEAR HER. IT WAS AS IF SHE HAD TURNED INTO SOME KIND

OF WILD ANIMAL. SHE HAD MOVED AWAY FROM THE CORNER, SO OFFICER B██ WENT TO RESTRAIN HER FROM BEHIND. L██ GAVE A HOWL AND BIT INTO HIS HAND, THEN TURNED ON ME. I WAS TRYING TO GET HER OFF MY FELLOW OFFICER WHEN SHE LUNGED TOWARD ME AND SCRATCHED AT MY FACE, GOUGING OUT A DEEP GASH. I PULLED MY WEAPON AND TOLD HER TO PUT HER HANDS ON HER HEAD. INSTEAD SHE CALMLY LICKED THE BLOOD FROM HER FINGERS.

I KEPT MY WEAPON TRAINED ON HER AS OFFICER B██ CALLED IN FOR MORE BACKUP. THAT'S WHEN L██ STOOD UP STRAIGHT FOR THE FIRST TIME AND ADVANCED SLOWLY TOWARD ME, EVEN THOUGH I STILL HAD MY WEAPON AIMED AT HER AND WAS ORDERING HER TO STOP. SHE IGNORED MY INSTRUCTIONS AND BEGAN SPEAKING IN A WEIRD INHUMAN VOICE. I DIDN'T BELIEVE A VOICE LIKE THAT COULD COME OUT OF AN ADOLESCENT FEMALE. I DIDN'T RECOGNIZE THE LANGUAGE, BUT IT MAY HAVE BEEN LATIN.

THEN SHE SUDDENLY CROUCHED DOWN FOR A MOMENT AND STARTED MOVING BACKWARD ACROSS THE ROOM USING WEIRD JERKING MOVEMENTS, AS IF HER BONES WERE POPPING OUT OF THEIR JOINTS. I THOUGHT ONCE SHE REACHED

THE WALL BEHIND HER, SHE WOULD BE FORCED
TO STOP, BUT SHE DIDN'T. SHE KEPT MOVING UP
THE SIDE OF THE WALL. I DON'T KNOW HOW SHE
WAS DOING IT. IT DID NOT SEEM TO BE HUMANLY
POSSIBLE.

WHEN SHE REACHED THE CEILING, SHE LET
OUT A SHRIEK AND FLIPPED OVER, LANDING ON HER
BACK ON THE FLOOR, STILL HISSING AND SPITTING.
OFFICER B▬ LEFT THE ROOM WHILE R. S. AND I
MOVED TO RESTRAIN HER. SHE THRASHED FOR
A COUPLE OF MINUTES, BUT BY THE TIME THE
AMBULANCE ARRIVED, SHE WAS PASSIVE, THOUGH
STILL NOT COOPERATIVE. THE EMTS LOADED HER
ONTO A STRETCHER AND TOOK HER INTO THE
AMBULANCE.

I've served on the ██ police force for thirteen years, and six years before that in ████, and in all my experience I have never seen anything like this before. A teenage girl as strong as two trained law officers, who walks up walls and curses at you in weird languages? I'm not an expert in these things, but that's not normal.

Officer D— and I were totally unprepared for the situation we walked into. I understood we had a noncooperative fifteen-year-old female who needed to be brought into custody, and when we got there, that's what it looked like. She was crouched in the corner, crying, but as soon as she turned around, there was something in her eyes that made me cold. It wasn't human. And she was biting and barking like a mad dog, and she caught me by the hand and bit me. It was a severe bite. I had to go to the emergency room. Officer D— was trying to control her, and she scratched his face.

I've never seen anything like it. I was terrified, and I made the decision to radio for more backup. While I was talking to the dispatcher, I heard a voice speaking some strange language, but it definitely didn't sound like a teenage girl's voice. And it didn't sound like English—maybe Russian? Or German. I don't know. When I heard that, I turned to look, and she was running backward up the wall. Even in the Olympics, they can't do that. Then she jumped off and fell to the floor.

I had to leave the room after that. I had no idea what she might do next. I just thought, This isn't a situation for the police. This girl needs a priest.

CHILD AND ADOLESCENT
DIAGNOSTIC EVALUATION

Date: 5/2/2014

Patient Name: L�▬

Patient #: ▬▬▬▬

Interviewer: Dr. ▬▬▬▬

Justification: Court ordered

Consent: Yes **X** No___

IMMEDIATE RISK ASSESSMENT

Suicide: Yes___ No **X**

Aggression: Yes **X** No___

Patient was admitted yesterday after an altercation with police. Patient was unconscious upon admittance. Patient regained full consciousness this morning, and was examined for diagnostic purposes this afternoon. Initial diagnosis of schizoaffective disorder may need to be revisited. Patient admits to delusions and hallucinations, but her described hallucinations are sufficiently atypical, as to render diagnosis difficult. Patient also appears to be an accomplished liar, and therefore her descriptions of her own symptoms must be treated with an appropriate degree of skepticism.

Patient claims no memory of the event that resulted in her hospital admission, nor any memory of previous similar events. Again, her symptoms are markedly atypical for amnesia resulting from physical or psychological trauma.

Evidence from the patient's file suggests an alternative

diagnosis: possibly folie à deux, or a form of shared delusion with another person, in this case, her mother. As is typical of such scenarios, the mother's stronger personality has overwhelmed the daughter's weaker one, until the patient is forced to modify her entire conception of the world to fit her mother's various delusions. In this case, the mother has shown a persistent belief (going back at least twelve years) in the presence of demons and malevolent spirits in her life, affecting every aspect of her and her family's existence.

During analysis, the patient described a very intense relationship with her mother that may exhibit features of codependency. The patient may have unconsciously determined that love, attention, and support would only be granted to her in this household as long as she supported and participated in her mother's delusions.

As yet, there is no conclusive evidence of sexual, physical, or emotional abuse or other latent trauma, but it would be unwise to rule out any or all at this stage.

RECOMMENDATION:

Patient should remain in hospital care, under close observation, until her physical and psychological states can be stabilized. It may be necessary to keep her separate from her mother for an extended period of time in order for the shared delusions to dissipate and the patient to become more cooperative. Though every effort must be made to reunite this family, it is likely that this patient will ultimately fair better in a foster care environment.

If, however, the mother seeks treatment for her own delusions and successfully overcomes them, this recommendation may be reconsidered.

MEDICATION:

Patient was previously prescribed a course of antipsychotic medication, but that treatment plan needs to be reconsidered in light of an updated diagnosis. The current treatment plan emphasizes daily therapeutic sessions with the attending psychiatrist, plus group therapy sessions (contingent on the patient remaining nonviolent). Low-dose sedatives are also indicated until the staff can be sure the patient is not a danger to herself or others.

TUESDAY, MAY 6, 2:59 P.M. (PRIVATE)

I have my laptop back! It feels like it's been ages since I updated here, but I guess it hasn't been that long. It just feels like a long time because a lot has happened. I don't really remember too much—all I know for sure is, Renee showed up at the house on a surprise visit, asked about the damage to my room, she and Mamma started arguing, and I . . . I don't know. Sometime later I came to in this hospital bed. Everything in between is kind of a blur.

I was really confused and upset when I woke up here, strapped down and surrounded by strangers. And for the first few days no one would tell me anything. They just hooked me up to machines and fed me pills, and sometimes they let me out of bed to meet with a psychiatrist, but that was about answering *his* questions. He wasn't at all interested in answering mine.

He won't tell me anything definite, just that I had some kind of "episode," and keeps prodding me again and again to tell him everything I remember. I keep saying there's isn't anything! He knows what happened a lot better than I do. It's all a blank to me. I really don't see the point of going over it again and again when there's nothing to go over.

But now finally they've let Gramma Patty come to see me, and let her bring me some of my stuff, including my phone and my laptop. (The screens are still cracked, but I can see what I'm typing, for the most part.) She brought me clothes, too, but no belts, and they took all the shoelaces out of my shoes. And they've banned all my wigs and makeup, for some reason. It would take a more ingenious brain than mine to figure out how to kill myself with a bright pink wig and sparkly eye shadow. They won't even let me have my bandannas and scarves, which seems really cruel. Without at least those, I feel naked. Like a sick person.

Which maybe I am.

Gramma Patty has told me *some* stuff the doctors and nurses wouldn't. Though as usual, she begs off and says she doesn't like talking about this stuff, as if she thinks it's somehow dangerous to even tell me what happened. She did say that when Renee saw the condition of my room and heard some of what Mamma had to say about it, she decided I needed to be removed from the house then and there. Renee asked me to come with her, but I didn't want to go, so she wound up calling the police, and eventually an ambulance. Gramma Patty says it took four full-grown men to wrestle me into the ambulance. I really can't picture that. I'm not a big girl.

I thought about this awhile, and then I asked her, "Was I

violent? Did I hurt anyone?" She didn't answer right away, and when she did, she just patted my hand and smiled and told me not to worry. Said everyone was going to be fine. I guess that means I did hurt someone, maybe more than one person, and I have no idea what I did or how bad it was.

I'm kind of afraid to ask for more details. I'm not sure I want to know what really happened. In a way, I'm glad I don't remember it.

Whatever that was back there, who hurt those people, it wasn't me.

THURSDAY, MAY 8, 12:50 P.M. (PRIVATE)

Gramma Patty visited again today. It is so good to see a familiar face in the middle of this nightmare, even if it's only for a few minutes at a time. I miss my mamma, though. Gramma Patty told me Mamma isn't allowed to come see me yet, but she'll come as soon as she can. Renee and some other people from social services have given her a list of things she needs to do to prove she can provide me with a stable home. Gramma Patty says they are working together to get it done as quickly as possible, but there's no way to rush these things.

I asked her if I could come home right away, once Mamma has done everything she needs to do. She said no. There's some stuff I need to do too. I have to convince the doctors here that I'm better, and that I can be trusted not to have another episode or throw any fits. I wish I could trust *myself* about that. But I think Gramma Patty's message was pretty clear: whatever I think might be going on inside of me, if I want to go home, I better figure out what the doctors want to hear and say it.

FRIDAY, MAY 9, 10:43 A.M. (PRIVATE)

Holy Jesus, I don't know what's happening. Am I awake or am I dreaming?

I was just reading over my last couple of entries and something weird happened. They looked strange to me. The screen started to swim in front of my eyes, like I had gotten some dirt in them, and I was tearing up, but I blinked and rubbed them and it didn't go away. Instead the screen was rolling and rippling and buckling right before my eyes. I thought I had to be hallucinating and that it was a trick of my eyes or my brain and not actually on the screen itself. So I took some screen caps to reassure myself, and look:

I just went back and looked again, and the entries themselves look normal to me now. But the screen caps are still messed up! Oh God, I just noticed something else, too. Those aren't the words I originally wrote. Mostly it is, but in the bubbled parts, there are other words that weren't part of the original post.

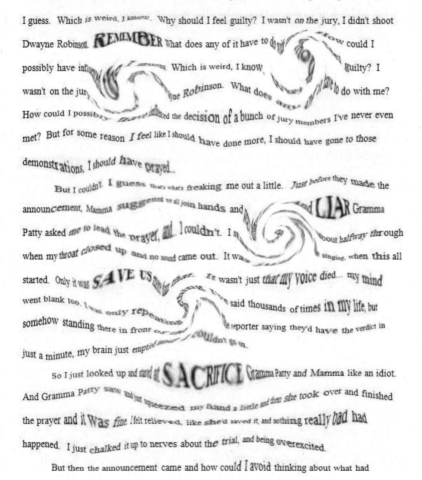

I guess. Which is weird, I know. Why should I feel guilty? I wasn't on the jury, I didn't shoot Dwayne Robinson. REMEMBER What does any of it have to do with how could I possibly have inf... Which is weird, I know, guilty? I wasn't on the jur... ...ne Robinson. What does ...rt to do with me? How could I possibly ...fluenced the decision of a bunch of jury members I've never even met? But for some reason I feel like I should have done more, I should have gone to those demonstrations, I should have prayed...

But I couldn't. I guess that's what's freaking me out a little. Just before they made the announcement, Mamma suggested we all join hands and LIAR Gramma Patty asked me to lead the prayer, and I couldn't. I s... ...bout halfway through when my throat closed up and no sound came out. It wa... ...singing when this all started. Only it was SAVE US ...before... It wasn't just that my voice died... my mind went blank too. I was only repeating said thousands of times in my life, but somehow standing there in front ...couldn't go on. reporter saying they'd have the verdict in just a minute, my brain just emptied...

So I just looked up and stared at SACRIFICE Gramma Patty and Mamma like an idiot. And Gramma Patty saw and just squeezed my hand a little and then she took over and finished the prayer and it was fine. I felt relieved, like she'd saved it, and nothing really bad had happened. I just chalked it up to nerves about the trial, and being overexcited.

But then the announcement came and how could I avoid thinking about what had

605

REMEMBER
LIAR
SAVE US
SACRIFICE

Where the hell did they come from? And what do they mean? I don't understand why this is happening.

TUESDAY, MAY 13, 6:23 A.M. (PRIVATE)

I've been wanting to write in here, but I kept holding back because I didn't know what to say. I think it's time I admit to myself what's going on here. It's time to face all the things I keep denying.

There are things I know. I didn't want to write them down because I was afraid that would make them real, but they are real, and I can't hide from them anymore.

Those words that appeared in my journal . . . *Remember . . . Liar . . .* I said I had no idea what they meant, but I do know. They're talking to me. Because I am a liar. And I do remember.

What I said before was all lies. What I told the doctors, and Gramma Patty, and even this journal. I said I didn't remember anything from my "episode," and my attack on those cops, but the truth is, I knew just what I was doing. I knew what I was doing, and I liked it.

I've been lying to everyone this whole time, and even to myself. That's what people always do, isn't it? When they've done something terrible, and people ask them about it? They always say, one minute we were arguing, and the next thing I knew he was dead and the gun was in my hand. I must have blacked out the rest.

It's easier that way, and it's what people want to hear. They think they want to hear what you were thinking, what it felt like, but they don't. It's too horrible. They'd turn away from you if they knew, and call you a monster. So instead you give them the same old script: *I blacked out. It's like something took over my body. I don't remember a thing.* That way, you get to still be human.

But now I know what a lie that is. I do remember. I remember the whole thing as clear as anything. I remember Mamma and Renee arguing, and I was trying to calm everyone down, and Renee said she had no choice; she had to get me out of this house. And I heard Mamma crying as Renee reached out a hand to me to take me away, and I felt this wave of anger and fear surge up in me, so I bared my teeth, and all my emotions came out of me in the form of a terrible, inhuman noise. I remember it all—cursing and spitting, biting that policeman, and even running up the wall. But it's almost like remembering a movie or a dream, because even as I was conscious of all those things, my attention was so much more focused on what was going on inside of me. And what was inside me was a rage so dark and thick, it seemed to fill me up, to replace my blood. It was like a black cloud, so heavy I felt almost like I could explode with it and send burning bile raining down over this whole city.

Although that's not quite right either. I'm trying to find words that fit, but something in me keeps wanting to phrase it so it sounds like some outside force that took over my body. So I can point to this or that and say, see? That's clearly not me. That's the demon. But the truth is, that's not how it felt at the time. At the time, there was no line separating me from the other, evil thing. There was only me all the way through. And that rage and evil were built out of every bad thing I've done or every wicked thought I've had throughout my whole life.

I'm not okay. I think I've known this for a long time, but I didn't want to face it. I came closest when I was talking to Miss Pierre, and she was trying to convince me that all this was happening to me because God chose me, but I knew even then that wasn't true. This whole idea of a demon possessing me . . . I don't think I ever *really* believed it. It's a nice story that makes me look like the good guy or like a victim. Like I was just some innocent who got attacked by evil out of bad luck.

But that was just a lie I told myself and everyone else to hide what's really going on. There isn't anything good in me, and there never was. Everything I have ever done on this earth has been in service not to God, but to my own glory and vanity and pride. To the Beast. If there is any demon, it's not possessing me. . . . It *is* me.

TUESDAY, MAY 13, 4:26 P.M. (PRIVATE)

My doctor here is "unhappy with my progress." I didn't tell him anything about what happened with the journal entries, or that I remember anything about my attack, but it's his job to get inside my head. I guess he can tell I'm hiding something. He seems to think I'm more in danger than ever.

Of course he can't know what's really going on, but in his way, he's probably more right about the danger—to myself and to everyone around me—than he even understands. He thinks this is some kind of mental illness, and if he can just find the right combination of pills, he can fix me up and I'll go back to being "normal." What he hasn't figured out is that this *is* my normal. There's no outside force, and there's no disease I've picked up. It's all the darkness that was always in me, just finally rising to the surface.

The only thing that's really changed is that I used to be able to control it better. I had all this wickedness and hate and anger and jealousy in me, but I was careful never to let it show. But now it's all just bleeding out of me, taking over my life. The visions I experienced, and the nails and bones and such that come out of me are just physical versions of the ugly thoughts and impulses that have always been there. The only thing that scares me now is what will happen if this process is allowed to go any further. What damage will I wind up doing once they let me out and there are no walls or straps or sedatives to stop me?

Maybe Miss Pierre or Mamma would say God could stop me, but I guess I don't believe it anymore. If God were real and good, He would have stopped me long ago. The fact that He hasn't just proves this world and whoever is running it is completely fucked.

But at least I still have some control. I think I finally understand what all those visions and dreams were. All the torture I was forced to see and experience. They were the tortures of Hell, and the visions were a message telling me where I belong. I fought it as long as I could, but it's the only answer that makes sense. The sooner I give in and accept my destiny, the safer everyone will be from me.

No one else is going to stop me, but maybe I can stop myself before I do any more damage.

INCIDENT REPORT

Patient # █████████

Patient Last Name: J█████

Patient First Name: L█████

Date of Incident: 5/14/2014

Approximate Time of Incident: 3:15 a.m.

Date of Report: 5/14/2014

After steady improvement over the last couple of weeks, the patient has regressed suddenly and dramatically.

Between three and four a.m. last night, an orderly making rounds notified the night nurse that loud noises were coming from the patient's room. The nurse notified the doctor on call, and proceeded to gather another nurse and orderly to assess the situation. Inside the room, they discovered that the patient had torn the metal bars free from the window casing, and was in the process of hurling herself at the glass. The glass panes are of double thickness and designed to be shatterproof, but even so, upon examination, the patient had clearly managed to damage the glass by repeated extreme force directed at the same spot. Lacking any blunt object in the room, the patient appeared to have used her own head to accomplish this.

For the next hour the nurse and orderlies tried to subdue the patient without much success. The orderlies both suffered deep lacerations to their faces, and the nurse suffered a broken wrist and three broken fingers. Eventually the patient exhausted herself, and a strong sedative was administered. The patient was then put to bed under heavy restraints.

It was only at this point that the nurse became aware of the blood, which was coming not only from the patient's head, and now from the orderlies' faces, but also from the patient's own wrists and mouth. The doctor on call arrived to perform an examination, and determined that the patient had chewed through the skin, veins, and tendons on both her wrists in an apparent suicide attempt. This process had also done considerable damage to her mouth: at one point during the examination, the doctor discovered a tooth lodged in the bones of the patient's wrist. A dental examination confirmed that this was her own tooth, ripped free by the exertion of her self-inflicted violence.

Although the patient was already unconscious, the doctor chose to increase the strength of the sedative being used on her.

CONCLUSION: Patient appears to be suffering from a critical level of suicidal ideation. She will stop at nothing, it seems, to achieve her goal of self-annihilation. She currently poses a severe danger to herself and others. It is difficult to say whether this condition was brought on by psychological factors or organic factors, possibly including a negative reaction to medication.

RECOMMENDATION: Restraints and heavy sedation until the patient is calm enough to engage in therapeutic treatment again.

Patient Notes, Dr. ███████████

Date: 5/16/2014

Patient # ████████████

Patient Last Name: J████

Patient First Name: L██████████

Patient is being maintained under heavy sedation and has not awoken since the incident. I would like to begin reducing the level of sedation so a psychiatric examination can be performed, but I am mindful of the orderlies and nursing staff, who appear nervous around the patient even when she is under heavy physical restraints. This is understandable, given the near superhuman strength she exhibited, necessary to pry the iron bars off the window. As yet, there has been no satisfactory explanation for how the patient was able to do this.

Nevertheless, tomorrow I would like to begin experimentally lowering the sedative enough to allow her to awaken. We cannot maintain her in this state indefinitely. This is an unusual case, so I am waiting on consults from colleagues before I make a definitive decision.

Patient Notes, Dr. ██████████
Date: 5/16/2014
Patient #: ██████████
Patient Last Name: J██████
Patient First Name: L██████████

    After affirmative consultation with Drs. ██████ and ██████, the process has been initiated to reduce the sedative and encourage the patient slowly and carefully back to consciousness. So far the patient is nonresponsive, but she is still under quite heavy sedation for someone her age and size. I will cut the dose again.

Patient Notes, Dr. ███████████

Date: 5/19/2014

Patient #███████████

Patient Last Name: J██████

Patient First Name: L███████████

Patient remains nonresponsive, even after considerable reduction in the sedative. I am growing concerned that some permanent damage may have been done to her brain as a result of overmedication by the doctor on call. This is in addition to the probable severe head trauma the patient inflicted on herself during her incident. I will order a brain scan for the patient tomorrow.

Patient Notes, Dr. ████████████

Date: 5/20/2014

Patient #: ████████████

Patient Last Name: J████

Patient First Name: L████

The results of the brain scan are not at all what I expected. The scan showed unusual hyperactivity in the patient's brain—not decreased metabolism, as would be expected from a traumatic brain injury or drug overdose, but heightened activity all over, even in normally dormant areas. Nevertheless, the patient remains unconscious. This is a very curious and surprising result. I may need another consult.

Patient Notes, Dr. ██████████

Date: 5/21/2014

Patient #████████████

Patient Last Name: J████

Patient First Name: L██████████

Some improvement today, in that the patient showed signs of increasing consciousness. Her eyelids fluttered repeatedly, and she attempted to speak at one point, though her words were unintelligible. However, it appears the patient has now developed a dangerously high fever that is so far resistant to drugs.

Letter from Ms. J█████ to L█████
Friday, May 23, 2014
(transcribed from handwritten letter)

Dear Laetitia,

I'm so worried about you, baby. It kills me that they won't even let me into see you, but they say it's too dangerous right now, with the fever you're running. But with all those doctors fussing over you, I can't help thinking you're bound to get better soon. I know you'll do it for me. You wouldn't leave your mamma all alone. Gramma Patty and I pray every day for you to recover and come home to us.

We are still working on getting things set up so you can live with us again. It just drives me crazy, because after all we've been through together, and then what happened when Renee was here, it really gets to me that no one will believe me as to what's really going on. There were witnesses! Renee and those police officers—how much more reliable can witnesses be? And those police officers will tell you what happened, how they saw with their own eyes how this family is being tormented by the Devil.

But still, social services insists I'm the one at fault; I'm the crazy one. Even though I'm just telling them what everyone knows is true. And they tell me the only way I can have my baby back home is if I say we made everything up. How is that going to solve anything? How is that going to help next time a demon comes around? It just makes us more vulnerable.

But don't worry; your mamma has an idea. I've been thinking about why we are experiencing these trials, and there has to be something inside the house that has brought all this on us. Some kind of cursed object or a portal that all the demons are traveling through. I learned about it on this TV show all about haunted places and possessions. If I can just find some evidence of that, some hard proof no one can disagree with, they'll all have to admit I was right all along, and someone will help us close the portal. We'll finally have peace. And then they'll let you come home.

I was going to call up those people from TV to come investigate, but their answering service said they were busy with other folks. But with God, anything is possible, so I prayed and prayed about it, asking God to show me where the demons were coming from, and the other day I got this feeling. You know all about my feelings, and how I have learned to trust them. And I'm just about convinced that what we're looking for is in the basement. You know I have never liked those basement stairs. They are downright creepy, and

I've always thought so. I hate going down there to do laundry, and I am sure that's why. That's where the bad spirits are coming from. I think something terrible must have happened down there, like a murder or a black magic ritual. Now I just need proof. There's a dirt floor, and if we dig around, I'm sure we'll find some evidence. I convinced one of those officers to come over and investigate, and when we find it, no one will be able to call me a liar ever again.

So you see? Mamma has the whole situation under control. Don't worry about a thing except getting good and healthy, and when you wake up, you'll be able to come straight home.

Love,
Mamma

TUESDAY, MAY 27
(TRANSCRIBED FROM CRAYON AND PAPER)

Finally they are letting me write again, though they won't let me
have my laptop back until I can prove I'm not going to freak out
again. I'm not, but I understand why they're afraid. I would be
too. But I'm not like I was back then. I'm the same person, but I
understand things better now.

They must have sedated me pretty hardcore, because I don't
remember anything from those first couple of days but bad dreams.
Then I started to wake up a little more and feel more conscious and
aware, but I was still miserable and just wanted to get away from
myself, from this world, from my body. I was too drugged up to
do anything, but I still had all those despairing thoughts from that
last incident, and I was almost dreading having to deal with normal
human life again. And I was tired of seeing the same old doctors
and nurses and orderlies come through my room.

I spent every day wishing Mamma or Gramma Patty would come visit me, just to see a familiar face, but I guess they weren't allowed. But there was this one woman who came every day and sat with me for hours. She's a nun, I think, from the way she was dressed. It's a Catholic hospital, so I guess they let the nuns visit with the patients sometimes. She's old, older than Gramma Patty, but she has a very sweet face, and just knowing she was sitting there, watching as I drifted in and out of sleep, made me feel better than all the doctors and psychiatrists and nurses put together.

She never said anything that I can remember. I don't even know her name. I wonder if she's taken a vow of silence. Up to that point, I'd been feeling so abandoned. After I saw those messages in my journal, I felt like everything was telling me there was something evil in me. Either something had taken over my soul, or maybe it had been dormant in my soul all along and had just been reawakened. And all I could think was that God would never accept someone as tainted and evil as me, so I was alone in the universe. I thought, if my soul was going to get sucked down to Hell, then so much the better because that would be where it belonged.

But if a nun is still willing to sit with me and hold my hand and pray over me, I can't be all bad, can I? It made me think there might still be hope.

Today before she left, she put a rosary in my hand. I don't think I've ever seen one before, except in movies and on TV. I know Gramma Patty would say that's all superstitious nonsense. She explained once that they're for counting out your prayers, but in our church, we don't pray like that, repeating the same words over and over. She said we speak from the heart as the spirit moves us. Still, I'm glad to have it. It's pretty, and it's nice to know someone hasn't given up on me.

WEDNESDAY, MAY 28
(TRANSCRIBED FROM PENCIL AND PAPER)

I slept through the visit from the nun today. Disappointing, because I've started looking forward to seeing her every day. But I know she was there because my dreams are always calmer when she's sitting by me. Sometimes she rests a hand on my forehead, and I get this peaceful feeling, like being a kid again and knowing people will take care of me and I have nothing to worry about. I haven't felt that in so long, and today, even in my dreams, I could feel it.

When I woke up, there was a new plant sitting on the table. I don't know what it is, but I took a picture of it. It's kind of strange. It doesn't have any flowers, just leaves. I wonder where she even got it. Still, I kind of like it. It makes the room feel less dreary.

I just asked one of the nurses, and I guess it's a palm leaf.

That makes sense—I guess it does look like it came off a palm tree. Not that I've ever seen a palm tree in real life. What a strange plant to bring to someone in a hospital. But it's nice.

THURSDAY, MAY 29
(TRANSCRIBED FROM PENCIL AND PAPER)

I tried to talk to the nun today, but she wouldn't answer. I asked her name, and if she works at the hospital, but she just smiled and put her finger to her lips. Then she put a book in my hands, heavy and leather bound. I assumed it would be a bible, but it's a book of the lives of the saints. I've always grown up with bibles around the house, but these stories are new to me. Our church doesn't talk about saints. The pastor says it's wrong to focus on anyone but Jesus. God. Whatever. I don't have anything else to read, though, since there's no Wi-Fi here.

It's full of illustrations, too, and some of them are pretty gory.

FRIDAY, MAY 30
(TRANSCRIBED FROM PENCIL AND PAPER)

I was reading those stories about these saints. A lot of them are very strange and seem not very realistic, like this story of Saint George, who saved a princess from a dragon, or Saint Ursula, who traveled all around Europe followed by eleven thousand virgins. That's hard to picture.

But then, most of the events happened a long time ago, and maybe some details got screwed up or exaggerated. Besides, if someone wrote a story of my life, I'm not sure how believable it would look, so maybe I shouldn't judge.

There's something strange about some of the stories, though. Something really familiar, which is weird, because I didn't grow up hearing these stories. It's not quite like I know the stories, but every once in a while there will be a word or an image that sticks out at me, and it's like a gong reverberating through my body, or something I've seen in a dream. Or déjà vu. But I can't quite put my finger on it.

FRIDAY, MAY 30 (LATER THE SAME DAY) (TRANSCRIBED FROM PENCIL AND PAPER)

I just figured it out! I was reading about Saint Catherine and how she was tortured on a spiked wheel, and I remembered the spiked and flaming wheel I used to see when I had my attacks. And the picture of it that showed up on my blog. And I flipped through and found Saint Apollonia, who had all her teeth pulled out. And here's Saint Lawrence, who was roasted alive on a grill, and Saint Lucy, who had her eyes ripped out.

There are other stories I've run across where I see weirdly familiar pieces of my life pop up. Famous pilgrims carried seashells, and one lady escaped her tormenters by growing feathers and turning into a bird, and a few made roses grow where they normally wouldn't.

What does it all mean? It feels like puzzle pieces fitting together, but I can't see the whole picture yet. Oh, and some of the pictures show the saints holding palm branches like the one that nun brought for me. Is that important? Does it have something to do with being a saint? Is she trying to tell me she thinks I'm a saint? I can't be, though. I don't even believe in that stuff.

But I remember what Miss Pierre was telling me before I got taken away and shut up in here. About how sometimes a possession is from the Devil, but sometimes it's a message from God that you've been picked out for something special. But what? I always thought God's purpose for me was to sing, but I don't really think that anymore. At least, not in the way I was picturing.

SUNDAY, JUNE 1
(TRANSCRIBED FROM PENCIL AND PAPER)

Miss Pierre came to visit me today. Funny, since I was just thinking of her. It was nice to see her, and she said she had been very worried about me, and has prayed for me every day. I must look like hell, because as soon as she saw me, she got a shocked and pitying look on her face, and she stroked my cheek and muttered a prayer or some other protective spell, I'm not sure.

She said she could see I'd "endured a great torment at the hands of the spirits." No argument there. She grabbed my hands and begged me not to give in to despair. She said there had been so many signs. Signs that I had been chosen. And then she said, "I know there is doubt in your mind, but there is no doubt in mine. You have been chosen for greatness."

I know I always dreamed of that. Of being recognized as

special or "chosen." If this is what it means, though, I wish I had dreamed of something else. I understand now: there's a lot to be said for being ordinary.

Besides, it's a nice thing to say, but how can I trust it? And if I've really been chosen for something, when do I find out what it is? Is there something I should be doing now? I don't feel like I'm doing anything very special at the moment. Mostly just lying in bed and trying not to vomit or faint every time I sit up a bit. I don't really see how that's part of God's plan.

Miss Pierre said not to worry too much about it. That I should just trust in God, and it would all become clear. She makes it sound so simple! But how can it be? How can I trust any voice in my head or my heart when God and the Devil sound the same to me? But Miss Pierre did tell me long ago that the Devil works for God. Is that true? Maybe they speak with the same voice because there is no difference between them. I don't know whether that's comforting or terrifying.

Excerpt from telephone interview between Professor M. Verano and Officer B██████ of the ████████ County Police Department.

Date: 11/24/2014
Subject: Results of the investigation of the ████████ residence for evidence of paranormal activity.

VERANO: AND SHORTLY AFTER THE INCIDENT WITH L█████, MS. C█████ J█████ CONTACTED YOU, IS THAT RIGHT?

OFFICER B████: THAT'S CORRECT.

VERANO: AND WHAT DID SHE WANT?

OFFICER B████: SHE WANTED ME TO COME BACK TO THE HOUSE. L█████ WASN'T THERE ANYMORE, BUT HER MOTHER HAD AN IDEA THAT THERE WAS SOME KIND OF . . . [UNINTELLIGIBLE] ACTIVITY IN THE HOUSE. SHE WANTED HELP LOOKING INTO IT. I GUESS SHE REMEMBERED HOW SPOOKED I'D BEEN DURING THE PREVIOUS INCIDENT, AND SHE THOUGHT I WOULD BE SYMPATHETIC TO HER MISSION.

VERANO: SO YOU AGREED TO RETURN TO MS. J█████'S HOUSE?

OFFICER B████: YES, BUT OFF-DUTY. ON MY OWN TIME.

VERANO: WHY DID YOU AGREE TO IT?

OFFICER B████: I WAS CURIOUS, I GUESS. I COULDN'T STOP THINKING ABOUT THAT GIRL. L█████. I KNOW WHAT I SAW, AND THAT WAS NOT NORMAL. THAT WAS NOT . . . IT WASN'T ANYTHING THAT BELONGS IN THIS WORLD. AT THE TIME, WHEN

I SAW THAT, I JUST WANTED TO GET AS FAR AWAY FROM THAT
HOUSE AND THAT FAMILY AS POSSIBLE. ACTUALLY, WHEN MS.
J████ CALLED ME TO ASK IF I WOULD COME BACK, AT FIRST
I HUNG UP ON HER. BUT THEN I STARTED TO GET CURIOUS.
YOU DON'T BECOME A POLICE OFFICER UNLESS YOU LIKE
MYSTERIES, YOU KNOW? I COULDN'T JUST WALK AWAY AND NOT
GATHER ANY EVIDENCE.

VERANO: DO YOU BELIEVE IN THE SUPERNATURAL?

OFFICER B████: I DON'T KNOW. [UNINTELLIGIBLE] I
BELIEVE IN GHOSTS, YEAH, BUT I NEVER THOUGHT THEY WERE
HARMFUL. DEMONS? NO, I DON'T BELIEVE IN DEMONS. AT
LEAST, I DIDN'T.

VERANO: SO YOU CONTACTED HER?

OFFICER B████: NO, I--I DIDN'T DO ANYTHING. BUT SHE
CALLED AGAIN A COUPLE OF DAYS LATER, AND THIS TIME I
HEARD HER OUT AND SAID I WOULD COME OVER TO HELP. I
WAS STILL SCARED, BUT I WANTED TO KNOW. I'M NO COWARD.

VERANO: SO WHAT HAPPENED?

OFFICER B████: I WENT OVER ON A SUNDAY AFTERNOON. I
WAS NERVOUS GOING IN, BUT THE HOUSE SEEMED PERFECTLY
NORMAL THIS TIME. IT WAS DIFFERENT WITHOUT THE
DAUGHTER THERE.

VERANO: CAN YOU DESCRIBE HOW IT WAS DIFFERENT?

OFFICER B████: DIFFERENT . . . ENERGY? I DON'T KNOW
HOW TO DESCRIBE IT. LIKE THE DIFFERENCE BETWEEN GOING
OUT ON A NICE SUNNY DAY VS. WALKING OUTSIDE AND

KNOWING A STORM IS COMING. SOMETHING IN THE LIGHT,
IN THE AIR . . . DIFFERENT SMELL, MAYBE. ANYWAY, MS.
J█████ MADE ME A CUP OF COFFEE, AND WE DISCUSSED OUR
APPROACH. SHE WAS CONVINCED THE NEGATIVE ENERGY WAS
COMING FROM THE BASEMENT. I WENT DOWN THERE WITH
A SHOVEL. . . . THE BASEMENT HAS A DIRT FLOOR. AND
I SPENT AN HOUR OR TWO DIGGING, MOSTLY UNDER THE
STAIRS WHERE SHE SAID THE [UNINTELLIGIBLE] WAS MOST
POWERFUL. MS. J█████ WAS CONVINCED SOMEONE LIVING
IN THE HOUSE HAD PERFORMED SOME BLACK MAGIC RITUAL
AND HAD OPENED A PORTAL THAT NEEDED TO BE CLOSED.
SHE SAID IF I DUG UNDER THE STAIRS, WE WOULD FIND
EVIDENCE. A OUIJA BOARD OR A MAGIC CIRCLE OR ANIMAL
BONES, MAYBE.

VERANO: WHAT DID YOU FIND?

OFFICER B█████: NOTHING, REALLY. JUST SOME RANDOM JUNK.
A KID'S BRACELET, FAKE EYELASHES, A PAIR OF UNDERWEAR.
I THOUGHT THAT MIGHT BE A CLUE TO SOME KIND OF TRAUMA
OR ABUSE, BUT SINCE THE WASHER AND DRYER ARE DOWN
THERE, THAT SEEMED LIKE A MORE LIKELY EXPLANATION.
NOTHING THAT SEEMED MAGICAL OR CURSED OR ANYTHING.

OFFICER B███: AFTER THAT I TOOK A FEW MORE PICTURES AROUND THE HOUSE, IN PLACES WHERE MS. J███ THOUGHT SHE HAD DETECTED SPIRIT ACTIVITY. BUT IT ALL SEEMED PRETTY NORMAL.

VERANO: THERE WAS ONE PHOTO IN THE BATCH YOU SENT ME. . . . ONE LOOKING DOWN THE BASEMENT STAIRS.

OFFICER B███: YOU NOTICED THAT ONE, DID YOU? MOST PEOPLE LOOK AT IT AND DON'T NOTICE ANYTHING STRANGE ABOUT IT. I DIDN'T UNTIL MY DAUGHTER POINTED IT OUT TO ME.

VERANO: THERE'S A SHAPE THERE. LOOKS LIKE . . .

OFFICER B███: LOOKS LIKE SOMETHING, I KNOW. IT'S NOT A COAT RACK, THAT'S FOR SURE. BUT I CAN'T FIGURE OUT WHAT IT WAS. I MEAN, I CAN'T BE POSITIVE IT WASN'T JUST A WEIRD SHADOW, OR SOME GRIT ON THE LENS. SO.

VERANO: I SEE. YES. THANK YOU FOR YOUR TIME.

END EXCERPT

DEPARTMENT OF SOCIAL SERVICES
FAMILY RESOLUTION PLAN

Date: 6/2/2014   Family Surname: ████████

PARENT/GUARDIAN INFORMATION

Father: Unknown, not involved   Mother: C██████
Other guardian: ████████, grandmother

Name of Child: L███
Age: 15

GOAL: Reunification of family

CURRENT SITUATION:

L███ has been removed from C███'s household and placed in state custody in response to severe instability in the home. Previous to her removal, L███'s school attendance was inconsistent, and her home life was dominated by constant threats of "demonic interference." Social services caseworker R. S. determined the situation was encouraging violent, delusional, and antisocial tendencies in L███. L███ is currently housed in a psychiatric facility. R. S. is working with C███ to improve the situation in the home, with the goal of L███'s eventual return. If C███ does not cooperate with the objectives, foster care is an alternative option for L███.

BENEFITS OF REUNIFICATION:

C██ is a caring and attentive mother who has no history of physically or verbally abusive behaviors. C████ has a history of seeking help and accepting guidance when her family's situation is struggling or threatened. L███ is polite, well behaved, and sociable when not under the influence of her delusions. L███ and C███ have a strong mother-daughter bond, and both are motivated to do what is required to end their separation.

RISKS OF REUNIFICATION:

C███ is overly reliant on supernatural explanations for challenges faced by her family. L███ is suggestible to her mother's influence and prone to "playing along" to support her mother's delusions. Both have in the past struggled to comply with plans designed to improve their situation, and can be stubborn or secretive when pressed.

OBJECTIVES FOR PARENT/GUARDIAN/CUSTODIAL CARETAKER:

- Mother will ensure child attends school on a regular basis
- All absences and tardies will come with a justified excuse from someone outside the household
- Mother will participate in a clinical psychiatric assessment and comply with the recommendations

- Mother will seek explanations for events not directly related to religion or demonic infestation
- Mother and child will not use demonic possession as an excuse for child's behaviors

Signed:

████████████████████████████

Mother: ████████████

Caseworker: ████████████

I have my laptop back! Mamma brought it when she came to visit today. I guess that's the other big news: Mamma's probation period is over, and the social services people have declared her fit to have me in the house again! Which means I can go home as soon as the doctors here approve it.

I asked Mamma what changed their minds, and she said it was *her* mind, really, that got changed. She was so sure there was some demon infecting our house, but the more she tried to tell everyone about it, the more crazy and unstable they decided she was. Finally she decided she'd get some hard evidence no one could disagree with, and they'd all see this situation wasn't her fault. She had this idea that there was something in the basement, some kind of portal or something, that was allowing demons to come through and torment us. She got the cops to come over and search it with her, but I guess they didn't find anything much.

After that, she decided to let it go. She wanted me back, and it wasn't worth the fight anymore. So she told Renee and a judge and a counselor that she didn't believe in demons anymore, and that from now on she would look for earthly explanations for problems facing the household. She even signed something saying she wouldn't get in touch with Miss Pierre, and she wouldn't talk about demons with me anymore. (She made an exception today because she couldn't figure out how to explain to me what the agreement was without saying it.)

Then she explained I could come home and live with her and Gramma Patty as soon as I was feeling better. She asked me if I thought that might be soon, and I told her yes, I hoped so. She'd heard about my incident with the window and had been worried about me, but I told her about the nun who visited me, and how she had changed my whole outlook. How without even talking, she had made me feel more positive about my situation. I expected Mamma to be pleased about this, but she looked concerned instead. She touched my head as if feeling for a fever, even though I told her I was feeling better.

I asked her what the problem was and she said, "Baby, this isn't a Catholic hospital. And no one has come to see you here except Gramma Patty and Miss Pierre. I saw the logbook."

I guess that means she doesn't believe me that the nun visited me at all. That, just like the doctors, she thinks I'm imagining things or making them up.

I started to argue with her, but I gave up before long. I was too tired to pull together evidence that what I remembered really happened. And anyway, after all I've been through, how do I even know to trust myself? I've long since given up any sense of certainty about what I see and feel versus what other people do.

And then Mamma took my hand and was like, "Baby, can you do something for me? When the doctors come in and ask how you are feeling, just tell them you are feeling fine, all right? Your story about the nun, that can just be between us. "

I guess I see what she means.

DR.▮▮▮▮: TELL ME ABOUT THE INCIDENT THAT PUT YOU HERE, IN THE HOSPITAL. DO YOU REMEMBER THAT?

L▮▮: WHEN I ATTACKED THE POLICE OFFICERS?

DR.▮▮: YES.

L▮▮ I REMEMBER.

DR.▮▮▮▮ AND WHAT ABOUT THE OTHER INCIDENT, WHILE YOU WERE HERE?

L▮▮ THE SUICIDE ATTEMPT.

DR.▮▮▮ IS THAT WHAT IT WAS?

I▮▮ PRETTY MUCH, YEAH. I THOUGHT IT WOULD BE BETTER FOR EVERYONE IF I WASN'T ALIVE ANYMORE. SO I DECIDED TO . . . YOU KNOW. WHATEVER IT TOOK.

DR.▮▮▮ AND HOW DO YOU FEEL ABOUT THAT NOW?

L▮▮ I DON'T FEEL LIKE THAT, NOT ANYMORE. I WAS ALL MIXED UP. NOW I JUST WANT TO SEE MY MAMMA AND GRAMMA PATTY AGAIN. GET BACK TO MY OLD ROOM, GO TO SCHOOL.

DR.▮▮▮ BUT YOU REMEMBER THOSE INCIDENTS.

L▮▮ YEAH. YEAH, I REMEMBER THEM NOW.

DR. ████ YOU DIDN'T REMEMBER THEM BEFORE? THE
MEMORIES CAME BACK TO YOU AT SOME POINT?
L ███ NO, I ALWAYS KNEW WHAT HAPPENED. I
JUST . . . I DIDN'T WANT TO TALK ABOUT IT
BEFORE. I DIDN'T KNOW HOW TO TALK ABOUT IT.
DR. ████ CAN YOU EXPLAIN NOW WHAT YOU WERE
THINKING DURING THOSE INCIDENTS? WHAT
CAUSED THAT BEHAVIOR?
L ███ I BELIEVED I WAS POSSESSED BY A
POWERFUL DEMON THAT WAS TRYING TO DESTROY
ME AND MY FAMILY.
DR. ████ BUT THAT'S NOT WHAT YOU BELIEVE NOW?
L ███ NO. OR . . . I GUESS I'D SAY MY
PERSPECTIVE HAS CHANGED. I BELIEVE NOW
THAT MY FAMILY WAS DEALING WITH A LOT OF
PROBLEMS, AND I WAS DEALING WITH SOME
PROBLEMS. ANXIETY. DEPRESSION. TRYING TO
FIGURE OUT WHO I WAS, WHO I WANTED TO BE.
I WASN'T GOOD AT TALKING ABOUT IT. SO MAYBE
THE DEMONS I BELIEVED IN GAVE ME A WAY OF
TALKING ABOUT THAT STUFF.
DR. ████ WHAT DO YOU MEAN? DO YOU MEAN LIKE A
METAPHOR?
L ███ YEAH, THAT'S RIGHT. I THINK WE ALL HAVE
OUR DEMONS, BUT THE ONLY WAY TO GET RID OF
THEM IS . . . IT'S NOT MAGIC AND EXORCISMS.

YOU HAVE TO JUST FACE THE PROBLEMS YOU HAVE
HERE IN THIS WORLD.

AFTER REVIEWING THE PATIENT'S FILE, IT IS
CLEAR PATIENT #███████ HAS MADE REMARKABLE
PROGRESS WHILE UNDER OUR CARE. SHE NO
LONGER SUFFERS FROM THE DELUSIONS THAT
PLAGUED HER UPON ADMITTANCE. THERE
WAS SOME CONCERN THAT CONTACT WITH HER
MOTHER MIGHT CAUSE A REGRESSION, BUT
THIS DOES NOT APPEAR TO BE THE CASE. BOTH
MOTHER AND DAUGHTER HAVE AGREED TO FACE
THEIR PROBLEMS AND NOT BLAME THEM ON
SUPERNATURAL INTERFERENCE.
THE PATIENT'S MEDICAL TEAM HAS DECLARED
HER TREATMENT A SUCCESS AND CAN SEE NO
REASON FOR HER NOT TO BE RELEASED FROM
THE HOSPITAL. HER DISCHARGE IS APPROVED
IMMEDIATELY.

DISCHARGE DATE: 6/3/2014

THURSDAY, JUNE 5, 4:30 P.M. (PRIVATE)

It's nice to be home, but I'm having some trouble adjusting to normal life. I can't help feeling removed from it. There's school, and there are chores and meals and TV shows, but none of it feels like it has anything to do with me. The doctors say that's normal, and that it will get better with time, but I don't know. I feel almost like I'm just biding my time until . . . well, I don't know what. But like Miss Pierre said, I'll just listen carefully, and hopefully, it will become clear.

I set the palm the silent nun brought me on my windowsill. Mamma asked if I wanted to just leave it at the hospital or donate it to another patient. She doesn't think it's very nice looking, as plants go, and she did bring me a nice bright geranium, but it seemed important to hold on to the palm.

Maybe it's because of what Mamma said in the hospital—

that the nun wasn't real. If she was just my imagination, where did the plant come from? And the rosary, and the book of saints? Those feel real enough, and other people can see them. I've thought about asking Mamma if she could explain it, or maybe Miss Pierre, but maybe it doesn't need to be explained. Maybe I already know the answer.

SATURDAY, JUNE 21, 12:30 P.M. (PRIVATE)

I was looking at the local news, and I saw the *America Sings* auditions are here in town. I could hardly believe it, but when I looked at my calendar, I had marked it months ago. Funny to think how important that once was to me, and today I almost didn't even notice it was happening.

I sort of checked inside myself to see if there was any part of me that wished I were there today, but I don't think there is. The person I was then seems so far away now. I flipped back to my blog posts from before all this started, and I hardly recognize who I was then.

It's been a while since I've even updated here. Honestly, I'm not sure what to say. I spend so much of every day repeating the things I'm supposed to say, it feels weird to acknowledge the other things. The things I'm not supposed to talk about. But I guess there's no reason to hide them here.

I know Renee and the doctors will send me away if they get the sense I'm "acting out" again. And I don't want to leave. This is where I'm meant to be right now, with my family, so I'll keep my mouth shut. But the truth is, I've still got a lot of the old problems; I just know how to deal with them better now. I still have bad dreams and visions, and days when I can't tell one from the other. I still sometimes feel like my skin is on fire, or I get a horrible stabbing pain in my side, but instead of falling to the ground or crying out and drawing attention to myself, I just accept it. It's serving some purpose, though I don't know what yet. But I trust that.

Anyway, there are more important things to worry about. Like the protests that are still going on about the Robinson trial. The riots pretty much burned themselves out while I was in the hospital, but that doesn't mean people have forgotten about the injustice that was done. The crowd gathering at the park is bigger than ever, and now I'm with them too, the way I always should have been. Mamma and I, we haven't talked about it directly, but we have kind of an understanding now. She still worries about me going over there, but she understands it's important to me, I know the risks, and I have to make my own choices. So the deal is, I keep quiet about all the weird stuff that is still happening with me, and she doesn't object when I go to the park to help out with the protests.

When Miss Pierre told me to look inside myself for what I should be doing, it didn't take me long to figure out that I should be with the protesters. But I wasn't sure what I had to contribute, so I asked around and found out they needed people to bring water and sandwiches. At first that seemed kind of dull and insignificant compared to all the stuff I've been through recently, but they told me, "People have to eat!" And I guess that's true.

So I just started making sandwiches and going around the park with a basket of them, offering them to anyone who looked tired or hungry. I didn't really want to draw attention to myself. I was afraid that would seem prideful, as if I were only doing it so people would be impressed with me. At first I just went around, my head wrapped in a scarf and not saying more than, "Hi, are you hungry?" to anyone. But then the other day an old teacher I had freshman year recognized me and said she remembered how I always used to have brightly colored hair. She said whenever she saw it, it was like a bit of sunshine in her day. Then she said people there in the park could use a little of that sunshine.

At first I felt awkward about it. The flashy hair was who I used to be, when all I cared about was being famous and singing in huge arenas and getting a lot of hits on my blog. It didn't feel appropriate to the serious work of protesting racial injustice. But the more I thought about it, the more I realized I missed it. My colorful wigs are part of who I am. What's the shame in that? And if they bring other people a little happiness and good cheer, maybe that's not such a bad thing. Maybe it could help raise morale.

So now I'm thinking I'll try it out. I've already played around with styling my turquoise wig tonight. We'll see what kind of reaction I get when I wear it tomorrow.

SUNDAY, JUNE 22, 5:32 P.M. (PRIVATE)

I showed up today at the protests in the turquoise wig with glittery pink barrettes. Other than that, I was just doing my normal stuff, walking around the park with my basketful of sandwiches. But it was weird—I felt totally different. I've gradually been feeling better about things ever since the old nun came to me, but this was the first time I could remember in ages where I really felt . . . glad to be me. To be alive. Confident and happy.

I think other people noticed it too, unless they were just responding to the wig. A few of them did mention they were happy to see me smiling. I guess I had looked pretty serious before. It was also useful, because people can spot me from far away. So if people need water or medical attention, they can tell someone to look for the girl with bright hair, and I'll come and help them. Now I'm not just handing out a few sandwiches. I can help a lot more people.

TUESDAY, JUNE 24, 6:53 P.M. (PRIVATE)

Guess who I ran into at the park today! Angela! I guess she's been coming to the protests for a couple of weeks, but she spotted me today because of the wig.

It was so good to see her again. We left things on kind of bad terms, but somehow it was easy to forget about all that today. She gave me a big hug and asked how I was doing. I thought about telling her all the stuff I've been through—the trances and the hospitalization and everything—but why drag up all that stuff? It doesn't really matter anymore. It seemed better to just talk about the Robinson trial and the demonstrations, and the work we're all doing together. She's excited about it too.

It's nice to have something in common again. Instead of fighting about whether to talk about my life or hers, we can talk together about something we both care about.

While I was catching up with her, one of Mamma's old friends from church came up to say hi. She told me she'd seen me around the park, but she didn't recognize me until I started wearing my wigs again. Then she asked me why I don't sing anymore.

I told her about how I used to sing, but one day I lost my voice. I kind of left it at that, figuring she didn't need to know all the other crap. Anyway, she just brushed it off and said it didn't matter. Singing is fun, and it doesn't matter if your voice is perfect or you sound like a professional. Funny, it's been ages since I thought of it that way. When I was a little girl and Mamma was teaching me songs, I loved to sing just for the joy of it. Then I started to get noticed, and it turned into a whole thing, with ambitions and pressures to succeed. . . . I still loved it, but in a different way.

I explained to her that it didn't matter—it's not just that my voice is no good; it's gone completely. But the woman hardly paid attention. She just started singing some old protest song, and Angela joined in, and so did a bunch of other people. And I sort of half knew the words from hearing other people sing it these past few weeks, and they all were having so much fun that I desperately wanted to join in. It's the first time I've really missed singing in ages and ages. So I just started mouthing the words so I wouldn't feel so left out. And then I was singing really softly under my breath . . . and then I tried it a little louder . . . and what do you know? I was singing again! It's true, my voice isn't as big and polished as it used to be, but it didn't seem to matter, because everyone around me was singing along and joining in, and no one was trying to be a soloist or be the best. We were all just having a good time and lifting one another's spirits.

That in itself would have been enough to make this a pretty amazing day, but then something else happened. I got all lit up with this sudden fire to write a song of my own. I don't know where it even came from! I've never been able to write songs before, not even a little. But as I was walking home that evening, I could hear the whole thing in my head—the tune and the words and everything. I was so excited, I actually started running the last few blocks, so I could write it all down before I forgot it. And once I sat down, I couldn't stop. Song after song just poured right out of me. I think I have six or seven written up now!

They're all just about joining together with other people for a cause. They're supposed to cheer people up, and maybe help our message spread wider. I hope people like them. I can't wait to go back to the park tomorrow and share them.

WEDNESDAY, JUNE 25, 9:42 P.M. (PRIVATE)

Today was amazing! I use to think singing was the greatest feeling in the world, but I had no idea what it would feel like to
hear other people singing songs I made up. And best of all, it's
supporting a cause that's really important. Finally I feel useful
to the world. And everyone—Gramma, Renee, my friends at the
park—they all say such a change has come over me in the past
few weeks.

  Though the truth is, a lot of that is just how I present myself.
I've learned how to share the good stuff and hide the stuff that's,
well . . . it's not bad, but it's harder for a lot of people to understand.

  That reminds me: I finally figured something out about that
plant the nun gave me.

I was curious, so I looked up palms online. Now I know why some of the saints are carrying palms and some aren't: the palm is a symbol of martyrdom. It marks out the saints who died for their beliefs.

I'm not sure how I feel about that. Was the nun trying to tell me that will happen to me? I don't want that, but the surprising thing is, I'm not as scared of it as I used to be. As I feel like I should be. Like most people, dying used to seem like the scariest thing in the world. Partly because I didn't know what it would be like, and partly because I was afraid I wouldn't get a chance to achieve my goals and dreams.

When I first read what the palm meant, I had this moment of . . . I don't know. It's like I paused a minute and looked inside myself, expecting to feel that jolt of terror most normal humans get when they picture their own deaths. But it never came. I just felt calm, and like I was finally understanding something I'd half known all along. Now I don't feel like death is a mystery. In the past few months, I've spent so much time and energy dealing with the spiritual world, it doesn't seem as foreign to me as it used to. And I feel pretty confident there is more than emptiness and nonexistence on the other side.

As for achieving my dreams, my dreams aren't what they once were. My new dreams are what I'm doing right now. All my life I was so sure I was special and I'd been marked for some kind of greater purpose. Now it seems crazy I ever thought I was fated to be a pop star when there are things in this world so much bigger and more important than celebrating my own glory.

Was the nun sent to tell me I'm going to die for this cause?

That I'll be martyred like the other people in that book? I don't want to die, especially not now, when I feel almost like I've just come back to the world of the living, but at least I know what I'm here for now, and this doesn't change that.

EDITOR'S NOTE
2/7/2015

The writer known in these pages as Laetitia did continue to volunteer at the protests in [redacted] Park. Though she apparently lost interest in updating her journal, she rapidly became known for the protest songs she would sing as she offered people food and water. During the next few weeks, she was struck by a rare creative energy and seemed to compose almost in a frenzy. Those close to her say she was more joyful and determined in this period than during any other time in her life.

Tragically, on July 2, 2014, there was an altercation between the protesters and the police at the park that turned violent and ultimately deadly. Details are still unclear and will perhaps never be known with any great certainty, but according to witnesses, a mentally unstable man who was not well known at the protests and had only participated occasionally was the root of some disturbance. Members of the police force allegedly fired their weapons at him, and a stray bullet struck Laetitia in her side. She died in a hospital downtown later that day.

According to her mother, the site of the entry wound was exactly the spot that had so frequently and mysteriously pained Laetitia in the preceding months.

Since the incident, the songs Laetitia wrote have become popular not just within her city but at peaceful gatherings around the country.

Though the lasting accomplishments of this author and the tragic injustice of her death are beyond dispute, it's not for me to say whether the forces that afflicted her in her last few months were demonic or divine. No doubt there are those skeptical few who will refuse either suggestion, and claim that all the described events can be explained as medical or psychological anomalies.

If I may make any request of those who read the preceding document, it is to put aside such disingenuous skepticism, and consider how such solitary suffering might be avoided in the future. Both science and compassion command us to recognize that Laetitia's ordeal had as real a cause as any condition described by the medical establishment. It is only through serious academic inquiry into such long-ignored phenomena that we may one day offer hope to the similarly afflicted.

Montague Verano, Phd
Professor, Department of History
University of Idaho

M. VERANO is an associate professor of history and curator of the North Idaho historical text collection. His research interests include new religious movements, occult and magical societies, and supernatural folk histories of Eastern Europe and America. His scholarship has appeared in *Archiv fur Altreligionsgeschichte*, *Transactions of the Continental Society for Hermetic Studies*, and *Memoirs of the Frances Yates Academy*. His most recent work is a monograph on Uqbarian catoptromancy. He is currently editing a series of first-person narratives documenting parapsychological activity.